THE RETURN

Marika stood on the deck of the boat and watched Günter emerge from the sea. He was wearing a wet suit that accentuated his wide shoulders and height. He stripped off his gear and Marika saw he looked much older now than she remembered, but magnificent all the same. She could not look away from his muscular, suntanned body. He was tougher, leaner, stronger.

Then he saw her, and the next moment she was pressed against him. She felt the leanness of him, the hardness. God, he was like steel, she thought, running her hands over his back.

Marika had been an untried girl when she first gave herself to this man. She was a woman now, with a beautiful daughter to protect, a husband to honor, and a full knowledge of who Günter Greiff was and the havoc he could wreak.

And none of it mattered. . . .

SONG OF THE WIND

SONG OF THE WIND

Madge Swindells

A SIGNET BOOK

NEW AMERICAN LIBRARY

Acknowledgments to Lawrie Mackintosh; Valerie Hudson; Owen Teasedale; D. W. Bulmer of the South African Minerals Bureau; and particularly to Susan Schwartz, my editor, for her invaluable assistance.

Acknowledgments to *Das Reich: The March of the 2nd Panzer Division through France, June 1944,* by Max Hastings, published by Pan; and to *Vogue Book of Fashion Photography,* by Polly Devlin, published by Thames and Hudson.

"Vengeance is mine, I will repay," *saith the Lord.*
—ROMANS, 12:19

CONTENTS

PROLOGUE

Chapter One

Johannesburg
February 1969

It was midnight. A storm was brewing on the horizon, the clouds mushrooming huge and menacing like a row of warring Impis; flash of spears and thunder of feet. Nearer came the sounds of the summer night: throb of cicadas, the bullfrog's mating croak, occasional cry of a predatory bird.

Keeping to the shadows, a man walked quietly past the secluded Parktown mansions; he looked and felt at home in the night and the blacks who passed him kept their distance; there was a certain fearlessness about him, a feeling of menace as he moved quickly through the streets.

He glanced around, crossed the road and sat on a wall overlooking the city. Below, the lights of Johannesburg glowed yellow, red and blue in stark rectangular patterns like colored stickers on a planning board, the roads exactly placed north to south, east to west; wide, new, uncompromisingly straight. South of the city were tall dumps of gold-mine dust and they, too, were blazing with the multicolored neon rash. Around him the city's affluent suburbs spread northward; leafy avenues and floodlit pools. Order imposed on Africa by a neat, fastidious people.

Just surface scratches. He smiled without humor. He had seen them before many times—Zaire . . . Uganda . . . Finally savagery won!

He was panting. He frowned and counted his pulse rate. Eighty-four! Momentarily he felt worried; a finely tuned body and superb reflexes were essential for his work. Then he remembered the altitude. At six thousand feet you are entitled to get out of breath.

Behind him on the crest of a hill stood Xhabbo, home of the mining magnate Günter Grieff. An old and historic house, it was carelessly placed among six acres of lawns and trees, relic of early mining times.

The man's name was Kramer, although his passport bore a different title. He had been in Johannesburg for only a few hours, but he knew the routine of the Xhabbo household as intimately as his own.

He knew, for instance, that the caretaker, whose name was Jim Hackett, had returned to the house for a last check, inspected the two Zulu guards stationed at the front and back entrances and retired to his cottage by the gate. He would remain there until morning. By now the guards would be comfortably settled in the front porch playing dice and halfway through their second bottle of wine.

The job was a cinch, yet he was uneasy. Grieff was in a Parisian jail on trial for his life. His wife attended the trial day after day. Grieff was a sensation: the richest man in Africa; handsome; reckless; owner of the Kwammang-a, one of the world's largest uncut diamonds, discovered when he had worked underwater with his divers dredging the dangerous Skeleton Coast. He piloted his own jet; raced his own racing car; was a qualified geologist and disappeared for months into the African bush prospecting and collecting native art.

The newspapers had been full of little else for weeks. The trial was the scandal of the year, bringing intimate details of the privileged few to the breakfast table of every household in Britain, Europe, the United States and South Africa. The public's suspicions were confirmed: riches and ruthlessness were synonymous and Günter Grieff was receiving the worst possible publicity. His wife, Claire, shared his fate. A tragic, broken woman, she was playing a supportive role and would have gained the sympathy of the press and public alike were it not for the hideousness of her husband's crime.

One A.M. The hour had passed slowly and Kramer studied the storm thoughtfully. Although the sky was bright with moonlight, in the southeast clouds were piling up thicker than he had seen for years. Forked lightning streaked across the horizon in a dozen places simultaneously and the thunder, although distant, was continuous. It would be one hell of a storm and it was approaching rapidly. It would wake the caretaker and send the guards back to their positions. It might even take the bloody roof off. He had experienced these highveld storms before. He would have to go in earlier than he had planned.

Kramer moved around the edge of the lawn. The central fuse box was unlocked. He flipped up the cover and switched off the mains. The lights went out and Kramer returned to the shadows.

A guard walked slowly along the path clutching his stick, his shadow huge and twisted against the moonlit wall. He was old: milky eyes and white tuft of beard. His dog whined uneasily as the old man rattled the window and the door. He left and shortly afterward the game resumed. Click of dice; a muttered curse; a bottle slammed to the ground.

Time to get started!

It took Kramer seconds to open the back door. He moved silently through the rooms, his mind like a calculator automatically pricing the items as his flashlight sent sudden stabs of light on either side. Rare books and maps, Chinese and Persian carpets, paintings, silver, cut glass, a few well-known masterpieces hanging on the walls among wildlife paintings. The house darkened as the moon was obscured by clouds. The cicadas were silenced. The bullfrogs fled to the fishpond. Then lightning crashed overhead.

Kramer hardly noticed. He found the safe traditionally placed in the study wall behind a large oil painting. He was sweating as he dialed the safe's combination. He stood up, took a deep breath and swung back the door.

Minutes later he could hardly control his disappointment. There were a dozen proof Krugerrands, worth a few thousand dollars apiece; a shoe box filled with small uncut diamonds looking like pieces of rough glass; several property deeds and share certificates and a bundle of one-hundred-dollar notes. He transferred the diamonds, the gold coins and the notes to chamois-lined pockets in his bag. But where was the Kwammang-a?

Leading from a door at the end of the lounge was a smaller anteroom and as Kramer entered a flash of lightning filled the room with surrealistic light. In that split second a thousand malevolent eyes leered from the walls. Then thunder smashed the house like a physical blow. Kramer shined his flashlight on statues, fertility dolls, death masks: stylized faces designed to terrorize primitive man. Idoma figure; Knono society mask; Kyuy serpent head. The room was cluttered with Grieff's collection of African art. Worth a packet, Kramer thought, but he had no idea of the value. He grimaced.

At 4 A.M., Kramer found Claire Grieff's safe ingeniously fitted into the ceiling of her wood-paneled closet. It was crammed full with diamond necklaces, earrings and rings, brooches of rubies, emeralds and sapphires, a belt of emeralds set into a silver serpent with ruby eyes. The pieces had been collected from all over the world. A fortune carelessly spent. But the Kwammang-a was not there and Kramer felt angry and, again, disappointed.

There was a bundle of papers among the jewelry and Kramer passed his flashlight over them. *Last will and testament of Claire Grieff née McGuire,* he read. *I, Claire Grieff, do hereby testify . . .*

As he picked up the documents, thin and yellowed with age, he swore. Shit! He was glad he'd never married. Here, locked in her room, was the evidence that would undoubtedly free her husband.

Looking around for a suitable container, he saw a photograph of the Grieffs against a desert backdrop. Günter had his arm around her and Claire was smiling proudly. The flight from London had been worthwhile after all, Kramer decided as he placed the papers in his bag.

Chapter Two

London
February 1969

It was a gray London afternoon following a night of intense cold. It would snow soon. There was hardly any light in the cafeteria of Charing Cross Station, which was stuffy and smelled slightly of recycled air, dust and old boots.

Among the busy scramble of commuters grabbing a sandwich and a cup of coffee sat Kramer, immobile, watchful, relaxed, observing the comings and goings with a predatory air as a lion will survey a herd of buck before selecting his victim.

A woman walked in and there was a sudden pause in the hubbub of conversation. Eyes swiveled toward her, attracted not so much by her amazingly extravagant clothes or her jewelry as by a certain arrogance, an intense self-awareness that seemed to make her stand out in the crowd. She was a short, thin woman, too slight for the tangle of red hair which gave her a top-heavy look.

She sized up the occupants of the neighboring tables in a brief glance and as quickly dismissed them. Then she sat down.

Mid-forties, Kramer decided. Her skin was lined and freckled from the sun, but there was something youthful about her nevertheless. Her eyes were deep blue; clever eyes; her mouth a thin scarlet line.

Ambitious, ruthless and tough, Kramer decided, watching Claire Grieff thoughtfully. The proud smile he had seen in the photograph two nights before was missing. She looked watchful and defiant. There had been no mistaking the fear in her voice when he had arranged their meeting this morning.

Kramer waited for a while. Let her sweat, he thought as

he calculated the value of her jewelry, hardly aware of the exercise: ten for the diamond ring; three for the emerald brooch—no, two, for the stones were too small. Its beauty lay in the craftsmanship and it needed to be restyled.

After a few minutes her eyes rested speculatively on him. One eyebrow shot up, the slash of lips curved, a red nail beckoned.

He stood up reluctantly. The bitch! She had turned the tables on him.

"Coffee?" she asked. Her voice was deep and authoritative, the sort of voice that only the very rich acquire.

He nodded and sat down beside her.

Claire felt more confident as she came to grips with him. She could sense the brutality in the man, the suppressed animosity. A bitter man, she decided, one who had extinguished his sensuality and his emotions long ago. She had seen men like him before in Africa; men who killed for a living because they had lost the reverence for life. Something about him sent icy shivers over her skin, but at the same time some of her anxiety was diminished. He was no agent—she was sure of that; an ex-mercenary turned crook. It was written all over him.

The coffee arrived and Claire toyed with the teaspoon as the two sat silently calculating each other's resources.

"I see you caught a good tan in Johannesburg." Claire's pale blue eyes flashed.

The man shrugged, unwilling to waste time. "Let's get to the point," he said harshly. "I have something to sell. You want to buy it. Make me an offer." His eyes glowed contemptuously.

Claire felt incensed. How dare he judge her. "Do you make a good living out of stealing other people's property and selling it back to them?" she asked coldly.

He leaned back, tilted his head sideways and watched her quizzically without speaking. Then he took out a notebook and pencil and scribbled a number onto a page, which he tore off and handed to her.

"If you want to make an offer, put it in writing in this

locker. You've got twenty-four hours.'' He stood up. ''Thanks for the coffee.''

Claire was startled and she showed it. ''No, wait.''

''That's it,'' he said quietly. ''You've got twenty-four hours. It's so simple. I'll be in touch.''

She gasped. ''I'm negotiating on my husband's behalf,'' she whispered. ''You better listen to me.''

Kramer watched her curiously. She was flustered and lying badly and she was afraid.

''Have you contacted anyone else?'' she continued eventually.

''No.'' How relieved she looked. ''But I have other appointments,'' he lied. ''I'll take the highest bid.''

Relief faded, anger took its place. ''Damn you!''

He shrugged, turned and walked toward the entrance. A moment later he felt her hand on his arm.

Her face was distorted into an ugly mask, her hands shaking as she tore his note to pieces. ''Tell me your price now,'' she said urgently, ''or you might miss out altogether.''

''You look very distraught, Mrs. Grieff,'' he said coldly. ''You're attracting attention. I wouldn't advise you to follow me out, at least not without paying for the coffee first.''

Claire sat down and fumbled in her bag for change. Tears of fear, anger and impotence left a crooked course down her makeup.

Outside the falling snow was thickening, low clouds reflected an eerie glow from London's lights, the north wind was gathering force. God, it was cold.

He walked rapidly through the streets. An occasional cab slowed beside him, but he waved them on. He had to think. The snow was taking hold, glowing white on hedges and gates, gathering in corners while visibility was down to thirty yards.

He began to jog through the blizzard, trying to shake off a feeling of vulnerability, a strange sense of being overexposed; something he had not felt since he was a mercenary. He slowed down and listened carefully. Some-one was running on rubber-soled shoes on newly fallen snow, not more than a few yards away. He heard the crunch of a stone dislodged and then a short skid from a misplaced step. He looked sidelong into the gloom. The night was full of white shapes and deep shadows, but none that seemed to have any living form.

He had been followed. He felt depressed by his lack of awareness as he waited in the nearest doorway.

His pursuer was running now, making no attempt at stealth and gaining rapidly. A second passed; then a man ran around the corner, paused and swore, uncertain of which way to go.

Kramer stepped behind him, grabbed him by the hair with one hand and twisted his arm viciously behind his back.

"What d'you want?"

"Hey! Hold it. Don't break my bloody arm."

Kramer thrust his arm higher.

"You Jones?" The man gasped. "There's someone wants to buy what you've got. Know anything about that? If you're interested you're to come with me."

Kramer watched him incredulously. "How'd you pick me up?"

The man looked away, but his face revealed his secret triumph. "That's my business. Don't start anything or you'll miss out," he said.

It was a large, red brick house in Hampstead, set well back from the road behind a tall hedge. His companion stopped the taxi and pointed the way.

"Well, that's it, then," he said. "No hard feelings, mate. I've done my job. I'd watch out if I were you."

A minute later a maid ushered him into the living room and left him there.

Company-owned, Kramer decided as he examined the large, impersonal room. Must cost a bundle, yet there was, nothing here of value, from the looks of the furniture and the prints on the walls. The house was worth at least half a million pounds.

Then the door opened.

Kramer gazed in astonishment. The woman who stood framed in the doorway was undeniably beautiful; her skin was white and flawless, her navy-blue dress fell in drapes from her shoulders in a fashion reminiscent of Grecian robes, her golden hair fell in waves over her bare shoulders. Yet her beauty was marred by her expression; she looked tired and shocked and there were deep shadows under her eyes. She was trying to hide her fear and Kramer wondered why.

"Hello," she said. "The famous Mr. Jones." She laughed as if the two of them shared an intimate secret. Then she moved toward him and stood too close as her eyes scanned his face, taking in the harshness of the man, the bleak eyes, the even suntanned features. "I haven't seen some-one like you for a long time," she said. "Not too long out of Africa," she went on. "Ex-mercenary I'd say, if I had to make a guess."

"You don't have to," he said uneasily, moving away as her hand rested on his arm. Briefly the thought came: She wants the papers very badly and she will do anything to get them.

"I'm sure you know who I am," she said softly.

Of course he knew: She had achieved fame and notoriety long before the scandal and the trial. Marika Magos, the fur queen, as the press had dubbed her. She was so much more beautiful than she had looked in newspaper pictures.

"What a busy man you've been, Mr. Kramer."

How the hell did the bitch know who he was? Kramer was unable to conceal his shock.

She laughed at his discomfort. "You mustn't get uptight if people play your game," she said sweetly. She leaned back on the couch, a feline gesture, spreading her arms along the back, crossing her legs. "Let's have a drink," she said. "Will you pour?" Kramer's gaze was snared and

for a second he splashed whiskey over the bar, over-
whelmed with an onrush of desire.

"I'd like to know what you want," Kramer said flatly.
He watched her carefully. Not the type to sleep around,
yet here she was offering her wares as persistently as a
Gyppo with a pack of dirty postcards. No finesse and
certainly no passion, but more than a trace of desperation.

"I want the papers . . . I must have them." Her voice
trembled with emotion. "And then . . ." She watched him
pleadingly. "I want you to kill my husband."

"I'm not a hired assassin" he said, draining his glass
and reaching for his windbreaker.

"But of course you are. That is what a mercenary is.
You kill for money, Mr. Kramer, and I can pay a great
deal of money."

"Sorry. I only want to sell the papers."

"One million pounds. Just think of it. You could retire,
Mr. Kramer."

"Or die," he said.

Lashes heavy with tears and lids drooping forlornly.
He'd seen it all before.

"Whatever you're offered, I'll pay more, much more,"
she said desperately. "I'm a very rich woman. You can
name your price. Anything!"

But not the Kwammang-a, he thought. "No dice," he
said, and let himself out.

Chapter Three

Outside the biting cold soon dispelled his desire and his
regrets. He walked briskly, stopping occasionally to glance
around for a passing cab, but in Hampstead they were few
and far between. He was almost home before he caught
one.

The blizzard was worse now. It was difficult to see through the falling snow; consequently, he almost stumbled over what appeared to be a large sack dumped on his front doorstep. As he bent over it the body slithered sideways and lay spread-eagled on the doormat.

A bruised mouth was opening and shutting, making curious mewing sounds. Kramer's first fleeting impression was one of disgust: the smell, the blood, the clumsy way in which she lay, the degradation of a young and once beautiful woman. Then alarm took over. He unlocked the door, picked her up and carried her through to the living-room floor.

Then he looked up and saw the chaos around him. His house had been taken apart, piece by piece, by experts.

He forced his attention back to the girl. Who the hell was she? Who had beaten her up? Her breathing was strong, but irregular, her pulse was beating rapidly, one side of her face was already swelling and signs of two black eyes were coming out unmistakably. Worse still, she was freezing to death.

He ran upstairs for a blanket and pillow and when he returned the girl was making mewing sounds again and rolling her eyes. He fetched a tumbler of brandy and tried to make her drink. Then he examined her arms and legs, but nothing seemed to be broken; merely superficial bruising by the look of things.

After a while she moaned gently and opened her eyes.

"Are you Kramer?" she demanded.

Kramer flinched. He wondered how she, too, had discovered his name and where he lived. In spite of the bruising he recognized her. Her face appeared nightly on the TV screen. "The warm, natural beauty of Sylvia Shaw draws $9,000 a day." He had read that somewhere.

"I've been mugged," she blurted out. "I was coming to bring you all the money I have. I drew it out of the bank this afternoon; and it's gone," she sobbed. "I must have the papers."

Childish tears, noisy and demanding, designed to summon help. Ignoring her, Kramer walked to the corner of the room and rifled through a pile of dusty magazines and newspapers.

"Who knew?" he asked over his shoulder.

"Knew what?"

"That you were coming here with the money?" He turned and watched her. "How did you know where to come; who I am?"

Her mouth closed obstinately, eyes trembled with tears.

"All right," he said. "This you?" He held up an American news magazine. The face on the cover was lovely; enormous violet eyes glowed with warmth and compassion; long blond hair floated around her as if she was gently returning to earth from some other world in the clouds where people who looked like her lived. "Unbelievable!" he murmured.

"Yes, that's me," she whispered. "You must sell me the papers. You can read for yourself how much I make. Whatever you want, I'll pay you off. Just tell me the price. It's a matter of life and death. You must understand."

"Yes," he said thoughtfully. "That's about the only thing I do understand."

Sylvia took her hands away from her face and watched him shrewdly. "Is it true Claire had the papers?"

"I'm merely negotiating . . ."

"Oh God. Don't lie."

She was only a child, he thought. Hardly more than nineteen; obstinate, too. She could be coaxed, but never bullied. He'd never had children, but if he had they could be around Sylvia's age, he thought, feeling strangely moved by her misery. He hoped he wouldn't be around when she caught sight of herself in the mirror.

"For God's sake," she burst out. "Just tell me how much."

More than she'd got. "I'll have to transmit your offer . . ."

She turned away with a hopeless, baffled look on her face. Then she kicked off the blanket and stood up shakily, holding on to the settee.

"They were here . . ." He gestured around. "When you arrived. Is that it? You disturbed them . . ."

"Yes, I think so."

"Did you get a look at them?"

"They had stockings over their faces. Horrible!" She shuddered. "Where can I find a mirror?" She began to prod her face with her forefinger. "Ouch!" She moved her head carefully.

"If I were you I wouldn't bother."

"That bad?"

He nodded. "Only superficial. You'll be as good as new in ten days' time. Like a drink?"

"Please."

Kramer poured her a stiff brandy and handed it to her. He studied her thoughtfully. There was no shortage of women in Grieff's life. One of them had the diamond. It might be her, he thought. Probably not, but she had something he needed. Information! He had once parachuted into Zaire with the wrong map—landed up in prison that time. He had the same feeling of insecurity now.

"Look," he said. "If I knew what was going on, maybe I could make a decision about your offer." He was lying and maybe he was being too obvious, for he saw doubt and distaste registered on her face, and he didn't like it. Abruptly he turned and poured himself another drink.

"All right," she said quickly. Then she hesitated. "I don't really know it all. There's only one person . . ." She broke off and prodded her face again.

"Leave it."

She removed her hand. "If you let me use your telephone, I'll take you to her."

"Go ahead," he muttered.

He pulled back the curtains and stared out at the blizzard. The snow was thick now, piling up over hedges and gutters, making the houses around look like a scene on a Christmas card. Suddenly he swore viciously. He hated England; hated the claustrophobic nature of the neat, small streets and houses; the trees; the hedged fields; the confines—mental and physical and moral. If he had to be in a blizzard he could bear it in Finland or Canada, but not here where there was little enough space to move, and now even that was filled with choking, blinding bloody snow.

He heard a voice behind him. "Gran, is that you? Sorry to wake you."

Shit! Why didn't he give her the papers now and get the hell out of this place? But then he might never lay his hands on the Kwammang-a. A moment later he felt her touch his arm.

"Let's go," she said.

The name beside the door read *Bertha Factor*. It stood in a small box above a mezuzah, signifying a Jewish home. He was startled. No end to the surprises for him tonight.

Sylvia had a key to the front door and she led him along a hallway to the sitting room. It was all there; the menorah on the sideboard, the silver candlesticks, the heavy lace hand-embroidered tablecloth and ornate chandeliers.

The woman Sylvia had brought him to see was exactly like her house: Jewish, middle-class, respectable and built to last. She sat erect and dignified in a rocking chair in spite of her excess bulk. She was somewhere in her sixties, Kramer decided. A shrewd, intelligent, resourceful woman.

She paled and gasped when she saw Sylvia's face.

"Oh my God! Bubeleh!" She moved across the room with amazing speed and cradled the girl in her arms.

"Oh, Boba." Sylvia buried her face in the woman's shoulder and hung on shaking for a few minutes.

"My name is Bertha Factor," she said, looking up at Kramer with coal-black eyes. "What happened to my granddaughter?"

"Boba, I was mugged. I didn't see their faces, but they took all my money. I drew it out of the bank, you see. I'm all right. You mustn't worry."

"Listen to the child! Her face is black and blue and she says I mustn't worry. Things have come to a pretty pass . . ."

"Boba, this is the man I told you about," Sylvia began. "The man with the papers. Mr. Kramer."

Kramer found himself looking past the wrinkled brown skin, the liver spots, the hooded lids, into eyes that had turned hard as agates.

Bertha turned away, led her granddaughter to a chair and hurried back with aspirins and a glass of water. She plied the girl with questions, ignoring Kramer, who felt increasingly uncomfortable, but eventually, when they were sitting with coffee and Bertha was sure that she had done all she could for her granddaughter's face, she said, "So, Mr. Kramer, you have blundered into a family tragedy; a family of powerful, headstrong people. Even tougher than you, Mr. Kramer, and shrewder, and their emotions have run wild."

For a moment her clever eyes appraised him, noting the strong, sunburned hands, the lean frame of the man, the veiled eyes which sometimes dropped their cover. "I doubt you could understand them. To tell the truth, most of the time I don't either and they're my family."

Kramer's eyes widened.

"I can see that surprises you," Bertha said, watching him shrewdly. "Unbelievable, isn't it? But it's true."

"Boba!" Sylvia's voice was shrill now. "Never mind that. You're wasting time. We must buy the papers from him."

"He didn't come here for money, Sylvia." Bertha leaned back and watched him hostilely. "No, Mr. Kramer, you have come here because you are unsure of yourself. You want to find out who would be your best bet."

Kramer cleared his throat and put down his cup. Violet eyes were watching him with an expression he did not like.

"I think that when I have finished you may well sell the papers to me," Bertha went on. "It's a long story. It goes back to Walvis Bay in 1940." She turned and frowned. "Don't cry, darling. We'll tell this Mr. Kramer what he wants to know and then we'll make a plan," she said.

"Those were terrible times. The Germans invaded Czechoslovakia in March 1939. So many tried to escape. Only a few succeeded and Marika was one of them. Just by chance

she was placed with a trainload of Jewish refugee children
being sent to foster homes in Africa. Or was it by chance?
. . . I wonder. When you get to my age, Mr. Kramer, you
begin to see a pattern emerging. You, too, are part of the
pattern; you have a role to play."

Kramer put his cup on the tray and leaned back in his
chair, wishing that the fire were not so warm, the room not
so stuffy and he not so tired. It had been a rough day, he
had to admit that, with Claire and Marika Magos and now
this incredibly beautiful, battered child. He had to struggle
to concentrate on what the old woman was saying. He was
so tired. If only she would get to the point . . .

PART ONE

PART ONE

Chapter Four

The sullen mist hung around wharves and cranes, cluttered the sandy street, obscuring the harshness of the settlement, so that buildings shimmered in shades of gray and merged with the gray sea as if nature were trying to hide man's crude attempt to carve a foothold in this, her most forbidding coastline.

To the uncompromising eyes of the child who watched dismally as the cargo boat neared the quay, nothing was hidden. The town lay bleak and forbidding, a joyless place without even a tree. She saw long wooden warehouses, the wharf, the harbor with whalers and fishing boats and beyond a heap of buildings and houses. There was nothing else except sand dunes which stretched out in all directions under a washed-out sky.

So this was Africa! She had imagined it a thousand times, but even in her worst nightmares it had not appeared so dreadful as it seemed now. The sun rose huge, implacable and blood red, and as the boat docked, the mist vanished, leaving the small settlement stripped to its pristine bleakness.

Marika shut her eyes, pressed her hands over her ears, but could not banish the sound of gulls squabbling, breakers crashing on the shore, the ship's siren.

She felt a hand on her shoulder and looked into the anxious eyes of the social worker who had accompanied her with fifteen other refugee children from Switzerland to their new homes.

"Look! Someone is waiting for you." She spoke softly in German.

Marika ignored her. She hated to hear German spoken and would not respond to it. She closed her eyes again and gripped the rails, but could not erase the image of a woman who had stood motionless on the quay for an hour while the ship docked. She was as ugly as the town she lived in, Marika decided.

The cargo boat was seven days overdue and the woman had stood peering into the mist every morning, praying that the boat would evade the German U-boats and bring her little daughter safely to her.

Her name was Bertha Factor and she and her husband, Irwin, kept the only import-and-export store in Walvis Bay. This morning Bertha was oblivious to the sand stinging her face and to the uncomfortable heat of the early-morning sun, for somewhere on the boat was her foster daughter.

Her own daughter! It was a fifteen-year dream come true, one that she had long ago given up, so now years of pent-up maternal need were bubbling out of her as a spring will occasionally appear in a dry riverbed.

She had imagined her child to the last detail. She would be small, plump and dark-haired, not exactly like her, but with a certain resemblance. Bertha was homely-looking and at thirty-five she looked fifty; the harsh sun and sand had spoiled her skin. Her hands were large and red, but they were capable, strong hands and her dark brown eyes were filled with compassion and intelligence. A hungry tribesman, a poor white or even a drunk sailor could count on Bertha's assistance.

She had not been pretty even when she was young; her husband had chosen her for her strength, not her looks. They had met on a liner, he bound for Walvis Bay after visiting his family in Holland and she, a Londoner, en route to Cape Town. She had not reached her destination. They had been married at sea and disembarked together.

For Bertha, the match had not been one of passion, but rather of trust and friendship. She reckoned that love would grow with the years and she had been right. Her life would be fulfilled with children, she thought. But this time she had been wrong, for they had not come. So she hoped and prayed and tried to come to terms with her disappointment month after month.

One day in desperation she went to see a rabbi in Johannesburg about adoption. He had explained kindly that there were hardly ever any Jewish babies available and by law she could adopt only a child of her religion. Now if she were Catholic . . .

Bertha looked older after her visit to the rabbi and her face was sad when she was not making an effort to smile.

Then, much later, the war came and among the flotsam and jetsam of unwanted people was a trainload of Jewish children from Czechoslovakia desperately needing foster homes.

Could Bertha offer one of them a home? the official letter from the Jewish Board of Deputies had requested.

Could she? Oh Lord, could she just? She had yelled aloud with joy, startling the fishermen in the store who were accustomed to her staid and placid ways.

Since then Bertha had heard only that the child was a girl called Marika Magos and she would arrive on the cargo boat, the *Tristan Belle*, sometime during January if all went well.

And here was the *Tristan Belle* safely berthed at last and coming down the gangplank was a middle-aged woman looking worried.

"She's here, isn't she? I mean, you do have her?" Bertha faltered.

"You must be Mrs. Factor," the woman said anxiously. "Yes, she's here, but I'm afraid Marika's not easy," she went on when she had introduced herself. She felt sorry for all of them. Walvis Bay looked like the worst place in the world and Marika was by far the most difficult of her charges.

She hurried up the gangplank and later returned pulling a girl by her arm.

"It can't be her," Bertha murmured incredulously to Irwin. She glanced at him and felt comforted by the sight of his shambling figure with long legs and balding head and his humorous eyes behind horn-rimmed glasses. She groped for his hand. "Please . . . not her," she whispered.

The child was tall and thin and she was clutching the rail, refusing to move. A torrent of unintelligible words poured out of her, ending in a high-pitched shriek. She lunged out; kicked the woman on the shin.

Looking up at her, Bertha saw humiliation and fear in her eyes. "It can't be her," she repeated. "Why, she's so big and so . . . strange-looking."

The child's head had been shaved and her hair had grown into a short golden skullcap shaped to her pointed skull. Her face was long and pointed, too; an adult face with high cheekbones, white skin and slanting amber eyes. Her mouth seemed too wide, her teeth too large, and she was abnormally thin. Skinny legs and arms protruded from clothes too small for her.

Bertha was reminded of a gazelle they had run over one day. She had never forgotten the look in the creature's wild and tragic eyes. This girl was just as wild, just as scared.

There was a sudden blast of sand and wind. Marika flung up her hands and rubbed her eyes with her knuckles. She was filled with loathing and despair. She did not care who picked her up and carried her off the ship. She was sure that this was the start of a new and terrible existence.

Chapter Five

Bertha hurried behind Irwin, watching the girl's face. Anger and sorrow seemed evenly matched. Occasionally, she kicked Irwin in the stomach with her long, skinny legs.

"Oh my goodness! What have I done?" Bertha murmured, hurrying to keep up with Irwin's loping walk.

Then she remembered how she had felt when she disembarked at Walvis Bay fifteen years before. It was the sand that had nearly driven her crazy. She had coped with the heat, the lack of any luxuries or entertainment, but the sand—oh Lord! Even now she hated it, and it was always there, clogging the bath, covering furniture, causing all manner of eye diseases, gritting between teeth at meals and finally expelled in sandy excrement.

The largest part of the small town's budget was spent on sand removal, but no one complained. What was the point? Walvis Bay was surrounded by the world's oldest natural desert, extending for two thousand kilometers from the Orange River in the south to the Angolan border in the north, and the dunes were the highest in the world.

The Factor home was an ungainly double-story structure built of wood, shedlike in appearance, balanced on stilts because of the disastrous floods which had nearly bankrupted them five years before.

The entrance was from a flight of wooden steps leading to double doors which opened to the store. Inside, the shadowy cavern was filled to overflowing with tins of fuel, fishing gear, household requirements, baby products, ships' provisions, bales of cloth, sacks of grain and sugar, dried fish and fruit.

Irwin was panting as he carried the child through the store and up the stairs, keeping up an incessant chatter of nonsense. Finally, he paused dramatically in front of Marika's room. Chanting "Tum, tara, tum-tum," he flung open the door.

Grinning gnomes, Mickey Mouse characters, fairies and a variety of cuddly animals leered from every available space.

Why must Bertha overdo everything? he thought treacherously. A nightmare! But how could Bertha guess the child would be so much older than they had expected? He knew Bertha was disappointed, he had seen it on her face when she first set eyes on the girl, but he also knew that she would never admit this to anyone.

By now he was almost collapsing under the strain. "Oy

vay!'' He lowered Marika to the bed, thumped a teddy bear in her arms and leaned against the wall, panting.

"You like the room?" Bertha asked anxiously.

Marika could not understand her, but the expression on Bertha's face was sufficiently explicit. She closed her eyes, blocking out the sight of both of them, their efforts to please and this horrible room. She flung the bear into the corner and buried her face in the bed.

The Factors looked helplessly at each other and back to the child. She was all smelly and sticky with the heat, but still clutched her tattered coat around her.

Why, she's so skinny, thought Bertha. A miracle she had survived. She needed feeding and loving.

She sat on the edge of the bed and tried to remove the child's old coat but Marika lashed out viciously. Bertha stood up, biting her lip.

"Come," Irwin said. "Leave her for a while. She's scared and it's all so strange for her. Let her be."

They tiptoed out, shutting the door, and clattered down the wooden steps to the office. But Bertha had second thoughts.

"Leave her alone there—heavens no—she's only just arrived."

"Let her cool off."

Bertha turned suspiciously. Irwin had never been a hard man, yet now his lips were pursed together obstinately.

"Listen to him, the child expert," she said, and hurried back to Marika with a glass of lemonade.

Marika grabbed the glass and hurled it against the wall. It landed in the corner on the bear, splashing jovial stuffed toys and a poster titled "Teatime for Teddy Bears."

"Why, look at this," Irwin said when Bertha returned looking chastened. He was riffling through the papers in the folder the social worker had given them. "Sunday is her birthday. January the twenty-eighth. She'll be twelve." He looked up sadly. "It says here she speaks only Czech and German. How's your German?"

"About as good as my Czech," Bertha said. "And yours?"

"Rusty," he admitted.

A fisherman came in for trawling nets and for a while Irwin was occupied in the outside shed where they kept the bulkier products.

Bertha blinked back tears of disappointment and went to the kitchen.

Only four days to her birthday and so much to do, she thought. Whoever heard of a birthday without a cake and candles? "So what if she's not exactly what I had imagined," she muttered to herself. "She's better." She kneaded the sugar with the butter. "Oy vay! What a temper she's got. But who hasn't? She's had to learn to stand up for herself, the poor, poor child." She tipped in the dried fruit. "Still, she's not exactly a child either. But she's in need of care and she's come to the right place. God knows I've been begging for a child to care for."

She vented her annoyance on the cake mixture with a wooden spoon. "She'll never think of me as her mother and when the war ends she'll go away." She paused and wiped a tear with the back of her hand. Then she renewed the attack on the pudding base. "Better she should be homeless, Bertha Factor?" she said sternly. She plopped the mixture into the baking pan. Then she turned her attention to her sewing machine. After a while she heard Irwin clattering up the steps again.

"How's the child expert doing?" she asked when he returned.

"Give her time" was the brief reply. Bertha was always surprising him. She wore plain clothes because she felt herself to be ugly. Her morning scowl into the mirror could never reveal the sensitive way she moved or her girlish smile or the compassion that shone out of her. Her brooding black eyes were startlingly observant. She often thought as a man and then, at the same moment, she could become infuriatingly feminine again. Right now, hunched over her sewing machine, she was producing the prettiest dress he had seen from the most expensive bale of *broderie anglaise* she could find in the store.

"If you ask me, it'll land up in the corner with the bear

and the lemonade," he said, bending over and pinching her ear.

"You think she should walk around in rags?" Bertha replied scathingly.

To Bertha the days ahead were traumatic, each one bringing new challenges, new heartbreak. The child was bitterly unhappy and unwilling to come to terms with reality. She closed in on herself and took to lying on her bed for hours curled up like a hedgehog. When Bertha tried to take Marika in her arms and comfort her, the child would push her aside. Sometimes Marika would walk out on the sand dunes and gaze at the harbor with an expression of such loathing on her face that Bertha would feel like crying.

"It's like a prison for her," she confided in Irwin. But what could they do?

At last Bertha found someone who spoke Czech. He was a deckhand on a Russian trawler in harbor for repairs and he arrived cap in hand the day before Marika's birthday in response to Bertha's pleas.

For the first time Bertha and Irwin listened to an eyewitness account of the invasion of Czechoslovakia and the forced removal of the Jewish community, all the more terrible as it was reported in such a matter-of-fact manner by a child.

For Marika the shock of hearing her own language produced a kaleidoscope of memories, vivid and traumatic. She was transported to the days before the Germans came; Mama's violet eyes were always shining then; she was always happy. Her mother was a commercial artist, the best in Prague, Papa always said. Sometimes she took Marika to work with her and even asked her advice.

"The child is talented, Janos, you mark my words," Mama would tell Papa proudly in the evenings.

At the thought of Papa, a lump came into her throat. How happy she had been when Papa took her to the hospital; how handsome he had looked in his long white coat; black hair gleaming.

When the Germans invaded Czechoslovakia, the family

left Prague and stayed with relatives in the country, but afterward Papa was taken away by the Germans. Then mother and daughter had prepared for their nightmare journey to the station at Brno, where her aunt had a friend who would smuggle them out of Czechoslovakia in a goods wagon. They were going to France, Mama had told her.

At the time she had cried for hours. Why couldn't they stay with her aunt, with the ducks and chickens and her dog, whom she loved? She had wanted to argue, but then, looking up, Marika had seen that her mother was crying. So she had squeezed her hand instead and helped to pack their rucksacks. But then came the terrible night when she lost Mama.

She remembered the long walk hemmed in between deserted warehouses and factories and the narrow strip of brilliant night sky above; occasional rumbles of thunder and sounds from the shunting yard; clash of buffers and sudden loud bursts of steam fading into silence. She could remember the soldiers, and her mother trying street after street to reach the station undetected. There was a scrap-iron dump where macabre, twisted shapes loomed into the night sky: giants, trolls and witches, but none as evil as the Nazis, Marika knew that.

That was all.

When she tried to remember more there was only a frightening blank and then—much later—running, fear and confusion and eventually being put onto the train with a group of children and sent to Switzerland.

"And then?" the deckhand prompted her.

She felt startled as she looked up at Bertha and Irwin and the man from the boat. Strangers' eyes! She could not explain to herself, so how could she possibly tell them?

Instead she fled to her room and remained staring sightlessly at the wall for the rest of the day.

That night Marika tossed and worried. It was nearly dawn when she fell into a restless sleep.

It was hot, unbearably hot. The desert wind whined with

anger as it clawed through the narrow streets of Brno. Trapped! It spat sand over the cobbles, rattled the windows of the warehouses, but there was no escape. Bertha had the wind by the scruff of the neck in one hand and it writhed like a demented genie from Aladdin's lamp. The other hand was holding Marika tightly and she, too, was struggling to be free. They were going back . . . back . . . back to Czechoslovakia and back in time.

There was the scrapyard and the wind kicked out with his hundreds of long legs, rattling the trolls and giants until they moaned for mercy, but tonight there was no mercy, they were breaking up and flying away in bits and pieces in the sandstorm,

"They won't last two minutes in a desert wind," Bertha said, maddeningly calm. They peered into the scrapyard and there cowed a small, frightened girl trying to shelter from the pouring rain. *"No, this is too late,"* Bertha said in a voice like a clap of thunder. The rain stopped and the clouds scuttled back to the horizon. Marika watched her other self running backwards like a frightened rabbit until she reached the doorway, where she cowered, clasping her arms around her knees, waiting for Mama.

Not here. This is not it," Bertha said, her voice like a peal of thunder again. *Back . . .*

Now she was creeping through the streets, she reached the corner of the warehouse, a dog howled and rattled its chains, Marika closed her eyes tightly and felt Bertha pulling her arm,

"Here we are," Bertha said. *"Now look, child, look well."*

"No," she screamed, *"No, I don't want to look, I can't, I won't, let me go . . ."*

"You prefer that you should never know?" Bertha's reply tolled like a death knell around her ears.

Bertha took both of her shoulders and shook her; the wind escaped and fled back to the desert where it was free.

"Wake up, Marika, wake up." Bertha shook her harder.

"I won't look, I won't," Marika sobbed, and stared up at Bertha and behind her Irwin, watching anxiously.

"It was just a bad dream," Irwin explained carefully in German. "You're quite safe here, go back to sleep."

"No," Marika sobbed. "It's not a bad dream, it's true and I won't look. I won't. You can't force me to." She was muttering in Czech, so neither Bertha nor Irwin understood what she said. Then she buried her face in the pillows and lay quivering.

Bertha sat beside her for hours, stroking her shoulders and her neck, and when at last Marika slept, she left and went to bed feeling exhausted.

Chapter Six

It was Marika's birthday.

It began with Bertha lighting the candles and Irwin reciting the blessing over the wine. To cries of "Mazeltov, Marika!" they then sipped the sweet homemade red wine shipped from the Cape.

Dinner began with the traditional soup and kneidlach, followed by gefilte fish and then roast chicken and tzimmes. Not exactly the best diet for the exhausting heat they were experiencing now, but this was a celebration.

Marika sat staring at the wall opposite, sullen and withdrawn, eating the barest minimum and then only after a great deal of encouragement from Bertha.

Irwin tried out his German to no avail and Bertha chattered away in English as if the girl could understand her. Then they cut the cake and produced the presents rifled from the town and the store: a canary in a cage; some ballet shoes which had been ordered for a customer's daughter, whom Bertha persuaded to wait another two weeks; a doll; some scarves; and a dressing-table set backed with mother-of-pearl, which Bertha had bought for herself two years before and then decided was too grand to use.

Marika hardly looked at the presents; from time to time she would glance fearfully at the bird.

Then Bertha said to Irwin, "Darling, I want you to read this to Marika, but in German." She pulled from her pocket a sheet of paper which she had filled with neat, precise handwriting. "Be very careful not to change a single word," she said.

Irwin eyed her suspiciously. His wife was prone to sentimentality to the point of becoming downright corny. Instinctively he knew that Marika would not be impressed.

"Are you sure . . .?" he began.

Bertha glared at him.

Irwin shrugged. He began to translate the page, speaking slowly and clearly.

"Marika, this is a letter to you from my wife, which I am reading because she cannot speak German and you cannot yet speak English." He cleared his throat, feeling embarrassed suddenly. "*Marika, I know that you do not want to be here, but you must remain here for a while.*"

Marika did not stir, but stared obstinately at the wall.

"*I want you to know that we are very happy for you to stay with us during the war years because we have no children and we have always wanted a child.*"

Marika tilted her head and made herself look at Bertha, noting the worn face, the double chin, the wart on the side of her cheek and her thick, ugly hands. She remembered her mother's delicate hands and turned her head away. How dare this woman try to take her place!

"*I know that you will never think of me as your mother,*" Irwin read on, "*and I would never expect you to do that, but I hope that you will think of me as your friend and call me Bertha, which is just right between friends . . .*"

Irwin broke off, feeling sorry for his wife, for only a few days ago she had been so full of happy anticipation.

"*My birthday present to you, Marika, is a promise,*" he read on. "*A promise that we shall do all we can to make contact with your parents, so that you will know how they are.*"

Marika's eyes wavered toward Bertha, with uncertainty

this time, and the sullenness was replaced by a small flicker of hope.

"*As soon as the war ends,*" Irwin read on, "*I myself will take you to Czechoslovakia and return you to your real home.*"

The clarity of Bertha's message brought Marika face to face with her problems and her hopes. She remembered the terrible train ride through Yugoslavia and Italy to Switzerland and the long wait in the camp; the daily expectation that her mother would come to claim her and the slow but gradual erosion of her self-confidence as her hopes dwindled. The children were always wailing and crying, but she never cried. Dry-eyed she had endured the loneliness, the cross-examinations, the lessons, the lectures and worse still the doubts and fears that Mama would never come.

Marika shook her head. A friend? That was nonsense. She would never trust anyone again. Never, ever again.

"*Next Monday,*" Irwin was saying, "*we shall start a savings account at the bank and each month pay some money into it for your trip home at the end of the war, and when you are sad, you'll be able to count how much there is. No one will be able to draw out the money except you, and that will only be when the right time comes at the end of the war. You will be paid pocket money here for your share of the chores and you can put this into the account, too, if you wish to . . .*"

Irwin got no further, for when he glanced toward Marika to see if she understood, he found she was staring at Bertha with such an intensity of sorrow and Bertha was gazing at her with that look he knew so well of monumental stubbornness. Surely the child would be frightened, and she was, for the next moment she burst into tears. Such a commotion! Such a wailing!

"Shame on you, Bertha, shame on you," he began, but Bertha was not listening. She had gathered the child onto her voluminous lap and was gently rocking backwards and forwards.

"There, there, Marika. There, there." She looked sadly

over the girl's head to Irwin. "So finally she cries" was all she would say.

"A child torn up by the roots and thrown away . . ." Irwin began. "A mother to the future! And so many millions like her." He shuddered.

Long after Marika had sobbed herself to sleep, Irwin and Bertha sat among the ruins of the birthday party, unable to shake off a sense of sadness.

Chapter Seven

When the German armies overran Holland on May 15, 1940, Irwin decided to join up. He informed the family of his plans at the dinner table, hoping that Marika's presence would curb Bertha's reaction. But even he was unprepared for the storm his announcement provoked.

Over the next few days Bertha tried bribes, threats and even tears, but when she saw he was determined, she did her best to look cheerful and kept up the façade. But inwardly she suffered. She was so sure she would never see him again.

From then on Bertha lavished her affection on Marika, but she was unable to form a bond with the child. Marika was like a flower transplanted into unsuitable soil; she would not take root. She was pale and skinny and obviously unhappy.

Her class teacher could not help either. After several meetings with Bertha and months of effort, she gave up and allowed Marika to sit by the window daydreaming. Marika had no friends and she would not learn English.

Marika would spend hours wandering along the seashore, watching the birds, and Bertha let her go, just so long as she stayed in sight of the store. After all, it was the only time she seemed happy. She became a familiar figure trudging among the driftwood, hunched and stooping. So forlorn!

Marika was not watching the birds when she stood gazing for hours without moving. Her mind was trapped by an image; one that had plagued her for months. It was of her mother's face caught in the searchlights: staring eyes, mouth open. And there was something else which Marika could not remember however hard she tried.

Until she understood she would have no peace. The key, she knew, lay in something terrible she had thrust out of her mind. Some vital memory.

That awful night; the broken memory of it had become her only reality. All the rest was a dream. If someone from this strange, new, unreal world tried to break through to her she resisted them with all the stubbornness she could muster.

Even at night her dreams played out her quest: she was searching for Mama and she always found her. Then the force of her joy would wake her and reality would come flooding back, reminding her of the pointlessness of her existence; so she would once again take refuge in daydreaming.

In October, Marika received a letter from her aunt which had been smuggled out of Czechoslovakia and sent via the camp and the rabbi. She wrote that Marika's father had escaped from the train taking him to camp and was in France working as a doctor and fighting with the Resistance. She tried to express her grief when she learned that Marika's mother had been shot and how grateful she was that her niece was safely in Africa for the duration of the war.

Marika read the letter with difficulty. It was over a year since she had spoken Czech. When she came to the part about her mother she threw it into the trash can. Insane and wicked lies contaminating her world.

That night Marika ran away. When she tiptoed to the window she could see nothing but fog which covered the sea and sky and sand. The curtains rustled softly in the cold sea breeze. Bertha was snoring softly when she left.

*   *   *

Irwin had always been the first to wake in the morning and it was in early morning that Bertha missed him the most. So she developed the habit of rising at dawn and going to the kitchen to make coffee. Then she would open the store and later, around eight o'clock, wake Marika.

This morning, however, the child's door was open and the room was empty. Bertha ran out and searched the seashore and the harbor and asked around town.

Within an hour there was no one in Walvis Bay who did not know that Marika had run away into the desert, for there was nowhere else for her to go.

Walvis Bay had only one police commissioner and two assistants who patrolled on camels, plus a small jail which was normally empty but today contained a Bushman awaiting trial for stealing a sheep.

It did not take Bertha long to muster the town's resources to search for her daughter. The Bushman was let out on bail of five pounds, which Bertha paid, and a stock breeder from Usakos lent Bertha his four-wheel-drive truck with an Ovambo driver who understood the Bushman dialect.

Everyone wanted to help, but no one held out much hope. The Namib was pitiless. So many prospectors had disappeared without a trace, their skeletons hidden by sand.

How tired she was and so thirsty, but Marika was afraid to stop. If she stopped she would have to admit that she was lost and so far she had managed to keep that terrible thought away. It was noon and so hot the air scalded her lungs. She felt dizzy, her pale skin was blistered and her eyes were burning so badly she could hardly see.

At first she had hurried away from the sea, confident that she would soon reach the end of this gigantic seashore, but she had walked all night and most of the morning and there seemed to be no end to it. How could there be so much sand in the world? she wondered miserably. Around her in every direction were ugly mountains of shining red sand. Nothing but sand.

Now she was frightened and she did not know which way to go, but she trudged on, forcing her legs to keep moving.

It seemed to Marika that hours had passed, but the merciless sun still hung overhead and the sand shimmered and trembled. When she tried to sit down she blistered her bare legs; her tongue was sticking to the roof of her mouth and brilliant white lights danced before her eyes.

In the late afternoon she heard a curious rattling sound which seemed to come from all around her, a strange hissing, shifting, creeping noise, and when she looked she saw that the desert had become alive. The sand was racing around in circles, lifting up and falling down. A sudden whoosh smothered her with sand in a single blast. Oh, how it stung her blistered skin. She screamed and began to run, but there was nowhere to hide, for the sand was everywhere.

She spat sand out of her mouth and tried to rub it out of her eyes and ears. The whistling became a roaring and the sand grazed her body with a million sharp impregnations. Shielding her eyes, she looked up and was terrified to see the tops of the mountains changing shape, blowing away and piling up again; twisting and turning. Suddenly the roaring stopped and then the whispering and the desert was deadly quiet again.

Marika was terrified. She wanted to cry, but no tears would come. Mountains of sand were squatting menacingly over her. They were waiting for the wind and then they would topple down and bury her alive.

Was she going to die? she wondered.

There was sand everywhere, in her eyes, her ears and her nose, enmeshed in her eyelashes, caught in her hair and embedded in the blisters that covered the skin. "Oh, oh, oh," she moaned. Even worse than the sand was the loneliness.

Then, ahead of her, she saw a curious green blob and she stumbled toward it. It looked like a crippled monster tree sprawled on its belly, green leaves writhing over the sand, but at least it was alive.

She heard the whisper again as the desert wind gathered strength from far away. She took off her dress with shaking hands and put on her coat, then she crept under the monstrous leaves, and wrapping her dress around her head she curled into a tight ball.

"Mary, mother of Jesus, send Mama to save me," she prayed. "Mary, mother of Jesus . . ." At last she fell into an exhausted sleep.

How cruel! If the wind had held off another hour or two surely she would have found Marika, or so Bertha thought as she urged the driver to continue. But it was impossble to search in a sandstorm. The Bushman climbed under the truck and Bertha and the driver sheltered under a tarpaulin while the wind raged and rocked the vehicle and whined through the sand dunes hour after weary hour.

How could the poor child survive in such a storm? She would be buried alive. Occasionally Bertha stuck her head out from under the tarpaulin but she could see nothing; visibility was nil and the sand battered her face, filled her eyes and drove her weeping back under the tarpaulin.

In the late afternoon the wind dropped, allowing them to resume their search, but there was no point in continuing, for the tracks had been obscured by the storm. Still, they tried until nightfall.

It was late that night when the sad party returned to Walvis Bay.

Dawn found Bertha waiting at the army camp for the aircraft and pilot detailed to help her.

The aircraft carried enough fuel for a four-hour search and they made for the point where Marika's tracks had been obscured by the storm on the previous afternoon.

As they traced and retraced the supposed route she had taken, the pilot glanced sympathetically at Bertha. He knew it was hopeless. The sandstorm of the previous evening had obliterated all tracks. In his opinion the girl was buried somewhere. One day the dunes would shift and a few more bones would litter the Skeleton Coast.

Chapter Eight

"Mary, mother of Jesus, save me; Mary, mother of Jesus, save me." A whispered supplication lost in the murmuring wind.

It was noon on the second day and Marika was dehydrated and exhausted, her tongue swollen and sore; her throat on fire. Her stomach ached and she was burning all over. Her legs were shaking so much she could not walk and she crawled over the stones and ridges on her raw hands and knees.

When she was too tired to carry on she lay on a rock and stared hopelessly around. It was then that she saw the hyena slowly approaching from behind her. She tried to scream, but only a croak came. When the great slobbering beast saw her staring at him it sat on its haunches and let out a mournful cry. Desperately Marika began to crawl forward again. If only Mama were here.

She began to think about the night she had lost Mama and it seemed so real. Once again she was back in the streets of Brno, following her mother and occasionally blundering into her swollen heels. She could hear the clatter of their feet on cobbles and knew they were making too much noise. The clash of trains in the shunting yard was closer now, mingled with distant thunder as clouds covered the sky.

"Sorry," she murmured after stumbling against her again.

"Shoosh!" her mother whispered.

They were approaching a scrap-iron dump; Marika looked sidelong fearfully as they crept past. Macabre shapes trembled in the wind and reached out to catch her. Suddenly she screamed loud and piercingly and hung on to her mother. Then brilliant light flooded the street. Her mother flung her back and away, but Mama was trapped in the blaze; her eyes were wide and staring, her mouth open.

"Run, Marika, run!" she yelled.

The sound of shots was like a physical blow; the pavement exploded as her mother jerked in the air like a puppet at a Punch and Judy show.

Marika tried to run, tried to do as Mama had told her, but she could not. Instead she crouched next to her mother, saw her head fall back.

She must run from the Germans, Mama had said so and Mama was dead, but when she glanced fearfully over her shoulder she saw only the slobbering jowls of the hyena and smelled its fetid breath. She forced herself to her knees and then to her feet and stood swaying for a few minutes. Then she stumbled onward.

Later she heard her mother calling to her. She saw a light flickering ahead and heard her mother's voice: "Come along, Marika, not far to go. Don't loiter or we'll be late for supper." They were coming down the hill on a narrow winding path through the trees toward the village where they would catch the bus for Ghubczuce. She could see the lights from the cottages and far ahead she could hear her dog barking impatiently. He was always in a hurry to go home. "Come along, Marika." Her mother sounded impatient now. "You're going the wrong way. Turn west. Turn west toward the sea."

The sea? How strange. There was no sea, but she turned obediently and followed her mother's lantern.

Oh, how tired she was. She stumbled and fell. "Marika, you're a big girl now, pick up your feet," her mother scolded. She tried to catch up with Mama, but the flickering light was always ahead.

"Wait, wait," she cried.

"Hurry, Marika, don't stop."

Then she heard her mother whisper close behind her. "Don't stop whatever you do. Remember Mama loves you."

Marika lurched on, through the night, hour after hour,

first one step then the next, each one a monumental effort as she followed the light of the lantern.

At last dawn came. Marika looked around and found she was alone. But of course she was alone, for Mama had died in Brno, she knew that now.

In front of her was a tall rocky outcrop and she crawled up onto it, amazed that she still had the strength to do so, and looking back she saw the hyena stand swaying on its long ungainly front feet, shaking its head from side to side. Then it turned and moved away.

Ahead of her was a narrow cleft between tall rocks and she could hear the thunder of surf, but there was no sea. Then, higher up along the riverbed she saw a mountain of water foaming white in the sunlight. The roll of thunder was the noise it made as it cascaded over the dried sand and rocks. The solid wall of water was as high as a room as it raced toward her.

Impossible, she decided. She must be dreaming again.

Terrified, she scrambled to the top of the rocks and hung on trembling as floodwaters from the uplands tore through the riverbed. There was thunder crashing around her ears and the air was full of spray. The rocks began to tremble as the breaker hammered the sand, but in a split second it had passed and Marika found herself lying beside a chocolate-brown river flowing sullenly to the sea, yellow foam bubbling on the surface.

Water! She scrambled down the rock into the river and, heedless of the force of the current, waded in, burying her head in the warm water and gulping huge mouthfuls.

She had no strength left to fight the flood as it sucked her under and bumped her on the sandy riverbed.

Rocks and sand tumbled about her as the river spread over the ground. Her feet touched bottom, but she was too weak to stand: she could only drift in the water. But the flood had passed and the last wave deposited her gently on a bank as the river seeped slowly down through the sand.

She sat up, aching in every limb, but when she tried to stand she found she could not. A multitude of small creatures were picking themselves up and scurrying back to the

sand dunes. Marika watched them and smiled. She felt
light-headed, giddy with relief. Strange, jumbled thoughts
flashed through her mind in rapid succession. Mama was
dead, but Mama still loved her. She had died because of
her daughter, but she was not angry.

A massive burden of guilt slid away and seeped into the
sand with the floodwaters. Mama had guided her back to
the water, back to safety, to her new home in the despised
shack over the store. Mama would not be angry if she
loved Bertha just a little bit.

At the thought of Bertha she felt strangely comforted.
Bertha was out there somewhere looking for her, Marika
had no doubt about that. But how would she find her? She
had walked so far.

"Mary, mother of Jesus, send Bertha to save me," she
prayed over and over. Suddenly she felt a tremendous
surge of comfort. She knew she could rely on both of
them.

It was sunset when they found her.

Chapter Nine

Within weeks Marika had almost recovered, but she never
lost her fear and hatred of the desert.

One day among the heap of presents left at her bedside
she found crayons and a sketchbook and she began to draw
the strange birds she had seen along the shore.

When Bertha left the store and ran upstairs to see how
she was, she said, "How lovely, darling. Who drew them
for you?"

"I did." Marika pointed to herself and smiled. Her
burgeoning English had to be assisted with numerous expressions and gestures.

"You think I believe you? What a little tease you are!"

So Marika had to sit and draw while Bertha watched, and afterward Bertha ordered several frames from the joiners so the sketches could be hung around the house and admired.

It was the same with her English. Was there ever a child who learned so quickly? Friends would be waylaid to witness Bertha's claims, so Marika tried even harder and was amazed how much she could remember from those hated lessons in the refugee camp.

Bertha was hoping that Marika would soon feel at home. On Tu Bi-Shevat she bought a large pot and a seedling tree, which she gave Marika to plant; Purim came and Marika politely ate the three-cornered cakes filled with plum jam which Bertha made; at Pesach she prepared the seder plate; and at Shavuot she helped decorate their home with flowers and plants.

Christmas time came and a huge tree with fairy lights glowed from the hotel window. One evening when they were passing, Bertha caught sight of Marika's expression as she gazed through the window. Even after Bertha explained why Christmas trees had no place in a Jewish home, Marika was filled with such longing, such poignancy! Bertha felt sad for her foster daughter.

So Bertha trod the well-worn, guilt-ridden path of compromise and bought a beautiful potted fir, shipped from the Cape, and told Marika it was a Hanukkah bush. On it they put eight burning candles and in the evening Bertha told Marika the story of the Jews who recaptured Jerusalem from the Syrian Greeks in 165 B.C. Of how they cleansed the Temple and relit the great menorah, and the legend of how they found a tiny bottle of oil containing enough for only one day, but miraculously the oil burned for eight days.

"That was the very first Hanukkah, which we have celebrated each year since," she told Marika, and was astonished to see the girl crumple in the chair, bury her face in her hands and sob as if in anguish.

Bertha stood up and put her arms around the child. She

was shuddering violently. Her face was flushed and she felt feverishly hot.

"Why, Marika. Darling! Whatever is the matter, child? Do you feel ill? Do you have a pain?"

"I'm sorry," Marika whispered, trembling in her arms, her head pressed against Bertha's soft shoulder while her hands gripped her arms so tightly Bertha could feel the nails piercing her skin.

"There's no sense in doing all this for me," Marika sobbed. "I'm not Jewish. I don't want to be Jewish. There's no sense in it, I tell you. I'm a Catholic. My father was Jewish, but my mother raised me in her church. That's the end of it. There! Leave me alone." She flung herself on the settee and buried her face in the cushions. "I'm sorry," Marika sobbed. "I know how much you wanted a daughter."

There was a long, awkward silence.

"Can't Catholics be daughters, then?" Bertha asked, more sharply than she had intended. "If you're a Catholic, Marika," Bertha said, more gently this time, "then tell me why you were put with a trainload of Jewish refugee children."

Marika opened her eyes wide. There was a look of fear on her face which Bertha could not help but notice. It hurt her.

"I never really knew," Marika sobbed. She buried her face in her hands, trying to remember. She could still hear the pounding rain, the thunder; she could remember running along the railway track until she heard the soldiers shout.

She looked up at Bertha. "It's so difficult to explain. An old man helped me because he knew my father at the hospital," she whispered.

Later Bertha said, "Suddenly I don't feel so guilty about having a Hanukkah bush. It's yours. It was really a Christmas tree anyway." She began to take off the candles.

"Can't we share it?" she heard a muffled voice say from the sofa.

Bertha bent over the sideboard pretending not to hear.

She felt confused and foolish, but she did not want Marika to see. "I think there's someone in the store," she lied, and hurried downstairs, wiping her eyes with the back of her hand. She began tidying the store compulsively, but her thoughts were far away.

Marika loved her. She fixed that in her mind. After all, she had shown it in so many ways. Bertha sighed. It had been so hard to come to terms with being a foster mother; to cope with the knowledge that one day Marika would go away and she might never see the child again. Yet she loved her like her own. Well, she decided, cutting through this futility, if Marika was a Catholic, then she would be a good Catholic. Surely there were some decorations left in the store.

"All right, we'll share the tree," she said a few minutes later when she bustled back carrying a box full of ornaments from the East.

"Who would believe it?" she murmured when Marika had finished. A Christmas tree with eight Hanukkah candles on top. Marika had insisted Bertha have pride of place, even over the Christmas angel.

"If you'd told me before, you could have had an Easter egg, Marikala," Bertha told her.

"I wanted to be like you, but I just couldn't make it," Marika replied. She turned and watched her so intently that for a moment Bertha was quite overcome with the gravity of the conversation.

"Perhaps if we lived somewhere else," Marika stammered.

"Why? Would that make a difference?"

"You see," she struggled to explain, "there's nothing here, nothing at all that was important to me at home. I have nothing left. Well, I have you, of course," she added hastily, watching Bertha's face, "but of the old me—well—really—what is there? When I think of all the things that were so important then."

"Such as?"

"Spring," she blurted out. "The changing seasons. Here it's always warm, hardly ever too hot and never cold.

No spring flowers, no autumn leaves, no roaring fires and snow. Mama and I used to collect flowers in spring and later pine cones for the fire and chestnuts.'' She broke off and bit her lip.

''There's no birdsong, unless you count the din the sea gulls make. Oh, just to lie in the grass, feel a cool breeze on my face, watch the clouds sail overhead, hear the bees buzzing and smell the grass. And people! I miss people.''

Jewish or Catholic, it made no difference. Marika was the center of Bertha's universe and as the months passed her daughter thrived; she became tall and sturdy; her face filled out and her hair grew longer. She began to look less of a deprived child and she gained a little confidence.

Once she had made up her mind to try at school, she quickly excelled and for two successive years she was top of her class. Bertha was proud of her. Marika had made up her mind to continue with her French so that she could live in France with her father at the end of the war, so Bertha organized extra lessons. She would be a famous model, she told Bertha time and again. The poor child spent hours drawing the dresses she would wear.

It was at times like these that Bertha felt sorry for her. She was so tall and gawky; her teeth were too big; her mouth too large; her features too angular. She looked like an overgrown elf with her slanting eyes and pointed ears. Admittedly, now that her hair was longer she looked better.

Yet, as the months passed, Bertha had to admit her foster daughter was a strange girl, introverted, secretive and obviously unhappy in Walvis Bay. She was never at home, she merely stayed there and although she did not shirk her share of the chores she remained uninvolved— until August 1942—the date when Irwin was killed at Alam el Halfa.

The telegram arrived on a crisp, delightful Sunday morning, the sea was sparkling blue, there was a hint of a breeze smelling strongly of ozone, the pelicans were wading in shallow water close to the store and Bertha almost forgot the war as they watched the birds—so she was momentarily off guard.

She collapsed and shortly afterward caught pneumonia. For the next month Marika ran the store and nursed her foster mother with the help of Rose, the nurse from the hospital who called daily.

Bertha recovered eventually, but she was more dependent upon Marika, and as if sensing this the girl drew closer to her and tried her best to be the daughter her foster mother needed so. She began to worry about Bertha.

"At the end of the war," she said to her unexpectedly one night, "you will come to France with me. We'll be happy there."

"I like it here," Bertha said sadly. "I've been very lucky," she went on defensively. And she had. She and Irwin had built their supply store into a complex operation and they had been happy doing it together. Over the years she had even grown to love the town, or part of it. She loved the comradeship of a small community when they gathered at the only hotel for the weekly cinema show; she loved the people; the busy harbor; the seals lazing in the bay; the multitude of sea birds. There was so much here, but Marika refused to see it. She looked at her sadly.

"As soon as the war's over," Marika went on, "we shall go to Paris and live there with Papa and perhaps you and Papa will marry eventually."

Bertha smiled, wishing Marika were not so immature.

"And what about the store?"

"Oh, you'll sell it," she said. "You're bound to get a good price. You'll have to come with me. After all, I'm all you have now."

Well, she wasn't lying. This awful thought chilled Bertha as she lay awake that night longing for Irwin. She had the strangest feeling that her roots were to be hauled painfully out of the desert sand.

Chapter Ten

There was little enough time for worrying about the future in the months ahead, for the Factor store had become the pivot of Walvis Bay. Bertha had to go to the bank for a loan to stock all the varied requirements of naval vessels on unscheduled visits. She employed a counter hand and then a second and finally she had to engage a full-time bookkeeper.

The Allies' fortunes were improving at last. RAF and U.S. bombing raids on Germany were well underway; Tunis and Bizerte fell; in July the Allies invaded Sicily; shortly afterward the Americans landed in New Guinea and the Russians retook Kharkov.

Marika spent hours studying the war news from magazines and newspapers which arrived from Europe months late. When naval personnel came into their store she always rushed to question them. Inevitably she would ask, "When do you think it will be over?" She was so eager to go to France.

The child was growing up. While Bertha was proud of the role she had played, she had to admit that the Catholic church had helped, too. Marika had regained a part of her past, she felt at home among the mysteries, the incense and the intoned Latin prayers and she was very devout, but God was not the object of her reverence. No, it was the Virgin Mary who had replaced her mother and as the months passed the memory of her mother underwent a metamorphosis until her features exactly resembled the statue in the church.

She had left school now and was studying bookkeeping at home. She often helped in the store: a strong and capable assistant who charmed everyone she met.

Sometimes Bertha would look at her and catch her breath with fright, for at a certain angle, or in a certain light, she would glimpse a rare loveliness and then, as quickly, it would vanish.

Was there real beauty hiding there, or was it just a mirage? A trick of the light and the situation? Or perhaps beauty was able to lie concealed like a cactus flower in the sand, waiting for that preordained moment when it would burst out and enrich the desert with its dazzling perfection.

What a silly woman you are, Bertha Factor, she would tell herself. The child had never even been pretty. But still, something about those slanting amber eyes was strangely compelling, Please, God, don't let her become a beauty. Charming? Why, yes. But beautiful? No! Bertha knew Marika would never be able to handle it. She was too gentle, too trusting. Goodness bubbled out of her from some inexhaustible inner spring.

Marika was unaware of Bertha's increasing dismay as she grew and grew. She looked in the mirror and saw a stranger, but no matter, for she was all bound up in her inner self. A sense of secret oneness pervaded her body and her mind; she quivered with the vibrations of the earth, her mother; and the air, her father; a child of their fertile impregnation. There she stood, vulnerable, thrusting forward; a bird balanced on the edge of the nest ready for that first irrevocable leap; a termite unfolding delicate gossamer wings; a moth emerging from the chrysalis. She was poised on the very lip of life and youth, and the excitement of it, the adventure of it.

Strange dreams would flit across her sleep: Prince Charming in myriad disguises, but always in Allied uniform; and he would carry her away on his trusty steed, but always to Europe. Such happy expectations. Somewhere, she knew, was the only man in the world for her. Once she met him she would love no other man.

Yet she was in no hurry to find him. She was like a novice at the shrine of life, a worshipper of goodness and mercy, trusting, secure in her world of God the Father, God the Son and God the Holy Ghost, plus the Virgin

Mary and a host of saints to boot. Prayers and promises! The world of flesh and spirit, neatly bound in a package deal and labeled "Life!" Soon, she knew, she would pick up the parcel, unwrap the wrappings, grasp the gift.

And then?

Oh, Marika! Oh, Marika!

The place was Oradour-sur-Glane, a small town near Limoges in southern France. The time: 2:15 P.M. on June 10, 1944. The town's population of 330, swollen to some 650 by the war, lingered over lunch this sunny summer afternoon; a scene which was destined to become frozen in history.

The town was crowded that day; the schools were full because it was the day for medical inspection and vaccination. The boys' school held sixty-four children, the girls' one hundred and six, and there was a new school for child refugees. By early afternoon the farm workers had come in from the fields, and a few weekend fishermen had come to try their luck on the Glane. It was a peaceful, rural scene.

The sight of Major Otto Geissler's 1st Battalion of the Führer Regiment, part of the SS division Das Reich, with their convoy of trucks and half-tracks driving through the main street of Oradour-sur-Glane, caused immediate astonishment and bewilderment. Why were they there? Why Oradour? No one knew.

The SS troops fired into the air, banged on doors with their rifle butts, burst into the school classrooms and called everyone into the small central square, known as the Champ de Foire. When at last all the villagers were assembled, the men were ordered to their feet—forty to fifty at a time— and marched out of the square to nearby garages and barns.

At 3:30 P.M., at a signal shot from the square, the Germans fired into the crowds of Frenchmen in their execution chambers. Then soldiers heaped straw and brushwood over the bodies, many of which were still alive. They set fire to the buildings and closed the doors.

Only five male survivors lived to testify about events in Oradour-sur-Glane that fateful afternoon.

Over four hundred women, children and babies were crowded into the village church. The doors were slammed shut and the church was set alight. The soldiers cocked their weapons, activated their grenades and killed the fugitives who tried to fight their way through the vestry door. Only one woman escaped.

Later, when the Germans left Oradour-sur-Glane laden with loot, and the French from neighboring villages were permitted to bury their dead, Oradour lay in smoking ruins, its population destroyed, an act of unbelievable savagery against a defenseless civilian population.

Only one Maquis leader was killed in Oradour-sur-Glane that day; a doctor, Janos Magos, of French and Czechoslovakian extraction, who had cycled into the village to collect his tobacco ration, issued every ten days. His body was charred almost beyond recognition and he was buried in a mass grave three days later.

The news was conveyed to Marika, his daughter and only surviving relative, for his sister had been shot at the time of the German evacuation from Czechoslovakia. It came by a devious route, via the International Red Cross and the Jewish Board of Deputies, arriving months after the crime. The rabbi from Swakopmund deemed it serious enough to travel to Walvis Bay to break the news personally to Marika.

"Never forget that your father was a very great man who devoted his life to the universal cause of good over evil. His death was accidental," the rabbi explained gently. "By chance he was in Oradour, which the Germans had picked for reprisals, and he died with the entire population. The Germans never discovered his true identity or that he was Maquis.

"A terrible crime against humanity," the rabbi said.

When the rabbi left, Marika walked slowly to the church and stayed there all that day and the next. At first she prayed, between torrents of grief and rage. She prayed for vengeance; that was all she had left to pray for. It seemed to Marika that the butchers of Oradour symbolized the nature of all Nazis. Emblems of savagery! On them she concentrated her loathing and her longing for revenge and more particularly the leader of the Führer Regiment, Major Otto Geissler, who had planned the destruction of Oradour. She prayed that he would die horribly and she would see him dying.

After a few days she realized that she was quite alone in the church. The sense of love and of oneness with God had vanished. Of course it had never been there, she persuaded herself. "Just silly imaginings. No one," she kept muttering. "There's no one there at all. Just some silly statues. There's no God—how can there be?" She would never come here again, she decided. Now only she was left to care and take revenge. The weight of her responsibility hung heavily on her shoulders as she swore a great, lonely oath. Then she went back to the store.

Marika was slipping away from her, Bertha noticed sadly after the rabbi's visit. Bertha knew she must plan for the girl's future, but she could not breach her defenses.

She tried to persuade Marika to attend high school as a boarder in Johannesburg, for no higher education was available in Walvis Bay, but Marika refused.

"I won't be here long enough" was her usual retort, yet there was nowhere for her to go.

Bertha went to great lengths to try to convince Marika that the store was half hers and one day she would inherit it all. Why not become an official co-director now? she argued, but Marika refused.

Marika became listless, depressed, and behaved badly to her friends and was particularly unkind to Bertha.

Bertha thought she understood. The poor child was grieving for her father, but she would recover eventually, Bertha comforted herself.

The weeks merged into months, and although Marika never mentioned her father again, Bertha noticed that the girl read all she could about the Oradour massacre and would talk darkly of revenge, one day when she was older and very rich. Her hatred of Germans was becoming paranoiac and this worried Bertha, too. When a farmer of German stock visited the store Marika would quietly slip outside. She would not . . . no, she *could* not serve him.

From that time on, too, she would not go to church.

"It was men who killed your parents, not God," Bertha told her repeatedly.

"There's no God," the girl would answer with a lost and hopeless look on her face. "Or if there is . . . why . . . then it's no one I want to know. My mother, my father, my aunt, all dead. And when I think of all those prayers and all those aching knees."

"Why, dear child, you mustn't talk like that," Bertha would chide her. "It's not what you get out of religion that counts. It's what you put into it."

"It's just a load of hot air," Marika would retort and a strange, obstinate look would come into her eyes.

When Marika turned seventeen in January 1945, she had become what Bertha had always dreaded, a woman of incredible loveliness. Her skin was porcelain white and quite flawless, her unusual golden hair hung around her shoulders, her features were perfect, her figure tempting and voluptuous with full breasts, a narrow waist and wide hips tapering to long, shapely legs. Perhaps her mouth was a trifle too large, but her face was dominated by her enormous slanting amber-brown eyes. Yet her appeal lay elsewhere. Perhaps it was her latent sensuality, of which she was quite unaware. Each man wanted to be the prince who would awaken the sleeping beauty.

Marika had become strangely self-confident. Bertha knew why, too. She no longer cared about anyone or anything, or what they thought of her.

Before long she became aware of her power over men, for even the toughest seamen were turned into grinning oafs when they saw Marika. As for the local youths, they loitered in droves offering gifts and promises.

Her fame spread along the South-West African coast.

Local fishermen began to think up all manner of foolish excuses to come into the store; stock breeders from up to a hundred miles away would pick on items they could purchase only from Walvis Bay and so they hung around cluttering the store, buying little and taking long enough about it.

Marika refused them all. She had no time for them, and the ruder she was, the more they tried to win her.

Bertha watched and said little. The softness had vanished; the sweet, youthful sensitivity, the compassionate eyes, the delicate shyness of her—all gone. In its place was a steel-like resolve to become strong and powerful; never to be trampled upon and destroyed. Yet underneath, the sweetness was still there, Bertha knew. One day Marika would find herself again.

If only she would fall in love . . . The more Bertha thought about it, the more it seemed to offer the solution. Besides, a son-in-law could run the store, which had become such a profitable operation; it would provide an excellent living and a good enough future for any ambitious young man.

But Marika was too beautiful and too ambitious, contemptuous of all lesser men. Bertha began to despair of finding anyone in South-West Africa good enough for her daughter.

Chapter Eleven

For Europe the war was nearly over. The Russians had captured Vienna and were pushing on toward Berlin, which lay in the jaws of a gigantic vise of Russian forces. The Allied advance to link up with the Red Army on the Elbe was marked occasionally by desperate resistance, but on the whole opposition was sporadic and isolated. Communications and command in the German Army had been entirely broken down.

This was not the case at sea.

The reconquest of the German-controlled coastline was the job of Montgomery's Twenty-first Army Group. British and Canadian forces were charged with clearing U-boat ports which could still serve as bases for damaging submarine raids against Allied shipping in the North Sea. Although the Battle of the Atlantic had been fought and won, a handful of powerful oceangoing U-boats were still at large. Their captains faced a unique and devastating defeat—they were forced to surrender as fuel and provisions ran out. Many chose suicidal battles in preference to prison camps.

One of them was Captain Max Erath, commander of the secret U-boat, the XLII. With its superior electric propulsion backed by Walther cycle turbines, this superb fighting ship, first of its kind, could cruise at a surface speed of over fourteen knots and at submerged speeds of eleven knots.

This boat was one of Germany's late, but effective, secret weapons, designed to wreak havoc on Allied shipping by avoiding detection for long periods underwater. Its revolutionary "schnorkel" could take in air for ventilation and expel waste air. The U-boat was crewed by fifty-six men, handpicked for fitness, intelligence, endurance and bravery, and each man had a first-class record.

In the past six months, the XLII had sunk twelve enemy ships and disabled another three. Now she was waiting off the South-West African coast for a British convoy of ten cargo boats and two escorting destroyers. Captain and crew alike knew that it was touch and go whether or not fuel ran out before the convoy was sighted.

In the control room the captain paced the deck tensely. The first mate, Steen, watched him in disbelief. In two years at sea he had not once seen the captain lose his composure. Yet now Erath looked like a beaten man.

"Up periscope," he ordered, his voice hoarse; unrecognizable.

Thrust into the atmosphere, the dripping glass revealed only whiteness, for the fog was so dense he could not even see the waves two feet below.

Erath swore and wiped his forehead. Normally he was a man of infinite patience and cunning; he possessed an almost uncanny ability to project enemy strategies. Steen understood, but could not share, the patriotic fervor that was driving him to destroy them all in this last, suicidal attack.

Steen sighed. It had been a long and difficult period for all the crew. The XLII was designed for speed, with a minimum of crew facilities. They had been submerged nonstop for twenty-eight days and the air was heavy with the smell of human waste. Green slime coated the walls and the charts, the crew were pale-faced and short-tempered. Only their supreme self-discipline saved them from squabbling with each other. They were nearing the war's end. They knew this because they maintained regular radio contact with Argentina and Las Palmas. What was the point in more loss of life? the first mate wondered.

In the engine room, the chief engineer, Hans Kolb, echoed Steen's sentiments but was in no way suffering from their long stint underwater. There was always something to do in the engine room and besides, Hans was blessed with remarkable fortitude, the ability to take almost any discomfort without breaking, plus an irrepressible optimism.

Right now his six-foot-three frame was curled under some low-slung pipes and he was totally absorbed in his beloved diesels. His assistant, Franz Schmidt, known as Smitty, was not so fortunate. The fetid air sickened him, he found the heat unbearable and it seemed as if the humidity was as high as it could be without drowning them. The pipes were leaking and dripping continuously, filling the air with the acrid stench of fuel, exhaust fumes and battery acid.

Glancing around, Hans noticed Smitty's face. It was as green as the slime coating the plating.

"Take a break," he grunted. "Two hours." He grinned

and returned to his task and was only dimly aware of the man still behind him.

The captain's voice came tinny and faint through the voice pipe.

"Take her up."

The U-boat surfaced gently and lay shrouded in fog off Swakopmund. Captain Erath mounted the ladder and opened the hatch to the conning tower and stared dismally around him. There was nothing to see but fog in every direction and the sea like a bubbling, boiling cauldron of milk beneath. He clattered down the hatch like a man possessed.

"Take her down," he said tersely, and slamming the conning tower hatch he secured the catches. Water splashed over the deck as the XLII dived steeply.

"Stop engines," he called into the voice pipe. Then: "Dead quiet."

In the engine room Hans squatted on a pump and listened to the monotonous drip of the leaking pipes, uneven and therefore disturbing.

A deadly hush settled over the U-boat, which seemed unnatural after the incessant hum of the diesels. The machinery was stilled, no one spoke. Five minutes . . . ten minutes . . .

Hans knew that in the control room the captain would be listening on the hydrophone for the telltale throb of the convoy's many engines. At this distance it was still more effective than any other instrument.

Hans stretched awkwardly in the confined space, leaned back and closed his eyes. He breathed deeply and tried to turn his mind away from the discomfort, the proximity of danger and the hopelessness of surviving the war.

He had a favorite dream, based on a poster he had seen once of a beautiful *Fräulein* in traditional peasant dress, her long golden hair blowing in the wind, her full breasts pressing against the white embroidered fabric of her blouse. She was walking in an Austrian field filled with spring flowers.

Hans sighed and smiled to himself as his favorite picture

faithfully emerged. Still, there was something missing; the stench of acid seemed to be overpowering. He tried to imagine the scent of fresh, sparkling mountain air; to hear the wind blowing through the treetops and the tinkling cowbells; the fragrance of wildflowers on the hillsides and the smell of the dairy at milking time.

Making a monumental effort of will, he held the picture for longer than his customary split second; then the monotonous throb of engines carried through the water drove the vision away. He scrambled to his feet and gripped the throttle, anticipating the captain's command.

"Full ahead."

Hans thrust the throttle hard forward.

Then: "Action stations! Action stations! We are engaging the enemy."

The full force of the Walther diesels sent the U-boat thrusting forward to reach eleven knots; the XLII wobbled slightly with backwash from the forward surge.

The convoy was approaching at ten knots, Hans reckoned. They were going in too fast. Annihilation! That's what he wants, he thought.

The crew had been together too long not to be aware of their captain's intentions. After years at sea, much of which had been spent submerged with the same companions, they had become extraordinarily sensitive to each other. Uncanny in a way, Hans thought.

He knew, for instance, that his friend Steen would be dead set against the captain's sentiments. Steen was a pragmatist, as Hans was. While he was prepared to die to win the war, he was not prepared to throw his life away needlessly; sentiments which Hans secretly seconded and most of the crew, too, although none of them had ever talked about it.

It was common knowledge that the captain had been ordered to destroy their U-boat rather than let it be captured, but now, when they were within weeks of the war's end, what was the point of it? All German inventions would be in the hands of the Allies shortly.

Hans could see no reason for further loss of life, either

theirs or the enemy's. Still, he had done his duty. Enlisting at the outbreak of the war when he was seventeen, he had been chosen for training in engines because of his superb grasp of anything mechanical. He had been picked for submarines because of his extraordinary ability to keep cheerful and calm for long periods under the most adverse conditions. Later, he had been sent to train on diesels. After the war, he would be able to find a job as a diesel engineer without much difficulty. But he knew that he was unlikely to see the war's end.

"Slow ahead."

The telegraph sent him into another flurry of activity. He found himself wishing that the fuel would give out there and then. He swore as he heard the whoosh of the first torpedo fired. Followed immediately afterward by a second. Hans could almost feel the tension in the submarine as the crew waited, counting.

A minute, a minute and a half, two minutes. Silence!

They had missed. There was another whoosh and the third was fired and then the fourth.

". . . sixty-one, sixty-two, sixty-three . . ."

Then came the sound of giant knuckles rapping on a distant hull. A hit! Hans froze, automatically counting. A second explosion came louder a minute later, and then a third, an enormous bolt of noise that hit the submarine at the same time as the backwash caught them.

Explosives in the cargo, Hans guessed.

The U-boat's bows lifted and she spun half around, like a live creature, throwing Hans and Schmidt together on the floor.

Slowly she righted herself and surged ahead, but now came a new and more ominous sound of destroyers approaching.

"Too close," Hans murmured. He longed to clutch the throttle, push it hard over to full ahead; instead they were moving slowly on a collision course. "Run for it, run for it," he murmured.

The captain's voice came tinny through the voice pipe.

"Ninety feet. Course two-three-oh." And then: "Full ahead."

Hans took a deep breath as he pushed the throttle.

The destroyers would have worked out their approximate position at firing, but they could not know of the tremendous speed of which the XLII was capable, or so Hans prayed.

He was right. The first explosion was well behind and above them. He heard the hollow thud as the depth charge exploded.

"Eleven knots," Hans murmured to Smitty. "We'll keep it up until the fuel runs out. Twelve hours, plus-minus. Enough! Then there's the batteries."

Smitty gave him a sickly smile.

"Come on," Hans clapped him on the shoulder, but at that moment there was a deafening noise as the second depth charge exploded, deeper and frighteningly close.

It was followed by another, slightly further off to starboard.

"Too damn close," Hans muttered.

"Stop engines."

The captain's command indicated that they could not hope to run for it. Even the XLII could not compete with a destroyer's speed. He was going to dive and sit it out near the bottom.

Sure enough, they were sinking rapidly. Hans heard the air hissing out of the valves and the water bubbling into the ballast tanks.

"Too fast, too fast, watch it," he wanted to yell. At last, after an eternity, the hissing ceased and the submarine steadied.

Hans wiped his forehead. He was wet through from the heat and from fright. In the dim light he saw Smitty do the same. His shirt was sticking to his chest and he looked exhausted.

"Dead quiet," the captain said.

Hans winked at Smitty: tried out a tense smile and pointed his thumb, The next five minutes seemed to last five hours. They could hear the destroyer's engines almost overhead.

Then a shattering explosion aft of the motor room sent the U-boat writhing like a harpooned whale.

For a terrifying minute, Hans hung on to a pipe and watched Smitty fall backwards, knocking his head on the engine. The U-boat tossed and heaved, rolled sideways and backwards, and there was a sensation of falling. As Hans watched, desperately trying to assess the damage, the lights slowly faded.

Suddenly he became aware of Smitty lying facedown in water which was already ankle deep. Then there was total blackness.

Fumbling in the dark, Hans reached out for Smitty and hoisted him over some pipes. He found his flashlight and switched it on. He could hear the captain's voice, sounding calmer now. Back to normal now that the bastard's achieved his target, Hans thought.

"Report damage immediately, Kolb," the captain was calling.

The flashlight revealed the damage all too clearly, for the explosion had wrenched most of the pipes askew. Water and fuel were dripping from a thousand cracks.

Hans made his way through the deepening water to the motor room. There he stared horrified at the jet of sea-water which was being forced at high pressure through a hole as thick as his fist where the depth charge had fractured the U-boat's plating. The hissing spray dampened his face while the water bubbled and frothed and foamed around his knees. The batteries were underwater already and the level was rising rapidly.

Hans backed into the engine room. Using all his strength, he forced the door shut and battened it down securely. By now the dripping from the pipes had become a trickle. The submarine had tilted over hard and was sinking rapidly aft down. Hans clambered up the sloping, slippery floor to the voice pipe, where the captain was still calling for information.

"Bad," he gasped. "The plating's holed in the motor

room and it's filling up fast. I've battened down the door; there's no possibility of any more power. The diesels are half submerged already and the pipes are leaking in a dozen places. Hopeless!''

''Batten down the engine room and get up to the control room,'' the captain said tersely.

Hans caught hold of Smitty, and was about to hoist him over his shoulder, when something about the lie of his head made him catch his breath. Smitty was dead; his neck broken.

As he laid him gently over the pipes, the thought came: Quick and clean; perhaps he's luckier.

For the first time in his life Hans experienced a deep, paralyzing fear. He had an insane desire to smash his way out. Adrenaline surged through his limbs and he began to shake uncontrollably. He reeled back against the pipes, fighting for control.

Trapped! They were all trapped.

The heat was becoming intense from the unstable fuel the Walther diesels used. He began to choke.

''Get control of yourself; get out of here.'' It was a stranger's voice, but he knew it was his own.

Fumbling through the galley, he heard the sound of praying; a hurried, mumbled supplication, as if the man had a great deal to say and not too long to say it.

The XLII keeled over to a forty-five-degree angle; it was next to impossible to manage the incline as he crawled through the petty officers' mess. Hans thrust his flashlight into his pocket and flung himself on all fours, clawing his way up the slippery deck plates.

Then the U-boat struck bottom. There was not much concussion, just a leveling out and the sound of crunching as she settled bumpily at a gently sloping angle. After that there was only the sound of water pouring into the engine room and the gurgling and dripping of pipes.

By the time Hans reached the control room he had calmed himself and a sense of shame gripped him. He, who had been through the Battle of the Atlantic and two years' service in the Arctic and who had expected death daily for five years, had suddenly crumpled. He knew why, too. They were so close to the end of the war and it was all so pointless. He stared at the captain with something close to hatred in his eyes as he stood to attention.

"Motor room and engine room hatches battened down, sir. Schmidt's dead. Broke his neck in a fall."

"Lucky fellow," the captain said, and laughed softly. "Well, a few more can escape, yes?" He raised an eyebrow significantly and looked at Hans. "Who do you suggest I choose first, Hans?"

"Senior officers, sir, or married men." Suddenly Hans felt overwhelmingly tired. "Permission to stand at ease, sir."

"Permission granted. And wear a life jacket." He stared at him long and thoughtfully. "Are you a married man, Hans?"

"No, sir. Never had time. I was too young before the war."

"Ah, yes, we haven't had much leave, have we? Well, Hans, take this and get up there." He handed Hans the oxygen lung and indicated the escape hatch overhead.

Hans stared at him, wanting to believe him.

"That's an order, Kolb. And you." He gestured to the first mate.

For a moment Hans and Steen stared uneasily at each other.

"Why me?" Hans asked, desperate and guilty.

"Because you are a dreamer, Kolb. The civilized world will need dreamers. How else can it be re-created? And then you were a champion swimmer, so you have a chance, yes?"

A sudden shudder seemed almost to wrench the ship apart. A sound of tearing echoed through the plating. Water surged into the hull with the pressure of millions of tons of the Atlantic around them.

Hans leapt up into the conning tower and reached back for Steen, hauling him up behind him. Too late, he thought, but he heard the hatch being secured. Then he wrenched open the top.

He could see nothing but searing white foam. He felt himself frozen, squashed and flattened, pushed up, rolled over and down. The force of the water wrenched the mask from his face, but he clung to the pipe and rammed it into his mouth, clenching it between his teeth.

Then he was rising and pulling Steen behind him. It was agonizingly cold and pitch dark, except for the occasional flash of phosphorescence. Up there, far above, was air. Life!

Around him was death. He knew there were pockets of air trapped in the cabins below. Men could live for days and die a terrible death. He was unable to control his fear as he kicked out blindly, surging upward.

Too fast, he told himself, too fast by far. Hold it, man, hold back. But the darkness was like an impenetrable wall around him. He gripped the precious pipe more tightly, taking huge gasps of oxygen and holding it in his lungs, letting it trickle slowly from his mouth. His eyes and ears ached intolerably, a warm numbness was sinking into his limbs. He had to fight against it.

He began to kick harder, using his powerful arms to propel himself to the surface. Later, he stopped again and tried to slow his ascent. He knew he was riding too fast and that he would get the bends when he reached the surface, if he ever reached the surface alive. Stygian darkness closed in from all sides.

Chapter Twelve

He had blacked out, but for how long? Hans had no way of knowing. It was still night and the thick fog which had covered the sea was now an eerie yellow glow and icy cold. Perhaps the moon had risen, he thought. He lay back in a state of shock, feeling bemused. He was dying and he did not care. He wanted to sleep above all else.

It was the bends that saved him; sudden red-hot stabs of incredible ferocity in his stomach, his arms and 'shoulders. He heard a voice, high-pitched, and inhuman screaming. The sound echoed forlornly over the empty sea. Then he realized that he was alone and the cries were coming from his own throat. Slowly he fought for sanity. The pain was worse than any he had experienced and he thought it would kill him, but eventually it passed.

Afterward he swam around, cautiously testing his arms and legs, getting to grips with movement and the joy of gasping in pure, fresh air. He called out, "Steen! Steen!" And then: "Hello! Hello!" There was no answer. Eventually he gave up searching for Steen.

Hans knew that they had been a few miles off Walvis Bay when they had sighted the convoy, but now, in this waste of sea and fog, the land could lie in any direction and he had no idea how many miles away. He had only one chance and that was to swim to shore.

Then miraculously the fog lifted momentarily and he saw the moon through the haze just above the horizon. It could be rising or setting. Sure that he had not been unconscious for long, he turned in what he guessed would be an easterly direction.

He set off at a crawl, but half an hour later his breath was rasping and his arms and legs felt as if they were strapped to lead weights. Shooting cramps tormented him. He changed to breaststroke and gloomily considered what five years in enclosed engine rooms had done to diminish his fitness. Good God, at school when he was seventeen, he had swum a five-mile race regularly and won more often than not. He turned and floated on his back and considered the problem. If he took off his life jacket, he would probably drown when fatigue overtook him, but if he retained it, he would never make shore, for the jacket impeded his arm movements and prevented the free flow of his body through the water. He would have to discard it. He struggled out of it, turned and resumed his painful crawl. Then he transferred his papers from his belt to his shirt pocket and discarded his trousers as well.

Hours later pain began to sink deeply into him; into his stomach, under his ribs and into the joints of his knees and shoulders. Too bad. It was necessary that his body became a robot and he would ignore the pain. He began to count, as he used to when training at school: "One, two, three, four; one, two, three, four." The pain was spreading outward to his fingertips but Hans ignored it and concentrated on counting. He carried on for half an hour, or an hour, he had no way of telling; he was mindless, merely a paddleboat as he churned his arms over and over.

Sudden cramps in his legs sent him screaming and threshing in the water. He turned onto his back, struggling to keep afloat and wishing for his life jacket. When the pains passed, he resumed his crawl. Now he was frighteningly aware that he had turned several times and no longer knew which way he was swimming.

If only the fog would clear, he thought sometime later, but it was thicker than ever. When dawn came he would be able to tell which way east lay, but that could be many hours away. Perhaps he was swimming in the wrong direction? Surely it would be better to wait, but when he turned and floated and felt the cold creeping into his limbs, he knew he would die if he did not keep going.

An hour passed and then another, but Hans was only aware of the agony of forcing his limbs to keep swimming as he fought his way through the water. He might have given up were it not for the memory of his comrades, dead and dying under the sea. It was he who had been given the chance to live. He had to live. He felt faint and sick, desperately thirsty. The salt coated his face, encrusted his lips and seared his eyes. His stomach was churning from the salt water he had swallowed. Occasionally he vomited into the sea.

"One, two, three, four; one, two, three, four." Then he heard the sound of water splashing, the rhythmic beat of his competitors, the screaming calls of the boys yelling for their favorite. He was at school, winning the five-hundred-meter crawl. He had to win, knowing that his mother was sitting there, a vision of blue in her blue taffeta dress and hat and her eyes as blue as the cornflowers that grew profusely around the kitchen door. His father was there, too, looking every inch the farmer, in his stiff, uncomfortable Sunday clothes, his arm proprietarily around his wife. Hans knew he could win, knew that the school cup would be on the sideboard beside the cups his father had won and which his mother treasured so.

He had always been jealous of his father, and however hard he tried, his feats never seemed to equal those of a man who was already a legend in the district. So he had fought his way through the water, turning his body into a machine, going faster and harder than he had ever known before, so that he not only won the school cup but had broken the school record and gone on to swim for Germany just before the outbreak of the war.

"One, two, three, four." Nothing else mattered except the necessity of forcing his arms and legs to perform feats for which they had not been designed. Soon, he knew that he had outdistanced them all. He was alone, but there was no end to it. Surely he must reach the bend in the river where the race ended and tape was tied across with gaily colored flags at each side.

He opened his eyes, twisted his head up and stared around. There was nothing but fog, icy and impenetrable, over the cold Atlantic. He turned and trod water for a few seconds. The sight of his mother's face had been so real. He could not stop the tears from racing down his cheeks and with them came the knowledge that this was the first time he had cried for her.

Briefly he contemplated the luxury of giving in and quietly dying here. What was the point of struggling when he knew his chance of reaching land was virtually nil? But he knew that he would never give up. As he turned and groaned with the effort of forcing his arms back and up over his head, he saw a flare at a forty-five-degree angle over his shoulder. He turned and made his way toward it, which he reckoned was only a mile away.

A moment of dizziness left him floundering in the water, spluttering from mouthfuls of sea.

"Goddamn you!" he screamed. "Swim, damn you, swim! Swim, you fool!"

Intolerable pain. His eyes searing, his limbs in agony.

"Get on or die!" he yelled, and choked again.

He could not remember when he began talking to himself, for he'd been lost in that strange world of half consciousness where spirit and body seem to part company. He watched the battered limbs beating the water and relentlessly he urged his body forward.

The fog took on an eerie luminous glow, like a candle flame, and strangely the sea became warmer and then hot. Beneath him a great belch of gas rose, scorching his legs, and the smell of sulphur filled the air. Sulphur and brimstone! He was in hell. This was hell—this endless waste of sea and fog.

Then another flare burst through the fog five hundred yards away and shattered his delirium. Summoning his last reserves of strength, he swam toward it.

He knew now that he would survive; that nothing would ever be quite the same again. From then on the solid earth beneath his feet would be revered and hallowed; each day would be a gift of life, something undeserved and gratefully accepted; he knew, too, that he would never be afraid again; he had conquered fear and pain. The fog was dispersing and for the first time he could see the surface of the sea for three yards around.

Then he saw the dawn. For a brief glorious moment the mist cleared away and the sky was revealed in a splendor of rose and lilac.

"I've made it," he muttered. Land was only a mile away. Not long afterward he heard shouts and a longboat moved toward him. Six sailors manned the oars and one stood in the bows.

"Over here!" he yelled.

There was a sudden silence. The boat towered over him twice as large as life.

"Bloody Kraut," one of them said. "Stone me, it's a bloody Kraut."

Hans grasped the edge of the boat.

"Here.. You a Kraut?" The seaman poked him with an oar.

They stared at one another. Hans had seen so much hatred. He longed with all his mind and body to run away from the war, but he knew this was impossible. He was desperate to stay alive; desperate to be pulled into the boat. He wanted to lie or pretend that he could not speak English, but instead he said, "Yes."

"Then we got the bloody U-boat?"

"Yes." Impossible to explain. He was so tired.

"You feed the sharks, mate."

The lookout kicked his hands off the edge of the boat and the oarsman pushed him away.

Kolb lapsed into unconsciousness.

"Don't be daft, he's probably the only survivor," another said. "They're bound to want him for questioning."

"He'll die anyway."

"Deserves to die," the lookout added as he reached over the boat and grasped Hans's arm.

"Cor, he weighs a ton. Help me pull him in, then."

Chapter Thirteen

Life was so boring in Walvis Bay. Nothing ever happened and not even a change of seasons broke the year. Then, one night, the town reverberated to the thunder of a great sea battle and the townsfolk quickly gathered around the wharf. There were Ovambo, Hottentots, Herero, a few Bushmen who worked as servants in the town, white settlers from English, German and Afrikaner stock, a sprinkling of Basters of Dutch-Hottentot descent and a rough, tough mob of men from every country in Europe who had settled more recently to grab a share of the sea's wealth.

By 2 A.M. they were restless and disappointed. Hours before, they had heard the sound of torpedoes and depth charges and since then there had been the brief glow when the Swedish cargo boat caught alight and sunk. Then the fog thickened and they saw only an occasional flare set off to guide the survivors to the longboats.

Several fishing boats had put out to sea to aid the search and the small Walvis Bay hospital had been alerted by radio. A few survivors who were too badly wounded to reach Cape Town were to be transferred to the tug and brought ashore.

The head nurse telephoned the doctor at Swakopmund and called her meager staff of two back on duty. She had only one qualified nurse, Rose Manners, who quickly prepared the operating room, and Claire McGuire, a young trainee from a local fishing family, who was sent to the harbor to supervise the transfer of the wounded to the hospital.

Claire was feeling tense as she waited at the wharf. At twenty, she was a self-possessed young woman, aware of her capabilities and common sense. She was a short, slight, wiry girl with a mop of frizzy red hair pushed under her cap. She clenched and unclenched her hands as her blue eyes peered anxiously into the fog.

Shortly afterward she heard the sound of the town's police siren approaching. The police commissioner hurried over to her.

"Well, Claire, this is a tough responsibility for young shoulders."

She scowled, feeling annoyed by his patronizing tone.

"Good luck, my girl." He bent and whispered, "The tugboat will be here any minute. There's a survivor from the U-boat. He's to remain under armed guard. I have to question him at the hospital, you understand. Well, I'll get up there and leave my assistant with you." He gestured toward a young constable.

"But surely . . ." she began. She reached out and touched his arm. "But what if he's badly wounded?"

"In this case, national security comes first," he said pompously. "They'll probably fly him to Johannesburg,"

"That will depend on his condition," she argued.

For a moment the police chief looked askance, "Ours not to reason why . . ." he muttered, thinking what a bossy young woman she had become.

Claire tried to conceal her temper. "I'd be glad if you'd assign your constable to keeping the crowd back," she snapped. "He might as well do something useful."

Behind her the tug loomed large and out of focus through the mist and seconds later seamen tumbled down the gangway and placed stretchers at her feet.

Like gifts, she thought, but only five, thank God. A moment later she was on her knees examining the wounded. After a cursory glance at them all, she turned to a seaman with a crushed arm, injected morphine and made him comfortable in the first vehicle.

Claire worked quickly, injecting, checking, dispatching. Three to go.

The crowd was strangely silent now and a low murmur of sympathy rose as she lifted the blankets from a blond, bearded man who was delirious and muttering in German. His face and one side of his body were badly burned and one leg was almost severed. It would have to be amputated, she knew. She handled the needle expertly, giving the maximum dose of morphine she dared.

"Tell Matron he's the worst," she called to the next driver and, looking up, saw that it was Bertha Factor in her station wagon.

Claire dispatched the next stretcher to the hospital and, turning to the last, lifted the blankets. That moment was to remain forever in her memory. A sleeping giant lay there and the overpowering maleness of him hit her like a blow. Even though he was unconscious she could sense the power and the willfulness. His face was wide—too wide—a broad brow plastered with damp ash-blond curls above thick, jutting cheekbones, and beneath, blond eyebrows startlingly straight. His eyes were closed and his long blond lashes brushed against his cheeks. His nose was short, straight and thick with flaring nostrils above sensuous lips and a jutting, obstinate chin. For a moment she was unable to drag her eyes away from his face. The overwhelming beauty of him took her breath away.

Then she groped under the blankets for his wrist, but she could not find his pulse. So handsome and so dead, she thought. Suddenly her eyes were brimming. She bent over him but there was no trace of his breath and no heartbeat.

Oh, but he was too strong to die, she thought. She thrust her mouth onto his and began to blow fiercely, forcing her breath into his lungs, willing her life force into him. She hardly noticed the crowd milling around her. At that moment she would have taken half of her own life and given it to him, so strong was the bond that she felt with him.

Later the color returned to his cheeks and the breath to his body and his pulse began to beat more strongly, but Claire had lost all track of time by then.

"Brandy," she called into the crowd.

She put her arm under his neck and lifted his head to guide the brandy to his mouth. Her eyes flickered over his thick, sinewy neck, the live and muscular body, and the long legs protruding from the end of the stretcher.

He swallowed and coughed and she found herself staring into eyes of cornflower blue.

"Are you English?" he gasped.

"Don't talk," she said gently. "Save your strength. Now you're conscious, I'll take you to the hospital."

He watched her gravely. "My name is Hans—Hans Kolb. I am a German."

"Don't talk now," she said sharply. "Just breathe deeply. Try to drink this."

"Ah, brandy," he said in heavily accented English. "I thought I was in hell . . . just now . . . but I know I am in heaven after all." He smiled.

Watching his strong white teeth Claire felt a pang of disappointment. He was so charming, so perfect. She could never, never hope . . . She felt burdened by his extraordinary excellence. If he were damaged, she thought treacherously, scarred or blemished, but he was not.

She looked up at last and saw black boots and severely creased trousers above them.

"So this is the German, is it?" The police commissioner had returned and he was frowning slightly.

Claire stood up and straightened her shoulders. "Oh, I don't suppose it is," she said. "I doubt that. Good heavens, but who can tell? They're all so sick. This one can't talk at all. Shock, I suppose, but the man I sent up first was speaking in German. I'd say more likely him." She looked down into cornflower eyes watching her strangely and she blushed.

"Too many questions," she told him later in the station wagon. "In a hospital nationality doesn't count, only people. There's only two sorts of people, sick and healthy." Her face was damp with embarrassment. "Time enough for all their silly questions. Good heavens, yes." They would fly him to Johannesburg, she thought dismally, or London. She would never see him again. But not right now. Oh, no. First he must rest for a day or two. What a lot of nonsense, she rationalized. After all, the war was as good as won.

Hans was sleeping when they reached the hospital. She took the bulky package out of his shirt pocket and opened it. The oilskin wallet was wrapped in an oilskin sheet, but the papers were soaked all the same. She would dry them for him and examine them later, she decided as she put them in her pocket.

The doctor had arrived and was in the OR with Rose while the head nurse was coping with the rest of the casualties. No time now for guilt or regrets, the man with the severed leg must be prepared for an operation. What a waste of time, Claire thought when she removed his life jacket. He had been caught in a blast, one side of his body was black and burned. He had no chance of recovery.

He was Swiss, she discovered from his papers when she

returned to the ward. Günter Grieff from Zurich. It was all there: his passport, birth certificate dated March 13, 1915, and an immigration permit for South Africa. His occupation was stated as fitter and turner. The documents had been wrapped in oilskin inside a waterproof wallet and they were undamaged. It was almost as if he wanted to be ready to produce them under any circumstances. Carefully she placed them in her drawer.

The night passed slowly. Between rounds she sat at Hans's bedside. Just the sight of him was enough to satisfy her. It was nearly dawn when he opened his eyes and smiled and Claire was overcome with joy and gratitude. He was going to live.

Rose was coming. She could hear her footsteps on the wooden boards. She bent over Hans and whispered urgently, "Pretend you can't remember anything. If they find out who you are they'll take you to prison and you're not well enough to be moved . . . really not well enough . . . if they find out . . ."

The cornflower eyes watched her gravely. Did he understand? Would he agree? The question tormented her all day during her off-duty hours as she lay tossing on her bed.

"Where are you going?" Marika asked when she saw Bertha in a silk dress and hat about to leave the store.

"I'm taking fruit and magazines to the hospital."

"Fruit?" Marika asked hopefully.

"That consignment of frozen apples arrived this morning when you were sleeping. I haven't had time to unpack ours yet."

"I'll do it," Marika said happily. "I'll have an apple for lunch."

"Eat a proper lunch," Bertha said sharply. "Absurd to diet. There's not an ounce of fat on you. Why don't you go to the hospital instead of me?"

"No, thanks," Marika said. "I'll mind the store."

When Bertha returned later that afternoon she was pale and upset. The sight of the wounded had reminded her of

Irwin. Had he suffered like that? The thought tormented her.

"All those horrible injuries," she kept repeating. "And as for that poor German. Why, he's so badly burned and maimed my heart went out to him, enemy or not."

Marika's eyes flashed with temper. "If he's German he deserves to die," she said coldly. "They should have left him on the wharf. Or better still, pushed him back into the sea. I would have."

"If you can't find compassion in yourself then I'm afraid life will teach you a lesson, my dear, and doubtless it will be a hard one. You'll see."

Marika laughed. She decided to visit the hospital the following day to see for herself how this German was suffering.

Chapter Fourteen

It was the afternoon of Hans's second day in the hospital and all he could think about was the joy of being alive. It was the young nurse, the sweet and steadfast Claire, who had saved his life. He would never forget her face at the wharf, willing him to recover, and her voice so close to tears, her eyes so fierce as she lied to the police.

Why? Because she fancied herself in love with him, he knew. Girls were absurdly romantic. All afternoon, although she was off duty, she had been popping in on one pretext or the other. He had taken her advice and pretended to have lost his memory, but he doubted Rose believed him. Like Claire, she was feeling sympathetic.

Thank God for Rose and Claire. He needed to rest. He knew he was shocked and weak. Worse still, he was eviscerated by guilt. The terrible fate of his comrades made him ashamed to be alive, and he had spent hours worrying about this, but eventually he decided that life on this beautiful planet was a gift from God and to be unhappy was to spurn the gift. So he lay propped on pillows, gazing out of the window, obsessed with the privilege of gulping down pure air, and seeing the lovely luminous glow of the sun through the mist.

Soon he would give himself up and extricate Claire from any blame. He would be taken to a prisoner-of-war camp, but eventually he would be repatriated. Then he would find the *Fräulein* of his dreams and marry her, or someone like her, and he would make a living as a diesel engineer. He felt quite confident of his future.

He closed his eyes, indulged himself in his favorite dream and fell asleep.

Later he heard a soft rustling sound beside his bed and, opening his eyes, saw the girl of his dreams standing beside him, carefully pushing some magazines and chocolates onto the table beside his bed.

"*Fräulein*," he murmured, caught in that strange state of being half awake and half asleep.

But it was her. Unbelievable! He was afraid to look away. He knew that if he even blinked she would be gone. "*Fräulein*," he called, and groped for her hand.

She pulled back and gasped.

In reality, she was a little different, he decided. Her hair was deeper gold, her eyes were amber instead of blue, her breasts were smaller than he remembered, but that was only because she was younger. Seventeen perhaps, but still it was the woman of his dreams. She had swum up out of the depth of his mind to find him here in this new life.

He closed his eyes and when he opened them she was gone. He was glad of that. Hallucinations, however pleasant, are not healthy things to have.

He sat up and reached for his water, but it was not in the accustomed place. A box of chocolates and some magazines were there instead. He touched them thoughtfully, opened the box and ate one. Real enough! He took another and then he rang his bell.

Rose arrived puffing a few minutes later.

"Have a chocolate," he said.

"Why, you wicked lad. D'you think I've nothing better to do than rush over here for a chocolate?" But she took one all the same.

"Mmm, nice. I'll have another."

"It was strange. Funny—you English say? *Ja?* Like waking in the middle of a lovely dream and finding it's real—not a dream at all," he said haltingly.

"How come?" Rose was in a hurry to get on with her work.

"I'm talking about the girl. The one who brought these." He pointed to the chocolates.

"What did she look like?" Rose asked, taking another.

How could he describe her? What words could possibly convey her perfection? "A face like an angel," he began. "Eyes like a fawn's. And her hair . . . you've never seen such hair . . . like golden threads."

"Well, well, well." Rose burst out laughing. "That must be Marika Magos," she said with her mouth full. "I've never looked at her that closely, but I guess she fits the bill. She's Bertha Factor's adopted daughter. Bertha usually comes in the afternoon. I hope she's not ill," Rose added. Then she hurried away.

Incredible, Hans thought. Then his analytical mind took over. Not incredible, but impossible. Perhaps because of his exhausted state he had seen a girl looking a little like his dream girl and imagined the rest.

He laughed aloud. Foolish fancies. But what a lovely name. "Marika," he said, exploring the syllables lovingly with his tongue. "Marika."

He awoke during the night ramrod hard and bursting with desire to find he was clutching the hand of his English nurse, Claire. He pushed her away, feeling foolish. "I was dreaming," he explained.

"Dream on," she said and, reaching forward, caught his hand and squeezed it. He summoned a smile, making an effort to be polite and to show a small part of the affection she so obviously craved. Poor, lonely Claire. He felt touched by her, knew he could take her now. He could read it in her eyes. He had only to pick up the blanket and she would scramble in. Why not? After all, she was alone on night duty. The ward was empty apart from him and the poor devil from the Swedish cargo boat who was dying behind discreet curtains at the end of the ward.

Hans was tempted, but when he thought about it he decided that it would not be an honorable thing to do. Hans had never loved a woman. Some nights in the U-boat, his need had been unendurable. In his lonely bunk he had often dreamed that he was performing the act which to him was still shrouded in mystery. He would wake in a sticky mess, and although physically relieved, he would walk around for days feeling lonely and depressed with a deep need to touch and hold a woman; feel the warm flesh. Well, here was one and she was both willing and able. Attractive, too.

"Penny for your thoughts?"

He looked at her and frowned. "I don't understand."

"What are you thinking about?" Her bright blue eyes were peering at him, alert and friendly, like a bird, but wary, too, like a bird.

"Many things all at the same time. You, for instance. Why are you being so kind to me? You lied to the policeman after I told you who I was. It was your duty to hand me to the authorities. I have expressed myself correctly? *Ja?*"

Evidently he had, for she flushed deep red and white in patches. Then she laughed nervously.

"Well, I'm Irish."

Was that supposed to mean something? he wondered.

"The war's as good as over," she went on, speaking faster until the words came pouring out. "You see, they want you for questioning. You would be flown to England. Something to do with the U-boat you were on . . . that's why I lied." She took a deep breath. "Good heavens . . . can you blame me? You aren't strong enough to go to a prison camp. There's no such thing as nationality in a hospital. I mean . . . no such thing at all. Friends or enemies . . ." She broke off and Hans had difficulty in not bursting into laughter.

Suddenly she flung herself upon him. "Oh, Hans, Hans," she murmured. She smelled of disinfectant and her frizzy red hair was tickling his nose. Hans turned his head aside.

"Claire, don't," he whispered. "Don't get fond of me. I won't be here for long and you'll get hurt."

She was not listening. She was lying along the bed, pressing herself hard against him, feeling exactly like a boisterous, wiry puppy. Any minute now, he thought, she's going to lick me. She was so sinewy and bony-hard. Even her lips, which she pressed firmly against his cheek, were hard and determined. Lips for giving orders, not for loving, he decided.

His hand stroked her hair, ran down her cheek, under her chin and over the horribly starched linen to her breasts, which seemed not to have ever grown.

"How old are you, Claire?" he whispered dreamily as he explored again.

"Twenty."

"I'm twenty-two."

"Oh, oh." She began crying. "Only twenty-two and just think what you've been through. I don't want you to be taken away," she sobbed. "After all, it's too late to change the war, isn't it? There'll be other U-boats for them, but never another you for me. Good heavens, just the thought of it . . . why . . . I can't bear to think of you in a prison camp."

Hans stirred uncomfortably. "Don't worry about me," he said, pushing her aside. "I'm alive. That's enough. A prison camp would be like paradise compared with the U-boat."

"But you don't have to go," she persisted. "You can take his papers." She gestured to the cubicle at the end of the ward.

Hans shivered and Claire said, "Poor darling. I'll fetch another blanket." She rushed away.

A muffled voice called from the end of the ward and Hans climbed out of bed and tiptoed cautiously to the end of the long passage. He pulled the curtain aside and leaned over the bed.

A corpselike figure was panting his life away through a small crack in the bandages. There was a long and terrible groan from the mound of dressings. Then, even more horrific, the groan became a voice, a man talking, or what had once been a man.

"You German, Hans?" The voice emerged eerily from the hole.

Hans murmured unhappily. "I've been on U-boats most of the war," he stuttered. At once he became horribly aware of his guilt as he looked down. How was it possible that this cocoon contained a man who was conscious and speaking lucidly? Suddenly he remembered all the losses they had inflicted on enemy shipping. Figures on a graph! But those statistics had materialized in front of him and become flesh and blood, maimed, blinded and suffering. How many more? At that moment Hans decided he would never fight again.

"I'm sorry," he whispered. "I'm so sorry for what's happened to you."

"Save your pity, Hans," Grieff whispered. "That's war. I'm getting better now. The pain's gone. Tomorrow I'll get up and walk." There was a long gentle sigh and the crack in the bandages showed two lips with the stubble of a mustache sticking out. Hans had the disagreeable thought that even when this cocoon was buried under the ground the hairs would keep growing.

Claire rushed into the ward. She was carrying a blanket, which she dropped on the floor, and some papers. "Look," she said. "It's you . . . really it is . . ." She flashed Grieff's identity documents in front of his eyes. "Only you must grow a beard. It says blond hair and blue eyes. Yes, you're really very similar. Of course, you're not thirty, but with a beard . . ."

"No," he growled. He felt hate rising in him, blocking out rational thought. "I tell you he's doing fine," Hans said loudly. "He's lying there listening to us."

"Oh, but you're such a fool," she gasped breathlessly.

"You'll see, he'll be buried tomorrow. You know what it's like in a hot climate. After all, a corpse decays almost immediately. It's not like . . ."

Hans flung himself at her and clasped his hand over her mouth.

"I tell you he's getting better," he said.

"Screw the bitch," the macabre voice growled in German.

"See, he's delirious again," Claire said, pushing him away. She picked up the blanket and he heard the staccato tap of her heels rushing down the long ward toward his bed. She was in a temper.

"She's very new, very young," Hans apologized to the heap of bandages, but there was no reply.

"Grieff, Grieff," he whispered urgently.

Was he sleeping, or unconscious? Hans did not know which and eventually he returned shivering to his bed.

"Be reasonable," Claire said when she had wrapped the blanket around him. From her tone it seemed that he was the guilty one, not she. Yet she was conspiring to steal and rob a dying man of all that he owned. Her voice went on and on.

"Once he's dead and buried no one will ever know or care. They'll have their victim . . . good heavens . . . that's all they care about. He always mutters in German. Everyone's sure he's German." She turned toward him, eyes glittering. "You'd be a Swiss immigrant. All his papers are here. You'd be safe. You must do it. You must! Say yes," she urged him.

"Claire." He reached out and shook her shoulders. "Listen to me. Pray that he lives. He's not dead yet. Poor bastard."

"Why won't you listen to reason?" she said petulantly. He stared at Claire and her eyes pleaded with him.

"Oh, but you're such fool," she gasped breathlessly.

Hans snatched the papers from her and pushed them into her pocket. Pity had changed to anger and he wondered why he had held back so long. "Why don't you take off that damned starched uniform, Claire. It feels like making love to a nun. Puts me off."

Her eyes widened, her face became deep red and then very white. She licked her lips; clenched and unclenched her hands.

"I want you to know that I love you," she said as she slipped off the overall.

She was so white with large brown freckles on her arms and legs and so thin he could count her ribs. Why does she bother to wear a bra? he wondered as she slipped off the starched white contraption.

"I don't love you, Claire," he said wearily. "I feel you should know that, too." Right now, he thought moodily, I don't even like her, but his state of virginity had become unbearable. No more excuses; the U-boat was dead and gone.

A man should be a man, he decided.

He was not quite sure how to set about it. Neither was Claire. They kissed too hard and their teeth clashed and once she bit his lip by mistake. Their hands fumbled, grasped and hurt. First she was too high in the bed and then too low.

Finally he entered her.

"Ouch!" she cried.

As he pounded her the bed rattled and squeaked. Hans could feel his skin being peeled off, layer by painful layer. He wanted to stop, but he could not. He was enmeshed in her; her arms were wound around his neck; her legs around his hips; her chin was hurting his shoulder.

Then pain vanished. He felt a strange excitement surging through his limbs. He was all goose bumps and sweet sensations.

Then it began; pleasure of frightening intensity. Hans cried out, more from shock than joy, and hung on tightly.

He heard an echo . . . anguished, involved, triumphant. He had forgotten Grieff. Like a spectator at a bullfight, he thought squeamishly, and rolled onto his back.

Claire was still there. He felt shocked by that. His pleasure had been so intensely personal; he had felt so alone.

Ugh! he thought, gazing at her gored thighs. She was brimful of love and gratitude; a mess of emotions.

"Go and look at him." He gestured toward the heap of bandages to get rid of her.

"But, Hans . . ."

He pushed her out of bed. "I'm going to shower," he said.

Claire stumbled across the ward and looked at the bed. Her face was twisted with disappointment; tears rolled down her cheeks.

"Why are you crying?" he asked, filled with remorse.

She looked up and nearly complained, then changed her mind. "He's dead," she said. "I told you so."

Hans turned and fled down the passage, away from guilt and the smell of love and death. He ran the shower fierce and cold and dived under it.

Chapter Fifteen

Marika gazed anxiously into the mirror. She saw a pale, insipid girl with staring eyes and a mouth too wide. She turned away, sighing, and reached for a women's magazine and the makeup box which Bertha had given her for her seventeenth birthday. Suddenly she blessed Bertha.

She tried the lipstick, but her mouth seemed enormous now. She rubbed it off. Perhaps the rouge would help; she rubbed it in desperately. When she added the face powder she was surprised to discover that her features became blurred and indistinct under this covering of beigeness, so she dabbed on more. Finally she brushed her hair and tried to achieve the Veronica Lake effect.

Marika had only one fashionable skirt, which Bertha had copied from a magazine. It was of blue cotton, trimmed with white lace, and it matched her white embroidered blouse with puffed sleeves.

She could hardly bear to look at Bertha as she rushed through the store, grabbed the basket of fruit which Bertha had prepared for the hospital and dashed through the doorway muttering, "I'll take it."

"Why . . . Marika, you look . . ." "Terrible" was the word that Bertha was about to say, but she swallowed it. "So smart. Why are you all dressed up?"

Marika felt embarrassed. She did not want to lie, but at the same time Bertha was trespassing; the thought came very strongly and it was the first time she had felt that way. Marika could not say this to her; she loved Bertha and would not hurt her for anything in the world; nevertheless her eyes answered for her.

Bertha understood and did not feel hurt, but she was anxiously wondering who had gained her daughter's affections.

There was Marika, flouncing and pouting, glancing in the mirror behind the door every other second and looking more and more disconsolate.

"Marika, come here," she said.

The girl paused like a bird about to take flight, breathless with glittering eyes.

"Can I show you how to apply makeup properly?"

"I like it like this," Marika gasped, and fled down the steps.

When she reached the hospital the familiar smell of disinfectant filled her with trembling, her eyes filled with tears and her palms became moist. What a fool she was. He would have gone by now and even if he were still there he would not notice her. She was so nervous she could hardly place one foot in front of the other, but she forced herself to go first to the maternity ward. It was filled to overflowing with black babies and their patient mothers. She handed the fruit around and hurried to the emergency room. After that she allowed her feet to guide her to the men's ward, which was along the passage to the right, but when she pushed open the door she found the room empty.

He had left. She nearly cried out, but managed to control herself. Instead, she leaned against the doorframe and closed her eyes, trying to cope with the disappointment surging through her.

Then she heard Rose's footsteps behind her.

"Oh, it's you, Marika."

She turned and saw Rose watching her curiously.

"He's not gone," she said. "That's if you're looking for our mystery man. You are, aren't you? Well, he's out in the back sitting in the sun watching the sea." She smiled when she saw Marika's expression. "He's lost his memory, he says, but it seems he remembers someone who looks like you."

Marika blushed deep red under the makeup. "Why, I was just taking fruit around," she stuttered.

"Is Bertha sick, then?"

"No," the girl gasped, and hurried away.

"Not that way, silly. This way." Rose laughed outright then and Marika began to run, her ears burning.

He was there! At the sight of him joy invaded her body; her skin glowed, her eyes began to shine and she smiled.

She wanted to say something gay and inconsequential, like "Hello," but her mouth had dried and the words would not come. Instead she could not look away from the sight of his eyes; the deepest blue she had ever seen. She could lose herself in them. If only he would look away, but he did not and she stood snared.

She found the courage to walk forward and sit balanced on the edge of a wooden chair.

"It's cool today," she managed to say eventually, to explain her trembling.

"Cool, is it?" he mumbled. Cool! He was on fire. His head was hammering, the blood was rushing through his body like an express train, so that he tingled all over. He could feel his cheeks flushing and the hair rising on his head as if he had received an electric shock. He had to touch her, had to reassure himself that she was real. He reached out and grasped her hand, leaning forward uncomfortably.

"Cool, is it?" he repeated oafishly.

"Oh yes," she said. "It's much cooler today." She was hardly aware of the words stumbling out of her mouth. Suddenly she had been tossed into another, strange and frightening world where her body took over. She was mindless, a prey to strange feelings of exquisite pain and pleasure. His fingers against her skin were huge, a thousand times larger than life, the only real and living thing in the universe. The fingers rubbed at her hand, at her skin, at her very existence, filling her with spasms of joy and breathlessness until she could not stand the pain a moment longer and she snatched her hand away. And then, oh, what woeful loneliness, so she thrust her hand back again.

"Cool, yes, very cool." She was nearly passing out with excitement.

"Perhaps if I were closer," he gasped, and moved his chair toward hers, laying his arm along her shoulder.

Oh, she knew she would faint with the force of the sensations ravishing her body and she was unprepared, so she sat on in a state of shock and forgot about conversation altogether.

When Rose passed by an hour later to see if he would like some tea, she saw the two of them sitting bolt upright in chairs pushed close together, he with his arm around her shoulder and his other hand enclosing both of hers. They were staring out to sea as if mesmerized by the birds and the fishing boats.

She giggled and the two of them sprang apart. "Watching the sea were you, then?" she said. "Perhaps you saw a whale. I hear there's one out there today."

"Oh yes," Marika sighed. "A whale."

Hans just smiled sleepily.

"I must go." Marika jumped up and rushed down the steps.

"But you'll come back." Hans stood up and looked for a moment as if he would follow her. "Come back tonight," he urged her.

"Visiting time is at seven," Rose said firmly, and watched Marika's attempts to look graceful as her four-inch heels sank deeply into the sand. She smiled mischievously. "Now, Günter, would you like some tea?"

At the sound of the stranger's name, Hans was overcome with guilt. Not Hans, he reminded himself, Günter, From now on he would think of himself only as Günter. All day he had been worrying whether or not to accept Claire's suggestion of stealing Günter's papers. Finally the desire to remain close to Marika had driven him to accept. But still, he could not understand how he could have sat all afternoon, completely forgetting it was Günter's funeral today. At that very moment they were probably lowering his body into the grave. Well, goodbye, Hans, he thought regretfully. He fingered Günter's papers in his pocket.

Claire was standing among a crowd of settlers of German stock who had decided to attend the burial of this unknown German sailor. Claire could not imagine why she was there, but she could not throw off a feeling of unease. It was almost as if she feared Günter Grieff would rise from the grave to repossess his papers.

Claire had no qualms of conscience; she feared only failure, and not for herself, but for Hans.

Uneasily she acknowledged that she should have given Hans's papers to the head nurse. Then the death certificate would have been made out in his name. But the thought of a tombstone marked with the name of her young lover was abhorrent to her.

Twice Hans had asked her for his identity documents, but she told him they must have been lost at sea. She had the papers safely hidden and the fact that she possessed them seemed to give her a strange power over him. It was as if she held the essence of him in her hands, pressed between her fingers, just as she had pressed the essence of him between her thighs.

He was hers and she was his: Mrs. Claire Grieff. She repeated these precious words every spare moment she had. She had saved his life, found him a new identity, thrust her life force into him. He was undoubtedly hers.

She could hardly wait for seven and she quickened her

pace as if that would speed up time. Still, a part of her fought against the madness that invaded her. "I am the sensible, hardworking Claire McGuire," she told herself. But she was not. Not anymore. She was a stranger who quivered and shook when she passed his ward, whose stomach churned when she heard his voice. Night and day she was filled with a terrible longing to be close to him, to touch him. For the first time Claire realized that her quick, incisive mind, her intellect, which she could always rely upon, was just a small part of her, a precarious minority rule over the dumb, emotional mass which made up the rest of her being.

"God help me," she muttered as she hurried home.

Chapter Sixteen

Starched and crackling, Claire rushed down the corridor, blue eyes shining, her unruly red hair bouncing to the rhythm of her strides.

She flung open the door and her words of greeting froze upon her lips. She paled and looked haggard, but no one noticed, for Günter only had eyes for Marika and he was gazing at her with an expression she had never dreamed she would see; all his watchfulness gone, replaced by sensuousness and . . . yes . . . there was possessiveness there . . . and so much tenderness. How could this be? When had they met? Her stomach lurched, her mouth dried and she gasped for breath.

Günter heard and glanced over Marika's shoulder. His eyes changed as he saw Claire. He looked startled, then sheepish, then irritated.

Claire backed out of the ward and fled down the corridor. When she heard footsteps approaching she crept into the linen closet, where she wept bitterly into a towel.

Humiliation and disappointment kept her quivering in the cupboard. He was a cheat, a faithless liar, a man without feeling. Marika would get her comeuppance in her turn. Yet even as she sobbed into the towel she knew that this was not true. She had seen the look in his eyes. Oh, what a fool she had been, offering all that she had without asking for reassurances. She had assumed that a passion as strong as hers was sufficient guarantee of being loved in return.

What was she to do? Fight back, she decided, and gave a long, shuddering sniff. After all, she had fought for everything she had. She was Buck McGuire's daughter, wasn't she? And he was the toughest, meanest fisherman on the West Coast. All her life she had had to fight—to get out of housework and go to school, for her clothes and pocket money, and after fighting Pa she had taken on the hospital board to gain admittance. Being Buck McGuire's daughter was hardly a recommendation, but she had one legacy—her toughness.

She crept out of the linen closet, washed her face, squared her shoulders and set about her evening chores.

The hour passed agonizingly slowly, and although Claire had decided to ignore both of them, she was unable to keep away from Günter's ward. She passed by on any excuse and endured the pains piercing her entrails each time she saw their silly heads together.

By eight she was stiff with tension, her stomach was aching and a lump had formed in her throat so she could hardly swallow. He would live to rue the day he fell for that hoity-toity Marika with her silly ambitions and her snobbish ways, Claire vowed. Good heavens, one word from her and he would be sent away, banished to a prison camp; she would do it, too, before she would let him waste himself on such a mismatch. She would rather go to prison than let Marika have him.

She told him so at midnight, when the hospital was quiet and the head nurse had gone to bed.

As soon as she saw his face she realized what a mistake she had made. His nostrils flared and his eyes narrowed as he scrambled out of bed. Swaying, he clutched the iron rail and peered up at her from under his heavy brows. She could see he was a dangerous man, but she was beyond caring.

"I'm nothing to you," she went on masochistically. "I'm sure you've seduced girls in every port you visit."

Guilt diminished his anger and Günter backed painfully against the wall. "You were the first," he said unhappily.

"Do you expect me to believe that?" she stormed.

Günter sighed. He felt sorry for her, the poor forlorn little thing. He was the culprit. He had taken away her virginity and left her with nothing in its place, not even love or caring.

"I'm sorry," he said. "I'm so sorry, Claire, but it's impossible. You and I. You see . . . I don't love you."

"But I love you." She was determined to torture herself to the limit.

"You have no right to love me," Günter said unhappily.

She flung herself on the bed and began crying.

"I . . . I want to say," he whispered, "that I'm sorry. I wish that I had not made you unhappy. And I'm grateful," he added stiffly as an afterthought.

"That's all?" She looked up, her face twisted with hate. "Is that all you can say? Well, what will you do if I'm pregnant?" Triumph displaced sadness momentarily when she saw how pale he had become.

"I'll not marry you, Claire, so don't be pregnant," he retorted coldly.

Then she jumped up and slapped him. "You're cruel and you're horrible," she whispered. "Tomorrow I'm going to turn you in to the authorities. They'll take you away and you'll never get back here . . . not for years . . . and when you do Marika will be married."

"You do that," he said icily. "But you had better hurry or I might get there first. Did you think that you had a weapon . . . that you could control me with it?"

Claire turned and fled from the hospital, forgetting that she was on duty.

Early next morning, when Günter was preparing to leave

the hospital and give himself up, Claire arrived. She looked a poor, crumpled thing with her puffy face and red eyes and he felt sorry for her.

"Don't do it . . . I mean, please . . . after all, we're both involved. You might get off scot-free, but I'll go to prison. Please, Günter."

He did not need very much persuasion. Claire might report him, but it was worth the risk to stay near Marika, Günter decided. Besides, he was so anxious to leave the hospital and be free; really free, for the first time in six years.

He borrowed twenty pounds from Rose to buy clothes and landed the first job he applied for, which was service manager of the fishing fleet owned by a canning factory recently established at Walvis Bay.

As the weeks passed, Rose watched Claire and wondered if she were ill. Until now Claire's ferocious attention to duty had amazed everyone. Her strength had always been her common sense and tenaciousness. She never gave up, never allowed herself to fail. Rose had often thought that she would make a good nun, for Claire had the ability to devote herself with single-minded attention to her ambition and so far that had been to become the perfect nurse.

Looking at her now, Rose was not so sure. Her discipline and devotion had dwindled. She was absentminded, bad-tempered and careless of the patients. Her hair began to look even more unruly; her fingernails were dirty and there were deep shadows under her eyes.

Weeks passed and as Claire's condition did not worsen or improve, Rose decided that she must be pining for Günter Grieff. The foolish girl! What was the point in that when everyone knew he was courting Marika?

It was a strange courtship, Bertha thought, for she, too, had heard the gossip. She knew her daughter was meeting Günter occasionally, but as yet Marika had not brought him home and their meetings seemed to consist of evening walks by the sea followed by coffee at the local café. Bertha became more and more curious.

Once a week the manager of the canning factory came to the store with his order and Bertha invariably questioned him about Günter's progress. He had nothing but praise for the boy: hardworking beyond belief, reliable, obsessed with learning. Günter lived in one room, spent little and studied English and navigation at night. He knew all there was to know about fishing, boats and engines. "I don't know why he stays here," he confided to Bertha.

Marika did not seem particularly interested in these conversations and she never mentioned Günter in the house, which was strange, Bertha thought.

Still, she had changed lately and Bertha was pleased about that. Her sensitive, lovable Marika was returning. Admittedly she was more introverted than she used to be and always daydreaming, but her hair began to shine, her eyes were soft and limpid and her skin glowed. Her sketches were better, too. She began to spend more time at the easel and she took long walks along the seashore carrying her equipment with her.

Bertha was puzzled. If Marika was in love, then why didn't she talk about Günter, or bring him home?

One day Bertha said, "Marika love, why don't we invite that nice young Swiss, Günter Grieff, for supper?"

"Why, no." Marika looked confused. "He'll come . . . when he's ready . . ."

"Ready for what . . .?"

"Why . . ." Marika was unable to explain. "When he's ready to come, of course . . ." She flushed.

"Are you"—Bertha searched for the right words, not wishing to offend her daughter—"going steady?" she asked.

Marika turned away. How could she explain when she did not understand herself? She no longer felt master of her own self, but merely a half of a whole, with Günter, working away in the canning factory, the other half. Even when she did not see him for days this strange feeling would not go away. It was all too, too strange. She could not understand why she felt this way. How could a stranger feel closer than any brother she might have had? Closer than Bertha? Sometimes she felt that she was losing herself and this frightened her. She let the days and the weeks pass without letting their relationship grow stronger. Perhaps if she remained aloof, eventually he would go away and then she would be free. So some days she met him at the café, as arranged, but sometimes she stayed away.

It was VE Day, May 8, 1945, and Walvis Bay trembled with the clamor of ships' sirens, guns and fireworks. For once the pilchard shoals were forgotten as fishermen and sailors gathered to celebrate.

Günter was in a bar with his new friends buying a round of drinks.

"What's the long face for?" Evans, the factory manager asked, clapping Günter on the shoulder. "Drink up, man. From now on the boys'll be coming back and this place will start humming."

"I'll drink to peace," Günter said. He drained his glass and slammed it on the table. "I don't feel right here," he muttered. "I didn't fight with the Allies."

He stood up, waved awkwardly and walked outside.

"Come on, Günter, not your fault. You're Swiss," one of the boys called after him. He was popular with the fishermen.

Günter walked moodily down to the wharf and stared out to sea. He was remembering home and the hours spent studying German culture; the pride in achievement which had been instilled in him at an early age; the desire for excellence. Yet the German genius had turned to madness and the entire world rejoiced in its downfall.

He thought about his comrades slowly rotting in their iron coffin, of Germans all over the world being rounded up and herded into prison camps; of Steen, his best friend, lost at sea; and of his parents behind Russian lines. What must it be like in Germany now with the starved and homeless and the occupation troops? he wondered guiltily.

Yet it all seemed so unreal. For him reality was the Namib, the fishing harbor and the factory. He felt an integral part of this wild and magnificent territory. He was at home here and happy. He hardly knew who he was anymore and it was hard to believe that he was an impostor. A man living a lie. He was carving a new personality for himself. Günter Grieff was his name—it belonged to him—and so did this country. He knew he would apply for citizenship soon; he would forget the past completely, he was so absorbed with the present. But he was a cheat and he had always been an honorable man. Suddenly he was choked with self-loathing and he vomited into the sea.

Chapter Seventeen

Günter had been in Walvis Bay for only six months, but already he loved the country more than he loved his own home and he longed to explore the hinterland. To Günter there was a haunting beauty in the silence, the wide-open spaces, the unspoiled desert. He was always intrigued to walk along the seashore, one foot in the ocean, fertile, abundant and teeming with life, and the other on a shore of utter desolation. Today the coastline was even more forbidding, for the wind was gusting up to gale force and the air was full of sand and salt spray.

He was looking for Marika and eventually he found her sitting on a tall rocky outcrop gazing out to sea with her long hair billowing in the wind.

He climbed up beside her. How lovely she was, but somehow frail-looking. Yet she was a strong girl, he decided. Perhaps it was her nose, a pinched, small European nose, sloping to a full mouth. Her amber eyes were so serious and concealed and when she looked down, which was often, her long lashes brushed her ivory cheeks. She'll still be beautiful when she's old, he thought. Her bone structure is fine and delicate and I shall look at her and remember how she looked today—flash of youth and virginal lips and those candid eyes which sometimes caught him unaware.

He wanted to explain how he felt about her, of the plans he had made, but shyness blunted his wits.

"There's a Christmas dance at the hotel and I've taken dancing lessons," he began.

One side of her mouth twisted into a lurking smile, while a frown hovered between her thick golden brows. "Oh, lessons, is it?" Then she giggled.

Günter frowned. Then he clambered back to the beach. He picked up some rocks and hurled them far out, venting his spite on the sullen waters.

"You better come down," he called. "It's not safe there. The tide's coming in and soon there'll be a breaker big enough to wash you off."

She scrambled down the rocks. Oh, my, but he couldn't be teased. "Oh, Günter, I'm glad you've been taking lessons. How silly . . . I mean to ask a girl to a dance . . . and then to find . . . but how very thorough of you."

"Well, what did you expect?" He was baffled by her laughter, but when she put one hand on his arm he smiled back.

She began to waltz around in the wind, her skirt and hair blowing wildly. "No, really . . ." Her voice came in snatches, dulled by the sound of breakers and the wind shrieking in the dunes. "And was it like this . . . one, two, three; one, two, three . . .?" She circled barefooted on the sand. "Show me, Günter."

He caught her hands and pulled her close to him and kissed her quickly on the lips. He felt embarrassed by the surge of passion which enveloped him and he was sure she would feel it, so he stepped back and swirled her around in the sand, humming the tune of "The Blue Danube Waltz."

"You can't dance," he said, letting go of her.

"No, but I can. It's the sand. After all, I have no shoes." She pursed her lips together and he could see the dampness on her forehead and her flushed cheeks.

"But you can kiss," he added teasingly. "I'd rather my girl could kiss than dance."

He pulled her close with a sudden movement which caught her off balance, but he held her up, hugging her close against him. The top of her head reached his chin, so he tilted her face back and bent over to press his lips upon hers. She tasted salty and cold.

"Oh, oh," she gasped, pulling her face away. Suddenly she felt feverishly hot.

"You're my girl, Marika," he said hoarsely, feeling as flustered as she. He caught hold of her more roughly this time and crushed her against his chest.

"You're hurting," she whispered, but pain faded as she became acutely aware of his body closely pressed against hers; blond stubble scratched her forehead; the hairs of his chest tickled her chin and the sheer bulk of him took her breath away.

She slid her arms around his waist, hugging him closer, feeling the muscled back and his hips hard against hers. Something strange was growing and pressing against her.

Desire swept through her body with the force of a desert flood and, like the desert, she was unprepared for it. Her skin felt taut and burning hot, her lips were cracked and dry, she was so dizzy she hardly knew if she was standing or falling.

She felt Günter lower her onto the sand, but she was scarcely aware of this. She was obsessed with her aching breasts and thighs and the touch of his hands on them.

"Oh," she groaned. "Oh, Günter! Go away. Go away and leave me alone."

Günter was feverishly exploring every part of her in clumsy, hurried movements. He tugged at her blouse and revealed her thrusting white breasts straining around the new bra already too tight for her. Then he buried his face between her breasts and pressed the soft flesh against his cheeks.

He was a time bomb fused and ready to explode. If she would not . . . if she refused . . . then he would burst all over the sand.

Fumbling fingers and panting breath. He was entangled in lace and elastic, but at last he revealed her thighs. The sight made him gasp and he lay bemused by her loveliness. Such long and lovely limbs, such pure ivory skin and a silky tangle of golden hair.

Marika sat up, saw her naked body and became quite overcome with shame. She gasped, pushed him away crazily, hauled up her pants and raced to the sea.

When Günter saw her plunge into the foaming surf, alarm banished his anger. He ran after her.

"Come out, you idiot," he called, but she laughed and splashed water at him. Her back was turned to the huge breaker thundering over her and a second later she was lost in the cascading roll of foam.

Günter yelled. She would be crushed to death before he could catch hold of her. He raced into the surf, caught sight of golden hair floating like seaweed, grabbed a handful of it and pulled her retching out of the water.

"Why, you fool," he shouted as relief turned to anger. He shook her. "It's lucky I saw you."

"Oh, but I had to . . ." She was choking and shivering. "Had to be cool . . . to be free . . . I can't explain," she exclaimed, and broke off coughing. Then she looked up at him with those candid amber eyes which always managed to turn his knees to water. "You see, I was running out of control. That never happened to me before . . . Look at my legs," she went on shakily. She was scratched from her thighs to her ankles.

"Serves you right," he said. "By now you might be washed out to sea and not a thing I could do about it if I couldn't find you."

"And would you look for me?" she asked mischievously. "Would you swim out in that to find me?" She pointed to where the waves were breaking. Now the sea was a cauldron of boiling foam bubbling between jagged black rocks. She shuddered.

Günter was about to tell her that he had swum for Germany before the war and of his long swim from the submarine, but he remembered just in time. His lips tight-

ened and his face took on a bleak expression. He was
living a lie and he was trapped in it for the rest of his life.
The prospect was not appealing.

"I'm cold and I want to go home," Marika said. She
seemed bad-tempered and remote as she hurried ahead,
answering in monosyllables.

So this is love, she was thinking as she glanced at
Günter. At that moment she wished with all her heart that
she had never met him. She had imagined being in love to
be rather different: gifts of flowers and chocolates; picnics
in wooded glades; listening to music by the fireside on
winter evenings. Of course, none of this was possible in
Walvis Bay, but still . . . The curious knowledge that she
was half of him and he of her alarmed her. She would
have to be firm with herself. After all, she was intent on
leaving Africa forever.

Günter was thoroughly out of patience with her by the
time they reached the store.

Then she paused, uncertain of how to say goodbye.
How angry he was. His head was lowered and he was
glaring up from under his brows as if at any moment he
would bellow at her. If she said goodbye now, just like
that, well, perhaps she might never see him again, although of course she was in no hurry.

"Perhaps I'll come to the dance," she said coyly. She
turned and fled.

Günter was left with an image of her dripping wet;
bedraggled hair and eyes half pleading, half contemptuous.
He lingered in front of the store, regretful and angry,
hoping that she would relent and invite him in, but she did
not and after a while he walked home.

Chapter Eighteen

Noon, but it was almost dark. The frenzied wind had tossed the sand high into the air and through it the sun shimmered blood red and menacing, distorted by the dust.

In spite of the sandstorm and the heat, a handful of German settlers were gathered at the grave, clad in stern and shiny black with handkerchiefs tied over their mouths and noses. No one could hear the words of the Lutheran preacher above the shrieking gale. No one cared!

It was over a year since the U-boat survivor had been buried in an unmarked grave, but lately news had come from England giving his name, rank and age, so the German settlers had clubbed together to pay for a tombstone, which was being dedicated now.

There was only one woman there, Claire McGuire, and she stood staring with morbid fascination at the tombstone. *Hans Kolb, 1923–1945, swam for Germany in 1939 and served his country well. Deeply mourned by his shipmates.*

How did they know the name? Claire had puzzled over this for days.

If only it were really Hans lying six feet under the sand. Claire closed her eyes and tried to imagine him dead; to see his skin decaying and macabre; the ants picking the flesh off his bones. Instead she remembered his blue eyes gleaming with love as he waltzed with Marika.

The two of them had danced together all evening at the Christmas dance and Claire had been so sick with misery she had been too ill to work next day.

Every evening since then Marika waited at the canning factory at five o'clock and then they would walk along the beach hand in hand like two silly sheep. Claire knew because she could see them from her window and she could not resist watching, however much it hurt. Her longing for Günter tormented her. At first she had hoped that she would gradually recover from this nightmare and forget him, but now she knew that she never would.

Day after day the spite lathered out of her, spoiling her looks, making her hair listless, her eyes haggard, her face pimply and pale. Nightly she planned her revenge, but so far she was the only victim of her jealousy. Oh, how she hated him. She clenched her fists and bit her lip as she turned away from the grave.

Günter would never marry Marika. He had chosen badly, taken in by looks and Marika's simpering manner. Well, just let him try. She would take his real papers to the authorities. Yes, she would endure prison rather than see the two of them bedded down happily.

He was hers by right and she would marry him, or no one would. With time and patience she would win him back, she comforted herself on the long walk back from the cemetery. He needed her strengths and resourcefulness for the life he had chosen here; and she needed Günter to be fulfilled, to be a woman. Without Günter she was nothing.

Chapter Nineteen

Dusk in the Namib. The twilight of mauve and rose was reflected on the sand and shone eerily around them. They had been collecting rock samples; they were hot and sticky and the sea loomed ahead invitingly. It was strangely calm this evening with flashes of fluorescence glittering among rocks and seaweed.

Günter parked by the sea, stripped off and dived into the water, leaving Marika to splash coyly in shallow water in her pants and bra.

Günter disappeared into the dusk and Marika leaned back and watched the flocks of cormorants and flamingos flying in formation along the coast. Down the shore she could see a colony of seals sprawled on rocks.

It was soon dark, but Günter did not return; she dressed and waited in the jeep. Eventually she walked to the water's edge and peered into the darkness, but there was no sign of him.

When he came at last he found her weeping, crouched among the seaweed tossed up by the tide.

He tried to explain: "I can swim for miles, Marika. You don't have to worry about me."

She refused to be comforted and they drove on in silence. From time to time Günter glanced slyly at her. She was in a bad mood, petulant, tearful and impatient with him. That did not bode well for what he had to say.

He slowed the jeep as he searched the dunes for a suitable place for a picnic. Then he parked, unloaded the food and scavenged driftwood for the fire.

Marika sat in the jeep watching, feeling astonished that he had not asked her to help. He was so self-sufficient, so arrogantly male.

When the fire was blazing and the meat sizzling on the fire, he uncorked the wine. "Marika," he called. "You can't sit there all night. Here's a glass of wine. Come and sit by the fire."

She clambered down and sipped the wine. It was raw and dry and she felt it surging into her bloodstream, making her toes tingle.

Was she supposed to do something? she wondered. All day she had contributed nothing. Günter had planned the trip, packed the food, made the conversation. He was collecting minerals and they had searched for the pieces he needed. She had been placid, compliant, uncaring. She had not enjoyed the day and now she wondered why. Broodingly she clasped the glass and watched the wine splash ruby red in the glow from the fire. She knew she resented his love of the territory, for this would be something she could never share with him. But it was far more than that. Right now she hated him. They were so close, yet they were miles apart. It was his maleness that stood between them, for she could not understand it. She regarded him with a certain fear and with contempt, too; the female antagonism for the male who was forever doing things, never relaxing. An overachiever, she thought, watching him.

She began to draw pictures in the sand by the light of the fire, but it became too hot, so she sat further away in the shadows. Oh, how busy he was, turning the meat, breaking the bread, and not even looking once in her direction. Why, if she were there or she were not, what difference would it make to Günter? She was simply an ornament to grace the occasion while they set about doing the things Günter liked. Oh, sometimes she felt so irritated with him. Looking at him now, she wanted to walk over and pinch him. The desire to hurt him was almost more than she could stand, so she lay on her back and stared at the stars which were appearing dimly in the darkening sky.

By the time the meat was cooked the full moon was rising from behind tall sand dunes.

"This is a strange night," she whispered. It was the first time she had spoken. "Really strange . . . can't you feel it? I feel strange, too."

"It's the wine," he said shortly.

Oh, but he could be irritating. There he was, snapping sticks, buttering the bread, capable, independent, reliable. Where were his faults, his doubts, his anxieties? It seemed he had none.

Could he not sense the terrors of the night? The desolation surrounding them? The future stretching ahead like a path to be forged through the desert, no signposts, no one to show the way, a lonely, tortuous route and at the end of it—why, just oblivion! Whatever gave him the right to be so self-complacent? To be sure of anything?

"Are you ever afraid of anything?" she asked abruptly.

"Not anymore, but once I was very afraid. One day I will tell you about it."

"Afraid of life, I mean," she persisted.

"Of course not. Life is good fun, to be enjoyed."

She gazed hatefully at him.

Watching her sidelong, Günter could see that she was still angry. What a strange, moody creature she was, but it would all change when she matured.

"Eat your supper," he said. He was determined not to gaze at her too much. All day he had been avoiding the sight of her beautiful breasts outlined against her blouse. When she walked barefoot in the desert the sight of her full hips and her slender waist nearly took his breath away. He was so afraid that he would lose control; the desire to grab her and toss her on the ground was almost uncontrollable. He had been ignoring her as much as possible, but even the sound of her voice, deep and vibrant, felt like a hot line to his groin. Right now he could moan with the agony of it.

They must be married soon. That was why he had planned the day, hoping to find a suitable opportunity to ask her. What a fool he had been to stay out so long enjoying the swim, for he had frightened her and now she was bad-tempered. Well, there was no point in hanging on any longer. Soon the picnic would be over. She was already gnawing her way through her second chop and drinking very little.

"I've good news," he began. "The company has given me a house and there's plenty of cash for the furniture. Already I have saved half the deposit for a fishing boat and soon I'll have the rest. The company will go fifty-fifty with me and secure the loan. I'll make plenty of money . . ."

He paused and glanced at her cautiously. She was gazing out to sea, looking completely vacuous. Was she listening?

"In five years' time, or thereabouts, I'll sell the boat and have enough to buy a business." There! Surely that should interest her. He glanced over his shoulder, but now there was a frown flickering on her brow.

She turned, grabbed a baked potato and bit deeply into it.

"And I?" she said, swallowing hastily. "How do you see my future?"

He beamed. This was his cue, but his face froze when he saw her expression. Careful, he thought. "It's something we must talk about," he hedged. Goddamnit. Why was he such a coward? "Marry me," he blurted.

Marika did not answer. Should she say yes? She owed him nothing. Yet she loved him. She had always known she loved him, belonged to him in a way. Yet a part of her rebelled against belonging. She wanted to be herself, not half of another, but still, she would say yes, she had always known that, for in all her life there would never be any other man for her. Not one whom she could love, really love, as she loved Günter.

She turned and frowned at him. She tried to imagine them married, sharing a house, sharing friends, sharing a bed . . . She had never allowed her sensuality to take over since that one afteroon on the beach when she had rushed frightened into the surf. Instead she had become frigid and full of tension.

"I'm worried about 'it,' " she said.

"Don't be," he said. "It's nothing."

"Oh!" She felt disappointed. "Of course, I've read books . . ."

"Everybody does. It doesn't help . . ."

"Have you . . .?"

"Once. Before I met you," he added hastily. He felt guilty again, but it was only a small lie, a difference of a day, that was all.

"Was it nice?"

"Messy." He remembered it all too clearly and shuddered.

"Of course, if we didn't like it we wouldn't have to do it, would we?"

"I suppose not."

"I've never seen a man naked," she went on. "That is . . . not until you . . ." She faltered. "Just now when you went swimming."

"We're not much to look at." He grinned mischievously.

"Well, if you took off your clothes, I could see for myself."

The grin faded. He felt shy. How absurd! He had never heard of a man being shy. It was supposed to be the other way around.

He brushed the sand flat with his hand, placed his glass on it, stood up and took off his pants. Then he kicked them over the sand and sat down. He picked up a chop and bit into it as nonchalantly as possible.

Marika was staring at him as if hypnotized. He felt desire rapidly rising and he was overcome with shame.

"Please look away," he said shortly.

"What's the point of taking off your pants if I can't look?"

He felt himself blushing and he buried his face in his glass of wine. Marika was inching over the sand, staring as if fascinated.

"Why, look," she said. "My God, it's growing enormous."

Günter jumped, grabbed his pants and clutched them over himself, splashing his wine into the fire, which hissed and smoked.

"Look at the sea," he said, and was furious to hear that his voice was hoarse and unnatural.

"You're shy," she said, and burst into laughter. Suddenly she was the strong one and she began to feel bolder.

"If you won't let me look I won't marry you," she said, suddenly aware of her extraordinary power.

"Don't play with me if you know what's good for you," he gasped.

"What will you do?" She stared at him challengingly. Her desire to touch, to hold, to grab and hurt was now beyond control. She flung her potato into the fire and snatched his pants away. His penis sprang up red and swollen.

Marika reached out and touched the tip with her finger. How smooth and round it was; a drop of moisture appeared and she rubbed it round and round. "How lovely," she said.

Günter sat up abruptly and grabbed at her wrist, but she evaded him.

"Better have a swim and cool off," she said teasingly.

"Bitch," he muttered. "Wait till we're married." But he ambled off obediently and she watched his white buttocks shining in the moonlight.

What a fool he was, she sighed. "Oh, Günter," she called petulantly. "Come back at once."

He returned at a run.

"Look, the fire's dying down; you can't leave me here alone."

He frowned and sat down. His clever blue eyes watched her thoughtfully. "I'm not going to rape you, Marika. Not if you tease me all night."

She stared out to sea again, flushed and breathless. "You see," she tried to explain eventually. "If we wait until the wedding . . . I mean on that night . . . I mean that night . . . with the jokes and everyone watching. I've thought about it . . ." She broke off.

"I understand," he said gently.

"You do?" She smiled. "Well, I thought that perhaps . . . I mean, we're engaged, aren't we?"

Günter could hardly believe his ears. His throat ached, his mouth was parched. "Darling," he muttered, hoarse and unrecognizable.

She began to take off her blouse. So matter-of-fact she was. "Then you see," she said firmly, "I could relax and enjoy the . . ." She was unfastening her shorts and Günter was watching as if hypnotized. "Why . . . all the fun of buying things . . . the arrangements."

She had slipped off her shorts, but now she crumpled and sat demure in her virginal white bra and pants with her arms locked around her knees.

"You're the most beautiful woman in the world," he said. "Please, please don't tease me." He was suddenly afraid of her. She could say yes or no; fill him with happiness or dash his hopes utterly. He knew there would never be another woman for him. He had loved her long before he met her and he would love her forever.

"You see, Bertha's so shy," she was explaining, and he struggled to listen to her. "She's never told me much about these things . . . I mean . . . what happens."

"More fun to find out by ourselves," he whispered. "Oh, Marika, I love you."

She sat back, looking forlorn. "I'm sorry . . . I simply can't . . . I thought I could, but I simply can't take off anything else. Oh dear," she said.

He undressed her slowly, his shaking hands fumbling with her bra and the elastic of her pants. He was so afraid that he would explode at the touch of her and shame himself. Then he said, "So sandy. Let's wash in the surf and we can shake the blanket."

"All right." She ran ahead, a vision in the moonlight, but Günter could hardly move with the strength of his passion.

The ice-cold water revived him. He splashed her and lovingly washed the sand from her body, watching the drops fall from her statuesque shoulders to her perfectly formed breasts and down to her waist and her wide hips and the triangle of silky golden hair. How long her limbs were and her skin was so soft, so vulnerable. He felt overcome with a tremendous sense of responsibility, for here she was offering him her body and her life so trustingly. He knew he would protect and fight for her, he would make a fortune just for her. He felt dizzy with the scope of his prospects. Then he picked her up and carried her to the blanket. Why, she was an angel, too good for him. He didn't deserve her.

"I'll be your slave," he began shakily. "Whatever you want, all your life."

Her skin was ice cold from the sea and she was salty to taste. He ran his lips over her body and she moaned gently. Then she wound her arms around his neck, pulling him roughly on top of her.

He wanted to woo her gently so that he would not hurt her. He could not banish the image of Claire spread-eagled on the bed; bloody and distressed.

"Wait, wait," he murmured as she wound her legs around his hips.

She would not. She was drenched and panting with the force of her lust.

He gasped as he felt her ice-cold breasts and stomach against his burning skin. She pulled herself up and clung to him as a young animal will cling to its mother.

"Do it, do it," she groaned.

Desire surged through his blood, his limbs felt heavy and stiff; then tenderness fled as he succumbed to his passion.

Thrust and pull and thrust again. Something tore and he felt warm stickiness around him.

"Oh God!" He pulled back, feeling thoroughly alarmed. "Are you hurt?"

How strange she looked. Her teeth were gritted, her mouth pulled into a grimace, and her eyes were rolling alarmingly.

She opened her eyes and frowned at him. "Don't stop," she said urgently. She reached up and caught his neck. Her fingers were probing and pushing with a life of their own. She hauled him down. "More," she commanded. Her nails pierced his skin.

But still he hesitated.

"Push," she gasped, and bit him on the chin. She dug her heels into the sand and her body rolled and rotated so that he was tossed up and down like a ship at sea: rising, falling; while she panted and sweated. Her strength was amazing. Then she let out a piercing shriek as her muscles gripped and contracted around him.

Günter sighed happily and a second later exploded inside her. For a while ecstasy clouded his vision and his mind, but when he recovered he found Marika was crying— her body convulsed with frenzied sobs.

"Oh God, Marika darling. Did I hurt you?"

"No," she said, looking up in amazement. "Of course not. It was lovely, Günter. Was it lovely for you, too?"

He was too relieved to answer as he lay back on the

sand wonderingly. After a while he felt the dampness rising. "Where's the blanket?" he asked.

"Who cares!" She giggled and propped herself on one elbow as she stroked him gently, letting her hand stray from his neck to his stomach.

Strange! he thought, watching her. He had been prepared for the disgust which had followed his fumbling attempts at love with Claire, but this time he felt only tenderness. He looked up and smiled at her. How beautiful she was. Her face was in shadow, but her eyes looked huge and shining, while her hair seemed dazzling bright in the moonlight and her skin shone white like alabaster. Deep shadows in secret places! He looked into her eyes and saw love there, tenderness, and there was something else: triumph! He smiled.

"Why are you smiling?"

"Because I love you."

"And I love you." She bent forward and laid her cheek on his belly. "I can hear your insides," she said. "Funny rumbles and gurgles. How hard your stomach is." She lifted herself on one elbow and pummeled his stomach with her fist.

"Does that hurt?"

"No, of course not."

She smiled happily and buried her face in his groin. "Such a beautiful body, such soft and silky hair. Oh, my Günter. You are mine, aren't you?"

"Yes," he whispered.

"Say it. Say it's all for me . . . all this . . ." She cupped her hand under his balls and weighed them. "So heavy . . . heavy . . ." she sighed.

"It's heavier sometimes, like just now," he said.

She laughed. Her voice sounded low and husky, more sensuous than before.

She thrust her face into his groin again, craving the taste and the smell of him, needing more intimacy than she had experienced. Her tongue explored him, sensing the soft and delicate hairs, the goose-pimpled skin, the saltiness and the musky odor.

"I feel so strange," she said. "I don't want to be me at all . . . not tonight . . . I want to be a part of you, to tuck myself into you . . . why, I would be one of these hairs in the pit of your arm." She reached up and stroked him there.

"Then marry me soon," he said.

"Whenever you like." She laughed again. "We are already married, you and I . . . don't you feel that?"

"Yes," he lied. In fact, he felt insecure. Each time she called him Günter his guilt frightened him and he wondered if he should tell her now. But what if he did not? Would their marriage be legal? he wondered. She would be marrying a corpse. He was filled with foreboding, so he pulled her up and onto him, feeling the weight of her body on his chest and his hips. Her hair hung around his face, tickling him.

Perhaps he should tell her after they were married . . . wait a month or two. Then they could go away and be married later in Europe, using his real name. But that would merely draw her into his lies and deceit. If only . . . He felt eviscerated by his guilt. Yet he knew that if he were to give himself up they would put him away and it might take years to get back. Perhaps Marika would not wait for him. What if she were to marry another? The thought was unendurable. He grimaced.

"Why, you're not listening to me," she burst out. "You are thinking of someone else, or perhaps of work, which is just as unfaithful. That's a man for you; no romance! Tonight you may think only of me . . . yes . . . you will."

She took hold of him and his penis stirred softly. "I defy you to think of work," she laughed.

"Oh, Marika," he sighed.

She was insatiable. She sat astride him, looking debauched and boisterous. Where was her womanly modesty? he wondered. His preconceived notions of women and sex were fast disappearing.

"Don't you want to rest?" he asked. "Come here." He

placed one hand on his shoulder. "I want to feel your head here; your body beside me.

She laughed and, holding his penis erect, sat on it, compelling him to participate as she slid her body backwards and forwards.

She looked statuesque, abandoned, inexorably female. The original Eve, he thought, devoid of shame. Her breasts were full and erect, thrusting forward aggressively, bouncing with the force of her passion.

"Oh, oh," she groaned. Her gleaming legs were shuddering. Then she covered her face with her hands and fell forward onto his chest.

"Do you love me?" she pleaded. The strumpet had fled, replaced by a child.

"Yes," he said.

"And shall we have a baby?"

"Yes, if you like," he whispered.

"Now my stomach's warm, but my back is cold," she complained.

He lifted her and placed her on the sand, tipping her onto her stomach on the blanket, noting her softly rounded buttocks, the square, brave shoulders, the tiny waist. Then he lowered himself onto her, nuzzling her with his mouth, tasting the soft hair in the nape of her neck.

"Oh, but you're heavy," she complained.

"I'll take you home." He sat up and looked around regretfully.

"Oh no, not tonight . . . why . . . I couldn't leave you."

Hand in hand they bathed in the sea, which was sullen and calm as if awed by the occasion. Then they dried each other with the sandy towel and Günter stoked the fire while Marika dressed. When it was blazing they wrapped themselves in the blanket and lay close together.

"No, but this is no good," Marika said impatiently. "I must feel you." She climbed out of the blanket, stripped off her clothes and then snuggled back. They lay still, overawed by the proximity of each other and the joy of feeling naked flesh against naked flesh.

The moon swooped down to the sea and dropped over the horizon, leaving the Namib in darkness, while the wind nuzzled the dunes and the two lovers fell asleep clutched in each other's arms.

Chapter Twenty

It was a stormy morning. Tall breakers raced across the bay; the air was choked with sand and the shrieking of the wind. The store was busy. It was too rough for the fishermen to set sail and they were passing the day by stocking up with odds and ends and repairing their nets.

Marika was helping behind the counter when a messenger arrived and handed her a letter. There was a vague smell of ether about it and she sniffed curiously as she opened the envelope. The note read simply: *Günter Grieff is dead. Come to the cemetery. Claire.*

Günter dead! Impossible! Marika tried to call Bertha, but only a croak came. Then she ran out of the store and down to the canning factory.

"It's nonsense," she muttered as she ran, but while her mind was thinking reasonably, her body was in a panic.

"Insane!" she blurted aloud. A vicious joke! But why? She could not banish a sense of foreboding.

"Where's Günter?" she called to a fisherman mending his nets.

He shrugged and jerked his thumb toward the canning plant. Ignoring the whistles, she ran on faster.

The workshop was empty, but she found Evans in the canning department.

"Where's Günter?" she gasped, trying to control her sobs.

"Calm down, Marika," he said, looking anxious. "He's around somewhere. I saw him ten minutes ago."

"There's not been an accident, then?"

"Why, no . . ."

Marika thrust the letter into his hands and ran on through the gale to the cemetery. It was deserted. She leaned against a tree, closed her eyes and stood shuddering. "Cruel! Cruel!" she whispered. She would wring Claire's neck when she found her. Still, something was wrong, she knew that.

How gloomy it was. The clouds hung low and sand obscured the light. She shuddered.

Marika had not been here before. She tiptoed along narrow paths, looking at the dead flowers and the sad attempts to prevent the graves from disappearing under mounds of sand. A bleak, depressing scene!

Then her eyes were caught by a bunch of fresh flowers in a jam jar. They had been placed there only minutes previously, yet there was no one here. *Hans Kolb*, she read, and with a shock realized that this was the grave of the German from the U-boat.

Dear God! There was a swastika engraved on the tombstone. She began to shake at the sight of the dreaded symbol. It had struck terror into her as a child. Men with swastikas had marched into Czechoslovakia; destroyed her home; taken her father to a camp; shot her mother and her aunt and later destroyed her father. "Oh God!" she wailed.

She closed her eyes and tried to banish the vivid memories which the symbol recalled. Instead she heard marching boots; saw her mother's face exploding. All the bitterness, all the loathing buried so long in her psyche surged up, blotting out reason. She hid her face in her hands.

Why was he buried here? His corpse should have been tossed into a lime pit. He would contaminate and poison the soil.

She grimaced. People were soft. They forgot, but she would never forget. She kicked over the jar and ground the flowers into the earth. Then she stamped again and again, forcing her heel into the sandy mound as loathing lathered out of her. "Filthy, filthy, filthy Boche," she muttered, her face contorted with rage.

She heard a low laugh and spun around.

Claire stood there, but how she had changed; she was even skinnier and her eyes were mean and full of venom. Suddenly Marika understood. "How spiteful . . . you bitch!" she stammered. "Oh! I detest you . . . and your stupid jealousy. Why . . . he could never want you!"

Eyes gleaming with hate, hands clenched. Then Claire flung something at Marika, hitting her in the face. "That's his," she gasped. "Give it to him." She ran away.

Marika stared down stupidly at the Iron Cross lying at her feet. His? Her mind was in a turmoil. She hardly heard the screeching brakes of the vehicle and Günter calling as he leaped over the graves. He caught hold of her, but she was icy cold.

"Marika. Look at me."

She looked up and saw that he was panic-stricken and once again a thrill of fear passed through her entrails.

"She said this is yours." Marika nudged the medal with her toe. Her eyes were full of pleading. "Say it's not," she whispered.

Günter bent down, brushed the sand from the medal and put it in his pocket.

"I blame myself. I should have told you before," he said.

"So you're German?" she asked in a small, broken voice.

Günter nodded and squared his shoulders.

He's relieved, she thought.

"I've been trying to tell you, but somehow . . . I never found the right time."

She looked away and the tears were rolling down her cheeks. "There is some curse on me," she said quietly. "All those I love are taken away."

"Your hatred . . . that's the curse," he said brokenly. "We'll still be married and in time you will forgive me for . . . for being German."

"Oh, but I could never marry a German. Why . . . to love one of those who destroyed my family . . . all my family . . ." She broke off.

"You must put it behind you . . ." he began, and paused, realizing the futility of his words. He licked his dry lips. "I love you."

"And I love you." The brightness had gone out of her eyes and her shoulders sagged.

After a while she squared her shoulders. "I wish . . . I wish you were lying there in the grave . . . I wish I had never met you."

Günter stepped back, looking shocked. "Go to hell," he said. "I'm proud of being German. In spite of everything. Proud of my parents; proud of my home. The war's over. Let's forget it."

"Over, is it?" She laughed sadly. "Where were you when they shot my mother? Goose-stepping your way through Europe with your Iron Cross?"

She looked up gravely. "You must have been a fine, patriotic German to win the Iron Cross."

There was nothing else to say. Günter watched her leave, noticing her bent head, her heavy feet. He knew that as long as he lived he would never lose anything so precious again.

It was a restless night; the wind whined through the sand dunes, the gulls screamed incessantly, but it was not the noise which kept Marika tossing and turning, it was a sense of loss. She loved Günter still, but she was intent on crushing each lingering particle of feeling. She would never marry a German. Never!

She would try to forget him. She planned to return to Europe and spend her savings on a modeling course. She was so sure she would succeed. At last she fell into an exhausted sleep and dreamed.

She had been offered a minor part in a movie. She was dressed as a Puritan wife and she was standing in a large field behind the cameras. A train was moving on the set—the original puffing billy. She watched as Red Indian film extras galloped toward the train in slow motion. Soldiers leaned out of the windows firing their rifles and the extras fell about groaning, blood gushing from their wounds.

"It's real!" She caught hold of the film director and shook him, "Stop it, they're real bullets!" she shrieked.

He turned and grinned and she realized he was Günter. Then she rushed on the set screaming, "Stop! You'll all be killed!" A bullet entered her stomach and lodged in her womb.

The actors sat up laughing and left and she staggered to the first-aid tent. "I've been shot," she told the doctor. "You have," he told her after a brief examination. "There's nothing I can do. The bullet will have to stay there." He shrugged and turned away.

Marika awoke shaking. The dream faded, but the bullet was real; a foreign body had lodged in her womb and was growing there; something hated and despised. She was impregnated with enemy seed and no one would help her; she would have to help herself.

A month later, after talking to the wife of a Herero fisherman, she bought a douche can and two bars of kitchen soap. She grated the soap and melted it in boiling water. When the water cooled, she forced the rubber nozzle into her womb, fainting twice with the pain, and tried to flush out the fetus with soapy water.

Bertha found her unconscious, spread-eagled on the floor, and called an ambulance.

The pregnancy was saved and a month later Marika returned to the store, unrepentant and furious. All Bertha's pleadings that she should marry Günter were ignored.

The chief source of gossip in Walvis Bay became Marika's spreading belly. She pretended that she did not care, but underneath she was seething with anger: forced to carry and nurture a German child. Sometimes her venom was so strong she felt she could run a dagger into her womb.

Bertha was sick with worry. She did not know why Günter and her daughter had quarreled, but she knew Marika well enough and feared that her next attempt to abort the baby might endanger her life. So she prayed for Günter's early return and tried to contact him, but he had left Walvis Bay and no one knew where he had gone.

Chapter Twenty-One

When Günter left Walvis Bay he had driven across the Kunene Pass southward through the flat highlands until he reached the Kalahari, where land could be purchased from the state for very little and payment could be deferred indefinitely.

There was only one proviso: a good water supply must be found, for the hardy karakul sheep, crossbred with local strains, could withstand the harsh territory and poor fodder, but water was essential.

Six days earlier he had left his jeep and set out on foot, for while the vehicle could cover the rough terrain, it was costly both in water and in gasoline. Along the route he had found enough melons to keep going and once he had shot a wild goose and dined sumptuously.

There was no shortage of fowl and most of them made good eating, but Günter was in no mood for hunting. He was searching for a water hole large enough to last through droughts and there he would create his farm out of the wilderness—twenty thousand hectares which he would stock with karakul.

So far he had walked along the eastern perimeter of the Kalahari Desert, but this morning he had turned westward and now he was trekking across wide valleys between gently sloping dunes, each one stretching for hundreds of miles from the north to the south. The deep ocher sand contained enough nourishment to sustain yellow grass and intermittent clumps of thorn trees.

Around him the veld shimmered in heat waves, looking blurred and unreal, and the air was sand-strewn and without moisture. The tops of the thorn trees were bending in the wind, goshawks were circling overhead, there was a hum of insects and the calls of many different kinds of birds. Around him were the spoor of buck and jackals, so he knew there must be water somewhere near.

Eventually Günter flung down his rifle and lay at the foot of another long line of sandy hills, watching the busy francolins gleaning insects. Beside him was a tsama plant. Its stalk, thick as a man's arm, wound over the veld and out of sight. Günter reached out and cut a melon from its tendril, sawed it in half with his knife and devoured the contents. The pulpy flesh was not particularly appetizing, but it contained enough moisture and sugar to keep him going for half a day.

He leaned back and grinned. This place was paradise.

By now Günter was unrecognizable. He had not washed or shaved in the time he'd been on foot. His shirt was in tatters and he was burnt dark brown by the sun, except for his nose, which was bright red and peeling for the fifth time. This was a man's world, he decided, untouched, savage, free. He loved the heat sensuously, the hum of the insects and the cicadas and he needed the loneliness of the arid bush. He was almost happy. Günter's thoughts were disturbed by the sound of a bustard calling from a tree. Something was exciting the bird, and Günter crawled up the slopes of the sand dune, feeling thankful that he was downwind. He peered over a wide expanse which might have been a dry riverbed.

Not more than forty yards away a battle was in progress between a secretary bird and a ringhals. The snake was glossy jet black along the back, merging to an ocher belly, with a pure white ring around its neck. Beyond the snake were three springbok watching curiously.

The battle soon began and Günter hung over the dune too surprised to move. For several minutes the contestants feinted and withdrew like sparring partners, but neither seemed to have the advantage. Then the secretary bird uttered a harsh cry, sounding like a sheep in pain. Günter assumed it had been wounded, but he was wrong, for a minute afterward it was joined by a comrade and both secretary birds attacked the snake, which was now losing, for it could not face both ways at once. Simultaneously the birds seized the reptile, one near its neck, the other further back, and bore the wriggling, struggling body aloft. Up and up they flew for nearly a hundred yards. Then they dropped their victim and swooped to earth with such speed that they arrived as their prey landed. The snake was stunned and in that instant it received a blow on the head which split its skull open.

The two comrades began to fight over the booty and Günter was so amused he burst into laughter and rolled down the sand dune. The secretary birds flew off and the springbok vanished. Günter climbed back and searched the horizon. It seemed to him that in the far distance there was a glistening vlei surrounded with trees. He wondered if it would prove to be a mirage, for he had been disappointed twice this way in the last three days.

As sunset approached, Günter began to feel hungry and tired.

Tonight there was something different about the veld. He tried to analyze it. Why were the francolins rushing before him with a sense of urgency? He had seen a small herd of springbok galloping in the distance and they, too, were taking the same direction as he. The birdsong was more varied, for there were more birds around, and the bush was becoming denser. Surely there must be water ahead.

Madness to walk through the bush at night, he knew, but a sense of excitement kept him going. The full moon rose and at last he was rewarded by the sight of an open vlei at least a hundred yards across, surrounded with tall reeds and several clumps of camel-thorn trees, and he knew he had found the base for which he had searched.

Günter never forgot that magical night in the bush as he crouched close to his fire. He heard the thrilling roar of a lion, followed by short, deep grunts. The sounds grew in intensity as the lion approached and the birds stirred uneasily in the branches above. He heard the high-pitched scream of the hyena and the howl of the jackal. An owl hooted, and there was a sudden call of a plover disturbed.

The sound of bullfrogs and crickets and the whisper of the wind was better than a symphony and the scent of damp earth and grass and the faintly stagnant odor of the vlei was finer than perfume to Günter.

He did not sleep that night. He was too happy. Dawn came too soon.

When Günter stood up and stretched, dozens of springhares hopped away through the grass; a small band of gemsbok came in cautious single file, their tall, straight horns erect and proud, and after them four springbok; a marabou stork hopped down from the branches of a dead tree and paddled in shallow water.

Looking around, Günter could see his camp as it would be soon. He took a knife and carved a sign on the largest tree trunk. It read: *This farm is the property of Günter Grieff.* Then he thought for a while and added: *Camp XLII,* for old times' sake.

Three months later Camp XLII looked very much as Günter had envisaged it on his first night by the vlei. There were three large thatched huts with walls a foot thick which were made of a curious compound: a mixture of pulverized termitaries, sand and water. Günter had discovered that this material was commonly used among the tribesmen.

He was amazed at the speed with which he had erected his three huts, one for living, one for the larder and a third for cooking, which was merely a roof on four poles. Günter's hut had half of a double story, for he had partially boarded the roof and entrance was by a rough ladder. He slept there on a camp bed and kept downstairs for living.

Günter was pleased with this camp and his only concern was the shrinking vlei. It was mid-April, autumntime, and there had been only a few intermittent showers during the summer rain season. Each afternoon, heavy thunderclouds would surge over the horizon and hang tantalizingly overhead, but the few drops that fell evaporated long before they reached the earth. So the vlei shrank, the grass shriveled and sandy patches spread. Even the camel-thorn trees had taken on a delicate, translucent appearance, offering only meager shade.

The wind arrived with the clouds, sending violent whirlwinds of dust and stones racing over the veld. Sometimes a few gigantic raindrops would fall on the parched and grateful soil, but the promise was not fulfilled and the clouds rolled away at dusk.

So Günter fenced off the vlei so that it was enclosed within the barbed-wire camp. Several animals had tried to break the wire, but the makeshift alarms alerted Günter and a few shots scared them away. By far the most persistent of the marauders were Bushmen who repeatedly tried to break in, but so far they had not succeeded.

Günter had made several trips to the Koes supply store for the gear he needed. Altogether, he felt satisfied with his home; there was game in the larder and provisions to last six months; there was a windmill, proud and tall some distance from the vlei, which operated a pump, and a wooden gate with his Camp XLII sign. All that was necessary was to purchase the land and buy some karakul and a dog. Then he would be in business. He decided to leave immediately.

The following morning Günter waited impatiently for the dawn. As always in the desert, the somber shadows and semi-darkness leaped into dazzling sunlight the moment the sun appeared over the horizon. Ten minutes later it was blazing hot and Günter was sweating as he left the camp in his jeep.

By now there was a rough track across the veld, but Günter loved the bush and he drove slowly, pausing now and then to search the terrain with his binoculars. It was an hour later when he saw two small shimmering black blurs against the shimmering ocher, but as they approached he could make out their diminutive ebony heads and the slender shafts of spears protruding behind.

Soon their shapes became more solid and complete. A man and a woman, and they were a heartrending sight, for they looked old, at least eighty, but Günter guessed them to be around thirty-five, for Bushmen aged badly. They walked with a strange, stumbling lope and closer now he could see their hollow cheeks, their sunken eyes and their skin hanging in folds over their meager frames.

They were dying, that much was clear, but Günter was not yet aware that he was the cause of their plight and he waited impatiently.

When they saw that he had seen them and he was not firing at them they became bolder and approached to within a hundred yards of the jeep. Then they paused, torn between fear and hope, raised their hands and uttered their strange, broken clicking sounds.

Günter took the water from the can and handed it to them in mugfuls and they rushed forward and gulped down one after the next until they had drunk about a gallon each. Uneasily he wondered if fencing off the vlei had contributed to their condition. The Bushmen sank onto their haunches and looked up with eyes so full of gratitude that Günter wanted to kick himself there and then, they were so dreadfully thin, but there were such sweet and childish expressions on their faces.

He transported them back to the camp and from sign language learned that other water holes were dry; the game had fled from the area, the tsama season was over and there was no rain. They had come from far away, and now that they had drunk they would be able to make their way to the Kalahari interior.

Günter was overcome with a deep and terrible shame. What vanity had driven him to take the water for his own needs and deprive others, upsetting the natural balance of the area? A sin against nature and against God, he reasoned.

He gave them food. Then he took an ax and a spade and, regardless of the heat and his bleeding hands, worked frenziedly until all traces of the hated barbed wire was removed from the vlei. He had a borehole nearer the camp, that was enough. Then he left without saying goodbye, hoping they would stay.

Chapter Twenty-two

Four months had passed since Günter disappeared and there had been no news since. Bertha had questioned everyone in Walvis Bay, but not even Evans had heard from him.

She was worried about Marika—the poor child. Admittedly Marika had brought the problem on herself by making love with Günter before their marriage, but who could blame her? After all, they were engaged. A justifiable impatience for which she was paying dearly.

The narrow-minded community of Walvis Bay suddenly seemed hateful to Bertha. Marika was the butt of every joke and she was known as Günter's woman. Bertha could not help admiring the way her daughter conducted herself. She was suffering, but no one would guess. She was aloof, calm and seemingly uncaring.

Not quite so admirable was her daughter's inability to accept her pregnancy. Just mention baby clothes or buying a pram or even the possibility of Bertha adopting the baby and she would shut herself in her room and remain there for hours, just as she had years before. Bertha could not understand her.

And why was she so quick to anger and slow to forgive? Young people often quarreled, Bertha knew that, but if they loved each other they made it up. Still, it was not Marika's fault. Bertha blamed Günter, rushing off like that, leaving her pregnant and alone. Whatever could they have quarreled about? It all seemed so unnecessary. Bertha knew Marika loved Günter. She heard her cry herself to sleep at night. Even now she was moping in her room with the door locked.

Marika was filled with self-loathing as she gazed at the

wall with bleak eyes. After her one unsuccessful attempt at abortion and the incredible pain which had nearly killed her, she had decided not to try again. She felt she was becoming enormous and apart from the burden in her stomach there were her aching legs, the nausea, her nervousness and lethargy. Yet she was unable to accept the growing fetus as having anything to do with her. It seemed to her that she was forced to play host to a parasite; an enemy child. Her body had been invaded and she was the victim.

She had only to wait and she would be rid of it forever, she promised herself. Never again. No more sex, no more love. She was finished with all that. She would go to Europe and pursue her ambitions. She would be a model. Yes, she would . . . she would.

Then one May morning when she was helping behind the counter, Günter walked in looking splendid. The sight of him sent shooting spasms of pain and excitement through her stomach. He was deeply tanned, except for his nose, so his eyes looked twice as blue and his hair astoundingly blond. His full lips were cracked and burned black and he was lean and strong and vigorous. Oh, how she hated him. How unfair it was. She was reduced to a pathetic, laughable state and he had got off scot-free. "Bastard!" she muttered, but pretended she had not seen him.

Günter was shaking with emotion and he turned aside to examine the nets so no one would notice. He could see her hair gleaming beautifully over the shoulder of the customer she was serving. Would he never go?

When he was about to leave at last, Günter caught sight of her belly. Pregnant! His face paled under his tan. His eyes flashed fire. He grabbed the counter. "Why didn't you tell me?" he whispered.

"It's none of your business," Marika's voice croaked with anger.

"Oh yes," Günter crowed. "It's mine. I can count." His eyes gleamed with triumph as he reached forward and grabbed her.

She pushed him away. "Keep your hands to yourself. You have no claims on me," she gasped. "It's to be adopted. Bertha's arranged everything."

Seething with anger, Günter made for the nearest bar and downed a scotch. The bartender pushed another glass in front of him, so he drained that one, too, and ordered a third. He was obsessed with the image of Marika; her golden hair tumbling over her sprouting belly.

"Hi, Günter! Hello, pal, so you're back." A crowd of fishermen from the canning factory came in and Günter glowered at them. He was not in the mood for company.

"Hey, come on, Günter. What's the matter? Didn't the farm work out?"

Evans, the manager, was with them, but he seemed strangely reticent.

Günter tried out a tentative smile. "Okay, fellows, what's it going to be?"

"I'll buy my own, thanks," Evans said quietly, but the rest ordered and set about teasing Günter good-naturedly.

"No water there? Surprise, surprise."

"Any good birds around? Just vultures. Tough luck!"

Their good humor was like salt in his wounds.

"So what are you doing in town, Günter?" they wanted to know. "Given up? Looking for a job?"

"Belt up," Günter snarled. "I came back for Marika, but she's more stubborn than ever. I don't understand her. After all, she's . . ." He looked at their faces; obviously it was no secret. "In her condition one would think . . ." His voice tailed off.

"Marika's always been self-willed," Evans said noncommittally. "Gave Bertha a lot of trouble when she was young. I wouldn't say much for your chances. Didn't you know she was in the hospital for a month after trying to abort?" he asked over-casually.

Günter looked shocked. "She tried to kill my baby?" Suddenly he understood Evans' unfriendly behavior. "Oh God." He seemed so broken by the news they felt embarrassed for him.

"Come on, drink up," Evans said. "Next round's on me. What'll it be?"

Four drinks later they were all making suggestions on how he could win Marika back.

"It's no good," Günter said hopelessly. "We had a fight. She'll never forgive me." He wondered whether to tell them the truth, but decided not to.

"Drink up," Günter said sadly. "I'll buy the next round."

Melancholy settled heavily on them with the alcohol and Günter's plight.

"Well," one said after a while, "if my girl got up the spout like, and then she got on her high horse because of a fight, or something silly like that, why, I'd take her back to my farm—if I had one, that is—until she came to her bleeding senses."

"Hear, hear," they chorused.

"You've got to be tough with women," his friend put in. "They respect strength. Women're like dogs that way."

"Get her back to the bush and she'll come round."

"Women change when they have babies."

"You can count on us, mate, but first we've got to prove she loves you."

Everyone had something to say and eventually they hit on an idea, although afterward no one could remember who had thought of it.

It was almost ten when Bertha and Marika heard loud knocking on the door and a chorus of drunken voices.

Bertha looked out of the window and then hurried down and unfastened the chains. Several fishermen stood swaying and grinning oafishly; they shuffled into the store.

Bertha glared at them.

"Begging your pardon, ma'am, but we've all had a bit too much to drink," their ringleader began.

"I can see that," Bertha said sternly.

"We've come about Günter. He's drunk and we can't do nothing with him. It's like this, see. He's taken his revolver and he's playing Russian roulette. He won't see reason. He says he'll shoot a bullet a minute until he's dead, or until Marika comes.''

"A likely story!" Bertha was looking exasperated. "I suppose he's drunk, too.''

"He's had one too many like the rest of us.''

"Oh, don't waste time, Bertha," Marika snapped, and Bertha glanced around in surprise. White-faced and trembling, Marika hovered in the doorway. For a moment she hesitated, then she rushed down the stairs followed by one of the fishermen and a moment later they were speeding across the sand in Günter's jeep.

"I'm too old to be fooled with a story like that," Bertha said crossly. She did not feel alarmed. She knew them well. They were good boys, just a bit rough at times.

"You see, Mrs. Factor," one of them tried to explain. "It seems a pity, don't you think? He loves her and she loves him—at least we reckoned that she'd go if she loves him . . . you can see for yourself she did . . .''

"Get to the point," Bertha admonished him.

"Well, her being pregnant . . .'' He was fingering his cap. Suddenly it did not seem such a good idea. Bertha could look ferocious at times.

"He's going to take her back to his farm. Maybe she'll give in and marry him once the baby's born. He's got a nice place there, he tells us. Günter says, will you pack her some things and he promises he'll take care of her.''

Bertha sat motionless, her mind quickly plotting. What was the point of Marika staying here, pregnant and miserable? At his farm, she might forget about the past. If there was a chance of happiness, then they must try for it—and how much better for the unborn child, she reasoned.

Ignoring the fishermen, she hurried upstairs and packed a few clothes for Marika, adding the baby clothes she had been secretly collecting, and she took three hundred pounds out of her bedroom safe and hid it in Marika's cosmetics bag.

"Günter's a good lad," one of the fishermen said awkwardly when she handed him the suitcases.

"Yes, he is," she said. "I always knew that. But tell

him to bring her back to Walvis Bay well in time for the birth. Please God they'll be married by then.''

When they had left, Bertha permitted herself the luxury of sitting down and crying, though whether it was from fright or relief she really could not tell.

Chapter Twenty-three

Marika sat in the doorway of her hut staring over the vlei; she had sat there for days watching the birds and the game which appeared intermittently. Günter watched her and swore silently. When he had first brought her back to the camp, he had tried to rekindle a spark of the passion they had shared when they met and to persuade her to marry him, but they had fought night and day, she would not forgive him and eventually he had given up trying.

Now she was placid and uncaring and Günter was more hurt by this than their fights. If he spoke to her she would answer, if he asked her to help him she would not refuse. She ate the food she was given, but did not care what it was. At night she locked herself in her cottage and unlocked the door only at breakfast. It seemed that nothing could disturb the calm acceptance of her days.

Eventually he offered to take her back to Bertha, but she refused. ''I'm not myself,'' she had told him. ''Leave me alone. I'll be all right.''

Günter was worried. It was difficult to find farmers who would part with their precious karakul stock, but old Weidinger, who had a ranch in the Maltahohe district, was retiring and auctioning his flock. Günter knew he must go, for in all likelihood this would be his only chance to acquire good stock; so he had serviced his jeep and arranged for a young Ovambo boy to start work at the end of the month. But still, he hated the thought of leaving Marika.

He watched her anxiously. She looked pale and miserable. He had promised Bertha to take her home before the baby was born. Well, plenty of time yet, he reasoned. She was not yet eight months. "Marika," he began anxiously. "I must attend the auction or I'll miss the chance."

"Go, then," she said without looking round.

"Aren't you afraid of being alone here?"

"Are you afraid?"

"No."

"What makes you think we're any different?"

"I'm not pregnant," he said uneasily.

"Aren't you lucky." She looked over her shoulder and felt dazzled by his amazing vitality. He was tough and lean and his muscles rippled under his sweaty skin. When he was near she had to endure the stupid flutterings in her stomach and the hated fetus seemed to sense her suppressed passion and kicked out jealously.

She moved away quickly so that he would not see, loathing herself for her vulnerability.

"It will take me three days at the very least," he went on, wondering again if he should take her to Walvis Bay first, but he did not want to lose her so soon. "Marika, come to the auction with me . . . please," he said.

Marika went into her hut and slammed the door and Günter waited for a while and then left, swearing quietly to himself.

Marika listened to the sound of the jeep bumping over the dunes; eventually the sound faded and she was quite alone. She opened the door, walked into the yard and sat on a boulder. She remained there for a very long time, or so it seemed, but when she looked at her watch she found that only half an hour had passed. She decided to make some tea. Surely that would take at least twenty minutes.

Marika was frightened, but not of being left alone. She was afraid of herself, for she knew she had changed. So many unwelcome desires were settling upon her. One

minute she would long to furnish her hut, then she would
feel like planting flowers. Worst of all was her need to be
loved and protected, to have a man of her own and to hold
his baby in her arms. But she would not give in, she knew
that. She would never marry a German or nurture his
child. Just let her weaken once and she would be trapped
forever. So she blanked her mind to these strange sensations and waited impatiently to be free of her burden.

The day passed slowly. At sunset she listened to the
shrill chorus of the geckos, followed by the cacophonous
chant of birds preparing for the night. The sun fled over
the horizon and darkness followed dusk so swiftly Marika
was always unprepared.

Perhaps she should not sit here by the vlei, she thought,
but she was unwilling to shut herself in the cottage. Although the moon had not yet risen, the sky looked brilliant, each star shining with amazing clarity. The wind was
cooling rapidly, stroking her skin; she became conscious
of the smell of the vlei and the damp earth and strange
whisperings in the branches.

Noctural springhares hopped around the vlei like minia-
ture kangaroos and she heard a high-pitched scream as one
was taken. Now was the time when the predators began
their nightly prowl; wild cats, jackals, foxes and caracals.

Her ears were finely attuned to the night and she could
see green eyes flashing in the bush.

How long did she sit there? She did not know, but she
had a curious, fleeting sensation that she was part of the
pattern of life . . .interwoven . . .indivisible; that she was
indestructible; part of a vast, intelligent life force which
throbbed through the universe and that if she were taken
by a beast of prey the chemicals of which she was made
would reassemble themselves into new forms and her life
force would return to the front. Home! Something dimly
remembered stirred inside her.

Her mood passed and she was left with a sense of loss.
Something vital had been almost understood, but now it
had vanished. Like trying to remember a forgotten tune,
she thought moodily. What was it?

She stood up shivering and hurried to her cottage. It was September, springtime, but although the days were warm and sunny the nights were sometimes chilly. Marika wrapped herself in a blanket and sat on the camp bed.

She heard the high-pitched scream of the hyena as it set off to hunt, and later its nervous laughter when it found its prey.

Then, in the distance, she heard a lion. There were several prolonged roars in rapid succession followed by a series of short, deep grunts. She felt terrified and sat shivering, listening intently. Then she heard them again, closer this time.

She tried to ignore her fears, but it seemed that the yard was filled with ghostly footsteps. Nothing could be worse than her imagination, she decided eventually. She must go outside and prove to herself that her fears were groundless.

She stood up, flung open the door and stepped into the dazzling moonlight.

Green eyes set wide apart stared at her and behind were several more. Kalahari lions! She had heard of them, but never seen them. Their pelts shone white in the moonlight, but she knew they were the color of sand. She could smell their fetid breath and the musky odor of their fur. Low growls turned her legs to jelly.

She shrieked, stumbled into the hut and slammed the door, squashing her finger with panic.

Then she sat on the bed wrapped in a blanket and waited for morning, listening to their grunts and snarls as the lions pawed the walls.

It was dawn when she went into labor. She endured the pains silently throughout the day, but at dusk her resistance weakened and she began groaning.

Much later she felt a hand lifting her head and looked up into the small, wrinkled face of the old Bushman woman who camped with her husband in the veld beyond the vlei. She was foul-smelling and almost naked, but her eyes were calm and she was smiling.

Marika was no longer alone. Gratefully she did what the Bushman woman indicated and the baby was born swiftly and almost painlessly African style, as the two women squatted on the floor, hands clasped, feet against each other, while they pulled back strongly.

Like rowing, Marika thought. How curious . . .As the baby opened its mouth and screamed, Marika fell into a deep, exhausted sleep.

Later she awoke to find the Bushman woman crouched beside her nursing the baby. The woman pushed the bundle toward her, but she shuddered and turned away.

All that day and most of the night the Bushman woman waited for Marika to accept her baby, but eventually she gave up and squatted outside the door rocking the wailing child.

When Günter returned at dawn, he heard the cries as he parked the jeep and, frantic with guilt and fright, he raced across the yard. Marika had survived and his relief was so great he flung himself beside her.

"I'll never forgive myself," he began. "Never. Are you all right? Shall I take you to a hospital?"

"There's no point," she said coldly.

"You have every right to be angry," he said, looking miserable. "How is our baby? Is it a boy or a girl?"

Marika did not answer.

Günter went outside and took the baby from the Bushman woman. He gave her some food and she vanished into the dusk.

Günter nursed the baby for a day while Marika refused to hold or even to look at the tiny bundle.

The following morning when Günter brought the baby to her, Marika could sense the fear in him.

"If you don't feed it, it will die," he said quietly, trying to control his temper.

Let him hit me, she thought. She did not care. "I did not want your baby, Günter," she said icily, "and I won't feed it. If you care so much, take it to the hospital."

She watched him standing in the shadow of the doorway, his legs tensed, his deep-set eyes glowing with anger, head lowered. "Leave me alone," she said.

He did not answer. The baby was crying again. The

sound was appalling. Marika thought she would go mad if it did not stop.

Günter tried to thrust the bundle onto her breasts, but she pushed it away violently. The baby fell, but Günter lunged forward and caught it.

Then Günter took the chair he had made and carried it to the center of the room. He took hold of her arms under the armpits, not roughly, but strongly, and hoisted her over his shoulder. She could feel his bones pressing into her sore stomach and her nightdress billowing around her thighs. There is no end to the humiliation here, she thought, but soon I shall go away and he can have his precious baby to himself.

"Sit down," Günter said. Noticing the stubbornness of the man, and the brute strength, she felt she was seeing him clearly for the first time. He would keep his precious child alive if he had to tie her down for a year.

He fastened her hands to the back of the chair and undid her nightdress. He swore when he saw how tightly she had bound her breasts with strips she had torn from a sheet. He unwound the cloth carefully and the milk oozed from her nipples.

Marika began to cry softly. "I won't do it. I hate it and I hate you. I want it to die. Don't you understand?"

Günter fumbled and his hands seemed twice as large as usual. The baby's head fell back, then sideways, and he cursed as he tried to get it into the right position. At last the howling mouth was firmly pressed on Marika's nipple, and as if it had been taught, the baby began to suck vigorously.

Oh, how sore it was, but there was a certain relief in feeling the burdensome milk being sucked away from swollen, burning glands.

Marika leaned back, closed her eyes and tried to ignore a sense of tenderness invading her whole being.

Günter arrived with the baby early the following morning and saw how her breasts were huge and swollen and how depressed she was, but he did not care. She was a spoiled and willful woman, unable to accept or give love.

He tied her hands more tightly, enjoying her gasps of pain, and thrust the wailing infant onto her breast.

"Oh, how I hate you," she whispered, "and I hate myself for giving the world another Nazi thug."

"It's a girl," Günter said shortly.

Marika stopped with her mouth open. A girl? She could not come to grips with this strange idea.

As the day wore on, Marika felt increasingly humiliated. She was no better than a cow, she had ceased to exist as an individual. How she hated them both. Yet, as she leaned back in the chair, eyes closed, legs spread-eagled with Günter kneeling between them holding the baby, she became aware of a strange bond forming between her and this whimpering, sucking, tiny thing.

Surely it was not just milk which flowed from her to the child, but her own life force. She could sense their communication. She bent forward and peered at the baby.

At that moment the baby opened its eyes and stared up at her. Marika gasped. "My mother's eyes," she murmured. They were huge eyes for such a small head and of the deepest shade of violet. "I have never seen any other person with eyes like my mother's," she said wonderingly.

"She's just like me," Günter said jealously.

Perhaps she had Günter's hair, Marika acknowledged, and possibly his wide brow, but for the rest she was the image of her mother.

Shortly afterward, when Günter took the baby away, Marika leaned back feeling puzzled and exhausted by her emotional turmoil. She could not understand herself at all! "How could I be so mistaken?" she murmured again and again.

How can she be so cruel? Günter was thinking as he clumsily washed the baby in a tub under the trees. Perhaps Marika was reacting from instinct, he thought, trying to excuse her, just as a wild beast in captivity will reject its young. He knew how unhappy she was here, yet there was so much of the wild in her, with her proud ways, her independence and her need to be free.

He dried the baby tenderly and rocked it to sleep. There

was only one person he loved more than Marika and that was his child. He felt amazed at the force of his love and humbled by the burden of his responsibility.

That night the baby cried intermittently for two hours while Marika tossed on the camp bed. Surely Günter must hear her cries? How could he sleep? The cloth-eared donkey!

When she heard the howl of a jackal close to the camp she flung open her door and rushed outside. The yard was bright with moonlight, and around the trees and huts were pools of velvet black. Strange rustlings were coming from the bushes and the sheep were huddled together in their enclosure. She heard the jackal again and the sheep began bleating and jostling each other as Marika rushed across the yard. She flung open the door of the hut where Günter was sleeping.

The baby was lying in her wooden cradle, red-faced and choking. Marika bent over her, slipped one hand under the baby's head and the other under her body. "There, there," she murmured as she lifted it. "There, there, there."

Tense and watchful, Günter waited while Marika soothed the baby and carried it back to her hut. Then he smiled softly and went to look after the sheep.

Chapter Twenty-four

It was mid-November, summertime. The damp earth steamed voluptuously; each blade of grass sparkled with dew; the trees were still dripping and flowers had appeared all over the veld. It had rained in the night—a magnificent deluge and the earth had opened her thighs gratefully.

There was joy in the air; in the murmur of the wind; in the light steps of the karakul trailing to new pastures; in the twittering birds bathing in puddles; in the springbok rolling on damp grass. Even the meerkats were too happy to be shy—mucking about in the mud.

Only Günter was joyless. Worse than that—he was afraid. He had no hold over Marika and she could leave whenever she wanted and take his baby with her. He feared her leaving so much that he was hardly able to think of anything else. He spent hours awake at night planning how to stop her, but there was no way he could find.

If only she would marry him. For the past three months he had showered her with promises until they lay between them as thick as ticks on a buck's back, but she would not. She was a headstrong, self-willed woman propelled by God knows what foolish pride and grudges, unable to forget the past and start again.

Watching her moodily as she rocked the baby in the cradle by the vlei, Günter decided there was only one thing he had not tried and that was pleading. Perhaps she would relent if he told her how much he needed her, how desperate he would be without his daughter. He walked toward her frowning as he tried to choose the best opening.

"Marika, I want to talk to you," he said, and collapsed on the ground beside her, aware that his mouth had dried and his hands felt clammy.

"I can't stop you talking." She stared doggedly at the water.

"I've done all I can to make you happy," he began, but his eyes were caught by the sight of her breasts thrusting against her blouse. Two damp patches showed through the thin fabric.

"What have you done to make me happy?" he complained. Goddamnit, what was he saying? He tried to stop himself, tried to remember the words he had been composing, but his anger and need were taking over.

"Don't you remember that night in the Namib? You needed me then."

He reached out and grabbed her arm, felt his fingers digging into her flesh. "I know you love me, however much you try to hide it. How d'you think I feel? I'm a man, aren't I?"

Her eyes showed contempt and Günter was stung to anger. "Goddamn you, Marika. What do you think about at night, locked up by yourself? Don't you long for a man? For me?"

At that moment he hated her. Could anyone have tried harder to make her happy? He was angry with himself, too. This was not the way he had intended to talk to her.

"Marry me!" The words came out like a roar and his eyes looked bloodshot, his thighs were stiffening and he was overcome with a desire to pound her into submission.

Marika became alarmed. "Let go of me," she cried, her voice high-pitched and ineffectual.

"Enough's enough." He flung her skirt aside and thrust his hand into her crotch.

"Take your hand away." Her eyes filled with tears. Then she struck him in the face. "I've told you . . . I'll never . . . never marry a German and you're wrong—I no longer love you."

"Then why are you all wet here? Why are your nipples hard? Your cheeks red? Why can't you learn to give way to your feelings?"

"You're wrong . . . you're wrong," she screamed. "I don't want you."

"You do, by God." Günter pushed her back on the ground and for a few moments they fought. But he won and, pinning her arms above her, he tore off her pants and pushed her legs aside.

Her eyes were open, but the pupils had almost disappeared under her eyelids; her mouth hung slack and her lips were dry.

Günter thrust into her, heard her sigh, felt her arms and her hips swaying beneath him. The motion nearly drove him crazy. Any moment he would explode inside her, but then he heard her scream, high-pitched, like a wounded hare, and they came together in a brief moment of shared ecstasy.

"Now tell me you didn't want me," he gasped.

"You beast . . . I don't want to love you . . . you're

cheating me . . . like you cheated me with the baby . . . forcing me to feel things I don't want to feel."

She stood up, snatched the baby from the cradle and ran
into the hut.

Günter lay on his back smiling. He felt a surge of
triumph thrill his body. So his instinct had been right, after
all. A little force—that's all it had taken. What a fool he
had been to wait so long. Marika loved him; he knew it
and she knew it. How could she deny it again? She would
always be his. He watched a kestrel circling overhead,
clouds were forming on the horizon. With luck it would
rain, too.

Then he heard the sound of the jeep's engine.

He jumped up with a roar of rage and disbelief and
raced after her.

Squeal of tires and cloud of dust, but Günter ran on
choking, Marika's words ringing in his ears.

"Goodbye, Günter . . . see you sometime . . . if you
don't die of hunger . . . or thirst . . . I'm going away . . .
did you think I could forget so easily . . . and marry a
German . . . I'd rather die . . ."

The jeep disappeared over a hillock and her voice was
lost in the wind.

"I'll find you wherever you are . . ." he hurled uselessly after her. "You stupid bitch," he added quietly to
himself and stood kicking at a grass root, eyes blinded
with tears.

Günter sank to the ground and looked around sadly. He
loved the bush, the loneliness, the freedom, and above all
he loved his farm, but he had to admit he would never get
rich here.

The loss of his daughter was a searing pain in his guts.
He must get her back . . . but how? He would have to
think of something, but not now. Tomorrow! Tonight he
was going to get blind drunk.

Chapter Twenty-five

There were footsteps on the wooden platform outside the store, yet it was past closing time. Bertha sighed and looked up from the accounts. She was tired, but she never refused anyone.

The door opened and Marika stood there.

"Darling!" Bertha exclaimed, too surprised and happy to stand up.

Marika walked in and shut the door behind her. Then she turned and faced Bertha and from the expression in her eyes Bertha could see she was glad to be back; she was trying not to cry. She looked older and thinner. Her long hair was plaited and wound around her head; her feet were dirty; her sandals torn; she was covered in dust and so was the bundle she clasped in her arms.

They've come back, Bertha thought. The farm hasn't worked out and now they're going to stay with me and run the store. "Welcome home," she said, trying to conceal her joy. "Where's Günter?"

Marika just stood there staring.

"I've left Günter," she said at last. "I'm going to Europe." She looked as if she was prepared for opposition.

"Oh, Marikala!" Bertha exclaimed, her hopes dashed. "I've missed you so. Well, you don't have to leave this minute, do you?"

Marika sat down abruptly and began laughing, but her laughter was too high-pitched. Then she managed to control herself. "Don't tell me," she said. "You're going to say: you'll make a plan."

Bertha laughed self-consciously and took off her glasses. They always steamed up when she felt emotional.

"Am I allowed to see your baby?" She reached forward

139

and then cried out, "Oh, Marika! Tiny babies must be kept clean."

"You try . . . my goodness . . . in an open jeep . . . over a dirt road for three days."

"But surely you stopped over . . ." Bertha was frowning as she examined the baby.

"I just drove like crazy."

"My, but it looks healthy," Bertha said. It was the best she could think of.

Her daughter laughed unkindly this time and Bertha sensed Marika was laughing at her.

"Is it a boy or a girl?"

"A girl."

Now Bertha was fussing and cooing and stroking the baby under its chin. The baby's eyes opened. Bertha gasped and nearly dropped the bundle. "Just look at those beautiful eyes. I've never seen such a color."

"Like my mother's," Marika said, her voice muffled a little. "So I took her. Otherwise I would have left her with Günter. He wanted her so badly."

"You would have left her?" Bertha sounded incredulous. She hugged the baby protectively.

Marika pursed her lips. She was too tired to explain.

"Well, enough of this 'her' and 'she.' What's her name?"

Marika shrugged. "No name as yet."

Bertha looked distressed and shaken. "You can be wicked sometimes," she said bluntly.

Marika felt startled. It was the first time Bertha had taken another's part against her and although it was her own baby she felt strangely perturbed.

"I'm going to bathe." She stood up slowly and stretched. "I ache everywhere."

"Didn't Günter . . .?" Bertha persisted.

"Oh yes. Dozens of names. Each day more and more . . . trying to find one to please me. But you see, they were all German."

Bertha heard the bathroom door shut and the sound of water running. She called the maid to unpack the jeep, but it was empty.

Clasping the baby, Bertha hurried upstairs.

"Where's your things?" she called.

"I left everything."

Bertha opened the door and looked at Marika questioningly.

"Please, Bertha. I'm tired."

"All right." Bertha gave in. "But later we'll have a great deal to talk about." She made it sound like a threat.

That night after supper, when the baby was sleeping, Bertha prized the story out of Marika: of how she had wanted the baby to die; of her loathing for the bush; of her disgust at the life she had led there, and her determination to go to Europe. She did not tell Bertha that Günter was really German, nor of her self-disgust at loving him, not even of her dream of seeing her father's murderers brought to justice.

Bertha went to bed feeling depressed and sorry for the little mite, whom she had decided to call Sylvia. She lay sleepless for hours. The wind had never whined so ominously, nor the gulls screamed so persistently. She, Bertha, was the guilty one, she decided. She had been given a child to rear to womanhood and she had failed. Perhaps she had spoiled her too much, or forgotten her femininity in her role of breadwinner. Where were Marika's womanly instincts? Only too lacking, it seemed.

Suddenly she had a vivid recall of Marika's twelfth birthday party. What was it Irwin had said? "A child torn up by the roots—a mother to the future." At the time she had blamed him for being pessimistic.

What sort of woman would try to destroy her own child? she asked herself. The answer came back loud and clear. Any woman faced with a life that was unendurable. Why? Why was it so terrible for Marika? Another woman would have turned the cottage into a home. But not Marika.

These questions plagued Bertha in the days that followed as she alternated between fits of despondency and bewilderment. She watched Marika closely, analyzing every word and action, searching for some quality to redeem her daughter in her eyes.

Marika was not lazy and she was not cruel, Bertha decided. Simply disinterested. She was only too happy to let Bertha take charge of Sylvia and could not wait to put her on the bottle.

She was leaving soon, Bertha could see that. Stitching, mending and sorting her old clothes; ordering new ones; packing baby clothes. Eventually Bertha came to a decision; she broached the subject at breakfast.

"I know you're planning to go," she said as lightly as she could. "Perhaps I've been selfish in hoping that you would settle down here. After all, I don't want to be parted from you and I like Africa. But still." She sighed and lost track of what she was saying. "Where was I?" She looked anxiously at Marika, who was gazing back with such compassion in her eyes.

"You can't look after Sylvia by yourself," she blurted out. "You don't care enough. Or maybe you care—but you just don't have that special instinct. Besides, with this silly idea of yours of becoming a model—how would you cope? It's wicked to leave a small baby alone." She took a deep breath. "You'll just have to wait until I've sold the store and we'll go together. The three of us." There! It was said. She glared defiantly at Marika.

"But, Bertha darling. I can't waste any more time," Marika said casually. "Sylvia will be all right. Other mothers work and their babies survive. When I'm rich I'll find a nanny . . ."

"You'll be working long hours. Sylvia will be neglected," Bertha argued. "If you stay here you'll be able to look after Sylvia properly.

"Oh, Bertha," Marika said, noticing her sad face. "Babies are awfully boring things. Just food, crying and changing diapers."

"Well, I never heard of anything so selfish . . ." Bertha stopped in midsentence, not wishing to say something she might regret, but she felt weighed down with sorrow.

*   *   *

The next morning, just after breakfast a ragged Ovambo came into the store carrying a sack and without asking unloaded his wares on the floor. Watching his glittering eyes and hollow cheeks made Bertha feel nervous. There was a look of desperation about him.

Bertha pursed her lips when she saw the carved figures he was trying to sell. Hopeless, she thought: she would have to buy one of them, he was so hungry. She looked around for a piece that resembled something real.

Then Marika came into the store.

"I'm buying one of these, Marika," Bertha said firmly for fear her daughter would be rude.

"Why, how lovely," Marika cried as she crouched on the floor and examined each piece carefully. "And all alone in the bush . . . just look what he's produced . . . but how will his work ever be noticed?" Her eyes were brimming with tears.

She bought half the pieces and placed them around the store. "One day," she told the Ovambo, "I'll take them to England." She wrote down his name. "Perhaps I'll be able to do something to help you."

"I can't understand you," Bertha said peevishly after supper. "After all, you need the money."

It was a hot night. Sylvia was whimpering and Bertha was rocking the cradle with one foot while her hands were busy knitting a jacket.

"I know you think badly of me nowadays, but you've never understood me," Marika began nervously. "If you had, you would never have thought . . . I mean never have hoped that I would stay here . . ." She stared strangely at Bertha.

"I want to go where it's all happening . . .where I can find myself. Give whatever I can back to the world . . . instead of always taking." She gazed into Bertha's eyes, lately so reserved and diffident.

"Oh, Bertha," she said. "You must understand. You and I . . . we used to walk along the shore and throw stale bread at the gulls . . . don't you remember how we used to feel when we forgot the bread . . . nothing to give?"

She was too full of nervous energy, pushing her fist into the palm of her hand, pacing the room, eyes alight and burning.

"If I can't find something in myself to give . . . well, really, Bertha, I think I'd rather die. You see, there would be no point in my existence.

"When I see dancers or listen to singers on the radio, well, there they are, the ones who give . . . giving their all. Then I say to myself: What are you going to give, Marika Magos?" She turned impulsively, crouched next to Bertha and flung her arms around her knees.

"Bertha, somehow I'm going to find a little bit to add to the world . . . there's got to be something." She sighed. "Creating something wonderful . . . that's what counts and that's why I loved that Ovambo. He's like . . . well . . . like my brother," she said, suddenly shy. "I have to do something, but I don't know what."

"Perhaps you should go to art school," Bertha said heavily after an awkward silence.

"Oh no," Marika said hurriedly. "I haven't time."

Bertha went to bed feeling disturbed. She felt she was in the same position as a hen who finds that her chick is of another species.

Looking back, remembering Marika's childhood, she realized that she should have guessed then. The child was always drawing, introverted and secretive. Underneath was the heart and mind of a creative person, unable to participate in normal life because she had been stamped "Messenger."

Yet where was the talent? Bertha asked herself. She painted, but not well enough. She had no other talents and she did not have the figure for a model, she was too voluptuous. Marika wanted to give, but was there anything there? Bertha feared that her daughter would be destroyed by her failure.

She tried to tell her this in the following weeks, but Marika would not give in. She had to go.

Finally Bertha persuaded her to leave Sylvia with her, at

least until Marika could afford a home or until Bertha had sold the store. Then Bertha would take Sylvia to London.

Once they had decided, Marika thrust her feelings into cold storage, as she always did.

"You'll miss Sylvia . . . all of us, more than you realize," Bertha warned her.

"No, why should I? There's nothing to miss. Just a wobbly bundle of flesh. When she's older, then I'll love her. Meantime there's no one in the world could bring up a baby better than you, Bertha."

Once again Bertha found herself standing at the wharf peering into the mist, trying to see Marika, just as she had years ago, only then the boat had been slowly appearing and this time it was receding—a blurred outline soon swallowed by the fog.

The poor, misguided child, Bertha thought. She'd be lucky to make a living, untrained as she was, never mind rich and famous. Oh, the young, she sighed. They would not listen, they had to learn for themselves. She'd be back soon enough, with a bit more common sense, please God. But what if she did not? What if she ran into trouble? She was too vulnerable and far too beautiful. "Oh, Marikala," she whispered.

Still she stood there.

Nine years! It seemed like ninety. Marika had come and irrevocably changed her life. Now she was gone.

Bertha remembered the small, frightened child with the shaved head and she remembered Irwin with his shambling walk rushing up the gangway to carry Marika to their home.

Tears were running down her cheeks and she smudged them with the back of her hand. Well, she told herself firmly, she had Sylvia to look after now and this was quite long enough to be out in the cold morning mist. She turned away reluctantly and trundled the pram back to the store.

PART TWO

Chapter Twenty-six

*The Kalahri Desert
April 1948*

Günter looked at the sky and cursed. Rain clouds gathered on the horizon daily, but although lightning flickered in the south and he heard occasional faint rumbles of thunder, the sky remained pitilessly clear and not a drop had fallen on the farm in the five months since Marika left. There was no grass and the thornbushes on which the karakul thrived were becoming more fragile daily, the leaves translucent with dehydration. Daily he fought ants, termites, jackals, flies and heat. No one could fight the drought.

Each morning Günter awoke before dawn, lit a fire and ate his maize porridge in the yard, watching the sky and desert change from gray to Technicolor. Then he would drive the karakul to a fresh patch of thornbushes and wonder how to endure the monotony of his daily routine.

On the first day of May, when Günter drove to the village store for provisions, he found a letter waiting for him. Was it Marika? His hands shook as he fumbled with the envelope, but it was from Claire; a long, rambling letter of little interest to Günter. She was still working at the Walvis Bay hospital, she wrote. He was about to thrust the letter in his pocket when his eye caught the name Marika at the bottom of the page. *Marika left for London on the Knysna Morn,* he read. *Bertha is looking after the baby.*

The rest of the letter was about Claire. Günter flung it away unread and drove home in a temper.

How would he ever see Marika? It would take years to save the airfare. The farm was a failure, the dam brackish, the rainwater finished and the karakul starving. There was no joy in sitting on his arse guarding sheep all day and no justification for hiring labor. It would take a lifetime to

build up a profitable farm, he knew. Marika would be lost
to him forever.

There was only one way to instant riches and that was
prospecting in the Namib. Just one good strike! Then he'd
have it made. He decided to sell the karakul and leave the
farm lying fallow.

Günter left the following month, taking only what he
knew he would need for prospecting. He locked the rest of
his possessions in his hut. He owned nothing valuable
anyway.

He drove by jeep to Aranos and from there to Mariental
and Maltahohe, across the Nanaja Plateau to the Zarisberg
Mountains, an immense ridge of black rock which forms
the barrier between the highlands to the west and the
Namib Desert.

By the following night he had driven over the tortuous
mountain pass and entered the flat, featureless gravel plains
which stretch between the mountains and the sand dunes.
Occasionally he had seen ostriches and gemsbok, but he
marveled that any creature could survive in such a barren
place.

Günter reached the first sand dunes by noon. Now he
was sweating in temperatures of over forty-five degrees
centigrade and the jeep made slow going over powdery-
soft valleys between peaks which soared a thousand feet
high.

Leaving his jeep, Günter stood up, shouldered his pack
and trudged over the dunes to survey the area, carrying a
rifle, flashlight, survey map, matches, pick, shovel and
water. He returned to the jeep at dusk and slept under it,
holding his rifle.

That night Günter lay sleepless, watching the stars. He
was remembering Marika and how she had looked the first
time he saw her and the way they had made love on the
beach. Oh God, he wanted her so. He must get rich. All
he needed was one good stake. Perhaps tomorrow . . .

In the moring he set off again . . . and again . . .

For months he endured the Namib, sweating and bent

double under the weight of his pack as he scrambled up slippery slopes and down again, goaded by impatience. He worked the territory section by section, making a figure eight, but always returning to his jeep to drive to the next base. There was a fortune to be found, he knew that, and it was lying under his feet. But where?

As the time passed, Günter became deeply tired; his eyes sank in their sockets, his face looked haggard and his flesh shrank on his massive frame. He lived on biltong and rusks and the occasional meal of braised venison when he came across game.

Months later he was still hoping for the big strike, but with less conviction. Admittedly, he had found lead and iron and he had registered his claims, but the deposits were not big enough to cover the high cost of transporting the ore through the desert. Günter had trekked southward in a zigzag route from Sossusvlei to the Fish River Canyon, but now, after thousands of kilometers of grueling search, he knew he would have to go north and prospect the desert behind Swakopmund.

He set off early next morning, but at noon he reached a dead end, his way barred by a twelve-foot fence. This was the forbidden concession area and it stretched as far as the coast, south to Alexander Bay and north to Walvis Bay. He would have to detour around it.

Günter stared angrily across the sand. There were diamonds for the picking there, littering the coast, millions of pounds of glittering gemstones. His eyes peered longingly through the grid.

God, he was hungry for the wealth that stretched out untouched before him. One day he would have his own diamond concession, he vowed. One day . . .

Chapter Twenty-seven

Claire parked and stared around in despair. Camp XLII showed unmistakable signs of an abandoned smallholding and she had passed enough of them in her long journey from Walvis Bay. The only tracks were jackal and buck; the karakul dung was months old; the doors and shutters of the three huts were fastened with long steel strips.

She tried to pull herself together, but disappointment kept flooding through her. Günter had packed up and left and goodness knows where he was or if she would ever see him again. It was all too much . . . too much. With Marika gone she had hoped Günter would settle for second best. He was alone here, and it was hard to find a woman willing to live in the bush. But he was gone and that was the end of her dream.

She was tired and far too dispirited to drive back. Besides, there was a strange comfort in knowing this was Günter's farm.

Eventually she climbed out of the jeep. She had driven overnight and stopped only for gasoline during the day and now she was stiff and her back ached intolerably.

She walked around the camp, examining the huts and the paddock. Nothing slipshod here, she told herself, and all wasted! Oh, what a fool Günter was.

It was dusk; a strange, lingering desert dusk when the amber light bewitched the landscape and colors were mellowed and brightened. The ocher sand glowed a deep and fertile brown, the bushes seemed thicker, the grass corn yellow. Birds were retiring, bats awakening, gnats in their millions swarmed over the vlei, a buck rose in fright from the water and leaped through the kraal and away over the dunes.

But where was Günter?

Chapter Twenty-eight

Early mornings were the best. The rocky peaks threw long purple shadows over the Namib and in the east the distant mountain range glistened like an ancient wall, the air was misty cool and when the sun rose the earth took on a luminous pink glow.

To Günter trekking northward toward the Kunene River canyon, it seemed that only he was at loggerheads with nature. His unquenchable desires—for food, for riches, for everything in the world that he did not have—seemed to be savage and vile.

Lately, he had been thinking a great deal about the nature of man and his place in the world—he had very little else to do—and it seemed that self-mastery was the very least he could attain—and the very most.

He singled out his anxieties and his weaknesses and he thought about them each in turn. Impatience! Surely that was his worst sin. Each moment must be a fragment of joy—and joy, Günter decided after days of thought, was when man was in full harmony with himself and his surroundings.

Yet he was not. And why? Because his belly rumbled and images of sizzling steak and liver were eternally floating in front of his eyes, so that when he saw the spoor of gemsbok or zebra he could think only of killing them. This was a terrible weakness.

This morning he had come across fresh tracks of gemsbok and now he was crawling up this narrow gorge like a beast of prey intent on killing. Rounding a rocky ledge, he saw two magnificent beasts within firing rage. When he lifted his rifle he found he was trembling with excitement—like a dog—and when the beast fell with a bullet through its heart Günter leaped forward with a yell and fell upon it as ravenously as any jackal.

He ripped out the entrails, dragged the beast some distance away and lit a fire. He fried the liver and ate it before skinning the carcass. Cutting the meat into thin strips took hours. The sun was blazing hot by now and burning his back, but eventually all the strips were hung in a nearby quiver tree.

When his hunger pangs were satisfied, Günter felt ashamed that he had eaten so savagely and so rapidly, while the blood was still on his hands. Surely man should be above such urgent, savage longings, he reasoned.

From then on, he swore, he would learn self-denial. Two sticks of biltong a day and some dried rusks would be his ration. He would hunt only when his biltong was finished and when he skinned and cleaned the animal there would be no frantic cooking and eating, but a patient wait until the meat dried.

The days became longer and hotter and the plateau was scorched. By late afternoon the red dunes lay beneath his feet like molten metal and Günter, toiling against the ferocity of his mental and physical needs, suffered the hell of his own private purgatory.

It was late January when Günter drove wearily into Walvis Bay. He was gaunt and his skin was tanned like leather. His hair was long and unkempt and his eyes shone with a feverish light. His lips were muttering, but no one could understand what he was saying. He staggered into the bar, climbed on the stool and collapsed.

When he awoke, three days later, he was in the Walvis Bay hospital. He looked up and saw red curls bouncing from the starched white cap and blue eyes glinting.

"You fool," she said angrily. "You crazy fool."

With hospital food, water and vitamin B injections, Günter recovered within a few days.

He could think more rationally in the hospital bed. He had gone too far. He knew that he must avoid primitiveness, but true savagery, he decided, was a system which smothered individuality and hindered man's spiritual development, reducing his capacity for moral judgment. He decided to study the primitive tribes, for he had noticed that they maintained dignity in spite of the daily struggle for survival. From now on he would learn from them, he vowed.

It was time to leave the hospital and Claire persuaded Günter to move into her tiny room until he was stronger.

For a week he slept in a sleeping bag on the floor and once they made love in her single bed with squeaky springs.

Claire tried to persuade Günter to give up prospecting and take his old job at the canning factory, which, she knew, was vacant. She threw herself down on her knees, wrapped her arms around his neck and held on tightly. "Oh, darling," she said. "Oh, please, darling. You'll die out there."

He stroked her shoulder and her neck. "Sh!" he said. "I need a week to stock up and the jeep needs servicing."

One day when Claire returned laden with supper and books for Günter she found he was gone. There was only a letter of thanks and a check on the mantelpiece.

"Oh! Damn you! Damn you, Günter," she wailed.

Chapter Twenty-nine

"Next!"

Marika looked up with a start of apprehension and hurried into the showroom. To her left was a man sitting behind a desk. He looked cold and bored; to her right was a cubicle. Inside a model was dressing to leave.

"What must I do?" she whispered.

The girl hesitated. "Look, dear, if you're not an experienced bra model you needn't apply."

Marika flushed and scowled at the girl.

The model looked embarrassed. "Sorry I spoke, I'm sure. Strip to the waist, walk down the room, turn around a few times in front of the sales manager, then go back to the cubicle, put on that bra and do it again."

It was 8 A.M., January 10. Outside temperatures were below freezing. To Marika it seemed no warmer in the factory. She shuddered. She had been in London for a year and during that time her optimism had been whittled away by constant failure. She loved London, loved the big-city atmosphere, the crowded shops, the sense of purpose in hurrying commuters, but she was unable to feel a part of it. She had dreamed of becoming rich and famous, but she was unable to find any sort of job. Was she the confident girl who had once vowed to find her father's murderer? she wondered. Surely not. Right now she could not even feed herself.

She had exactly nine pounds, four shillings and eleven pence left. The rent for her rotten room was due tomorrow—five pounds ten—and if she didn't get this job, she would not be able to pay.

She could cry when she thought of her foolish optimism, yet she had done well at the modeling classes. But all the learning and determination could not alter her bone structure. She was too broad in the shoulders, too wide of hips, too narrow in the waist and starving herself for six months had only changed her statistics by an inch.

It was her 36-C bust which had brought her to this dismal factory. The company was advertising for a house model for their larger bras. Hardly success, but any job would do now. She was desperate and frightened, for deep inside Marika dwelt the small child who had run homeless through Brno. She tried to rationalize her deep-seated anxiety.

This morning she felt wretched and the thought of appearing half naked was intimidating. Since Marika had been in London she had become accustomed to nudity, but she had never managed to acquire the blasé attitude toward her own flesh which other models flaunted. Perhaps because she had so much more of it than they. Shame-faced, she hung back.

"If you're ready, Miss . . . er . . . er . . ." she heard a voice call.

"Well, really . . ." she murmured to herself. "What nonsense . . . I mean . . . if they make bras, how many breasts they must see . . . probably hundreds every day."

Marika squared her shoulders, tossed her hair back, walked in a daze to the table at the end of the room and stood poised for an instant. Then she looked down.

The man was staring at her with a strangely impersonal look on his face, his eyes wandering from her face to her breasts to her hips and back to her hair. She felt vulnerable and exposed. Shame took hold of her and she blushed and grabbed her breasts with both hands. She was about to flee when a voice called from the doorway.

"What's your name?"

The sales manager leapt to his feet with a hurried exclamation. "Mr. Lymington! We don't often see you here his early."

Lymington, whoever he was, was watching her with a weird expression. Like a cat stalking a mouse. Yes—that was it—predatory! I've got to get out of here, she thought.

"Just a moment, please," Lymington called as Marika hurried back to the cubicle.

She fled and heard him call the supervisor. "Take that girl to my office. I'll see her in a few minutes."

Marika would have left if she could, but when she emerged the supervisor cornered her.

The man who wanted to see her was Quentin Lymington, chairman of the board. He was also a blunt man who did not waste time on unnecessary words.

"So you want to be a model?" he said when he had dismissed the supervisor. "Take my advice, forget it." His green eyes were glinting with amusement.

Marika sat absolutely still and gazed at her hands. "Then why waste your time and mine?" she asked, trying to control her temper.

He laughed briefly. "I hope I'm not wasting your

time—or mine. We have another vacancy—public relations officer, someone to take care of our out-of-town and foreign customers, organize hotel bookings and that sort of thing. There might be a small amount of modeling involved. It's really a question of''—he eyed her speculatively—''common sense. We like to keep up with international trends. Nothing's too good for our customers. Top salary for the right girl. Twenty pounds a week.''

"Twenty pounds . . ." she gasped with surprise. She had hoped for seven.

"Plus commission on big orders, of course.''

. . . so really it's a sort of selling job, she wrote to Bertha that night. *Thank goodness I've found something at last! I badly want to be a model, and the work will involve some modeling! I'm on a month's trial . . .*

During the next three weeks Marika's training was planned with care by Quentin, as she had learned to call him. He took her to restaurants and taught her to order and he was always correct. When he introduced her to friends or business associates it was always as Miss Magos, his public relations officer.

Marika glowed with pride. At last she was finding a niche in this tough city.

"You're coming along fine," he told her one evening as he dropped her in front of her dilapidated lodgings in Chalk Farm.

"There's a most important buyer arriving tomorrow afternoon from the Middle East," he said. "I think you're capable of looking after him. Meet him at Heathrow and keep him under your wing until he leaves. You know the ropes, and remember to introduce him to everyone at the plant.

"Good luck. Oh, and don't forget, Marika, there's a five percent bonus for you.''

Her month's trial was nearly over. A permanent position would depend on the way she handled her first big customer.

*   *   *

The man she met at Heathrow was from Iran and he explained that he was not simply a buyer, but the owner of several chain stores which sold almost everything as long as it was expensive. She took him to the factory; the salesmen brought in their house models and he took copious notes in his strange script.

They worked all day; his energy was inexhaustible, but it was fun. He would say, "How about it, Marika? You like? You think my customers like? What you think? You tell me what to do?"

They dined at the hotel where he stayed and he sent the suitcase of samples to his room. They would study them after dinner, he told her, and make the final choice.

"I'm not really sure . . ." she began nervously when he ordered coffee to be sent to his suite with a bottle of champagne.

"But it is your job," he reminded her.

Of course. Just a job. Funny hours, that was all.

She had never seen anything like his bedroom. A king-sized bed in a room paneled with rose damask.

"I think we should study the samples in the other room," she said. "The lighting's so much better there."

"As you wish," he said, suave and sure of himself.

When he took off his jacket and tie, she realized they were going to be working late.

"Try this on," he said offhandedly, handing her a bra and underwear set.

"I wouldn't dream . . ." she replied, watching his brow crease and a look of genuine puzzlement spread over his face.

"But *Mr.* Lymington said you were a model . . . that you would model the garments for me," he retorted.

"That's true," she said. "I am."

She tried to look casual. After all, Quentin had said there would be a little modeling. She walked into the bedroom, locked the door and stepped into the transparent lacy pink bra and the matching panties and petticoat. Thank God there was a housecoat. She put it over the underwear and walked into the adjoining room. "There's been a mistake,'' she said. "You see . . . I'm actually the company's public relations officer and I couldn't possibly . . .''

He caught her in his arms. Strong as a steel trap, she thought, for all her strength was ineffectual. It was like fighting a bear.

"We must fight a bit first. Yes? Pretend a bit? Women are like that,'' he said, pulling the housecoat from her shoulders and reaching behind her to unfasten her bra.

She hit him one stunning blow with her fist.

He caught her wrists in his hands and for a moment held her arms high in the air while he scowled at her. "But we don't want to make our little scuffle too realistic or we might get hurt? That is so . . . yes?''

"You've made a mistake,'' she said desperately. "I'm not available. This is not the way we do business.''

"But Mr. Lymington said you were a whore . . .and he should know . . . he pays you for it. Or so he said . . . nicely of course, tactfully. Very English, your Mr. Lymington.'' He smiled curiously at her. "He said you would bend over backwards to please me. Bend over, Marika, backwards, over the table. I like that.''

"I'll scream.''

"But you are undressed and your clothes are in the next room. How will you explain that? Your police, I believe they frown on whores. Silly, isn't it?''

She should have known; should have realized. She remembered Quentin's words: "We like to keep up with international trends.'' She felt disgusted with herself more than anyone. She was half smothered with his body over hers, the edge of the table was cutting against her legs and she could hardly see his face through her tears. Disgust lent her strength. She pushed him back, grunting with the effort, and kicked him in the stomach. For a moment he was doubled over. Then he opened his eyes and stared at her—puzzled and hurt, like a dog that doesn't understand why it's being beaten, she thought.

"I don't think Mr. Lymington will be pleased with you,'' he said, struggling to his feet. Then he smiled.

"But don't worry, I won't tell him. You have to be violent . . . is that it? All the world wants to be violent, even women. But you can overdo things, Marika."

She began to laugh hysterically and then cry and, finally, she took him and she never knew why. Perhaps it was loneliness—or simple lust—or to revenge herself on him; she had no way of telling; he was a man, that was all.

She straddled him, urged him to greater virility, nursed him while he recovered. The man-child and the man; he was both alternately as she sought his life force and his energy. Wanton! Insatiable! Until he nearly cried with tiredness, but still she was greedy for more. At last they slept.

"You're the best," he said next morning. "The best I ever had."

He smiled at her gratefully and she felt gratitude in return.

She bathed, ordered coffee, dressed carefully and picked up her bag.

"Aren't you going to wait for the order?" he asked her.

"No."

"You don't have to worry. It will be a big one—I promise you."

"I'm not worried," she said. "I no longer work there."

Then she left.

Chapter Thirty

It was Marika's last letter which jolted Bertha into selling the business. She had sympathized with her daughter when she battled to find a job, wept for her many disappointments, worried over her dingy basement room, but when the letter came telling her about the wonderful world of public relations, Bertha took fright.

She contacted a leading Johannesburg business broker and he sent an auditor to value the store. Thirty thousand pounds, he told her; two-thirds in stock and the rest for goodwill and the building. Bertha was amazed.

The following week the managing director of the canning plant flew from Cape Town to see her. Over a cup of coffee he explained that his company had always wanted to control the Walvis Bay store, but had decided it would not be fair to go into competition with Bertha. They agreed on a price and within days the store had been taken over, lock, stock and barrel. Bertha could live in the flat above until she was ready to leave.

"What a nightmare!" Bertha struggled with a pram, packages and a whimpering baby through customs and immigration. When she emerged on the gangplank at Southampton she was overcome to see Marikala again—and looking so thin and touchingly grateful to see them both.

Marika burst into tears, hugged Bertha and grabbed Sylvia.

"Oh, how she's grown," she sighed. "She's big for fourteen months and how pretty she is—just look at her eyes."

"She's going to be a beauty like you," Bertha said, watching her daughter carefully.

Marika stood without moving, as if she had not heard. Then she whispered. "No, Bertha. Perhaps by Walvis Bay standards, but here things are different."

Pathos suited her. She looked tragic and scared and very much as she had looked all those years ago on the cargo boat. Only her skin was paler nowadays and her hair a darker gold.

It seemed to Bertha that she had arrived just in time. Marika was broke and her clothes looked old-fashioned by London standards. She was not getting enough to eat and she had lost a good deal of confidence. Well, she would have to make a plan, but first things first.

Leaving Marika to get to know her daughter, Bertha

searched for accommodation and eventually settled for a small house in Finchley.

When Marika saw the house she became quite emotional with gratitude and spent the next few weeks redecorating. Her biggest joy was an old treadle sewing machine which she found in a secondhand shop. At last she was able to make herself some fashionable dresses and she spent most of her evenings crouched over the machine.

In the afternoons, she took Sylvia to the park and pushed her on the swings. As summer changed to autumn she realized how much she loved the changing seasons after so many years of endless summer in the Namib. Sometimes they took the tube to Hampstead and fed ducks on the lake. There was so much to see. As the weeks passed mother and daughter grew closer.

But the nights still tormented her and Bertha would hear her creep downstairs in the early hours of every morning to make tea and read a book until dawn. One night Bertha followed her.

"I can't bear it. You must tell me what's wrong," Bertha said sternly. And then, when Marika did not answer, she added, "This is what you chose, isn't it? You could have stayed with Günter. He would have left Africa if that was what you wanted. You know he'd do anything for you."

"Oh, Bertha, Günter's German." Marika wept silently into her hands. "He fought in the war. He even earned the Iron Cross. I've seen it. Somehow he got hold of false papers. I didn't ask how. I don't want to know."

Bertha was too shocked to speak. This was the last thing she had imagined.

"Did Günter say he was German?"

"Yes."

Bertha made tea and after a while Marika stopped crying and wiped her face on the kitchen towel.

"But it's not just Günter," she said. "Here everything reminds me of home—the city, the shops, funny things like rain dripping, birdsong, cars passing on wet roads. I never heard those sounds in the Namib. I was sort of numb. Suddenly I find myself remembering and grieving. Honestly, Bertha, I can't stand it.''

''Tell me about your home,'' Bertha said, bustling around the kitchen. The more she talks, the better she will feel and the quicker she will recover, Bertha reasoned.

So Marika told Bertha all manner of inconsequential things: the silver cups on the mantelpiece Papa had won for athletics; her mother's new blue silk dress she had worn on her birthday; her dog whom they had left with her aunt.

Dawn came, but Marika was still talking. ''I feel so helpless,'' she told Bertha when at last she had agreed to go to bed. ''I can't just accept things and forget. Because . . . you must understand . . . if I do that . . . if we all do that . . . then we'll never be safe,'' she said sadly.

Chapter Thirty-one

Bertha was sitting at the small writing desk by the window where the soft spring light found purple and brown shades in her ebony hair. Watching her surreptitiously, Marika noticed for the first time that Bertha was not an ugly woman. Admittedly she was overweight, but her eyes were huge and almost black and her features quite regular. The English climate had improved her skin. It was smoother and younger-looking. Marika calculated quickly: Bertha was forty-two. Good heavens! Not old at all.

Bertha was forever scribbling in her notebook. Pages and pages of figures. Was it the household accounts? Surely they couldn't have eaten that much. Marika felt so guilty because she was not contributing toward the household. She had tried office work, but found it unendurable. She wanted to do something meaningful and creative, but what? Why was she such a failure?

"What's in that precious notebook of yours?" she snarled eventually, soured by guilt.

"Ours . . .not mine. Ours!" Bertha looked up smiling. "I invested half the money we were paid for the store in karakul pelts. As a matter of fact, I paid the farmers in advance. We could make a good profit on the deal."

Marika forced a smile. "How very clever of you, Bertha." She was unwilling to reopen an old argument. Bertha insisted that half the money from the store belonged to her—and Sylvia, too. What a lot of nonsense, but there was no point in arguing when she was still out of work.

"We'll find out how sensible I was at the fur auctions next week. You must come with me, Marikala."

Their next-door neighbor, Myrtle, minded Sylvia for the day and the two women set off in a taxi for the Hudson Bay Company at Garlick Hill, London's fur center.

The auction room was vast. Gazing around at the tiered seating, Marika reckoned it could seat five hundred people at least. It was soon full.

Bertha felt proud of Marika. Everyone seemed to notice her and she had to admit her daughter looked a million dollars in the tailored tweed suit she had made herself with the blue gorget blouse. You'd swear she patronized the best couturier in town—and why not, with her looks?

Marika never forgot her first auction—the smell of the pelts, the babble of foreign languages, the suppressed excitement as the bidding mounted, the staccato voice of the auctioneer and the sharp smash of his hammer.

There were over two hundred different qualities of karakul in the catalogue and the pelts were to be sold in "lots" of two to three hundred a batch.

She was examining the pelts in the tea break when she met him. For a moment she stopped and stared. There was something about him that was so familiar. His dark brown hair was curly, almost kinking, and rose up from a wide, square brow. There was some gray at the sides, she noticed. His face was square-cut, his eyes blue-gray, and his

ears were too big. Put a white coat on him and he could be
my father, she decided.

Feeling strangely moved, she hurried off and sat hunched
on the seat waiting for the auction to begin.

The crowds came surging back. Bertha missed Marika and
sat looking for her until someone sat in her daughter's
seat. He introduced himself: Mendel Sidersky, furrier, and
then chatted away about nothing in particular. He had a
soft-spoken voice with a pronounced London accent, and
there was a trace of something foreign as well; Polish,
Bertha decided.

Bertha listened good-naturedly, puzzling why he should
be interested in a plain woman like her. She did not have
to wonder for long.

"And that beautiful young woman I was talking to in
the tea break. I believe she is with you."

The silly old fool. He was her age at least. Forty-five,
she'd say at a guess. "She's my adopted daughter and
she's twenty-two," she added pointedly in case there should
be any doubt about Marika's age.

"She's lovely," he said. "I envy you. If I'd had a
daughter I suppose she would have been around the same
age."

Bertha warmed to him, and he kept her amused until the
bidding started soon afterward. Then he became so en-
grossed he hardly said another word.

When the auction finished he stood up and gave her an
oddly foreign little bow. "Perhaps you would like to visit
my factory next week to see what happens to your pelts
after tanning? I'll show you and your daughter around."

Bertha was pleased. They would go on Wednesday, she
told him. Then she went off to find Marika.

Mendel was nervous. He couldn't remember how many
years it was since he'd been this nervous. He glanced at
his watch again and again. Perhaps they had changed their
minds, or perhaps Bertha would come alone.

Mendel was a solitary person. He seldom made friends.

Only in the war had he built up a special camaraderie, with soldiers in his regiment. He had been lonely when he was discharged after a minor wound.

He saw himself as a plain, uninteresting person, and he was quite overawed by Marika's appearance. He found it incredible that she would soon be here in his factory. Not that he entertained any notions of an involvement with her. Good God, no, he told himself.

It was just that he longed to see her from time to time. He had decided to ask her to model his collection. On her statuesque frame his coats would look superb.

He glanced at his watch again. They had said "around three," and it was already ten minutes past. Suddenly he was hurrying upstairs. The plant was working at full capacity; his twelve machinists were bent over their machines; and at the end of the row a particularly gorgeous ermine coat was nearing completion. He would love to see her in it. Briefly he thought of giving it to her, perhaps as a modeling fee, and then as quickly he banished the thought. He wasn't Rothschild, after all.

Mendel's business was located on Copenhagen Street in an old, four-story building wedged between two large warehouses. It took Bertha and Marika some time to find it and so they were late.

Everyone stared at them curiously as Mr. Sidersky led them from floor to floor. Marika had the impression that this had never happened before.

The factory was a study of contrasts, which she found thoroughly confusing. There was the showroom, a huge and pompous place with a deep crimson carpet, gilt mirrors, chandeliers, and a stage which could be concealed by velvet curtains, with a changing room behind. Mr. Sidersky was very proud of his latest technical advance: a pushbutton curtain operator, which he demonstrated to them several times.

The showroom led to the street via a small, but attractive reception area. Behind the showroom was another world entirely: a kennel-type office where the doorkeeper,

Jim Landon, sat; the bookkeepers, Mrs. Brown and Miss Brompton, known as the two bees, shared a vast old desk pushed between partitions made of shelving crammed with box files. Next to them was an even shabbier office, which was Mendel's.

The manufacturing plant was housed on the next two floors. Here it was light and airy. There were two rows of machinists on the second floor next to the cutting department. When the pelts were machined together they were wheeled upstairs on trolleys for buttons, linings, collars, embroidery and the final touches and checking.

Suddenly Marika was full of questions. She wanted to know every detail of design and makeup, and Mr. Sidersky, or Mendel, as he insisted she must call him, explained it all proudly.

On the top floor a large strong-room door faced the stairs. Once inside, Marika found that the entire floor was a huge strong room with a cooling plant. It was almost freezing and overcrowded with stacks of pelts and racks of made-up furs hanging from rails. No wonder the windows were barred, Marika thought, looking at the fortune lying around her.

She was fascinated by the stacks of beautiful furs: mink, possum, karakul, beaver, pelts of every possible texture and color. Just the sight of them conjured up images of fabulous coats and stoles. Marika was in a daze with all the ideas racing through her mind when they walked downstairs. She lingered a long time in the finishing room while Bertha went down to the showroom for tea.

But how disappointing! Mendel's coats were so dull and old-fashioned. If she had these facilities and these wonderful pelts she could make coats that would make your mouth water. If only she had a chance.

"Ghastly," she said aloud, peering at a full-length ermine coat which was being passed to the end of the row. "What a waste!"

"Pardon?"

She turned, not realizing she had spoken aloud. The machinist beside her was glaring angrily. She looked like a mouse, Marika thought, with her little beady eyes, mousy hair, sharp and slightly protruding front teeth. The young woman was watching her enviously.

"I think the coat's lovely," the mouse went on in a strong cockney accent, her eyes glittering with suppressed animosity.

Marika flushed. She would have liked to retort, but that would have been even more disloyal to Mendel.

The supervisor was hurrying down the aisle.

"Keep working, Tanya," she said sharply to the mouse.

Marika turned away and made for the stairs. She lingered long enough to hear her say, "There's no fool like an old fool."

Ears burning, she hurried downstairs.

Mendel was smiling complacently as he offered tea with quaint, old-world mannerisms. "So you like my coats, yes? How would you like to model them for me at my next show?"

Marika mumbled self-consciously, not wanting to hurt him.

"Of course I'd pay you," he said, suddenly looking anxious. "But not much, of course."

Marika remembered the supervisor's comment and the machinist's unconcealed envy. For a moment she hesitated. Yet the feeling that this was her world, too, overcame her doubts. Besides, Mendel looked so anxious.

"I'd love to," she said, and then wondered why he looked so happy.

"I'd like a chance to see your next consignment of karakul pelts," he told Bertha. "Perhaps we could do business together. I can promise you a good price."

Mendel arrived at their house a week later and bought Bertha's new batch of pelts. Everyone was happy and when Bertha suggested he should stay for supper Mendel accepted.

Bertha was looking very pleased the next morning as she scribbled in her notebook. She smiled happily at Marika.

"You might like to know that although we did well at

the auction, we're doing far better now that we sell directly to Mendel. He's going to take all our pelts in the future. By the time we've received them all—in two years, more or less—we'll have doubled our capital. Quite a nice sum if it's properly invested. We'll have a small income for life.''

"You will," Marika said determinedly. "I'm still out of work."

After that Mendel called regularly. He became a familiar sight sitting in the old velvet armchair under the bay window reading the newspaper while Bertha made tea or supper. Anyone could see that Mendel was at home there.

Before long, Marika felt that she knew Mendel very well indeed. He was so easy to talk to and she felt comfortable with him. It seemed that she had known him for years. She learned that he had emigrated from Poland in his early teens. During the war his London factory had been converted to making army clothing and his two retail shops had almost gone into liquidation. Now he was rebuilding the business and it was tough going. Soon Mendel forgot his shyness with Marika and the two of them had long conversations in the evenings while Bertha was cooking.

When Marika learned that Mendel's family had been killed in Poland in the war, she felt they had a great deal in common. She wanted to talk about it, but Mendel did not.

"Best to put things like that behind us and concentrate on the future," he said.

"But why? I can't agree. That's just what people should not do," Marika repeated nightly. Eventually she told him about Oradour and her father's death. "I think a lot about that terrible massacre," she said. "Most of the soldiers who survived are in prison. But will they ever come to trial? Why are they delaying it for so long? It's so that people will forget."

Mendel decided to give Marika the address of a friend of his. "It might help if she felt she was doing something constructive," he confided to Bertha. "I'll speak to her tomorrow."

Chapter Thirty-two

The following day Marika took the tube to Swiss Cottage and walked along the High Street. When she saw the dingy building she began to have doubts. But Mendel had recommended him, so he must be good.

The office was spartan. Several rough wooden shelves along one wall were filled with box files. A desk, a chair and a telephone were set in the middle of the floor—nothing else—and the man behind the desk was like the room, stripped of all extraneous emotions.

"Are you Klaus Greenstein?" she asked.

He nodded. "Miss Magos, please sit down." He spoke heavily accented English. Polish, she decided, plus a long spell in America.

"I'm sure you know about the massacre at Oradour-sur-Glane," she began nervously. "Over six hundred people . . ."

"Yes, yes, I know . . . I know . . . the world knows." Then he bent forward and his eyes were bright and curious. "You don't sound French, Miss Magos. What are you? Your name is Hungarian?"

"South African, Czech-born," she told him. "My father's family came from Hungary, but he was a French Jew. A doctor. My mother was Czech. We lived outside Brno before the war."

"Well, to cut short a long preamble, I know why you are here." He smiled. "Mendel Sidersky told me all about you."

Marika stared at her hands without replying. "I don't think you do," she said eventually.

There was a long silence. Then he said, "Tell me about yourself."

"There's nothing to tell," she said. She looked up nervously, not knowing how to begin. She stammered as she blurted out, "I want you to give me a job. I want to help . . . to find these monsters . . . you must give me a chance. You see, I care. Hardly anyone seems to care anymore. It's all forgotten."

He sighed. "Marika . . . may I call you Marika? . . . you would be wrong to imagine that you are the only one who cares. The problem is—there is so little that any one person can do. Take you, for instance." He leaned back and smiled. He hardly knew how to tell her how absurd her offer was. "You want to hit back—avenge your father's murder, but you don't know how to set about it. Am I right?"

"Mendel told you," she said tremulously.

He nodded. "Marika, I have an army of helpers, Jews from the camps spread throughout the world. They don't want wages, or recognition, they just want to track down these criminals. They're trained, experienced—more important still, they know what they look like." He paused and gazed at her compassionately. "And they care, I promise you.

"Marika, what I need most of all is financial support. The agency is non-profit-making, that goes without saying, but there are expenses: travel, bribery, legal fees . . . I rely on backers like your friend Mendel Sidersky."

Marika tried to conceal her disappointment. She reddened with anger. "Then you must find Major Otto Geissler, and I will pay you."

He laughed briefly. "Let me tell you, the world would be looking for Geissler—if he were not dead, that is."

"But there's some doubt about his death," she argued.

"I see you've been doing your homework."

Greenstein stood up and opened a filing cabinet in the corner.

"Major Otto Geissler," he began at last. "Commanding the First Battalion of the Führer Regiment, which murdered the citizens of Oradour. At the time it was thought that Geissler was motivated by thoughts of revenge because his best friend had disappeared at the hands of the Maquis a few days previously. Certainly that was his excuse for taking his regiment to Oradour, I won't tell you about the massacre; obviously you know it all. Since then countless acres of paper have been filled and gallons of ink spilled in exploring the motivation of the men who did these things. This particular massacre has developed a fascination of its own.''

He leaned forward again and riffled through the file. ''On the thirtieth of June, 1944, Major Geissler foolishly moved outside his bunker without his helmet and was caught by a fragment of shell in the head, which killed him instantly.

''There was some speculation among his colleagues that Geissler had lost the will to live and was committing a suicidal act. It's certainly difficult to imagine he was stricken by remorse, but it's possible that he was exasperated by the inquiry being pursued into his actions at Oradour.

''No doubt his death was a relief to Das Reich and indeed all of Army Group B,'' he mumbled on as if speaking to himself.

''Of course, there is another alternative: that he was not killed at all; that his comrades covered up for him, knowing that he would face the wrath of the Allies when the war ended.'' He closed the file and leaned back. ''That, actually, is the only possible avenue of inquiry we could pursue. The chances are he was killed.''

''Please go on,'' she said.

He shrugged. ''It would be a long and lengthy investigation. We could try to contact members of his family, find out if they are meeting or writing to some unknown relative in South America. Whether any of them are living there.''

He looked up and spread his hands, palms upward. ''If we could find Geissler's grave it could be exhumed. Perhaps we could check his dental work with his dentist in Germany, assuming we could find his dentist and assuming any records have survived the war. One could check among the German community in South America. We have our informers, you know, even there."

He smiled bleakly. "In other words, my dear, it's a long, costly road which will undoubtedly end in failure. Nevertheless, I will reopen the file, regardless of any action you may take. If you decide to become one of our benefactors you would be helping with all our agency's operations—not just the search for Otto Geissler, because this could never become a separate entity."

Marika waved her hand angrily. "How much will it cost?" she asked crudely.

He leaned forward, looking a trifle colder. "It's not a question of how much it would cost, but how much you can afford. You don't look as if you can afford very much. Forgive me for saying that." He scribbled a bank account number on a sheet of paper. "If you decide to go ahead, make it a monthly debit order," he said. "The amount is up to you.

"I will—just as soon as I start working," she whispered.

Marika walked out feeling disappointed. Was that all she could do? Just pay? Well, if money was the key to revenge, then she would have to become very rich, Marika decided as she hurried home, because she had so much to avenge.

Marika had been invited to visit Mendel's factory whenever she liked and she could not resist, although she knew the machinists resented her presence. Oh, how she envied them, for they were a part of this wonderful world of fashion while she was just a bystander.

As the time for the collection drew near there was a great deal of excitement tinged with concern. Mendel had not shown his fashions since before the war and he had financed the new machines with a large loan. To survive he needed far more business.

Marika did not know this, but she sensed his anxiety. Mendel was a gambler, it was part of his makeup, like his sense of humor and his compassion. Poor Mendel, she thought. The coats and capes were so dull. She knew that he would not be as successful as he hoped.

Her fears proved all too real. Several buyers and the press left before the end of the show. There was a good deal of polite approval, but no real enthusiasm. Mendel was looking downcast afterward, but it was his own fault.

She told him so when everyone had left—guests, musicians, caterers and the compere. Mendel was sitting contemplating his notebook.

His eyes glinted with temper and his mouth folded into a tight, hard line.

"I don't care if you're mad at me," she said, although she did. "If you can't take a bit of criticism, then it's going to be tough."

He poured a stiff scotch and sat sipping it moodily.

"I'll have one, too," she said.

He poured her some wine. "That's your lot," he said. "Reckon I should get a good designer, do you?" he went on when he had simmered down. "I used to be right at the top—before the war."

What was, was, she thought practically, but she only said, "I could give you a few ideas—I mean, show you how the fashions are right now, since you obviously have no idea, that is."

"You?" He laughed.

"Mendel," she persisted. "You didn't do as well as you'd hoped, did you?"

"Too early to tell," he said, and his blue eyes narrowed.

"But you can tell?" she insisted.

"All right, all right. Don't rub it in."

"Well, I don't need the modeling fee if it's any problem."

He threw back his head and laughed. "Here, hark at her. I'm in the red for sixty thousand and she wants to lend me her miserable five quid."

"I'm only trying to help," she pouted.

He looked so anxious that she put an arm on his shoulder and gently kissed his cheek.

"I just want you to know that I'm very happy about you and Bertha," she said by way of explanation.

She looked far from happy, Mendel thought, watching her carefully. In a moment of insight he realized that, emotionally speaking, Marika was very young, despite her grown-up ways. She was still looking for that father of hers who had been taken away so early in her life.

"Really happy," Marika lied. Noting the compassion in his eyes, she began stammering badly. "You'll be one of the family, won't you?"

"No," he said quickly. Suddenly he looked embarrassed. "Oh Lord! Is that what Bertha told you?"

"Oh my . . . of course not . . . she said you're lonely. But I mean . . . I can see how at home you feel with her."

"I like Bertha," he admitted. "But I like you, too."

"Oh." She couldn't think of anything else to say. Then she smiled, suddenly sure of herself again.

Watching her, Mendel felt a strong bond. Marika needed him and he had never been needed before. He wondered why he felt happy when she was around and why he wanted to help her. Perhaps it was just that he was showing off. God knows, she was beautiful. But he knew it was more than that. In some inexplicable way she was his life line to the future.

Suddenly Marika threw her arms around him and hugged him. "It's just nice being together," she said, looking relieved.

"Now, now, none of that," he said, disentangling himself. "Time to go home. Just to show there's no ill feeling I'll throw in the price of a taxi with the five quid. O.K.?"

The following weekend, when she knew Mendel would not be at the factory, Marika persuaded Jim Landon to let her in. He knew her well by now, but he was puzzled all the same. Usually the girls did not work overtime unless Mendel was there. He decided to telephone him, just to be on the safe side, but it was evening by the time Mendel arrived.

He found Marika sitting despondently on a chair with a lopsided coat on a hanger beside her.

"Oh, Mendel." She felt embarrassed to be caught out. "I wanted to show you how the fashions are right now. You see . . . it's a hobby of mine . . . I wanted to make something beautiful for you to sell."

Mendel walked to the bench by the window and flipped through her sketchbook. "You drew these?" he asked.

"Yes, but they're only roughs just to give some ideas, but I can see now . . . well . . . to be honest, it's more difficult than I realized. I never have trouble making dresses. I made this one," she said, suddenly pirouetting. "Fur is more of a problem than fabrics. How do they produce those beautiful furs I've seen at the cinema? Coats that make the wearers look gorgeous. Your customers walk out looking like grizzly bears."

Unaware of how much she had hurt him, Marika was glowering at her effort, trying to tug the fur straight. "For goodness' sake, how can I get this right?" she moaned.

Mendel raised his eyebrows and scowled at her. "You want to know how? Fine, I'll tell you how—you'll start right at the bottom, learn the business properly and go to night school, learn dress designing and pattern making for two years. God help you if you waste my time or cash.

"You'll learn about the pelts, how to put them together and how to make them flow, you'll learn how to buy them and how to check the tanning and the dyeing—such as it is nowadays. But first you'll damn well unpick this mess and if I see a single stitch mark or a single thread you'll get the sack—on the turn." He flipped her sketches over. Then he dumped them in the wastebasket. "Not one of them's suitable for furs," he told her. "In six months' time you'll know better."

"Oh, Mendel," she gasped.

"I don't have shirkers here. You pull your weight or you'll be out before you're in. By the way," he said as he was going. "Those sketches of yours. I think you've got talent. I really do."

"Thank you, Mendel," she said, hoping that he would not notice she was crying.

Chapter Thirty-three

It was nine months since Marika started work at the plant and Mendel had learned to rely on her. Sometimes he wondered why. Certainly not for her experience, for she made mistakes every day. She was improving—give her that, he thought. No, it was something intangible—something to do with her ferocious will to succeed. She was a go-getter and success was all she wanted out of life. Her dedication was infectious and Mendel was swept along with her.

Marika's days began at six, when she dressed and ran downstairs to find Bertha waiting with coffee and toast. She would spend ten minutes with Sylvia before racing to the underground. Before eight she was at her drawing board, which was in a tiny enclosure next to the pattern-cutting department. Usually she worked from eight until five and then there was just enough time to rush home to spend half an hour with Sylvia before evening classes began.

Marika had worked hard at night school and become expert at pattern making and cutting; she could take her place at any of the machines when necessary, and it often was when a machine hand was absent. She even checked the bookkeeping.

Mendel had persuaded Marika to take driving lessons and lately she often borrowed his car to deliver new coats to the shop, or drive down to his Bournemouth retail outlet to check sales. She had even tried her hand at window dressing at both of the shops. It saved expenses and she was quite good at it.

Increasingly, she had to endure the jealousy of the staff, and particularly the mouse, Tanya, who never tired of complaining about Marika's designs. If she made a mistake, and she often did, it was always Tanya who picked it up and told Mendel. One day, when she was rushed and careless, she designed a coat with two right fronts. Tanya, who was on the cutting bench nowadays, followed the pattern. "Who are we to argue with the boss's favorite?" she said spitefully. It was a valuable fox jerkin and there was no more matching fur in stock.

But it was Mendel's happy-go-lucky attitude toward business which irritated Marika the most. She would watch him coping with creditors badgering for payment, suppliers demanding cash on delivery, the bank manager bullying him, and machines breaking down, but he was always cheerful and the first to crack a joke however perilous his situation. She reckoned he had a break-even phobia. He would work like a slave to meet their commitments, but that was all. He always had his back to the wall. He seemed to like it like that. You'd think "profits" was a dirty word, she would mutter to herself daily.

When she had worked at the plant for exactly a year, Mendel gave her a raise and the promise of a company car in the future if she continued to dress the windows so well.

Marika rushed home early to tell Bertha the good news. She found her lying on her bed with a wet flannel over her face pretending she had a headache, but it was easy to see she had been crying.

Marika felt panic-stricken. This had never happened before; at least not since Irwin was killed. Her stomach lurched.

"Where's Sylvia?" she cried.

"Playing with Myrtle's children."

"So what's wrong?" Marika asked, feeling puzzled.

"I'm feeling sorry for myself," Bertha snapped. "In other words, nothing's wrong." She walked heavily down the stairs. "Want some tea?" she asked Marika, who was following close behind her.

"Please tell me," Marika begged her.

"I'm just homesick. Ridiculous! Tell me something, Marika," she said, peering sharply at her daughter. "Don't you ever long for Africa, for the heat, the desert, even for Günter?''

"No, never," Marika lied. "You can keep the desert." She turned away so that Bertha would not see her face. It was impossible not to think of Günter; his child-support checks arrived regularly each month with a letter carefully stating his progress, which appeared to be negative, and apart from that, just looking at Sylvia was a constant reminder. The older her daughter became, the more she resembled Günter.

"It's not like me to be depressed," Bertha went on. "Can't think what's come over me lately."

Marika noticed the sagging features, the graying hair, the sadness in Bertha's eyes. How selfish she had been, she thought guiltily. Then she thought of Mendel. He never came anymore. They were so busy at the plant. She remembered how she had imagined Mendel was courting Bertha. Suddenly she felt a wave of resentment. Damn Mendel. Couldn't he take the trouble to call?

"At the end of the year you'll have finished your classes at night school, so you won't have to stay out evenings. Surely you could put Sylvia into nursery school," Bertha said. "There's quite a few around. Have a look. If you're kept late you could take her to the plant. Other working mothers cope. It seems to me you do pretty much as you like there, anyway."

Finally it was all arranged, although not without a few arguments. Bertha would go back to Africa when Marika finished studying and Sylvia was booked into a nursery school near the plant.

Bertha felt guilty. It was no life for the poor mite, but, she reasoned, another lonely year like the last one and she would go quite mad. Besides, she rationalized, Marika and Sylvia did not spend enough time together and in the future Marika would have to cope with being a real mother.

At the beginning of January, Marika sadly helped Bertha to pack and saw her off at Heathrow. Bertha was to return to Walvis Bay for two weeks and then on to Johannesburg, where she had friends and relatives.

Sylvia cried at the airport and all the way home and Marika realized just how difficult it was going to be to cope with two conflicting roles. "Other working mothers cope," she kept repeating to herself anxiously.

From then on Marika fetched Sylvia at four each afternoon and brought her back to the factory. It was not long before the machinists complained. Tanya had put them up to it. Marika knew that.

Marika restructured her working day and converted Bertha's bedroom to a workroom. She brought home her drawing board and equipment and evenings and weekends she designed there while her daughter played. Marika's bright red Morris was a source of great pride to both of them and on fine weekends they explored new places. Marika began to enjoy her newfound responsibilities.

Chapter Thirty-four

Mendel was both amazed and dismayed when he received a formal invitation to supper at Marika's home one Saturday night. "What's all this about, then?" he wanted to know.

"You eat, don't you?"

"Sure, I eat."

"Well, that's what dinner's about—eating," she said with more than a slight touch of asperity.

She'd gone to a lot of trouble. Give her that. Beef Stroganoff, crepe suzette and a bottle of vintage wine.

"So what are you up to this time?" he asked when he had read Sylvia a story and she had been put to bed. They were sitting in the tiny lounge listening to classical records played on the gramophone Mendel had bought Marika for her birthday.

"I've been designing for you for nearly eighteen months," she began. "I think it's time I had a little public recognition." She laughed awkwardly.

"If you're after a raise, young lady, just forget it," Mendel said sourly.

"Look," she said. She went to the sideboard and returned with some labels. They were very pretty labels, silver writing on pale gray: *Designed by Marika Magos*.

Mendel looked as if he had been punched in the stomach.

"Marika, come off it. I told you when you started—it takes years to learn the business. You've only been there eighteen months."

"But it hasn't taken me years," she argued. "I want these labels on my garments. It's good for both of us. After all, Sidersky's is a very reliable name, but it's hardly modern. Twenty-five percent of the coats sold now are exclusively designed by me."

"That's what you're paid for," he said sourly.

"Well, that's not enough. You pay me a pittance, anyway."

Mendel was turning the labels over and over in his hand.

"Did you design these?"

"Of course."

"Pretty," he said, and threw them on the table. "The answer's no."

"You're being ridiculous, Mendel!" Anger flashed in her eyes.

"Marika," he said gently. "Take it from me, you're a very talented young woman. You're also a beautiful young woman. How about finding yourself a boyfriend, getting married and having some fun. You work all hours; far longer than necessary. I think you owe it to yourself to lead a more balanced life."

"What cheek!" she exploded with temper. "Don't try to soft-soap me."

"Come on, Marika, you know I'm right."

Suddenly and unaccountably she burst into tears.

Mendel produced his large white handkerchief with a flourish. "Won't have a handkerchief to my name soon. You never give them back," he moaned.

"Damn," she said. "Damn! Damn! Damn! Why did you have to hit below the belt? I wanted a tough business discussion. I think you're unfair," she sobbed.

"Because of Günter?" he asked gently. "Haven't you got over him yet?"

"Yes, of course I have," she lied. "I've got over love, too. Anyway . . ." She looked at him so candidly that Mendel realized that he was going to hear one of her rare confidences. "There isn't a man in the world to touch Günter. There! I've said it, but I'll never marry a German. Never! Oh dear. Oh dear." She began to clear off the table. "Well, that puts paid to our business talk, but don't think I've forgotten," she said.

"I couldn't be that fortunate," Mendel moaned.

A week later she brought up the conversation again. They were having lunch: cottage pie and draft beer at the pub around the corner. Marika was feeling particularly aggressive.

"I deserve recognition because my garments are selling the best," she said. "Why, only last week Jennifer Johns, the actress . . ."

"A few successes hardly entitle you to your own label," Mendel interrupted her. "Let's see if you can keep up the pace. Now listen," he went on in a conciliatory tone of voice. "You're coming along nicely. I'm going to include a good many of your designs in my next collection. There's plenty of time, so don't panic." He sat back beaming.

"Oh no, you're not," she said. "At least not without my name on them."

Mendel gave in eventually, but first, he insisted, Marika must sign a five-year restraint-of-trade contract.

"Five years," she gasped.

"I'll give you ten percent of the profits on the garments you design."

"But you never make profits," she grumbled.

"Exactly," he said.

They spent the afternoon planning the next show. They would launch several Marika Magos designs for the younger set, fur and fabric combination designs so that they would be less costly, Mendel decided, as well as a few really way-out, stylish fur coats and capes.

From then on the days fled by. When they discovered that the factory next to Mendel's plant was coming on the market it seemed like a good omen. Mendel decided to ask for a three-month option so they could test consumer acceptance at the launch.

Marika threw herself into the joy of planning her own collection and worked long hours, sometimes taking Sylvia to the plant weekends and letting her play there with her toys. After discarding dozens of designs she felt satisfied.

Then came the buying of the furs and fabrics and accessories, which took weeks. She had to shop around for a cut-make-and-trim house for the fabric makeup. Best of all was the makeup of her own furs. Finally came checking and last-minute adjustments.

At last she was ready and it was well before time. Good heavens, yes . . . still another eight hours to go. How would she survive the day?

Chapter Thirty-five

The day passed agonizingly slowly and by evening Marika was in despair. She would be the laughingstock of London. When she looked at her designs hanging on rails they seemed gauche, garish even. Who was she, after all? Just a bumbling amateur. She would ruin Mendel's reputation.

"Mendel, don't let's do it," she urged him as he hurried past. "Let's forget about it. They're awful."

"Did you think you would be perfect on your first showing?" he asked gently.

"Don't humor me," she yelled. She flung an ashtray at him, missed, and it shattered on the floor.

"Pull yourself together," he said, suddenly harsh and unfamiliar, "or you'll ruin the show." He stalked out, stiff with offense.

Marika could not bear to be alone, so she hurried to the showroom and gasped when she peered through the door; it had all happened so quickly. The reception desk was gone—a Persian rug in its place—and a table with a huge bowl of roses stood just inside the door. The showroom was filled with rows of gilt chairs and there were flowers at the side of the stage where the curtains were firmly drawn. She could hear frantic voices in the dressing room, waiters were arriving, caterers were rushing around, models were frantic. "Ice! For Pete's sake, where's the ice?" Tanya sounded panic-stricken. Musicians were tuning up softly at the back of the room. Albert Sandler! Obviously Mendel spared no expense at his shows.

Marika turned away and collided with a waiter. "Hey, miss, cheer up. Things can't be as bad as you look," he said sympathetically. "Have a glass of champers. Make you feel better." She took the glass and drained it. Then she took another.

She was to wear only Magos furs. A suitable punishment, she thought, as she slipped into her black leotard and tights.

A model darted into the changing room. "Come on, Marika. Margaret Lockwood's in the front row and Glynis Johns is three rows behind. Hurry!"

"I can't stop shaking," Marika wailed.

"Swallow this," the model said.

Marika changed, feeling light-headed and sick. When she glanced in the mirror a wild-looking woman stared back with huge frightened eyes, disheveled hair and a face as white as chalk. Tanya rushed into the room.

"Marika, the compere has announced you. For goodness' sake, come on."

Doom was approaching. Well, she might as well get it over with, and taking the most absurd of her creations, the one she had fought Mendel bitterly to keep in the range, she shrugged into it and glided onto the platform. The shocked faces of the audience glimmered out of focus: pale anemones in an English field. She heard gasps, but she no longer cared.

"Shit," Mendel muttered. "why did she have to wear that coat first?" It was supposed to be last. The compere would get everything wrong. He grabbed the microphone.

"This is the most avant-garde creation in the new Marika Magos collection," he said, "and we've decided to show it to you first to get you in the right mood. By the way, Marika is modeling her own designs. She has named this style Oryx because of the curious triangular brown-and-white pattern which was inspired by these desert deer. You'll notice that the coat hangs in a triangular shape to follow the distinctive pattern of the fur. You might call this a market tester," he went on bravely.

Marika stood still, legs apart, ready for flight, like the oryx after which she had named her coat. There was something incredibly forlorn about her, Mendel thought.

The stunned silence which had accompanied Marika's appearance suddenly changed to a hum of conversation. There was some laughter and flashguns popped.

Then Mendel heard an American voice behind him, strident and impatient: "I'll take that! Hey, you! Waiter! Take this note to the guy up there and tell him it's mine. Okay?" she yelled at the waiter's retreating back.

"Thank you, Marika, that was lovely," Mendel said nervously. He took the note the waiter had handed him and grinned delightedly.

"Well, this is a little unorthodox, but I'd like to tell you that the first Marika Magos model ever shown has been bought by none other than Lucy Vanderbilt, who, as we all know, is a great trendsetter."

Marika seemed to come to her senses and swirled out to a burst of applause.

Mendel handed the microphone to the compere and went backstage, where he found Marika with her face in a basin of cold water Tanya was holding.

"Don't you ever do that to me again," he shouted. "Now fix your hair and sober up. I'll have something to say to you when this lot's over."

But by then there was nothing left to say to each other except "Mazel tov!"

Chapter Thirty-six

Success had entered her life, nuzzled her and curled up in a corner. Marika liked the feel of it, but she knew that only hard work could coax it to stay. Nowadays the telephone was always ringing with orders for her latest designs and Marika was spending more time at her drawing board. Mendel engaged another two machinists to cope with the extra business. She began to receive invitations to first nights and parties thrown by people she had never met, and a variety of handsome young men hung around trying to date her.

Marika refused them all. She did not go out at night, except to attend business meetings. She had no time to waste on frivolous matters. She had work to do.

It was 1953—a traumatic period for Marika, for the final war crimes trials of the 1st Battalion of the Führer Regiment were drawing to a close. Since 1951 they had proved an embarrassment to the French authorities and almost everyone else concerned—and a matter of great personal sorrow for Marika and all other relatives of the victims.

*   *   *

When World War II ended, the remnants of the Reich
Division were mainly in Hungary or Austria fighting along-
side the flotsam of the Third Reich. A few of the SS
reacted to news of the surrender by attempting to fight
their way across Europe and escape the Russians. A few
succeeded, but most of them were imprisoned by the
Allies.

The French, of course, claimed the survivors of the
Reich Division, and several hundred were sent to France,
where they were held in prison ships at Bordeaux until the
late forties and early fifties, awaiting trial or release.

Twenty-one NCOs and men of the regiment were in-
dicted for their part in the Oradour massacre, but the real
criminal, Otto Geissler, was dead. Even more embarrassing, from the French point of view, was that fourteen of
the accused were from Alsace, which lately had been
reunited with France.

The Alsatians blamed the French government for per-
mitting the trial of these young men, who they claimed
were as much the victims of Nazism as were the dead of
Oradour. Six of them had already surrendered to the British in Normandy and told everything they knew of the
massacre. Two had subsequently served with the French
Army in Indochina.

At last, in February 1953, the Military Tribunal at Bordeaux gave its verdict. An Alsatian volunteer named Sergeant Boos was sentenced to death; nine other Alsatians
received hard labor and four prison terms, none of which
exceeded eight years. A German warrant officer was sentenced to death in absentia. One was acquitted; the remainder received prison terms of from ten to twelve years.
Forty-two other Germans were sentenced to death in
absentia.

France was wracked by the storm that followed, first
from the relatives and survivors of Oradour, outraged by
the leniency of the sentences, and second from the people
of Alsace-Lorraine, convinced that their young men were
being made scapegoats.

It was too much for a struggling French government

trying to create national unity. Sentences were commuted, five of the seven Germans sentenced were repatriated at once, and all the Alsatians, except Boos, were amnestied. Both death sentences were commuted.

The French authorities had opted for the future, not the past. They knew that a strong, united Europe would need the active help of West Germany. Besides, the real criminals were either dead or missing, they reasoned.

When she heard about the amnesties, Marika became quite sick with frustration and tension. She spent several sleepless nights, the nightmares about her parents began again and for days she could not eat. She walked around the plant looking heavy-eyed and thin and eventually she contracted pneumonia.

Myrtle minded Sylvia until she recovered and three weeks later she was back at the plant, looking drawn and pale.

She discovered a message waiting for her. Klaus Greenstein had telephoned and wanted her to make an appointment to see him urgently.

I thought you might like a progress report,'' he said, looking smug. ''Well, sit down, sit down.

''Sorry to drag you here, but I didn't want to tell you over the telephone. Geissler's alive! Or he was alive long after his death had been filed. That's the good news. The bad news is that we have no idea what name or nationality he has assumed.''

Marika leaned back and closed her eyes. She felt swamped with a flood of conflicting emotions. Horror that the monster had escaped the net of Allied wrath for so long, pride that she had helped with the search in some small way—and fear. Geissler was out there—he was living among normal, unsuspecting people. She tried to imagine what Geissler would look like in civilian clothing—sinister eyes and butcher's hands!

''I've just returned from South America,'' Greenstein was saying. ''We've handed over a war criminal to the

Israelis. A big fish, I can tell you . . . a very big fish indeed.'' Watching him, Marika decided she liked him better when he looked mournful. His face was not designed for smiling.

"Under interrogation he admitted to seeing Geissler in Paris after his supposed death," Greenstein went on happily. "He doesn't know where Geissler went and unfortunately that's all we managed to extract from him."

"It's a start," Marika said, trying not to show her disappointment.

She left soon afterward. It was such a fine day, she decided to walk in the park. She found herself surreptitiously scanning passersby. One of them might be Geissler. She knew she would recognize him; after all, she had studied his photograph so often. There and then she decided to increase her monthly payments from ten to fifteen percent of her salary.

Chapter Thirty-seven

Günter awoke to the sound of sand and schist being hurled against the sheer sides of the canyon like pelting rain. His hair, ears and eyebrows were filled with sand and his possessions were buried in small sandy heaps around him. The east wind had reached gale force during the night and it would probably last for three days. When it dropped it would be even hotter and already the temperature had reached forty degrees centigrade.

Günter was tired and at twenty-eight his face was stamped with a maturity born of deprivation. There were deep lines on his cheeks and at the corners of his eyes. He was strong, but emaciated. His skin was like parchment and only his eyes showed signs of his youthful optimism. He had been in the desert for nearly four years and during that time he had pegged over ninety claims, which were registered on his infrequent trips to civilization. None of them were currently viable propositions and he was beginning to lose heart.

He was prospecting through the moonscape region of the Namib, a desolate area of tortured black basalt mountains with deep canyons between the sheer slopes. The area stretched for hundreds of miles without a desert shrub or even a bird.

He stood up, blinked and looked around. The sun was trembling over the highest black peak, filling the ugly canyons with a strange purple glow.

Günter shook the sand off him and dug for the water container. No chance of a wash, water was too precious, but he drank deeply and took a piece of dried meat from the pack and gnawed at it for a while. Then he shouldered his pack, took his rods and shovel and set off in a north-easterly direction to where he had left his jeep.

The lunar landscape seemed to be unending. Easy to get lost here, he reckoned, without a good knowledge of navigation.

The sun rose, the temperature soared, the air trembled with heat and mirages shone in the distance like sparkling mirrors of water.

Günter kept going through the wasteland. Around him lay untold riches, he knew, but he would need more capital if he were to carry on prospecting much longer as well as more sophisticated equipment to find the minerals. It would take a fortune to mine his claims. The best he had achieved so far was selling his claims to established mining groups in order to earn the cash to carry on.

By noon Günter was close to fainting from dehydration. It was the hottest day he had ever experienced. He had to bend almost double to drag his feet out of the hot clinging sand and the air was so dry it seared his lungs. Seeing a deep ravine in the side of the canyon, he crept into its shade. He leaned back, drank some water and, looking up, saw a vivid emerald scar with patches of turquoise in a gully above him where a recent rockfall had occurred.

Copper!

*   *   *

It took half an hour to scale the steep slope, but it was worth the effort, for this was a particularly rich vein, and Günter sat fondling the glittering fragments.

Currently the price of refined copper was two hundred and fifty pounds a ton; raw ore brought in only twenty pounds a ton, but this mine was a winner. The rocks contained at least twenty percent malachite, a semiprecious stone for which there was a keen market in Japan, so he could demand four times the usual price of copper per ton and ship the ore in the raw state.

Günter collapsed on the slope and drank a treble ration of water to celebrate. He wondered how far the vein extended. The green scar showed for at least eighty feet on the mountainside. All he had to do was dig it out of the mountain, transport it through the moonscape area and across sixty kilometers of the Namib to the docks.

Not impossible, he speculated.

He set about pegging his claim and after some thought put two claims next to each other. He built four conical pillars of rocks as center and corner beacons, each with iron poles impaled in them, giving his prospecting license number and the size of the area. Then he laid out stones in rows showing the direction in which the claims lay.

That should do it, he thought, three hours later. This was the best find he had yet made, and taking a few fragments in his rucksack, he set off happily for his jeep.

At sunset he reached the end of the moonscape and as he entered the dry bed of the Kuisseb River he saw the first feathery ana trees and a clump of camel-thorn trees, their roots going deep down to find the subterranean water. Further up the rocky hillside he saw occasional quiver trees, standing like silent sentinels over the canyon, their bare branches stretching up like candelabra with small green powder puffs at the tips.

Later he came upon water seeping over a rock halfway up an incline in the side of the canyon. He had heard about this spring; it was the only one in the Namib which never ran dry and around it were spoor of zebras, springbok, baboons and ostriches.

He drank some of the brackish water and hurried on toward his jeep. By eleven he was in the pub at Walvis Bay.

It took Günter five days to register his claim, buy a van, recruit the labor he needed, stock up with food for them and transport them back to his copper mine. He put a lock on the water drum, for water had to be carefully guarded. He set up a tent for the workers, and detailed one of them as cook. At dawn the following morning, the five men attacked the mountainside with picks. The copper fragments began rolling down the hillside, forming a heap far below in the canyon.

The miners sweated in the sun and Günter sweated beside them. At eleven-thirty he called a three-hour break; at two-thirty the miners began work again and at three they dropped their picks and demanded immediate transport back to Walvis Bay. The work was too hard and the sun too hot, they complained.

Günter argued and threatened the six Ovambos, but they would not give in. He offered double pay and then treble, but still they refused.

They were not antagonistic toward him, but simply afraid of the heat. "we will die here," their leader told him. "No living thing should come here. Look around, you can see for yourself—nothing can live in this terrible place."

Günter drove them back that night. He, too, was exhausted and he stumbled into the nearest bar, sat on a stool and ordered a pint of water, much to the barman's surprise.

"God, it's Günter. I never would have recognized you, man. Life's tough in the Namib, eh?"

Günter looked like a wildman with his unkempt beard and ragged hair.

"You stink worse than a meerkat, man," the barman complained, but Günter was too tired to retaliate. He drank the water, ordered a cold beer and went to his room for a shower and a good sleep.

The word soon went around that Günter was back in town and by dusk the next day most of his old friends had gathered in the pub to see him, but by then Günter had showered, shaved and visited the barber and he arrived grinning to find everyone wanted to buy him a drink. Günter's stubbornness and endurance were becoming a legend, and although he was thin, he was tough and strong with sinews knotted over his body. Not a man in town would dare to pick a fight with him.

Toward midnight Günter followed Evans to his truck. He tried to look casual as he said, "Heard anything from Bertha and the family?" He could not say Marika's name, for when he tried his lips became stiff and his mouth dried.

"She was here—Bertha, that is. Stayed two weeks, just to look up a few old friends. She's gone to live in Johannesburg. Evidently she has relatives there. Oh my, she doesn't like England. You should just hear her talk about the place."

"And the rest?"

"Well, they're still in London."

"For Christ's sake, Evans. Is there or isn't there any news?"

Evans laid a hand on Günter's shoulder. "I know how you feel, Günter. We all know how you feel. She's a beautiful girl, but I think you're out of the running, pal."

"What d'you mean?"

Günter could look really mean at times, Evans thought. "Marika's designing furs, doing well, according to Bertha. Reckon she won't be back here in a hurry."

"What about Sylvia?"

"She's lovely. Looks like you, too. Bertha gave me some snaps. I said I'd probably bump into you sooner or later."

Evans took an envelope from inside his vehicle and passed it to Günter.

He did not look at them until he was alone, but once in his room he spread the pictures on the bed. There were six and Sylvia was lovely in each one of them. Nearly five years old and the most beautiful child he had ever seen, with her huge eyes and her ash-blond hair. He'd known she'd be a beauty, but she was better, far better.

"Goddamnit!" he exploded, and pummeled his fist on the bed. He must make money. How else could he get to London?

But what was the point of hoping? Here he sat sweating in a cheap Walvis Bay hotel with a few hundred pounds left and an abandoned mine in the desert.

Common sense told him to forget Marika, but he knew he could not. He loved her, he had loved her even before he met her, but what was he to do? His plans to get rich quick were not working out. Yet he had the copper. Hundreds of thousands of pounds of it—if he could only mine the ore and transport it to Walvis Bay.

Günter sat for a long time considering his prospects. This was likely to prove his only chance to strike it rich. He would have to mine the copper himself, he decided reluctantly. The prospect was terrifying—even for Günter.

Chapter Thirty-eight

It was noon. The savage sun scorched the barren landscape and towering basalt mountains shimmered under the pallid sky.

To Günter, toiling on the mountainside, only the heat was real. It blazed around him, blistering his body, searing his lungs, scalding his eyes. He felt shriveled and old; every movement was agony, but Günter had set his mind on selling the copper and he would not give in.

He lifted his huge blackened arms and hurled the pickax into the rock. The jar sent shivers of pain through his back, his shoulders and down to his fingertips. Thud!

Thud! Thud! The noise echoed in the canyons every ten seconds. It was the only sound for hundreds of miles around.

The emerald-green scar lengthened and deepened; the copper tumbled down the mountain slope and piled up in the canyon. Slowly the mine took shape.

It was the thud of the pickax that led Claire to Günter's camp. She had left Walvis Bay two days before in a hired truck with a local tour guide and slept in the desert. It was only a day's drive to the edge of the moonscape region, but no one knew where Günter was and they had spent two days searching for him. On the second morning they heard the persistent clang of a pickax on iron-hard rock and Claire leaned back and sighed.

Günter had visited the town twice since he had been in the hospital there three years before, but he had not contacted her. At last, in desperation she had gone to his hotel room one night.

It was a year ago now, but the memory still haunted her. Günter had made love to her as he would to a prostitute.

"You need me," she had sobbed. "You don't believe me, but you'll find out one day." They had fought bitterly and she had left in a temper, blaming herself for being such a fool.

Her determination to forget Günter had led her to bed down with several ship's officers and later to become engaged to an American mining prospector. But it was no good; night after night she dreamed of Günter and she longed for him all day. Eventually she had broken her engagement.

When she heard the clang of the pickax Claire's throat constricted with emotion, but whether it was compassion or anger she did not know.

What a fool Günter was, but what a magnificent fool. She loved him, but she hated him, too, because she could not keep away from him.

So here she was again . . .

*   *   *

She shuddered and sat up. She was drenched with sweat and sticking to the seat; every breath she drew was too hot, burning her nostrils and her lungs, and she was swollen and itching. The sun was a tyrant—watchful and malignant. Every movement she made seemed a declaration of war.

They had been climbing all day and it was rough going as the truck inched forward through crevices and over rocks. They were approaching a flat plateau on a mountain which overlooked the moonscape area. At last they parked and the view made her gasp. It was so . . . she searched for a description . . . so alien.

She could not see Günter or the mine, for the slope twisted away in a curve beneath them, but far below she could see a pile of turquoise ingots glistening in the sun. As she watched another few rocks hurtled down the slope.

"Come back for me," she said.

"When?"

"Tomorrow morning."

He shrugged. "That'll cost you another day."

She nodded and turned away.

The tour guide watched her climbing rapidly down the steep slope. Her red hair shone like a flame in the sunlight. She looked up and smiled, but her shrewd blue eyes were not smiling. Then she waved.

That's some tough woman, he thought.

Surely that could not be Günter? Not that skeletal frame clinging to the rock face? Claire's stomach lurched and she nearly fell.

Then Günter looked up and she saw his cornflower eyes. He looked surprised. Then he frowned.

"Hi, Claire," he croaked "I see you never give up." He bent over wearily and laid the pickax on a rock.

"Do you?"

"No, I suppose not."

"Well, neither do I."

That was something he understood. Suddenly he smiled. Then he took the pickax and brought it crashing down. She flinched when she saw his body shudder with pain. The clang hurt her ears.

"Hey, Günter," Claire yelled. "It's taken me two days to get here. Aren't you going to let up?"

"Sunset," he said briefly, unwilling to waste energy. "Camp's down there."

Claire's eyes pricked with tears as she slithered down to the canyon, keeping well away from the rocks bouncing past.

"Bastard!" she muttered, but she knew it served her right and in a way she was glad. Perhaps now she would learn to forget him.

She found his spartan camp in a shallow cave under an overhanging ledge and in the sweltering heat she lay down and fell asleep.

She woke much later to see Günter standing beside her. It was sunset and the rocks glowed with an eerie purple light.

"What d'you reckon that's worth?" she asked, gazing at the pile of copper a hundred yards down the canyon.

"There's about eighty tons so far and, working on a guestimate of fifty pounds a ton, about four thousand pounds, I should say, less the cost of getting it to Walvis Bay harbor."

He spoke softly, conserving his movements as he stripped off his clothes. He took a basin of water and a rag and began to wash himself. He looked haggard and ill, there was no flesh on his bones and he was scarred and badly bruised.

The sight of his damaged body brought a sudden shaft of joy like a spear thrust through her entrails.

"I'm glad," she said fiercely. "Glad! Do you understand what I'm saying? Glad you're destroying yourself just to be rich, but that won't change anything, Günter. Marika will never marry you. She hates Germans and she hates the Namib."

"People change," he said. "Besides, the war's been over seven years . . . nearly eight. People forget."

Claire stared gloomily at him. "Seven years . . . so

long . . . and all that time . . ." She broke off and bit
her lip.

Watching her, Günter felt sad for her.

She gnawed at the biltong. "You make this yourself?"
she asked after a while.

"Yes."

"It's terrible. Look what I've brought." She fumbled in
her rucksack.

"Save it," he said. "I don't want to spoil my stomach."

"Jesus!" she gasped. "Now I've heard everything."
She hurled her biltong down the canyon.

Günter stood up mildly and ambled after it. He took half
a cup of water, washed the biltong and hung it back on the
hook.

"You don't understand," he said. "It took me months
to get used to this diet, and now if I change it, it will be
tough again. You understand? *Ja? Ja?*"

She noticed his German accent was more pronounced,
perhaps because he was tired. "Jesus, Günter, what are we
going to do?" she asked earnestly. "You and I both."

"You are going back to your job and you'll find a nice
man and marry him and be happy." He put his arm around
her and she snuggled close, glad of the touch of him and
the nearness.

It would be so easy to love Claire. Sometimes he wished
he did. Often he wondered if this passion he held for
Marika really was love. Or was it just that she was the
trophy and he had to win? At any cost. Claire was the
consolation prize.

"So you still love her?" Claire asked bitterly.

"It seems like that now," Günter replied uneasily, wishing that he could take the words back. He did not want to
hurt her more than she was hurt already.

"But, Günter, what if your dreams come true, what if
you make a fortune and still she won't have you? Say in
five years—or even ten . . . have you thought . . .?" She
broke off. "Oh God," she wailed. "I hate myself . . . I
hate myself for begging. I'm like a dog . . ."

Günter was overcome with compassion. Poor, poor Claire.
She was not half as tough as she thought. At that moment

he wanted nothing so much as to ease her misery. "Then I'll marry you," he said.

"Promise?"

Good God! Why had he said that? He looked into her eyes naked with misery and saw a glimmer of hope there, too. "Yes," he said. "But, Claire. Don't hope . . . You see, I know Marika loves me."

"Oh, Günter," she burst out. She threw herself on him again.

She was no longer puppyish or inexperienced, but still wiry. There was the same feeling of hugging a wound-up spring. "You haven't changed much, Claire," he whispered. "But neither have I. Nothing's changed. Remember that."

He pulled her under him. Then he sighed. There was none of the soft ripe womanliness of Marika here. Her skin was hard and firm, her buttocks were rounded lumps, her breasts childlike and unformed. Yet she loved him. No man should be loved this much. The thought came: Perhaps if her passion were not quite so fierce he might not be so repelled by her. He should have more feeling for her, but he did not. Yet she was a woman and he needed a woman.

He stood up, lit a hurricane lamp and hung it from a hook in the overhanging ledge. Then he took off her clothes, her shorts and her panties, her blouse and her unnecessary bra, and stood back staring at her body half hidden in the shadow of the cave.

"I want to look at you," he said. She was really pretty, standing there looking coy. He had never taken the trouble to study her, but her face was pert and heart-shaped, her turned-up freckled nose was delightfully girlish and her hair was quite lovely even though unruly.

"Come here," he said, smoothing out the sleeping bag, and when he lay on top of her he thought: She's got a good cunt, she always had. It was tight and stiff, quivering and pulsating around him.

They were lying in a pool of sweat, wet skin against wet

skin. The days were unbearable, but there was no relief in the night, for the rocks stored the heat and they were oven hot. The moon rose and the canyon became filled with a ghostly light. After a while the wind came and sighed through the mountains.

Claire could not sleep. This night was too precious to waste, for she could see the outline of Günter's cheek and his nose jutting against the moonlit sky. Each strand of hair shone and gleamed like burnished silver. He was like a statue lying on a tomb in a deep dark cathedral; the thought frightened her.

If money was what he wanted, she would help him. One day he would be hers, she knew. She had heard of Marika's marvelous good fortune; who hadn't? Claire was not envious of Marika. There was only one thing she wanted in life and that was Günter and he was lying next to her.

Well, the sooner he became rich, the better, she thought. Then he could get this silly obsession over and done with.

She sat up and looked at the copper gleaming emerald in the moonlight. All Günter's hopes were centered there.

At sunrise, Günter woke, stretched and stumbled sleepily to the water container.

"I'm leaving," she told him. "But I'll be back. I'm going to get help."

"Don't bother," he told her. "I've tried. You can't get the blacks to work in this heat. I offered treble the normal wage."

"Convicts," she said.

"Forget it. They might die in the heat."

Who cares, she thought, as long as Günter survives, but she kept her thoughts to herself.

She was at the first peak when she heard the thud of the pickax against the mountain. How tired she was but happy.

She was smiling when she crawled over the last peak on her hands and knees.

The tour guide saw her coming and grinned. "Must be some guy down there," he said.

"Yes," Claire answered proudly. "Some guy! In fact, he's my fiancé."

Chapter Thirty-nine

Clarie took three weeks to obtain the workers. First she had to convince the prison authorities that Günter was establishing an experimental farm settlement in the Kuisseb River bed and that she could show evidence of two armed guards and provide adequate housing. Eventually they agreed to let her have six prisoners convicted of minor offenses.

She borrowed hunting rifles from her uncle in Windhoek, hired two down-and-out whites and bought a road workers' tent.

The journey was a nightmare. The convicts, manacled together, sang mournful dirges of freedom; the guards swore, sweated and smoked incessantly; she could see they were nervous and the van she had hired threatened to break down over every pass.

It was dusk when she arrived at the plateau. She hurried down to Günter, leaving the convicts to unload the gear and pit props.

The mine was forty feet deep now with overhanging ledges and she could see Günter toiling in the gloom below.

"Günter!" Her voice, shrill and urgent, echoed around the rocks. "For God's sake come out of there. I've brought pit props and six prisoners."

He emerged swaying heavily on the rough rope ladder. "I don't like using prisoners," he said, and his voice sounded slurred. She could feel his exhaustion. "They're not strong enough for this job."

She shrugged. "Let's give them a try," she said.

For the next few days the hole deepened, although not as fast as Claire would have liked, because Günter insisted that the convicts work short two-hour shifts with three-hour breaks in between. He alternated with them, stripped to his waist, toiling in the stinking hole. But any fool could see he was doing most of the work, Claire thought.

When there was about two hundred tons lying in the gully, Günter decided to take off a few days to fly to Johannesburg and negotiate a deal with a Japanese mining consortium.

"You can't stay here with these guards, it's not safe," he urged Claire repeatedly, but she was adamant.

"The guards can't be left without supervision," she said.

It was excessively hot on the day Günter left, with temperatures soaring to forty-five degrees centigrade in the shade. After he had gone the convicts became moody and lazy. They worked slower, and the more Claire shouted at them, the more sullen they became.

Claire watched them, hating them. If only they worked half as well as Günter she would have no problems. Günter would be kept busy transporting the ore. She cared only for him. He must survive and to hell with everyone else.

Eventually she decided that the convicts' water ration and food would depend upon the amount of copper they sent up each hour. She reckoned they should be able to produce as much as they had done when Günter was there.

By noon the heat was so intense that Claire hid in the camp and lay under a ledge in a pool of sweat.

It was 1 P.M. when Johannes, one of the guards, ambled down the hill toward her.

"The natives are on strike," he said nervously, and went on toward his tent.

"Where's Gideon?"

"Up there trying to talk sense into them."

She toiled up the slope, but her head began to ache until she thought it would explode and blinding flashes danced in front of her eyes. She reached the top and peered over the edge of the mine.

"If you don't work you won't get water," she called.

Half an hour later the convicts agreed to work, so she sent the water bucket down.

For four days she kept them working. She saw how lean they had become and how the whites of their eyes turned yellow and their skin hung on their frames like parchment, but she did not care. She must keep Günter out of the mine. Convicts were replaceable, Günter was not.

By the end of the week the mine was sixty feet deep and the tunnel followed the copper vein into the mountain another twenty feet. The cavern was held up by a series of pit props.

It was then that the convicts complained of heatstroke. Johannes came to tell her.

"Oh, but they're bound to be ill just because Günter's gone," she said angrily.

She climbed up and peered into the gloom. "Hey, you . . . you there, Jason," she called to their leader. "Listen to me. Can you hear me?"

"I hear you," a deep voice replied.

"You must work," she yelled, hoarse and fuming.

"You have done wrong to bring us here," Jason called out. "This is not a farm and the heat is bad."

"The boss has been working here every day for three months."

"We're not working." Jason's voice was low and obstinate. Then the convicts began to sing, their voices drowning hers.

"Pull up the ladder," she told Johannes as she stared down malignly.

"Bloody heavy, ma'am."

"We'll do it together." She moaned with the effort, but eventually they succeeded in hauling it out of the mine.

"You and Gideon take turns to guard them," she told Johannes. "They can get out if they try. No food nor water. They'll work before nightfall."

Johannes laughed evilly. "Now you're talking," he said.

She slithered down to the camp feeling furious, clenching and unclenching her hands. They must work. If she took them back to prison she would never get another batch when they discovered the convicts had been used for mining instead of farming.

The sun rose and hung remorselessly over the mine and eventually even their singing was stilled.

At dusk she sent Gideon to replace Johannes and when she went to peer into the mine she found it quiet, but the smell turned her stomach. She returned to her camp, washed with a meager cup of water in a basin, ate her biltong and a rusk and made some black tea.

At last she fell into an uneasy sleep.

She did not know what time it was when she woke. She had heard something, but she did not know what it was, only that her skin was prickling with fright. Something was wrong.

There was no moon and it was pitch dark in the canyon. She crawled to the edge of the ledge and listened, but all she could hear was her panting breath.

She heard the sound of a stone falling and a sharp exclamation which changed to a hoarse scream—cut short brutally. Silence! Then someone shouted and there was the sound of footsteps running away. Somehow the convicts had escaped and killed the guards.

When she tried to light the lantern she found her hands were shaking so badly it was hard to hold the match. She waited for what seemed like an eternity, but there were no further sounds. No doubt they hd taken the rifles and escaped into the Namib.

Relief changed to horror and amazement when she saw the shaggy, sweating figure of Jason. His shadow loomed like a giant on the wall of the canyon behind him.

She felt powerless. Too panic-stricken to move. The next minute he was bounding upon her, his black eyes staring out of his head. His mouth was twitching and his hands reaching for her.

"Bitch! White whore! Bitch!" he screamed, seizing her arm.

He was going to kill her. The thought jolted her out of her trance and she began to fight like a cat, spitting, clawing and biting.

Jason dragged her heavily back into the cave.

"No, no," she screamed.

Claire felt herself being pushed down and down. They were falling heavily, but he never let go of his grip on her, not for a moment. She felt a dull, stunning bruise somewhere. He held her arm and she struggled until it seemed to be dislocated.

It couldn't be real. Oh no, not real. Not this. Not death. She clawed at him horribly, but she could not get up. Jason and she looked into each other's faces. His head was only inches away. His eyes looked yellow and his lips curled back like a snarling dog's.

She whimpered with fright, spent now, all the strength gone out of her. She could not fight.

Sensing this, he dragged her to her feet. "I'm a man. A man, you hear," he panted. He glared with a strange ferocity, willing her to understand.

"You left us there . . . without water . . . in that hell hole . . . stinking in our own shit."

He pushed himself out of his trousers, holding her with one hand, and ripped at her skirt ferociously. Then he tore her clothes off.

Hatred was rising through her, replacing fear. His body was touching hers, strange, violent, powerful. A horrible convulsion went through her, wracking her. His face was livid, but she could sense the savageness leaving him. It was the sight of her naked body.

Shuddering violently, he stepped back and stared at her as if hypnotized. Then he moved forward. She knew he would rape her now and then kill her.

Reality became unreal and time switched to slow motion. The lantern, Claire thought. Her hand stretched toward it, but it was slow . . . so slow . . .

Jason lurched forward like a runner caught by the camera in a moment of triumph; each jerking movement seemed to be made with lethargic grace.

Her desperate fingers caught the lamp and swung it . . . but oh . . . so painfully slowly . . . in a wide arc up and over toward his face. As he leaped forward he seemed to be poised in midair.

The paraffin trickled down his face, slowly . . . slowly the flame flickered on his hair and crept down . . . and down . . . while he screamed and rolled on the floor, clutching his hands over his eyes.

Time returned to normal. Claire watched in a trance as the flames engulfed his face and shoulders. She smelled his burning flesh.

Then there was darkness and the sound of his sobbing breath. Then that, too, was stilled. Why? Perhaps because he was coming after her. If only she could see, but the darkness was impenetrable.

She cowered into the corner of the cave, fumbling for her gun under the mattress.

She could hear him now, smell his burnt flesh. Oh God, he would get her before she found the gun.

Then she had it in her hand. She slipped off the safety catch as hands groped toward her.

She fired again and again. Later she became aware that she was screaming and pulling the trigger of an empty gun. She could hear low moans and someone crawling away. Then she heard the clatter of his body falling down the slippery slope to the floor of the canyon. After that there was silence.

When Günter arrived next day he found the guards tied back to back, their rifles gone, and Jason groaning on the ground with bullet wounds through his right kneecap and his left thigh. His face was burned raw and so swollen that Günter could not see his eyes.

When Claire heard Günter calling she left her hiding place and hurried to the camp.

"He tried to rape me," she said.

Gideon had told him why the convicts had refused to work. He felt horrified by the extent of their suffering. He left at once to take Jason to the Swakopmund hospital, leaving Claire to return the guards to Windhoek and explain to the prison authorities why the convicts had escaped.

She had a right to defend herself, he knew. But why had Claire treated the convicts so badly? They could have died. There was a cruel streak in her which frightened and repelled him.

He shuddered. Claire's hatred was as ferocious as her love and he knew he would see both sides of her before they were through with each other.

Chapter Forty

After the success of Marika's collection, Mendel had taken the vacant factory next door and increased his mortgage by twenty thousand pounds for working capital.

They had decided to keep the Marika Magos collection small and exclusive to start with, catering to the top end of the trade, and Marika had engaged an assistant designer, a pattern cutter, six machinists and a secretary. For the rest she shared Mendel's facilities.

Mendel was a traditionalist, but he had the sense to see that the world belonged to the young and that Marika was in the forefront.

At last Marika had an outlet for her pent-up creativity. The months flew by as she worked from early morning until bedtime. It was only a few weeks before she launched her next range and she had worked for nine months on it, but still she was worried. Would she be good enough? Perhaps her last success had been a fluke. Mentally she reviewed the twenty-four coats and capes hanging in her strong room. Was that pocket just a little too bulky? Did possum really go with mink?

Suddenly a small, cold body hurtled into bed beside her.

"You're late, Mummy," Sylvia complained, snuggling

closely against her and placing two small frozen feet on her warm thighs.

"My, but you're cold," she gasped. "what were you doing out of bed?"

"I was drawing."

"You're not allowed up without your slippers and bathrobe."

Sylvia wrapped her arms around her mother's neck. "The kettle's on and you better get up or I'll be late for school."

"Oh Lord. Stay here and keep warm while I cook breakfast."

Marika scrambled out of bed and raced to the kitchen to cook eggs and bacon.

She had just finished when a call came from Landon, Mendel's caretaker. There was a fire at the factory, he told her. He had called the fire brigade and Mr. Sidersky.

"A fire? Which plant?" she stammered.

"The new one."

Marika shuddered as she replaced the receiver. Their new collections were there.

She raced to school, and after dropping Sylvia at the school gate, took half an hour to reach York Way. At the end of Copenhagen Street she paused in horror at the sight of smoke pouring from windows. Firemen were still playing their hoses on the building.

She parked and rushed down the pavement. The staff were gathered on the ground floor looking scared.

Mendel was next door, assessing the damage, they told her.

She raced around the corner to the Magos entrance.

"Sorry, miss, you can't go in there," the fireman on guard said.

"Mendel," she yelled in panic.

Mendel leaned out of a second-floor window. His face was covered in grime. "Calm down, love. I'll be there in a jiffy. We're having a look around. Don't come in, you'll get dirty."

"Dirty," she gasped. "what about my furs?"

The fireman let her pass and she rushed inside. There was dirty water sloshing around the floors and it was very smoky. Coughing, she made for rickety stairs and stumbled up to the stockroom.

"Oh no," she moaned. The pelts and the rails of made-up furs were sooty and soaked. Some were still smoldering.

Then she remembered her sketches and raced down to the drawing office. The place was dripping with water and soot, but the drawings were in a steel filing cabinet and they were saved.

It was impossible to make up the collection again, or even replace the pelts, in time for the launch.

Mendel walked in. "what's the damage?" she whispered.

"Rough estimate—half a million—plus the cost of redecorating."

"We're insured, I suppose."

"Yes, of course. Don't worry."

She watched him narrowly. Mendel was a worried man, she could see that.

"What's wrong?"

"We're underinsured," he admitted. "I never updated the figure when we bought the pelts for the show. It was a quick in-and-out job, or so I thought."

It was another hour before the firemen deemed the fire out and the building safe, although sodden.

"I don't know about you," Mendel said contritely, "but I could do with a pint and a ham sandwich."

"Me, too," she said unenthusiastically.

But then chaos arrived with the insurance assessors and an electrical engineer in tow. It was nearly three by the time the emergency quieted enough to allow them to think.

Then Mendel walked into her temporarily converted office in the reception area, put out his hand to squeeze her arm and crumpled. For a moment she thought he had tripped, but when she rushed around the desk to help him she saw that he had passed out.

The ambulance took ten minutes, but it seemed more like an hour. Mendel was still unconscious when they carried him out. Marika was about to follow when she remembered Sylvia.

"Oh God," she wailed. How could she forget her own daughter? It was nearly half past three and dark and the north wind was coming up to gale force.

Her heart was pounding as she arrived at the school. There was no sign of Sylvia. Looking up the long driveway, she saw the building, dark and ugly. There were no lights on. She had difficulty in making her legs obey her as she ran up the drive and around the school calling her daughter. She found her eventually. She was curled up in a doorway, blue with cold.

In the evening Marika drove to the hospital, but Mendel was still in intensive care and unconscious. "Get better quickly, Mendel," she whispered. "I need you."

Sylvia was waiting outside the ward, a pale child wrapped in a blanket and shivering with the cold.

"She should be in bed," the nurse told Marika sternly.

In the morning Sylvia was running a temperature and Marika called the doctor. She had bronchitis, he told her, and not to worry. She must stay in bed for a few days.

What was she to do? She wrapped the child in a sleeping bag and took her to the plant. She found the staff were hanging around looking miserable and no one was working. She sent the machinists back to work, grumbled at the supervisor, Mrs. Hanson, for being so lax and began to return the telephone messages: her insurance broker, the police, who told her the fire was caused by an electrical fault, electricians, decorators and all their business associates, who wanted to know if they were closing permanently.

For fourteen days she drove herself to a standstill, keeping Sylvia at the plant, sending out for snacks, putting her to sleep on a camp bed and carrying her home in a sleeping bag.

She ordered a fresh supply of furs, not exactly as she wanted them, but they would do, and she hounded the machinists into working overtime to complete existing orders. She begged an additional credit line from the bank to cover her until the insurance money arrived and she coped with their badgering creditors.

Each day seemed like a year, but there was one consolation: Mendel was getting better.

Mendel returned to the plant at the end of the month. He grinned weakly. "Never knew I had a weak heart," he lied. "I still can't believe it. I feel fine now. Give me a day or two and I'll be back to normal."

By December 15, the beginning of their annual holiday shutdown, most of the fire damage had been disposed of, the factory had been rewired and they were waiting for the new machinery to arrive. Using Sidersky's facilities, Marika had fulfilled their orders, although showing their latest ranges had been canceled. They would make up for it in the spring, they decided. Mendel seemed to be fully recovered and refused to rest.

The real victim was Sylvia, Marika thought, watching her daughter sadly.

"I'm taking Sylvia to Bertha," Marika told Mendel. "I've made up my mind and Bertha's pleased, too. I can't look after her properly and I can't do my job. It's a no-win situation—and Sylvia's suffering the most. She'll be happier with Bertha. It's for the best," she added fiercely.

"You could work part-time and stay home afternoons," Mendel argued. "Plenty of women do; you'll still have your profit share and the same salary."

"No, it wouldn't work," she said firmly. "When I'm with Sylvia, I'm neglecting my work; when I'm working, I'm neglecting Sylvia. I always feel guilty."

"Just as long as you know it's possible. I've never wanted to boss you around, but I think you're making the wrong choice."

He was disappointed and the expression on his face angered her. "Just worry about my designs," she snapped. What right had Mendel to judge her?

Chapter Forty-one

Günter soared over the horizon, insignificant as a fly against the vast waste of sandy plains and mountainous dunes, until he reached the Fish River Canyon and there he saw the river, like a thin brown snake, writhing in deep canyons carved into the basalt mountains.

It was unique and awe-inspiring; Günter gazed until his skin prickled with goose pimples, then he yelled, pushed the throttle forward and plunged toward the river. Soon he was twisting and turning over sluggish water with sheer black rocks towering on either side. He whooped with joy and landed on the riverbank. Stripping off his shorts, he waded in, letting the brackish water soak the grime and sweat from his skin. Then he sat on the sand drinking a beer before taking his chisel and sample bag.

Whistling to himself, Günter went a mile downstream and eventually returned to the helicopter. He labeled the samples, looked around and regretfully took off. Shortly afterward he was following the course of the river toward the sea. Twenty miles inland it stained the crystal-clear waters of the Orange River a deep ocher as the two mighty waterways joined forces to the sea.

Günter grinned with joy. This was the way to go prospecting. "Beats footslogging," he murmured.

It was over a year since Günter had exhausted the viable copper from his mine. He had made enough to buy a clapped-out Bell helicopter and the spare parts he would need to recondition it. Then he had paid back Claire for the equipment she had purchased for the mine and said goodbye with relief. He still flinched when he remembered the scene she had created and that, more than anything else, had precipitated his trip to Johannesburg, where he had trained for a helicopter pilot's license.

It had taken him six months and almost all of his remaining cash to service the helicopter and replace worn parts, and only when he was confident it was in prime condition had he flown to the Namib.

He had spent four months prospecting the northern regions. Using an abandoned desert police station as his base, he had worked his way slowly across the territory. It was approximately twenty-five miles northeast of Seal Bay that he had discovered strong traces of uranium and excitedly he had staked his claims.

He had flown to Windhoek to register them and on his return investigated the area more fully. Then he had become very excited. Untold wealth lay under the sand. Right now the uranium market was weak and oversupplied, but within a decade the world would need much more; coal and oil reserves would eventually become depleted and nuclear power would be the source of the world's energy. One of these days, Günter reckoned, scientists would start planning for the future and they would need all the uranium they could get.

The fact that it was there and registered in his name made him feel good. More sobering was the knowledge that it would take a fortune to mine it. Eventually he would be forced to sell out to one of the established mining groups.

Günter was in no hurry. He was thirty-two and time was on his side. He felt good. He decided to celebrate by taking a few days off in Swakopmund.

The sand dunes glistened pink and rose in the morning sun like an ancient whore promising fun and forgetfulness. Three thousand feet above, Marika watched them from the windows of a light aircraft. She was not impressed. She knew the Namib intimately and feared it.

She leaned back, closed her eyes and thought about Sylvia and Bertha and the way they had looked at the airport that morning. The memory hurt.

When she left London with Sylvia two weeks before, Bertha had met them in Johannesburg. What a reunion! Boba and Sylvia! They were meant to be together, Marika thought with a twinge of jealousy.

They had searched for a school and a cottage and they had been lucky with both. The Morningside School was set among acres of lawns and shrubs and in spite of its good scholastic record it exuded a happy, informal atmosphere. The thatched cottage they had rented was within walking distance of the school. Bertha was only too happy to leave the boardinghouse and have a real home again.

They had moved into the cottage just before Christmas and spent ten happy days together, but when the time came to leave Sylvia had cried all day.

Oh hell, Marika didn't want to think about it. She knew she could have stayed two days longer, too, but she was feeling guilty and sad and she wanted to run away from both of them. So she had used the excuse of buying more karakul pelts in South-West Africa and had flown to Swakopmund. Then Bertha had asked her to sort out the final payment problems with the canning factory which had taken over her Walvis Bay store.

Marika was afraid of flying. She shuddered as the aircraft descended, circled the small town and landed.

A limousine was waiting and three hours later she had concluded Bertha's business, kicked the sand of Walvis Bay from her feet—forever, she hoped—and gratefully returned to Swakopmund. At her hotel she wondered dismally how to pass the day. She tried to read, but the memory of Sylvia's tearful face kept intruding. When she could no longer stand her recriminations, she went downstairs to the lounge. There would be the usual rough, loud-mouthed crowd of fishermen, but anything was better than her own company.

He was sitting on a high-backed chair, legs dangling on either side, like a cowboy on a diminutive horse. His hair was so blond it looked white, and his skin was deep brown except where his shirt had been and even there it was tanned golden. The long pale hairs on his arms and legs glistened in the dim light so that he seemed to be covered with a silver sheen. He was wearing a striped shirt and shorts and thonged sandals.

Against the puny, darker local boys, the stale beer fumes and tobacco smoke, Günter stood out like some magnificent desert creature captured and tethered among the riffraff. Watching him, she thought: If I were to meet him now for the first time I would fall in love all over again. And then she thought: If he were not German.

He turned and looked at her and the moment was quite shocking. He open-mouthed, eyes round with disbelief, and she feeling quite shattered by the cornflower blue—so blue—how could eyes be that blue? It was unnatural.

So in her moment of shock, good manners deserted her and she stared longingly at his massive shoulders, his arched, muscular neck, the broad brow, which was more lined nowadays, and the proud curve of his cheeks. There was more—much more: the scarcely veiled danger of him, his flaming strength, the sensuousness and his strange, ethereal sensitivity. She wanted to groan with the force of her desire, and at the same time she wanted to turn and run. All she could do was stand still and try to smile, but her features were rigidly set into a mask of lust and her hands were clammy with fright.

He, on one side of the room, and she, on the other, but there was more than just glances running between them, surely, for the room was suddenly quiet; frozen in time; and the air was heavy with unspoken words.

Günter glanced around at the gawping faces staring at Marika and back to him. Then he stood up, walked across the room, put one hand on her arm and said, "Come."

Later, five minutes later, or perhaps longer, Marika returned to sanity and found she was in Günter's jeep and they were driving out of Swakopmund along the lonely sea road that runs north between the Namib and the wild west coast. They were going to inspect Günter's uranium claims.

"Where's Sylvia? Who's looking after her?" he asked as they raced along the sandy road.

Marika found she was trembling. Absurd, she told herself. It was none of his business. What had Sylvia to do with him?

"With Bertha," she answered sulkily.

"In London?"

"No."

As he prized her miserable story out of her, Marika began to feel even more guilty. Yet Günter was smiling. How strange, she thought to herself.

They turned east, and drove off the road, across vast, sandy plains with here and there tall basalt cliffs, but nothing else. Just rocks and sand—mile after mile of it. The desolation frightened Marika. "Nothing could live here," she murmured. "Nothing at all."

Günter drew up; she must get out, he explained patiently as if to a child. No, he insisted. She must examine the multitude of life around her. That was Günter! She had criticized his beloved desert. She sighed and examined the black and crimson mosses that covered every rock and learned that they took their moisture from the morning sea mist. And from the moss, and the damp sea air, the termites lived; and from the termites, the spiders and scorpions lived; right up the line to snakes and moles, horrible burrowing creatures in the sand.

She shivered and climbed back into the jeep. They drove mile after tortuous mile across featureless gravel plains in this heat—this insufferable heat—so why was she shivering? And why was she here? She felt powerless to resist the confusion of emotions ravaging her body. So finally she sat still—as still as she could in the rocking jeep—and let whatever would be, be.

At last he drew up and gave a great flourishing sweep of his arm. "Here," he said, "and there—and look over toward the mountains. All mine—all this uranium—millions of pounds lying here under the sand."

But that was all there was to see. Only sand.

"How lovely," she said falsely. He was disappointed in her; she knew that. But sand? Ugh!

Then, as they tramped around the perimeter of his various claims, there was a low whine in distant dunes which changed in a trice to a frenzied wail and before they could reach the jeep each breath was a mouthful of sand. Marika crouched on the floor of the jeep under a sleeping bag as Günter drove through the mounting sandstorm down into the canyon, where they raced along the dry bed of the Kuisseb River to an ancient oasis, built around a natural spring, and the abandoned German police station of World War I.

When they reached the door the sand was so thick they could not see two yards ahead. They groped their way to the door and she hung on to the handle as Günter fumbled with the lock. The door swung open and she fell inside. Then it slammed shut. The howling and shrieking was outside and they were inside.

"Oh, oh," she croaked. "Water!"

"Don't swallow." A mug was pushed into her hand. "Rinse your mouth and spit. And again."

"You've been living here," she exclaimed when she had washed the sand from her eyes. Günter had hung a paraffin lamp from the hook in the ceiling and in the dim light she saw the camp bed with one blanket neatly folded, a towel on a nail and books heaped on a table. The windows were glassed and the shutters tightly fastened.

She sat on a folding chair and looked around in bewilderment. "How civilized," she said.

"It suits me fine when I'm in this area," he replied. "Maybe I'll buy this place one day. I like it here."

The storm was worsening. Rampaging outside the strong walls like a wild beast, huffing and puffing. Yet not one draft penetrated the old building. Here it was cool and dark and peaceful.

She laughed shakily, trying to retain her grip on normality and fight this uncontrollable urge to open her heart and her thighs and say, "Love me."

"No one ever comes here," he told her. "Look!" He pointed to a nozzle attached to a pipe which protruded from the roof. It was placed over a galvanized iron tub in the corner. "You can have a shower."

"No, really, it's too much. I can't believe it." She laughed and her laugh sounded hollow even to herself. What am I afraid of? she asked herself. Of Günter? No, she answered—of herself.

"Go on. I mean it. Have a shower. There's a tank full of water up there." He jerked his thumb toward the roof. "I pump it from the riverbed. It's down there—far below the sand."

Günter could not sit still. His urge to grab her, push her down and down onto the ground under him, to thrust himself on her and in her and batter her into submission, was becoming stronger than his self-control. Where was the discipline he had fought so hard to attain?

"Well, really, I simply can't stay here," she said decisively, trying to recapture her independence.

"You know we can't leave, either," he said, watching her narrowly.

How long? she wondered. A night at least, maybe a day as well—or even a night and a day. Good heavens . . . she remembered storms lasting days.

Slowly she turned her head toward him and for a long time they gazed at each other. "It's fate," she said at last. "Why bother to fight it?"

"I still love you," he said hoarsely. "There'll never be anyone else. Do you think of me sometimes?"

What could she say? There was no future for them.

"Do you?"

"I don't want to talk about things like that," she said. "What's the point?" The storm would end eventually and they would .leave this place, and she would return to London on the next plane. She was not free, she reminded herself. She had responsibilities—to the factory and her staff and not the least to her conscience. She had a mission in life and nothing could be allowed to stand in her way. Yet she loved Günter. At that moment she felt that she loved him more than she ever had. Why? she wondered. Why did it happen? Why am I here? Why is all this necessary?

As if sleepwalking, she crept to the shower and took off

her clothes, moving with slow deliberate movements, not
coyly or coquettishly, but purposely, like a woman in
love.

Watching her, Günter knew without doubt that she loved
him. "Whatever you say, or wherever you go, I know you
love me still," he said hoarsely.

He became acutely aware of all that he had lost and for
a moment he was awash with sadness. Then lust took over
and he stared as if hypnotized, watching her every movement, his face brick red, his eyes smarting.

She wrapped the towel around her and held out her
arms. "Yes," she said. "Of course. Oh, Günter, my dear.
Yes, but that changes nothing."

Chapter Forty-two

After Marika left, Günter's anger and his need were like
snake venom in his bloodstream; it incapacitated his body
and poisoned his mind.

So he had flown inland and spent a few weeks prospecting the gravel plains around the Tiras Mountains. He had
regained his composure, but found nothing worth pegging,
and this morning he had decided to fly south again to the
Fish River Canyon and up the coast to Lüderitz. He could
never forget his dream of owning his own diamond concession. The land was tied up from Walvis Bay down to the
South African border, but, he reasoned, no one owned the
sea. Not yet!

Soon he was passing over the forbidden concession
areas and as usual he gritted his teeth and tried to control
his envy.

From Alexander Bay to Lüderitz, the coast was barren
and forbidding, but beautiful. Desolate sand dunes hung
over the frenzied surf like chalk cliffs and the occasional

black rock rose out of the sand, steep and inaccessible. Sheltered bays were scarce and they were packed with hundreds of thousands of seals basking in the sun while packs of jackals skirted the fringes of the colonies, searching for the young or feeble.

Along the coast were numerous rocky islands overcrowded with penguins, cormorants and pelicans, each jealously guarding their own territory, and flocks of flamingos veered around the helicopter.

He reached Lüderitz at noon and circled the small town perched on a rock overlooking the bay. Günter wondered that an entire community could live without a tree or a flower as he hovered over the ruins of the old whaling station, the only one in the world where they had harpooned whales from the shore.

The airport was a flattened sand dune behind the town adjoining the old ghost mining settlement, which nowadays was three-quarters buried under the sand. There was no sign of anyone around, so he left the helicopter and went in search of gasoline and a night's lodging.

Lüedritz was a dying town; no soil, no natural water— water here cost more than anywhere else in the world, he had discovered—and, worst of all, no hinterland, just a narrow strip of beach fifteen kilometers long for Lüderitz's citizens to walk along. Beyond was a tall wire fence with the now familiar, but hated *Forbidden* sign in three languages.

Nevertheless, Günter found the hotel congenial and the quaint old German buildings fascinating.

The local garage owner also serviced the airstrip. "Next time you come, just circle the airport three times before landing and I'll drive out with the Avgas tanker," he said.

Günter hired a jeep from him and scuba gear from a local diving enthusiast.

Next morning Günter ate a light breakfast and drove his jeep through the fog along the fifteen-kilometer stretch to the high wire fence and parked it underneath the *Verboten* sign.

"Watch out you don't go beyond the sandbar," he had

been warned by the hotel manager. "It's worse than it looks. Bad currents, thick mud and sharks. If the undertow gets you it can grind you to pieces on the rocks."

It was years since Gunter had swum any distance, but he reckoned he was still fit enough and half a mile out to sea he veered southward and swam parallel to the shore for five miles.

The fog cleared and the water took on a dark blue sheen. A dolphin circled him for a while and the sun burned the back of his neck while his face tingled with salt spray. It was like a welcome home.

Günter veered inland toward a rocky outcrop white with foam a hundred yards from the shore. He was still fit, he discovered with pride. Must be the mining, he thought, but at the same time his arms and legs were beginning to throb. He turned on his back and floated for a while before swimming closer to shore. Here Günter took his mask, switched on the oxygen and plunged down to the seabed.

Visibility was less than a yard in the sandy water and the strength of the undertow alarmed him. He fumbled over the bottom for a while. A hopeless task. Abruptly he returned to the surface and swam on toward the sharp black rocks where the spray was rising fifty feet into the air. It was safer underwater, Günter reckoned, and he plunged to the seabed and felt his way cautiously southward.

There, the undertow caught him and tossed him forward and backward—out of control—but he managed to catch a jagged rock and hung on, feeling the water swirl around him with a force that he had never encountered.

When the sea calmed slightly, he felt his way over the rocks, pushing his fingers into cracks and crevices and putting the stones and shells into pouches on his belt. When his fingers became too numb to continue he swam away from the rocks, keeping close to the sea bottom, and surfaced at a safe distance.

He felt dizzy and tired. Danger signals! So he set off in a leisurely crawl along the coast while curious seals circled him playfully.

It was dusk when he returned to his jeep lugging six crayfish as a reason for his swim. He did not empty the pouches around his belt until he was safely in his hotel room and there, among the stones and pieces of rock, was a rough diamond the size of a pea. He felt elated and went downstairs for a beer.

At the end of five days Günter was dog tired and aching in every muscle, but he had five diamonds. It was a pointer to the future.

That night Günter lay awake for hours trying to think of a way to dredge the diamonds cheaply and efficiently. Eventually he gave up trying to sleep and went down to the bar and from there found his way to a discreet brothel on the outskirts of town.

Günter had not been to a brothel before and he felt ashamed of himself, but he had a deep, uncontrollable longing to hold a woman in his arms.

There was a girl there who reminded him of Marika although he did not know why. She was of mixed parentage; dusky skin and slanting Oriental eyes.

She was not surprised when this handsome but drunk blond giant called her Marika. She had been called a hundred different names by so many lonely men. In the morning, when he paid her, he gave her a small, uncut diamond as a bonus.

Chapter Forty-three

Claire was working in the ward of the Windhoek hospital when she heard the news about Günter from a patient. He was in prison in Lüderitz on charges of diamond theft and smuggling. Claire told the head nurse a fictitious story, begged a week's leave, packed and booked a flight. The following morning she was in Lüderitz.

As the prison loomed ahead a wave of uncertainty settled on Claire. Günter did not give a damn about her, unless it suited him. She had lost her last job at the Walvis Bay hospital after taking unauthorized leave to help Günter with his copper mine and it had taken her three months to find another. Memories of that dreadful experience still haunted her sleep.

The car drew up in front of the prison. Claire paid the taxi and looked around uncertainly. Why bother? she wondered. Let the bastard stay here. It would serve him right.

It was not visiting day, the Prison Commandant explained, but nevertheless . . . He smiled gallantly and made a special arrangement. Half an hour later she was shown into the visitor's cell. She heard footsteps approaching and seconds later the connecting door was thrown open and Günter stood there.

Claire gasped when she saw him. He was so pale and he looked depressed. Thoughts of revenge faded. "How could you be such a fool?" The words came rushing out. "You know how strict they are. No one gets away with it. No one! Oh, Günter, you'll get two years—at the very least, that is." She broke off, looking depressed.

"Cheer up, Claire," he said gently. "I swam five miles down the coast and found the diamonds in rocky crevices underwater. Well outside the concession area." He turned away and gazed out of the window. "I wanted to see if it could be done, but I made a mistake in giving one to a friend." He flushed as he spoke. "I suppose she reported me to the mining company."

"If what could be done?" she interrupted him impatiently.

"Underwater diamond recovery—with some type of dredging equipment." He rubbed his hands together nervously. "It can. The problem is, if the diamond mines find out it's so easy to pick them up offshore, they would extend their concession area. At present they don't think it's a viable proposition."

"Perhaps it's not," she said.

"It is. With small boats—keeping expenses to the minimum." Günter's face lit up with excitement. Then he grinned. "I'd rather sit in prison two years than lose out on a chance of an offshore concession."

"What chance would an ex-con have?" she asked scathingly.

"What else can I do? They won't give me bail. They're scared I'll skip. If I could get out of here I'd tie up a concession."

Claire stood up and sighed. "We're wasting time," she said. "They only gave me half an hour. Tell me what to do."

The dumb fool, she thought as she was leaving. When was he going to learn that he needed her?

The next morning Claire flew to Johannesburg and tried to get an appointment with Tex McGregor, but it was two days before she saw him.

McGregor was an American miner with a reputation for being anti-establishment and getting his own way, or so Günter had told her. He had been on a collision course with the established South African and British mining groups since he sank his first shaft and founded his company, Western Minerals. He had mines in Australia, Canada and South Africa, with headquarters in London and Johannesburg. Although most of his working mines were in South Africa, much of his assets were unmined claims that would come to fruition later.

McGregor was quite unlike anyone Claire had ever seen. He was short, but built like a sumo wrestler. Rolls of fat ran around his neck and his wrists, but the rest of his bulk was solid muscle; his skin bristled with thick black hairs, like a wild boar's, but worst of all, Claire decided, were his eyes, which were large, shrewd and devoid of any emotion. He was in his mid-forties and Claire found him repulsive.

"So you want to make a deal for this boyfriend of yours?" He came straight to the point. "You want me to bail him out and buy half his company, which owns some uranium claims that are unminable until the price rises and the amazing discovery that there are diamonds in the sea?"

"Günter thought you would be interested," Claire said. And Günter's no fool, she thought to herself.

He leaned back and smiled. "Everyone knows there are diamonds in the sea, but they're scattered all over the seabed. Impossible to recover them—or the established miners would be there. They have the best engineers in the world. I admit they tried dredging once, but laid off because of high costs and poor recovery. They found they were up against the sheer impossibility of sifting the sea-bed, plus rocks, currents, shifting sand, sharks, storms, mud and God knows what else besides. They lost a few divers before they called it a day. It's the worst coastline in the world—I'm sure I don't have to tell you that. Now, does that tell you why I'm not interested?"

"But Günter found five diamonds," she persisted. "And he can do the exploratory work because he's a good swimmer."

She leaned back biting her lip.

McGregor frowned and stood up. Behind him, one wall of his office was covered with survey maps on movable aluminum frames. He pulled one forward. "Where did you say these uranium claims are?"

Claire rose impatiently. "Don't waste my time, Mr. McGregor," she said. "Günter told me the uranium will be worth a fortune one day with or without the diamonds. You must know that. Yes, or no, Mr. McGregor?"

"Hey, wait a minute, honey." He stood up slowly and his gaze moved lasciviously from her face to her ankles. "Call me Tex. Decisions like this can't be made in a matter of seconds. How about dinner?"

She smiled. She understood men like McGregor. Günter was as good as free.

Chapter Forty-four

Each day seemed to last longer as Günter worried about whether or not Tex would accept the deal. On the tenth day, when he was beginning to give up hope, Claire arrived with McGregor's lawyer.

The lawyer had a proposition; Günter was offered a fifty-fifty partnership in the Western Minerals Exploration Company, which would start an offshore operation as soon as the concessions were tied up. Five thousand pounds would be deposited in the company's bank account in Walvis Bay and Günter would run the operation. Günter agreed and signed, subject to the diamond-dredging rights coming through. As soon as the concessions were tied up, the lawyer explained, Günter could reveal where he had found the diamonds and charges against him would be dropped. With McGregor's influence the lawyer saw no difficulty there.

As soon as the concessions were legal, Günter would sign his desert claims over to Western Minerals, of which he owned half, and the company would mine them as and when the time was ripe.

Not bad, Günter thought. He had lost fifty percent of everything he owned, but Tex would put up the cash and equipment. It was a fair deal and he accepted, subject to Tex getting the concessions.

After this Günter was in a fever of impatience to get out of jail and start work, but there was no news for several weeks. Claire visited him regularly and acted as go-between. "Tex says it's the red tape from the government that's delaying the deal," she told him anxiously.

At last the lawyer arrived with a ninety-page contract listing the diamond-dredging concessions granted to the

company. They ran down the coast from the Orange River
to the border from one hundred meters below the low-
water mark.

It was far more extensive than anything Günter had
envisaged and he felt absolutely great as he signed his
desert claims over to the Western Minerals Company.

Three weeks later Günter was a free man. He met Tex
for a lunchtime drink and celebrations lasted well into the
night. There was only one source of friction between them;
Tex did not have the cash to start diamond dredging right
away. Just give me a couple of years, he kept stalling.

Eventually they argued and Tex shouted, "For Pete's
sake, go ahead if you want to, but raise the cash yourself."

He'd do just that, Günter decided when he had recovered from his hangover the following afternoon.

He went to his Walvis Bay bank manager, who had
always been a good friend in the past, taking a copy of his
partnership agreement with Western Minerals plus a list of
all his desert claims.

"Must be worth a few hundred thousand," he said
confidently. He left them with the manager and returned to
his hotel.

A few days later, Günter was having a snack and a beer
in the bar when the bank called him. "I've been checking," the bank manager explained patiently. "These uranium claims are owned by the Western Minerals Exploration
Holding Company, but you showed me your stake in the
Western Minerals Exploration Company, which is a new
and entirely separate company set up to control only the
offshore diamond dredging. Now do you or don't you have
a stake in the Holding Company? Because it appears that
you've transferred all your assets to it."

There was no way out. The top business brains in Johannesburg could not get the uranium claims back.

Eventually Günter's lawyer persuaded Western Minerals
to hand over the other fifty percent of the Exploration
Company to Günter. He used the threat of prolonged legal
action, which Günter had no hope of winning, but which

everyone knew could prove severely embarrassing to McGregor in his bids to obtain more claims and bring in cash from overseas investors.

Günter took stock. He had his helicopter, an old jeep, five thousand pounds in the bank, the mining rights to most of the sea along the Skeleton Coast, but not enough cash to do anything about it. His Namib Mining and Minerals Company, which now had no assets at all, took over the bank account and the offshore dredging concessions. Just the sound of Western Minerals made him feel sick. Never again! Never again would he sign anything unless he had the best legal brains standing behind him, Günter swore. He had been defrauded of millions of dollars— worse, much worse, he reasoned, was years of grueling toil in the Namib—all wasted.

A telephone call to their Johannesburg office confirmed where Tex was—in the Namib, at the stolen uranium claims near Seal Bay.

Günter flew there the following morning. The desert was hidden in a thick mist and the ground was visible only eight meters before he landed.

Tex heard the helicopter and walked toward the sound of the engine. He heard the engine switched off and then Günter appeared through the mist.

As soon as Tex saw him he looked around for a weapon. There was an iron bar lying five meters away. Maybe he'd get it—if he was quick. It was worth a try. He went after it, bent double, hands outstretched, but he was too late.

Günter charged. His right fist lashed out at Tex's head. Tex ducked, but Günter's momentum sent his shoulder crashing into Tex's chest. They fell with flailing arms and legs into the yielding sand.

Günter caught the thick wrestler's neck between his hands and squeezed. Tex knew the score, knew he was fighting for his life. He knew the right moves, too, but it was like wrestling in water, his feet could get no support in the soft, shifting sand. Desperately he grabbed a handful of sand and flung it in Günter's face.

Günter laughed savagely. Tex was gasping for breath; his eyes bulging, his face turning blue. In a last effort to free himself he brought up the outside edges of both hands in a sharp swing, chopping Günter across both ears.

The pain was intense. For a brief moment Günter relaxed his grip.

Tex grabbed his hair, jerked his head aside and twisted free. He rolled to his feet and bent forward like a grizzly bear, trying to anticipate Günter's next move.

As Günter lunged in, Tex swung his heavy boot and caught him with a ferocious kick on the side of his jaw.

Günter's head snapped back and he sprawled on the sand and in a flash Tex leaped forward and kicked viciously at his body.

Günter grunted, but felt no pain. He caught the boot, flung the huge body sidelong and kicked out, knocking Tex's feet from under him.

They were both down, but Günter was first to his feet. Tex was built like a wrestler and solid muscle; Günter was untrained, but lighter and fitter. He knew he must rely on speed and endurance. Tire him out, he thought, circling Tex. Tire him out and go in for the kill when he's spent.

Already Tex was snorting and bellowing like a bull elephant. Suddenly he charged. Head down, arms thrashing.

Günter fell backwards in Tex's path, brought up his feet and sent Tex hurtling over his head, propelled by his own momentum. Tex landed on the side of a tall dune and suddenly he was scrambling up it, panting with the effort.

"Run, you bastard," Günter muttered. "Wear yourself out." Then he went after him.

Tex was halfway down the other side when Günter sprang and, with a roar, landed on Tex's back, propelling him down the slope. Then he grasped his hair and pushed his face deep into the sand.

Tex could not stop panting. He was filling his lungs with the quartz dust of the Namib. He could no longer see or hear, his eyes and ears were filled with sand. He was choking.

He struggled violently, tried to rise, but Günter shifted

up until his full weight was pressed on the back of Tex's neck.

Flailing the sand with his arms and legs, Tex tried to get one gasp of air. He failed.

Slowly his struggles quieted. He was half unconscious when Günter pulled his face out of the sand, hauled him to his feet and struck him with a savage jab which split Tex's nose wide open. A flood of blood and sand gushed from his nostrils.

He hauled him up again.

"Now you hear me good," Günter sobbed. His breath was coming in great painful gasps, his face contorted with rage and exhaustion. He backhanded Tex across the mouth and as he fell back caught him up again and held him swaying on his feet.

"I'm going to finish you one day. Don't think you've seen the last of me." Then he drove his fist like a giant piston into Tex's stomach.

Tex crumpled and lay on the sand retching.

"You pollute everything, you bastard, even the desert," Günter said, prodding him with his foot. Then he staggered back to the helicopter.

Chapter Forty-five

Günter left Swakopmund at dawn and flew low over the Namib, hugging the coast, although it was out of his way, because he wanted a last look at the sea—his sea—since he owned the offshore mineral rights from Walvis Bay to Alexander Bay.

Günter was impatient to start dredging for diamonds. He had found a way to do it; his technique was simple and economically feasible, but he needed more capital than he had. The answer, he knew, lay in coal. South Africa had limited resources and it was vital that new fields were found.

Besides, if he made his headquarters in Johannesburg he would be near Sylvia.

The next morning Günter felt apprehensive as he walked up the driveway to the small whitewashed cottage set under thatch. Bertha was not expecting him. He should have telephoned her, but somehow he couldn't bring himself to do so. He had not seen his daughter since she was a tiny baby at the Kalahari farm. Now she was seven and a half. Legally he had no claim on the child, although he never failed to send the monthly check for her support.

So much would depend on whether Sylvia liked him or not. He knew that. His mouth was dry and his palms were sweating.

Did she know she had a daddy? Did she know he cared and that he was always thinking of her?

Sylvia was playing on the grass with a puppy and she was beautiful. There was so much of Marika in her, and so much of him. Here was the living proof of their unforgettable night in the Namib. For that reason alone he would love this child with all his heart.

Suddenly two large violet eyes were regarding him curiously.

"You're not allowed here. You're tres . . . tres . . ." She frowned.

"Trespassing."

"That's right."

"No, I'm not. I came to talk to you, Sylvia." He sat on the grass beside her.

"How d'you know my name?"

"I know lots of things. I know your granny's name. It's Bertha."

"No," she said. "It's Boba." She smiled delightfully. "You don't know everything."

"Look," Günter said. "We've both got the same hair and the same-shaped eyes. You look very much like me."

Sylvia stood up and caught hold of his hair and examined it for a long time. Then she stepped back and stared hard at him while Günter stroked the puppy.

At that moment Bertha peered out of the window and recognized Günter. She almost ran out, but then she smiled and hung back.

"What's your puppy's name?" Günter asked.

"Pluto."

"And what's your daddy's name?"

She frowned. "You seem very silly to me," she said. "You should know what your name is."

"What makes you think I'm your daddy?"

"Because I've seen a picture of you, Boba's got one, and because Boba said you'd come one day, and because Mummy always says I've got your hair; and 'cause Boba says when we say our prayers, if we're good, God listens. I've been very good lately," she added.

"Why should you want a daddy, when you've got Boba?" he asked huskily, staring hard at the puppy.

"All little girls have daddies. I'm the only one in our class who doesn't have one." She looked away sadly.

"Well . . ." He did not know what to say. "Tell your friends that now you've got one."

He picked her up and hugged her.

"They wouldn't believe me," she said. "I often tell them that you've come. I say you're the biggest, most handsome and most clever daddy in the world. And that you took me up in your helicopter."

"Did Bertha tell you about the helicopter?"

"Yes. She reads me your letters when they come with the money you send me every month."

"I think it's time we took Bertha out for a really super treat. What do you think?"

"Can I come, too?"

"Of course you'll come, too."

"Would you take me to school on Monday? I want the girls to see I was telling the truth this time."

"Sure I will, honey."

"Do daddies always cry like this?" she asked. "Bertha told me grown-ups don't cry."

"Only when they're happy," he said.

*   *   *

Günter applied himself to his new ambitions with a thoroughness which defined all his actions. First step was to find a place to live which was close to Sylvia's school. When the time was ripe, Günter intended to persuade Bertha to bring Sylvia to live with him.

It did not take long to find a suitable plot in Bryanston. Four acres of wooded parkland with a tiny rondavel set on it; just one room with a kitchenette and shower built on. Without a house it was virtually unsalable, he reckoned, so he offered them half the asking price and obtained a ninety percent mortgage.

The next step was to transfer Namib Mining's bank account to Johannesburg.

From then on Günter worked all hours. He drove around remote farming areas prospecting the land and when he found promising signs of coal he bought up the farmer's mineral rights for a song. Next he developed the mine with the minimum labor, relying on his own energy and resources, and when he had proved the mine to be a viable proposition, he sold out to one or other of the large groups. His capital was doubled within a year and he was regaining confidence in himself.

Günter planned a huge party for his daughter's eighth birthday. As the time drew near Bertha was kept busy with the catering and Günter raced to finish the swimming pool he was building beside his rondavel. The class was invited to the party and Günter took the children on flights in his helicopter.

From then on, weekends and holidays were kept exclusively for his daughter. They went on camping trips and they slept in a tent in the bush and Günter taught her how to navigate by the stars, how to pick up the spoor of a jackal or a hyena, how to tell a rough diamond from a piece of glass, how to recognize minerals in the Namib, and a hundred other things for which she would never have any use, but which made her world sparkle.

In May, Bertha and Sylvia flew to London for a short holiday with Marika. Günter was filled with anxiety in case they did not return. But they did, at last. All the same, he could not help noticing that Sylvia seemed strangely remote. From then on she spent hours alone and even camping did not pull her out of her gloom.

Sylvia was worried. She had hardly seen her beautiful, dazzling mother during their brief holiday, for Marika had worked for much of the time and she had spent most evenings chatting with Bertha. Sylvia was only young, but instinctively she had sensed the effort it had taken Marika to spend a whole day on the beach at Brighton with her. Maybe her mother did not love her. This dismal thought preoccupied her for hours at a time and tormented her increasingly as the months passed.

Eventually Sylvia wrote to her mother, telling her about the party Günter was organizing for her ninth birthday and begging her to come. "Please fly over, Mummy, please do," she wrote. "I am so frightened because when I close my eyes to think about you I cannot remember what you look like."

Marika had telephoned to explain that she could not come. The plant only closed for ten days at the end of this year and she had to be back "on the road," as she put it, when the factory reopened. September was out of the question, she told Sylvia. It was her big selling time. But she would send a photograph—which she did.

Sylvia tore it up and buried it in the garden. She was too hurt to tell anyone and for a while Bertha thought she was sickening for something.

The following May, when Bertha and Sylvia flew to London again, Sylvia behaved badly and everyone was glad when the ten days were over. Bertha tried two more holidays, but eventually gave up trying to reconcile mother and daughter.

From then on, Sylvia lavished affection on a weird collection of pets: a bush baby, a meerkat and a three-legged tortoise as well as her beloved dog and cat. She would play at being "Mummy" fiercely and intently and the only time she became angry was when one of her precious pets was threatened.

Sylvia often spent the weekend with Günter, for Bertha
had started a one-man catering business which usually kept
her out late on weekends. "Business" was too grand a
title, she told Günter often enough, for she was hiring her
services as a kosher cook, except that she prepared most of
the food in her own home and transported it in her car.
Günter had grown extremely fond of Bertha; his parents
had died in the war and she was all the family he had. He
knew how lonely she had been and this business took her
out to meet people.

It was Günter's devotion to his daughter and Marika's
failure to visit Sylvia which finally persuaded Bertha to
move into the cottage which Günter had built for them in
his large garden. She reasoned that Sylvia should have a
strong bond with one of her parents. A granny wasn't
enough.

Günter took Sylvia with him on every holiday. School
holidays were spent prospecting in the Namib and hunting
for their food. Sometimes they went on expeditions to find
African art and the highlight of Sylvia's childhood was a
trip to the Kinshasa Forest in Central Africa for a Janus
headpiece used by the Ba-Bembe tribe which was very rare
and which her father coveted.

Bertha wondered angrily if Günter knew the difference
between a boy and a girl, for Sylvia wore jeans and
T-shirts and her hair was cut as short as a boy's. She never
loved the dolls Bertha kept buying, but she was the best
shot in the school, and she knew more about engines than
anyone else there.

Sylvia had one problem in her life and that was Claire.
Claire was a nurse at the Johannesburg hospital and it
seemed that she had known Dad and Boba for a long time,
for she was always arriving with gifts and pleas for Günter
to take her out somewhere or other. Sometimes she tagged
along with them when they went on expeditions and that
annoyed Sylvia. She liked to have her father to herself.
Sylvia considered Claire to be very thick-skinned. Anyone

could see Dad didn't really want her, but somehow she was always around.

On Sylvia's twelfth birthday, Günter took her and two close schoolmates to their Kalahari farm. They flew for hundreds of miles over the ocher sand and arrived at dusk. As the vlei at Camp XLII came into view Sylvia shrieked with excitement.

Over the following days they helped Günter to repair the camp and the huts and they cooked under the thatch roof. Günter showed them how to follow the spoor of animals and track game for their supper, told them the names of the many different wild birds and recounted old tribal stories to them when they sat round the campfire at night. He showed them the rondavel where Sylvia was born and where the Bushman woman nursed her until her mother was feeling well enough; and the place where the white Kalahari lions had frightened Marika.

That night in the camp bed in the hut, Sylvia tried to imagine her lovely mother coping with the farm, cooking food, loving them both. She had never understood the gulf between her parents, and while she tried to convince herself that it was modern and daring and terribly worldly to have parents who were not married, secretly it hurt her. Besides, she always sensed her father's sadness when he spoke about her mother and she loved her dad more than anyone in the whole world.

Why could her parents not be like other girls' parents and live in the same house and do ordinary, sensible things together? Worst of all was the annoying matter of names. All the girls knew her father was Günter Grieff and she was Sylvia Magos, so there was no point in making up stories. But she would console herself with the thought that her father was the most handsome man in the world and quite the best father a girl could have.

Chapter Forty-six

Marika was in a frenzy of impatience with the buttonholer, who seemed to be taking forever to finish the coat. Not just a coat, she thought proudly, a work of art—too good to be worn. Why, oh why did they always have to sell every damn thing?

It was of white fox, a long, shuddering sexy fur, with a tie collar to wind around the neck and fall over the shoulders. The line fell like an inverted V to just two inches above the kneecap. Why not, she reasoned, pacing up and down. This was an era for breaking fashion taboos, the era of the young. Youth was in, age was out, and if you had good legs—well, flaunt them.

It was ready at last. She grabbed the coat and raced to Mendel's office. He was crouched over the accounts, as usual.

"Look!" she said dramatically. She flung the coat over her shoulders.

Mendel looked at it and frowned. "Where's the bottom half?"

"Oh, come on, Mendel, don't be old-fashioned," she pouted.

"It's quite out of the question," Mendel said primly. "Knees are women's worst feature. If you don't believe me take a look in the mirror. Unladylike. No one would ever wear clothes that length."

She groaned. "Ladylike is a very unfashionable word this year, or hadn't you heard?"

He sighed, wondering how many pelts she had cut up. "Never forget the great classic outline," he said. "Then you won't go wrong—particularly with furs. Now unpick it. Oh and, Marika, be careful.'' He turned his attention to the books.

''I will not!'' The words came out like a whip crack. ''When will you learn, Mendel? It's the youth market we're after.''

Mendel put down his books and smiled at her. She was so impetuous. ''Aim for timelessness in furs. You can go a bit wild with your fabrics—not too often, mind you.''

''Timelessness!'' she screamed. ''Learn some new words, like sexy, dazzling, modern. Then you wouldn't have to spend so much time crying over the books.'' Mendel wasn't even listening. She rushed off in a rage.

It was an old argument. No one won, but at the same time, no one gave in.

She went home early, saying she had a headache. She knew she was sulking and she did not care. She took the coat with her in case Mendel should ask someone to unpick it. On impulse she turned off and drove toward the New Bond Street wholesale shop.

She would . . . yes, she would. The shop was closing and the manager was not pleased to see her.

''I'll miss my bus,'' she grumbled.

''You go,'' Marika told her. Half an hour later Marika locked the shop door and gazed happily at the window. Her coat was center stage and it looked even better there. Humming to herself, she drove off.

She felt tired and it was good to be home. She loved the little Finchley house, the comfortable confines of small rooms, cozy homemade touches, tiny plants in tiny pots— the wilderness was not for her. She cooked liver and bacon for supper, ate it while reading a novel. Then she put the book aside reluctantly and went to her drawing board.

That night she saw her future stretching ahead comfortably, predictably. She and Mendel, working hard together. They would prosper eventually and she would become famous.

It was 1 A.M. when the telephone rang. It was Mendel's housekeeper. Mendel had been taken ill and she had called the ambulance. Now he was in the intensive-care unit. It had been just after supper . . .

"Just tell me where he is," Marika interrupted her. She found it was hard to dress, her fingers were shaking so badly.

It was dawn before Mendel recovered consciousness. He was removed from intensive care and placed in a ward.

He smiled weakly and tried to hold her hand. It took a long time for him to move his.

"Just rest," she whispered.

Mendel looked up and saw her amber eyes looking sad and scared and he felt sorry for her.

"I'm sorry, Marika," he said. His voice was so weak she had to bend over him to hear what he was saying.

"Wish I could stick around a bit longer to help you."

"Mendel, stop it," she implored him. "You're talking yourself into . . . into being worse instead of better."

"All right . . . all right. It's just that I wanted to get it all tied up . . . nice and watertight . . . for you. Don't like to leave you in the lurch."

Marika stared hard at the wall, trying to ignore the painful lump in her throat.

At seven she kissed Mendel goodbye for the day and hurried to work. At ten the Bond Street shop telephoned to say they had a buyer for the new fox coat in the window and how much was it?

"Who cares? Who cares?" she muttered to herself.

At three, when she visited the hospital, Mendel was asleep. She sat there for a few hours and eventually left and looked in again in the morning, but he was still sleeping.

The nurse telephoned her at the plant that afternoon. "Mr. Sidersky is sinking," she said. "You're his closest friend. You'd best come."

She could not trust herself to drive; instead she called a taxi and left immediately.

Mendel was sleeping and he looked tired and maybe a little weak, but otherwise normal. They're making a mistake, she told herself. Hospitals make mistakes all the time. He'll be fine.

When the rabbi came, Marika glared at him defiantly. "He'll be fine when he's had a rest," she said.

The sound of the rabbi's prayer depressed her with its sense of sadness and finality, so she walked outside the ward to wait. People didn't just die—not young people. You couldn't call Mendel old, could you? People got shot, or murdered, or burned to death, or else they died of old age . . . didn't they? She felt so helpless and alone.

The rabbi left and Marika crept back to Mendel's bedside.

"Mendel, get better," she murmured urgently. "Get better, I need you."

After a while he opened his eyes and looked up at her and something about his face made her feel quite relieved. He looked happy; obviously he was getting better.

She held his hand and smiled confidently.

"Marika . . ." he whispered. "Marika . . ."

He fell asleep and she sat holding his hand for a long time, until the nurse came; the nurse ran to call the head nurse and the head nurse looked at Mendel sadly and told Marika that she must go now because Mendel was dead.

Chapter Forty-seven

Marika hardly knew what was happening in the dreary days that followed. She closed the plant for three days out of respect for Mendel, but they could not afford to shut down for longer. Soon after the funeral the will was read. Marika was Mendel's sole beneficiary and she inherited an insolvent business. Until this moment she had never understood the extent of Mendel's debts. For every asset there was a corresponding liability. The plant had operated on ninety-day credit lines from the fur traders and Mendel had always tried to get the pelts made up and sold in the minimum time. She could understand why. There were large overdrafts for both shops and neither made a profit. Worst of all, the factory operated on a fifty-thousand-pound trading overdraft—much of which had gone toward purchasing the new machinery when Mendel reestablished the manufacturing plant at the end of the war. Only Mendel's house in Hampstead was not mortgaged and he had transferred it to her name years before, without telling her.

Marika walked back to the factory, feeling confused, unhappy and very, very scared. How would she manage? How could she bear it there without Mendel's cheery voice to encourage her? How could anyone manage with these massive debts? She was too miserable and shocked to try to think. She would just try to exist, day by day, until she recovered, she decided.

It was Friday morning. Marika sent the messenger to the bank to collect the wages and he came back looking frightened, with a message to phone the bank manager.

The manager told her that Mendel's credit line was closed and the bank wanted immediate repayment of fifty thousand pounds or they would foreclose. There was a registered letter in the post to her, they explained. She had one month.

She was still reeling with shock when a supplier telephoned to say that her check had bounced. "I'm so sorry, but the bank closed our facilities when Mr. Sidersky died," she explained shakily. "Won't you give me a week or so to make other arrangements?"

"One week" was the angry reply. "Then I'm suing."

The pelt delivery was two days late. This had never happened before and their machines were standing idle. When Marika called to complain, the foreman sounded embarrassed.

"I've been told it's cash on delivery," he said.

Marika tried to control her shaking voice and demanded to speak to the general manager, but she was transferred to a credit clerk.

"We cannot extend Mr. Sidersky's line of credit to you." The clerk sounded triumphant, as if she seldom had the chance to throw her weight around. "If you need credit, fill in our form and mail it back. Your application will be considered in the normal manner."

Marika raced around, filled in the form and explained the urgency of the matter, but when she called back two hours later she was told that her financial position was not sufficiently viable to warrant credit.

Now she was badly frightened. Sadly she gathered the staff in her office and explained why she was unable to pay them, but promised she would withdraw her savings first thing in the morning . . . if they would kindly come in at ten.

They all knew the score because the messenger boy had spread the news. Nevertheless, this had never happened before and Marika knew she had failed them. Then she noticed Tanya hanging around and she wondered why. She probably wanted to give notice; Marika could hardly blame her.

"What is it, Tanya?" Marika asked. The woman did not appear to know how to begin.

Tanya looked hesitant, her gray eyes glittering with the effort. "I've never really liked you, Miss Magos," she began hesitantly.

"Oh, I know that, Tanya," Marika said. She glowered at the girl. What a time to pick a fight.

"I always thought you were too hard, you see. Pushy! Far too pushy for Mr. Sidersky, but over the years I've learned to admire you," she said, ignoring the interruption. "You're a survivor. I'm going to put my money on you—if you want it, that is."

Marika leaned back with her mouth open.

"Well . . . I . . . really don't think so," she said. "It's extraordinarily kind of you . . . but really . . . I don't want you to spread gloom . . . but we don't have much chance of pulling through and I couldn't let you waste your money."

"I'm putting my money on you, Miss Magos. I'd back you against any odds."

Marika turned away, feeling quite overcome and unable to speak. "All right," she mumbled. "If you really feel that way."

"I don't know how much I'll have. I'm mortgaging the house my mother left me. Then there's my savings. You can count on about ten thousand pounds. I was hoping for fifteen percent."

Of course, Marika thought, what a clever idea. She would apply for a mortgage on Mendel's house first thing in the morning.

"I took the names of the staff who can manage without their wages for a couple of weeks. Of course, they'd want the money back when you get fixed up at the bank."

"Of course," Marika repeated, trying not to show how emotional she felt about this strange declaration of loyalty from someone who she had thought was her enemy.

"There's one or two who are dissatisfied and you probably won't see them, come Monday morning. You're better off without them," she went on hurriedly. "Well, that's settled, Miss Magos, is it?"

"Since we're partners, don't you think you should call me Marika?" She tried out a shaky smile.

On Monday morning half the staff did not come to work, including Mrs. Hanson, the supervisor. Tanya was put in her place and she hunted around for good machinists to fill the gaps.

By ten, Marika was talking to Mendel's lawyer. "Can you buy me time?" she demanded. "Keep the bank off my back for a year or more? Give me a chance to clear off the debts?"

He laughed drily. "Dear lady," he said. "You'd be crazy to try. Mendel was a gambler; he was going for bigger stakes, mass production, but he needed more time. Unfortunately the worry hastened his death.

"My advice to you is: Go bust! I'll handle everything

for you. We'll get a friendly liquidator and you won't feel a thing."

Marika leaned back and waited for the lawyer to stop talking. How could she give up? She must become rich! Without money, nothing was possible. There was Sylvia to think about. She was longing to bring her daughter back, but to do this she must employ a nanny. Never again would she endure the guilt of neglecting her child. She must pay Greenstein, too—more money—much more money—how else could she persuade him to put more agents onto her search? Give up? Well, it was good advice—if she were free . . . if she could afford to live a normal life like any other woman . . . if . . .

"I'm not giving in," she said eventually, trying to stop her voice from quaking. "I'm mortgaging the house for working capital. How long can you keep the bank off my back?"

"I've no idea. I can only try my best. There's any number of matters we can dispute. For one thing . . ."

"I don't want to know," she snarled. "Just do it."

That week Marika raised a loan on the security of the Hampstead house. She opened an account with another bank. Then she went to the fur traders and paid cash for her pelts.

She was back in business.

A month later she sat at her desk poring over the figures and feeling depressed. Since Mendel's death hardly any orders had come in. The machinists were working part-time and the amount of business the factory was doing would not cover their overhead, let alone pay back the debts.

She called Tanya into her office. "Would you be prepared to go to night school and study management techniques, personnel and cost control—learn to run this plant in the daytime, while I'm out selling?" she asked.

Tanya's eyes glittered with joy. She almost smiled. "Try me," she said.

*   *   *

Marika sold the company car and bought a secondhand van, which she had redecorated in pale gray with silver writing almost exactly like the labels she had designed so long ago. Inside, her latest garments were hanging from movable racks. She had a list of past customers and she intended to show her furs to every one of them.

It took her a long time to pluck up courage to make her first call. She sat outside in her van longing for the warmth and security of her office and drawing board. Eventually she walked in quaking, but she walked out with an order.

During the next four years Marika became a wizard at selling, but she never came to like it. She traveled the length and breadth of Britain, driving at all hours and in all weather, not getting enough to eat or to sleep. She knew all her customers by their first names, and all their problems. Gradually she whittled out the competition and gained a growing share of the fur market. Then she gate-crashed the department stores. It was a tough life, but by the end of her first year orders were rolling in and they had to increase production facilities. They were still poised between profit and loss, but at least they weren't losing. By the end of the second year she had repaid some of her debts and from then on her hard work began to show a profit. Two years later she had ten thousand pounds saved. Strictly speaking, it was not her money, but the bank's. Marika was keeping it aside while she considered her alternatives. There was so much she could do with it: the machines needed replacing, the factory needed redecorating, Tanya needed an assistant and a holiday, while she needed a new van. Worse still, the bank would like the overdraft repaid. She sighed.

She had to admit that Mendel had been right. Mass production! That was the only way to get rich.

Chapter Forty-eight

It was a lovely June morning, with a hint of a breeze and small, puffy cumulus clouds were sailing gaily across the sky.

Marika asked the messenger to pack the sample line, but when she climbed behind the steering wheel she found she simply could not face it. "No," she said aloud. "I've lived in this van for four years. That's enough punishment."

The next morning she drove to the West End to see John Sidwell, public relations officer and management consultant. He had been recommended by a friend, but watching him now, she felt doubtful.

John Sidwell was tall and bookish-looking, perhaps because of his horn-rimmed glasses and pointed nose; his mouth was too small and he had a habit of puckering it like a maiden aunt; his eyes were gray, his hair sandy-colored and thinning, but it was his arrogant expression which irritated her the most.

She introduced herself hurriedly. "I want you to make me famous," she said before she had sat down.

He stared at her with a glimmer of a smile.

"And how long do I have?"

"A year," she said.

"I'll have to see your work," he went on arrogantly. "If I decide to take you on, it will be a thousand pounds a month in advance for the first six months; incidental expenses are payable on invoice."

"I don't think I can afford you," she moaned. "I was thinking in terms of a few hundred pounds—at the most."

"I can see how much you need me," he said infuriatingly. "Let's go!"

*　　*　　*

Marika could not sleep that night. She worried about money, and about Sylvia and Bertha and whether she was sending them enough each month and how long it would take her to become rich and bring them back to London. Then she worried about Greenstein and why he was taking so long to unearth her father's murderer. Was he really trying? she wondered. After this she worried about Tanya and what would happen to the business now that she had taken their hard-earned savings and squandered it. Finally she worried about that arrogant man with the mean eyes.

Eventually she gave up trying to sleep and made some coffee. "Marika Magos, you've done the right thing," she told herself. "If you want to get on you must be famous. Then the orders flow in, the credit flows in and down goes the red carpet."

Next morning she arrived at the factory earlier than usual, but John was there and Tanya was looking peeved.

Marika called her aside. "Tanya, I've blown half our cash on John Sidwell. He's a management consultant," she explained sorrowfully. "Please cooperate."

"Just keep him out of my hair," Tanya muttered.

John worked out a better layout for the plant and Tanya fought bitterly over it. John won.

"When did you last show a collection?" John asked Marika.

"Not since Mendel died. There's no point, because I visit our customers regularly and show them everything. Nowadays I spend most of my time on the road," she explained.

His probing gray eyes scanned her face. "It shows," he said eventually. Then he left.

At noon the telephone rang. It was the manager of the New Bond Street shop. She was almost hysterical with rage because John had given her two months' notice and there were signwriters painting over the Sidersky sign.

Marika raced round in time to see *Marika Magos* go up in silver lights.

"I couldn't possibly allow . . ." Marika stammered, and shook she was so angry. She tried to explain that she had loved Mendel and his name must stay. Furthermore, it was unthinkable to sack someone who had been employed by Mendel.

"It's a tough world," John agreed.

That was the sentence that he fell back on increasingly in the weeks ahead. Marika was by turns annoyed, bewildered, furious and sad, but she was impressed all of the time.

Marika was installed in the New Bond Street shop together with her design equipment and John found an eager young salesman to take over.

"You'll find the customers will come to you now," he said. "And you can receive them in style here. When you're not selling—design."

"I do my designing at night," she told him.

"Nights are for getting famous," he retorted.

From then on John organized a whirl of first nights, operas, parties, film debuts, press conferences and interviews with journalists from the fashion press. In September, Marika appeared on television.

The program was an in-depth study of women in the next decade—the sixties—and she appeared with a panel of experts in various fields. Marika made sweeping statements such as: "Fashion must typify women's new energy and furious pace," and "Romantic heroines and society leaders are out," and "I want to let some fresh air in to the rarefied atmosphere of fashion."

The orders began rolling in, but there was no cash for expansion. She must have credit, Marika knew. How else could she afford the pelts to make up all these new orders?

So, cap in hand, she contacted the fur traders again and this time she managed to obtain an appointment with the general manager.

"My dear young lady," he said, pouring coffee from the company's best silver service. "It's the first time in my memory that a designer of your talents has made such imaginative and versatile use of furs. I see your face in the newspapers nearly every day.''

''I'm expanding, that's true,'' she admitted with a winning smile. ''But I need a bigger credit line.'' She took a deep breath. ''I'd like to have the same line of credit Sidersky's used to have here.''

''Well, naturally,'' he said before she could continue. ''Just tell us your requirements. Don't worry about filling in forms. Your name is very highly thought of here.''

Feeling dazed, Marika shook hands and swept out.

At the end of the year she paid a surprise visit to John's office. ''You're lucky to catch me in,'' he said. ''Safer to make an appointment.''

''The year's over, John,'' she said. ''You made it. Now I'd like a complete statement of account.''

''How about starting again. How about: 'Good morning, John, how're you keeping?' I'm not sure I'm ever going to teach you anything.''

She grinned. ''Now about that statement.''

''Take my advice. Don't ask.''

She sat down and took off her gloves. ''When you first asked me for more than half of all I owned, I felt I might have been taken. I didn't sleep nights. Lately I'm worrying about how much I still owe you.''

He leaned back and smiled.

''So we're famous enough now, are we?''

''Enough for the time being,'' she said. ''Enough for what I want to do.''

''Which is?''

''Franchise my name and my fashions around England. The Bournemouth shop is doing marvelously. I want to sell seventy-five percent of it and maintain quality control and of course my name. Fifty percent of their stock must be my furs.''

He looked startled and she laughed.

''I often wondered what you were after. For some reason I didn't figure that one out. Silly of me,'' he said.

''If it works in Bournemouth I want to franchise my name all over England,'' she said modestly. ''Would you like the job of selling it? After all, I'm your only client just now.''

"You've been doing some homework," he said.

She smiled. "Ten percent," she said.

For a moment he stared at her shrewdly. "It would have to be handled right," he said. "If I went into your business full-time you'd have to promise to show a collection twice a year. To succeed you need more publicity—much more."

She frowned. She had not shown a collection since Mendel died. She knew she should, but it was safer to show her fashions privately, toting them from shop to shop. This gave her the chance to make changes and adjustments as the comments and sales came in. She dreaded the instantaneous and public verdict which followed the launch of a collection. Overnight the fashion press could ruin her. Then she shrugged. "I had to start sometime," she said.

Chapter Forty-nine

Marika returned to the drawing board and attempted the near-impossible task of squeezing some creativity from herself. Day after day she spent hours sketching, but all her work was discarded the following morning. She was badly in need of inspiration, but she felt empty. She became more and more despondent. So much would depend upon this collection.

Her fashions must be an encapsulation of the times. She must express the aspirations of a woman who rose at six to send her children to school and then competed in a man's world. Woman's surge into the world of business was still in its infancy—women were feeling their way—the right clothes could mean so much to them—or so Marika reasoned.

But how? She lost weight, became haggard and bad-tempered, but still her collection did not hang together.

Then one night, when she was tired and not even thinking much, but doodling, her subconscious took over. She sketched sculptured dresses worn to the knee—modest and smart with snug shoulders, hip-fitting, and wildly extravagant collars, cuffs, and trim. The look was bold and adventurous—a real space-age collection worn with pop art costume jewelry. The furs were new and different, too, smartly exaggerated, shorter; furs for having fun. The whole collection was exciting, daring, new.

When she showed John the sketches a week later, he became madly excited and hired an advertising agency to create a space-age backdrop for the stage and rig up some fancy lighting. The models would descend in a flying saucer made of aluminum tubular frames covered with foil, he decided, and pour out onto the stage.

Everyone was worried because there was so little time left. The cutters, pattern makers, furriers, machinists, buttonholers, embroiderers all worked day and night and their house models were permanently on call. The last trim on the last garment was still being stitched as the flying saucer descended to the wonder of the audience, who broke into delighted clapping.

John had employed dancers instead of models and they were backed by modern pop music and free-and-easy intermingling with the audience. The press had turned out in force and cameras were clicking. Marika could see they were all delighted.

"This is the start of the swinging sixties," Marika said at the very beginning of the show. "Haughty couture is out. Today's fashions must be designed for women on the move. Women are in the limelight and facing up to it beautifully, but they need the right clothes, clothes that move, clothes that can stand up to a busy day in the office and dinner afterward."

The show moved with a swing—with clapping, astonished gasps and even some cheers from the audience.

The next morning rave notices appeared in every daily: "Ravishingly unpredictable." "Enormously stylish." "There is a candid quality about Magos' clothes which wins through every time." "Impeccable, glittering, wonderful!" "The way every woman wants to look . . . snap, crackle and glitter in the Magos range."

At last Marika Magos had been acclaimed Britain's leading designer.

Chapter Fifty

The Bournemouth franchise was quickly sold and proved successful. Retailers in London, Edinburgh, Glasgow and Torquay followed their lead immediately afterward. Within a year John had added six more retail shops to the Marika Magos franchise and he had contracted a factory in Rome to make Marika Magos fashions under license.

At the end of the following year Marika engaged a financial director. A wizard of a man who quickly sorted the complicated list of debtors and creditors which had become a nightmare for Marika.

"Am I solvent yet?" she wanted to know.

"Depends how you look at it," he said. "On paper you're a millionaire. How does that feel?"

"Penniless," she answered truthfully.

"You have assets in the form of twenty-five percent of ten furriers, you have the New Bond Street wholesale shop and the mortgage is now paid off, you have the plant and machinery—you also have some outstanding loans. Nevertheless, the money's beginning to come in faster than it goes out. In two or three years' time you'll be a very wealthy woman, but remember this, Marika: You're not designing only for your own company, but for very many others. You're on a treadmill. In the fashion world—you must keep ahead.''

She shrugged. She had always been on a treadmill. Now, at last, it was going to pay off. She did not feel particularly pleased about the accounts. Success was only a small part of her ambition. Her real target was as unattainable as it had ever been.

John decided that Marika was the company's most valuable asset and he insured her against every conceivable mishap. Then he engaged three top designers to assist her.

Marika had always worked alone and she did not know how to cope with a team. Her life became a blur of work and three months after showing her collection she collapsed and was taken to the hospital. The press reports said she was suffering from overwork, but Marika knew that this was not true. It was guilt which was sapping her strength and her morale.

She threw a tantrum and left the hospital without her doctor's permission and, summoning a taxi, went straight to Greenstein's office.

Little had changed, she thought as she climbed the rickety wooden stairs. Greenstein was in and he looked surprised to see her. She could not help noticing how old he looked.

''Lately I spend more time in the office and leave the youngsters to do the legwork,'' he told her. ''Nevertheless, it's best to telephone first.''

Marika nodded, unwilling to waste time. ''I had to see you,'' she said. ''I'm going crazy. All this money—all this fame—and it was all made for a purpose. I have the money, but Geissler's still free. I can't take it. You've got to do something.''

She leaned back and took a deep breath. She was still paying fifteen percent of her income to Greenstein's agency, but there had been no further news of Geissler since the first doubtful report that he was still alive. Sometimes Marika felt she would go mad with all this waiting. She tried to explain this to Greenstein. "I'm going to increase my monthly stop order," she told him.

"My dear, all the money in the world is not going to find Geissler for you. We need luck—or perhaps he's dead," he told her. "Sometimes I wonder if what I'm doing is right. Do you know what Churchill said at the end of the war?" He quoted mournfully: " 'Revenge is, of all satisfactions, the most costly and long-drawn-out; retributive persecution is, of all policies, the most pernicious.' " He sighed. "War crimes! I've come to the conclusion that all war is a crime and both sides are equally guilty."

Marika flared up in sudden anger. "You have a responsibility—to all of us who've trusted you—and paid you. You can't give up. Try harder!" She insisted on trebling her donation and eventually Greenstein gave in and promised to put more agents on the job of tracking Geissler.

"Maybe you're right. Perhaps I'm getting old," he said.

The knowledge that there was a network of agents working in Europe and South America with Geissler as their number one target made her feel a little more confident of her eventual success, but to her surprise that did not make her any happier. She was plagued with a feeling of emptiness and she spent hours worrying about the absurdity of existence. "What's it all about?" she asked herself night after night.

In her career, Marika was right at the pinnacle, but as a mother and a woman, she had failed dismally, she knew. She had been only too happy to leave Sylvia with Bertha. Now, for the first time, she began to question her motives. Was it for Sylvia or for her own well-being that she had sent her child away?

Marika was an honest woman and, looking back, she had to admit that maternal love had been pushed into second place by the hatred that had motivated her and propelled her to the top.

Perhaps it was not too late to try again, she reasoned.

Chapter Fifty-one

It was an unusually clear winter's day and Marika could see the snow-clad Alps glistening thirty thousand feet below from the first-class compartment of the BOAC airliner.

She leaned back and closed her eyes and tried not to worry. Marika had not seen Bertha or her daughter for over two years and she was ashamed. This was a journey she had put off for far too long and she was frightened, too. For the first time in months she allowed herself to think about her daughter as she had last seen her. It was hurtful. Why, oh why do I have this terrible ability to block out people who are close and dear to me? she wondered.

Her introspection was interrupted when they landed in Johannesburg at eight in time to catch her connecting flight to Lüderitz, where the family was vacationing with Günter.

The flight was a tourist's dream and several foreigners were enthralled as the pilot flew low over the sand dunes. They saw gemsbok fleeing before the plane's shadow and they drooled over the beauty of the Namib, the space, the uniqueness of it all. Marika was not impressed and closed her eyes until they landed on a wide plateau of sand.

There was a gale blowing as Marika hurried down the gangway to the Volkswagen van and in spite of her scarf and sunglasses her face was stinging with sand by the time she reached the safety of the bus.

There was only one hotel in Lüderitz. Marika had arranged with Bertha that she would arrive sometime during the week and give Günter and Sylvia a surprise.

"They're here today, I assume?" she asked the receptionist. "Where else could they go in a sandstorm?"

"Mrs. Factor and her granddaughter are here. Mr. Grieff is at sea," the receptionist said, eyeing her curiously.

When she stood outside Bertha's door she could hardly stand the suspense. Would she be welcome?

Then the door was opened and a moment later she was clasped in Bertha's arms.

"Marikala. Oh, how wonderful to see you—I was so worried about your flight in this terrible gale." Soon she was dabbing her eyes and drying her glasses, which had steamed up.

Sylvia hung back, looking furious, but Marika was so happy to see her. How tall she had grown . . . good heavens, at fourteen she was nearly as tall as her mother. Marika held her daughter at arm's length and studied her. Her features were almost perfect, yet there was so much of Günter in her wide brow, her hair and her wide-set eyes. But Marika could see herself, too. Sylvia had her white skin and her small nose. Thank heavens she hadn't inherited Günter's nose.

"Don't I get a hug?" she asked, and the girl hugged her reluctantly.

"She's a real beauty." She smiled over Sylvia's shoulder at Bertha.

Bertha snorted. "For all the good that may do her," she said tartly. "It didn't do you much good, my girl."

Marika smiled and released Sylvia.

"You knew," the girl said accusingly to Bertha.

"It was a surprise for you," Bertha said, and gazed compassionately at her granddaughter. "Your mother's been missing you so much."

Something was wrong, Marika knew. It was not just her arrival that had brought such an anxious expression to her daughter's face. Sylvia had walked back to the window, and she was standing there twisting her hands, her eyes glittering with alarm. Then she turned abruptly and rushed out of the room, slamming the door.

"Sylvia's upset," Bertha explained. "We're supposed to be here on holiday, but the day before we arrived one of Günter's divers was lost at sea. Now he won't let anyone down but himself. He says he's got to prove it's viable. You know what Günter's like. At first he took Sylvia out on the boat with him, but she worried too much and caused a scene, so now he won't take her."

"Well, let's forget Günter for a few minutes," Marika said. She put her arms around Bertha and gave her a hug. "It's good to see you. I've missed you—and Sylvia. Terribly!"

"Wouldn't have thought you'd have time to miss anyone," Bertha said, but she looked pleased all the same.

"I think I'd better go and find my daughter," she said eventually, feeling confident and happy. After all, the battle was half won.

Sylvia was in her room gazing out to sea. She hardly bothered to look at the presents her mother had brought her. "Since you're here," she said quietly as if trying to control her emotions, "perhaps you could talk some sense into Dad. He'll be killed out there."

"He's a wonderful swimmer," Marika said. "Don't you want to look at your presents?"

Sylvia turned away.

"All right," Marika said. "I'll go and talk to him—if that's what you want."

Give her time, Marika thought. She felt confident she would win her daughter back eventually.

Chapter Fifty-two

When the launch left the calm bay and roared out to the open sea Marika realized she had made a mistake and if it weren't for Sylvia she would have turned back.

Huge waves rolled implacably toward the shore, smashing the towering cliffs of sand. The heat was oppressive and burned her skin through the plastic raincoat she had borrowed from Bertha. Her senses reeled from the heat and the sudden contrast of icy salt spray.

She was scared. One moment the boat was poised on a mountain of water, their outboard engine whirling uselessly in the air, and a moment later they were plunged down into a deep green trough which threatened to engulf them.

Suddenly the engine was silenced. They were rocking over the swell. She plucked up courage to open her eyes and saw Günter's fishing boat tossing like a cork in front of them.

"We'll circle and wait for a drop in the wind, then come up from the stern," the boatman said.

Then there was a sudden lull. The boatman expertly maneuvered them under the stern and a moment later she was climbing the rope ladder. Strong arms grasped her and hauled her painfully over the side.

"What the hell are you doing here, lady?" It was a strong midwestern accent and Marika looked up into eyes of green and carroty hair. This must be Günter's skipper, Tom.

"I'm a friend of Günter's," she said. "Where is he?"

He pointed his thumb to the seabed.

"You planning on staying here?" Tom asked curiously as she shook her wet hair in the wind.

"I came to see Günter," she said. "Call him up."

"Just like that?"

"Please call him up." She tried to dazzle him with a smile.

"Ma'am, if you knew him as well as I do you'd wait until he's ready," the skipper said harshly, and turned away.

Marika felt amused. So Günter had a reputation with his colleagues. She wondered if he had changed much in the past seven years. To while away the time she examined the operation.

The boat was a converted fishing vessel, a sixty-footer, with the usual mainmast and foremast, but toward the stern was a vacuum pump and from here a wide plastic suction

hose led over the side of the boat and down to the sea.
Presumably Günter was hanging on to the end of it trying
to vacuum the entire seabed. Well, that was Günter for
you. She smiled to herself.

In the center of the deck among the wire rigging was a
complicated structure containing three wire grids, one beneath the other, with the finer mesh at the bottom. Salt
water was gushing from the pump through the grids, washing the debris caught in the wire and sending the ooze
flooding over the deck and back to the sea.

It's so simple it's brilliant, she thought, watching the
rocks and shells being washed clean.

"Those diamonds?" she asked the skipper.

"Maybe."

She reached forward and took one. "This is," she
exclaimed in delight.

The skipper grabbed it and put it in the chamois bag
dangling from his belt.

"How many d'you reckon on finding a day?" she yelled
above the roar of the wind.

He shrugged. "Varies," he said noncommittally, obviously unwilling to give her any information.

After this he ignored her, so she sat in the stern and
tried to dry her clothes.

Later she felt the boat shudder and sway, out of tempo
with the rise and fall of the swell.

Tom jerked his thumb over his shoulder. "Günter's
coming."

A few seconds later Günter climbed over the side.

Marika gasped and bit her lip. The black rubber wet suit
accentuated his wide shoulders and height. He was massive, she thought. She felt intimidated and wished she had
not come. This was Günter's territory.

Then she saw how tired he was. He stripped off his gear
in slow, jerky movements and dumped the equipment on
the deck. He looked much older than she remembered, but
magnificent all the same. She could not look away from
his muscular, suntanned body as he stripped off his gear.
He was tougher, leaner, stronger. Age suits him, she

thought. He'll go on looking better and better. Watching him made the blood surge through her body.

Then he saw her.

His face changed; a look of infinite tenderness softened the harsh lines, made his eyes glow, while his sensuous mouth turned up at the corners in a grin.

"Hi," he said. "Nice surprise." His voice was husky. Then he cleared his throat.

Marika had her speech ready. He must return at once and stop frightening Bertha and Sylvia. She wanted to say this, but her mouth dried and she could not speak.

"Hi," she croaked.

The next moment she was grabbed off her feet, whirled around the deck and pressed against his body. She felt the leanness of him, the hardness. God, he was like steel, she thought, running her hands over his back. Then she forgot everything except the proximity of Günter and how much she loved him.

By sunset the gale had dropped and Günter, who had insisted on working another shift underwater, was sprawled on the deck dressed in an old pair of trousers and a polo-neck sweater, drinking beer, with Marika stretched out beside him on a rug.

"Look over there." He passed her the binoculars. "There's an old abandoned mining camp built by the first miners to come here. There's the cemetery. Most of them died of thirst or hunger. Still, in a way I envy them. No concessions in those days, no limitations, a man was free to go where he liked and what he found was his."

"And free to die," she said icily, "which is what will happen to you here, if you're not careful." She shuddered.

He turned. His penetrating blue eyes stared into hers. "Would you care?" he asked.

"Sylvia would be desolate."

Slowly his big hand slid over hers and clasped her tightly. "You care," he insisted. "You always have, but you won't admit it, not even to yourself."

She laughed shakily, only too aware of him pushed hard against her side. She felt frightened here, particularly as dusk set in, and Günter seemed inviolable, a haven of refuge, indestructible.

She felt herself clinging to him, shuddering.

Soon it was dark, with only an occasional flash of fluorescence as the boat disturbed the water.

Marika felt herself losing control, slipping away, falling hopelessly into a state of desire where she could think of nothing but the nearness of Günter and the need to be impaled upon his hard, strong body. Her face was burning, her skin felt cracked and hot. She moved her head a few more inches toward his, her mouth feeling for his in the dark, tasting the saltiness of his skin, the softness of his lips and his tongue. At that moment there was nothing else but Günter in the world. She moved restlessly toward him.

"I'll take you to the cabin." His voice was hoarse. Unrecognizable!

Fleetingly she thought of Tom and the deckhands; as quickly she dismissed them. Only Günter! Nothing else counted. Only him and her need, which was so strong she could make love here, on the deck, without caring.

She would never forget that night, squashed with Günter on the comfortable old bunk with the eiderdown that reeked of oil and fresh sea air.

He loved her frantically at first, throwing her on the bunk, pulling her clothes off with clumsy fumbling movements and thrusting deep inside her, while his fingers dug into her shoulders and his body pummeled hers and she felt him throbbing with passion, exploding too soon, leaving her still craving the thrust and pull of him.

"Oh God, Marika, keep still," he murmured. "Just wait a minute." He lay inside her, his face two inches from hers, gently kissing her cheeks with moist, sensuous lips.

He nuzzled his lips in her hair, her ear, her neck. The delicious, never-forgotten smell of him was overpowering. She burst into harsh, wracking sobs, crying out her loneliness and her need into Günter's shoulder.

Why was she crying? Günter wondered. Why was it

necessary for her to punish herself and him, too? All these wasted years. But he did not want to waste the night, now that he had her once again.

He knew Tom well enough. He would take the boat out to circle the bay indefinitely. Well, he'd do the same for him.

He pushed himself up on his feet and hands in the narrow bunk.

"Where are you going?" she murmured, disappointed and cross.

"To light the lantern. I want to look at you." He lit a match and put it to the wick of the storm lantern hanging overhead. It flared briefly and then steadied, swaying to and fro to the motion of the ship.

Then he sat on the edge of the bunk and stared at her.

"Come," she said. "I want you here. Come back."

"Marika . . ."

"Shh." She reached up and laid her fingers over his lips. "Don't let's spoil it."

Whenever he saw the statuesque, untamed beauty of her naked body it took his breath away. Inexorably female, there was something debauched about her when she let herself go. All the bravado, all the coldness melted. Then she seized sex and bit into it with concentration, like a starving man at a crust of bread. At that moment, he knew, only lust was filling that beautiful head. She was brimming over with it, he could see from the pallor of her face, the swollen red lips, her eyes half closed voluptuously.

He crouched beside her and began to run his lips over her shoulder, over her face, softly, gently, moving down the curve of her breasts and her belly.

She groaned softly and dug her nails into his shoulder. "Fuck me," she commanded.

"Wait." He bent over swiftly, plunged his face into her soft and secret places, his tongue seeking, probing teasingly. She was all woman, he thought, feeling his own passion in his bloodstream again; his skin was goose-pimpled, the hairs on his arms erect.

"Oh, you must, you must," she whispered, but still he would not.

Marika lay with her eyes screwed tightly shut. Intolerable need filled her; she could scream, she could bury her face in the bunk and cry out her need, she would . . . she would . . . soon . . .

She sat up angrily, her face swollen and red, and grasped Günter's neck, using all her strength to pull him on top of her.

"Now . . ." she commanded. "Now . . . do it . . . do it . . ."

Then she was rising and falling with the gentle movement of his passion. She was one with him, she felt united, feeling as he felt, knowing the throb and ebb of his passion.

Arms locked around each other, legs entwined, they thrashed the bunk, churned the eiderdown, came together and then lay, wet body against wet body, feeling at peace for one brief ecstatic night.

At dawn the boat chugged into Lüderitz harbor.

"We must talk . . ." Günter began.

She shook her head.

He was losing her again. She had withdrawn into that secret world of her own, her emotions neatly packed back into the isolation ward where she kept them out of the way of harmful germs and nasty Germans.

He felt bitter and regretful, hungry for another night . . . and another.

"Haven't you punished me enough? Fifteen years! That's a life sentence."

"I'm not punishing anyone," she answered sulkily.

Günter stared at her long and hopelessly. Could she not grasp that she was using him to get back at the entire German nation? And why could she not see that the real victim of her spite was herself? No, he could tell by her face that she was not open to reason. He turned and went quietly up on deck.

Chapter Fifty-three

It was Sunday morning and the hotel was sleeping, bathed in the morning sea fog. Marika did not want to wake Bertha and Sylvia when she returned, so she crept into her bedroom and fell asleep.

She woke much later and went to find her family. Bertha and Sylvia were sitting on the balcony gazing out to sea; Sylvia's angry eyes told her that Günter had gone diving again.

"Your father is a magnificent swimmer," she told Sylvia. "I told you that yesterday. And besides, he's as fit as a man could be. You're making yourself unhappy for nothing. He'll never give in. You should know him by now."

"But it's Sunday," Sylvia complained. "None of the divers are out, so why should Dad go?"

Marika looked questioningly at Bertha, who nodded toward the sea. "Look! It's as calm as a lake today. I have no doubt that Günter's searching around the rocks for the body of his diver. He's been fretting for calm weather. If he waits until tomorrow the gale might get up again."

Half a mile out to sea, at a depth of six fathoms, Günter was feeling his way through a treacherous underworld of razor-sharp rocks and dangerous currents. Shining his flashlight into the murky depths, he was searching for a place where a body could lie trapped, wedged in crevices or tangled in seaweed.

Visibility was less than two meters in this muddy region where even the slightest swell disturbed the ooze and great fronds of seaweed tall as trees hid the sunlight. Ahead he saw a gaping black hole and dived toward it. As he approached the cave his flashlight beam encountered a sudden prismatic gleam of color and he twisted around and down.

As he did so he felt a stunning thud on his shoulder as a gigantic black shape soared past, dragging him behind in its wake. Shark! For a split second he was paralyzed with shock at the realization of his miraculous escape. Then he reached out and grabbed the nearest rocky ledge and hung on as the shark circled and disappeared into the gloom.

When it attacked it was with the speed and strength of a torpedo. Günter ducked and his hands shot up with all his strength, thrusting the knife into the shark's belly. He hung on, degutting the fish as he was dragged through the water. Then the threshing ceased and the shark turned belly up and drifted toward the surface. Günter stuck his knife into his belt, grabbed his flashlight and swam back toward the cave, looking for that strange brilliant gleam that had saved his life.

He found a rough diamond, as big as an egg, wedged into a crevice. It took a long time to prize it out and as he worked he wondered at the strange chance which had saved his life and shown him the diamond. Perhaps it had lain there for thousands of years.

An hour later, Günter gave up the search for the diver's body and swam back to his dinghy.

Breathlessly he examined his find. For a while he was too shocked to think, but eventually he pulled himself together. He reckoned he was holding at least ten million pounds in the palm of his hand. The diamond was huge, a thousand carats at least. He wondered how it would take to cutting. Even uncut it was worth a fortune, one of the world's great treasures. And it was his!

The next day Günter sent the divers back to work. He was too excited to work and he wanted to spend some time with his family. They wandered around the old ghost town and the whaling station and then they explored the Fish River Canyon in Günter's helicopter. He did not tell them about the diamond.

It was bliss, Marika decided, watching father and daughter together. At first she had tried to pretend she was doing all this for Sylvia, but there was no point in lying to herself and she knew that the few days she spent in Lüderitz with Günter were the happiest in her life.

The nights were best, for when the hotel was quiet Günter would creep into her room and she would snuggle against him, her knees behind his legs, her arm around his waist, and sleep blissfully until the following morning.

It did not take long for Sylvia to find out and then she became wildly jealous and at breakfast asked them when they were going to be married.

"Anytime your mother wishes," Günter said blandly, wolfing his eggs and bacon.

Marika stared at him, feeling very much on the defensive.

"Stay here with us," Günter urged her.

She gasped. "I love you all so much, but I have my business . . ."

"Sell the business and marry me," he persisted.

Marika put down her cup and glared at Günter. "You put her up to this, didn't you? You had no right . . ."

"No, I didn't," Günter said quietly. "I'm sorry. I should have stopped her at the beginning. Sylvia," he said, turning to his daughter. "When grown-ups decide whether or not to get married it's between the two of them and nothing to do with anyone else."

Sylvia's eyes were suddenly brimming over. She fled from the room and Bertha hurried after her.

"I was going to ask you, you know that," Günter began awkwardly after a long silence. "She jumped the gun."

"What a lot of American slang you've picked up lately."

"Don't hedge."

"No, I wasn't, but why must we have this painful conversation?" She sighed. "Can't we just enjoy the holiday?"

"It's nearly over."

"Yes."

"I know you love me."

"You don't have to be a genius to know that," she

replied painfully. "Nothing's changed. My reasons for not marrying you haven't changed. I will never marry a German. I have certain standards. Like not spitting on the graves of my parents. If they had graves. Where does that get us?"

"Damn you, Marika!" Günter's fist came crashing down on the fragile table. Spoons and forks shivered and the milk jug toppled over. Suddenly the dining room was quiet as everyone stared toward them.

Günter lowered his voice. "You should have stayed in London nursing your ancient vendetta. I'd almost forgotten what you looked like."

She buried her face in her hands. "I've been wrong, you are right." She put on her sunglasses hastily.

"Günter, I don't expect you to understand how I feel. Perhaps it might help if you knew that fifteen percent of everything I earn goes to a certain agency which specializes in catching Nazi war criminals. The war is very real to me. The loss of my parents, my culture, my homeland, it's a permanent loss, something that I live with every day of my life. Can't you understand that?"

"I lost my parents, too. And I loved them. That doesn't stop me from loving you. Marika, I swear I'll make it up to you." Günter reached across the table and grabbed her hand. "I'll find something to replace everything you've lost. Give me a chance. You're the only woman I'll ever love."

Marika pulled her hand away and stood up as Günter fumbled in his pocket.

"This is for you," he said, producing a cardboard box tied with string. It was the size of an orange and it had contained a spare part for an engine once, she could see.

"No, please," she whispered. "It's no use."

"Take it," he said, his voice hoarse and furious.

She grabbed the box, wondering at the heaviness of it, and fled to her room, where she locked the door and flung herself trembling on the bed.

Why had she come? She'd been a fool. How could Günter be so deceived as to dare to hope. She was a woman of principles and standards which she would never abandon. Or if sometimes she did . . . why, then . . . it was only a temporary weakness.

For a few moments she sat on the bed contemplating the small box Günter had given her. It was unusually heavy for its size and Marika was curious. She opened it and gasped. Nestling in cotton wool was a rough diamond wider than a golf ball, but more elongated in shape. For a moment she was too confused to think. Incredible! Surely it could not be real . . . yet she knew that it was. It looked like an enormous ball of frosted glass.

But the size of it! Surreptitiously, she weighed it in her hand. Then she carefully covered it with the cotton wool. She wanted to laugh. She was sitting here holding a fortune in her hand. Unreal!

After a while she plucked up courage to look at it again. It was still there. She had not been dreaming.

She unfolded the note which she saw in the bottom of the box. It read: *You've never regarded South-West Africa as your home, Marika, or taken an interest in the people here, which is a pity, because one can learn so much from their culture. Strange to think that you, a sophisticated Londoner nowadays, can be as confused and unhappy as the poorest Bushman woman, because you hide from your emotions. There's a beautiful song the Bushmen sing. It's called "Song of the Wind" and it goes like this:*

"Oh, listen to the wind, you woman there; the time is coming; the rain is near; listen to your heart; your hunter is here."

I hope you like the present. I've named the diamond the Kwammang-a, which is Bushman for "God's rainbow." I found it quite close to where you boarded the boat.

Marika closed her eyes and leaned back, feeling stunned with the force of emotions surging through her. She thought of Günter, sitting in his hotel room, writing out his Bushman poem with his blunt pencil. Hoping! Then she felt the tears starting out of her eyes and rolling down her cheeks. She must go back to London at once. She had the impression that if she were to stay another day she might be lost forever.

*   *   *

Günter was in the courtyard tinkering with the engine of his jeep. "You'll be able to afford a new one and much more besides." She laughed shakily and pushed the box into his hand. "What are you going to do with it?"

"I gave it to you. That's what I planned when I saw it. There's all the money you'll ever need there. You can forget about your business."

"I don't want to forget about my business," she said as gently as she could. Günter was still staring obstinately at the engine, trying unsuccessfully to conceal his anger. "Will you have the diamond cut?"

"I suppose so," he said eventually. "If I can find someone good enough to attempt it."

"It's still worth millions, even if it shattered," she said.

"I'd hate that to happen. I Want the Kwammang-a in one piece. It could become one of the largest diamonds in the world."

"What a sentimental fool you are," she said. "It's the money that counts."

"Marry me," Günter whispered.

"No, never. I never will. I'm leaving today."

Günter smiled painfully. "Claire always warned me that one day I'd make a million and you'd say no."

"Oh, so it's Claire now, is it?"

"If you won't have me," he said spitefully, "I'll marry her."

Marika looked wounded and he felt glad.

Making a poor attempt to look cheerful, Günter slammed the engine cover down and went off to find Sylvia.

Marika packed and left. She had no regrets as the plane took off, although sometimes she couldn't help wondering what it would be like if life had allowed her to marry and live a normal life, just like everyone else. Her life's work was still ahead of her, she decided. There was no time to waste on stupid regrets.

A week later Günter returned to Bryanston with his family. He moped around the house for a few days and then pulled himself together and banished Marika from his thoughts.

One morning he plucked up courage to take his treasure to the Van Zijl's Corporation, who were the best in a city famous for its diamond cutters. He was unprepared for the consternation caused by the Kwammang-a.

The managing director, a thin, pale, aesthetic man, emphatically refused to keep the diamond on his premises until it was insured, and Günter had to sit and guard it while their broker was called in. He contacted Lloyds in London, who underwrote the Kwammang-a's insurance for ten million pounds.

Next the firm's experts were called in to examine the treasure in the top-security floodlit cell where the Kwammang-a would be kept during the cutting process—which could take a month, they told him.

There was a good deal of excitement and speculation as to how the stone could best be cut, and Günter waited impatiently while the managing director warned him of the slender chance that one really huge pure diamond might be salvaged from the mass. "Good God, man," he exploded. "There's nearly three thousand carats of rough diamond there. It's almost as big as the Cullinan diamond before it was cut—and that was the world's biggest." He made a visible effort to calm down.

"Well, we'll know our chances soon enough. Meantime I suggest coffee in my office."

Shoulders hunched, Günter followed the diminutive figure, feeling more like a naughty schoolboy than the stone's owner.

"Mr. Grieff, it's unlikely that news such as this will remain your secret for long, but I suggest we try to maintain silence about the stone until cutting has been completed," the director said. After that he tried to discuss business, but Günter was too worried to respond.

An hour later the head cutter called him.

It gave Günter a strange feeling to see his diamond firmly clamped in place under a series of brilliant lamps and reflective glasses. Around the table were numerous diagrams and several men in white coats were arguing heatedly over them.

"In there," the cutter said, "might be the world's largest cut diamond." The sweat was glistening on his forehead. "It's too early to tell, but first examination shows a stone of remarkable purity. There are flaws, but only on the peripheral."

"Cut it, man. Let's find out."

"I'm afraid to take the responsibility. With your permission we intend to send to Amsterdam for two experts—the world's best. Anything less would be an insult to a stone of this size. They should be here within three days. In the meantime . . ."

Günter shrugged.

"You must understand the risks," he persisted. "You might end up with a number of smaller diamonds. Up to sixty-nine percent of the weight of the uncut diamond could be lost in the process. The chance of obtaining a large pure diamond of any outstanding size is remote, but I think it's a chance you should take. Meantime, as it stands now—uncut—we'd like to make you an offer."

"No deal," Günter growled.

"Very well. I quite understand."

"I'll leave it in your hands," Günter said. His voice was so hoarse he could hardly speak.

Three weeks later, after exhaustive testing and planning, Günter saw his diamond cut. The speed of the operation, after such drawn-out planning, left him gasping in amazement. The result was the Kwammang-a, an oval-shaped diamond of amazing brilliance, purity and weight. At 419 carats it was second only to the Star of Africa, and he knew that he had just witnessed the birth of one of the world's great treasures.

Small wonder he and everyone else there were drenched with sweat. Apart from the Kwammang-a, Günter had eight large stones and over seventy smaller ones, which he had agreed to sell to the diamond cutter.

Later, after a celebration at the cutter's premises, he held a press conference in the company's boardroom. He hoped that this would free him from further harassment, but the Kwammang-a was headline news, and it seemed that everyone wanted to know about how it was found. For weeks to come, Günter was bombarded with telephone calls from all over the world.

Günter now found himself in a curious situation, as he explained to Claire one evening. The sale of the smaller diamonds had paid some of his debts, but he was still operating his offshore diamond dredging business on a massive loan, which was hardly secured by the trucks, boats and equipment.

Apart from the equipment, all he owned was the Kwammang-a. Admittedly that was priceless and if he sold it the money would set him up for life. But Günter was unwilling to part with the diamond.

The answer was to use the Kwammang-a as collateral, too, but Günter knew this was a dangerous move. If he did not repay the loan in time he might lose the diamond.

As the weeks passed he found that he had no alternative. He needed cash for expansion. He envisaged a long line of dredgers, all the way down the South-West African coast. It would cost a fortune.

Regretfully he pledged his diamond to an international merchant bank for a six-year loan of ten million dollars. The Kwammang-a disappeared into the merchant bank's vaults.

Apart from converting twenty fishing boats into diamond dredgers, the ten million enabled Günter to acquire interests in several vanadium, magnesium and coal mines.

The months passed, and one day, true to his promise, Günter married Claire. The ceremony was performed simply at the Johannesburg magistrate's court, with Sylvia and Bertha as witnesses. Günter reckoned that the marriage would stem his longing for Marika, and that slowly he would fall in love with his wife.

Now Günter set his mind to becoming very rich in the shortest possible time. He had a goal, which was to recoup his uranium mines in the Namib together with the entire Western Minerals stable and ruin Tex McGregor for all time.

Slowly and cautiously Günter was buying Western Minerals shares. He bought them through various investors, so that Tex would not suspect that any one person was holding a large part of his group.

It was a gamble and Günter knew he was staking his diamond on beating Tex. All his profits went into acquiring more and still more Western Minerals shares. He could well lose out: if the bottom dropped out of the uranium market . . . if he could not acquire the majority voting share . . . if the diamond-dredging profits dwindled . . . if . . .if . . .

"Play safe, Günter," Claire urged him repeatedly. "You've struggled so hard for all you own. Don't risk it for the sake of revenge. Forget Tex. You've made it on your own."

But Günter never forgot and Günter never gave up.

Chapter Fifty-four

Marika's small house seemed like an empty shell when she returned to London. She was lonely and filled with regrets, so she threw herself into her work and for another year everything she touched went well for her. John Sidwell franchised another fifteen shops; they extended the plant and updated the machinery. Marika learned to work with her top-rate design team; her task was merely to guide them. She liked to train the sales team, too, and Tanya had become an expert supervisor and production manager.

Marika's days were filled with activity, but she dreaded the nights. There was no excuse for loneliness, Marika told herself repeatedly. There were dozens of parties around, no shortage of escorts, and she gave regular dinners which were always entertaining. She redoubled her efforts and became a regular first-nighter. She was seen at all the best parties. If she tried hard enough, she decided, she might eventually succeed in having no time to think at all.

The plant closed for the annual holiday, but Marika could not face the family now that Günter was married to Claire, so she stayed in London and endured a week of loneliness. Not another day, she decided. There must be hundreds of ways to forget Günter. She went to the local travel agent and examined the alternatives.

"I want something exclusive," she told the woman, "but away from tourists. Is that possible?"

"Depends on how much you want to pay."

"Make it fabulously expensive," she said, "but quiet and out of the way.

"I've just the place for you." She showed Marika a photograph.

Winter sports . . . skiing . . . that was just what she needed. She left the following morning.

Her mood lightened as they neared the Alpine resort. Below, the lights of the village twinkled against the white and purple shadows of the evening snow and on the train the people smiled at each other with an air of camaraderie in their brightly colored skiing clothes. It was easy to see who were the natives and who were the visitors.

As Marika took the horse and buggy from the station to the inn, she felt relaxed and pleasantly tired and even a little happy for the first time in almost a year.

When she reached the hotel she stopped and gazed around at snow-capped mountains and the lights in the valley below. She breathed in the crisp, sparkling mountain air and felt great. Why . . . this was better than moping in London. Instinctively she knew she was going to have a wonderful time.

The inn was all that she had demanded. The innkeeper and his wife were like caricatures of innkeepers and their wives, dressed in rosy cheeks and jolly smiles. Her room was large and extravagantly comfortable with central heating, timbered ceilings and a view of the mountain slopes down to the village in the valley.

Marika had a natural aptitude for skiing, perhaps because she remembered from her early youth. She had a few falls, but nothing serious, and before long she was flying down the beginners' slopes, abandoning herself to the thrill of it. Every day she went further afield and tried new and more daring runs.

For three days Marika skied, returning at sunset too stiff and tired to do more than stumble into a hot bath and have a drink. She had supper sent to her room.

On the fourth day, when she returned, she found a note on her bed. It read: *Dear Ms. Magos. Quite by chance I saw your name in the inn's register. One of my Rome factories makes Magos Fashions under license. That makes us business associates, although we have never met. Would you care to have dinner with me tonight? Or tomorrow night? Angelo Palma.*

Damn! She wanted to get away from business. She decided to send a note to Palma explaining that she was under doctor's orders, could not eat supper and must rest a great deal, but would meet him briefly for a glass of soda water on the balcony at six.

She arrived late, but there was no sign of Palma. The skiing crowd were all young. For the first time in her life she felt old. At thirty-four she was probably the oldest person there, she realized with a start of annoyance. She recognized at least two famous film stars and an American model and they were all chattering in English. Everyone seemed to know everyone and to be having a wonderful time. She felt left out and wished she had stayed in her room. Then she recognized one of her furs and it made her feel more relaxed.

A young man at an adjoining table stood up and walked over to her. "I hate drinking alone. How about you?" He spoke with a strong American accent.

She looked up uncertainly, but something about his face put her at ease. He was young and aggressively handsome in a rugged sort of way and his eyes gleamed with mischief. He was smiling now with a sort of cynical good humor. He was certainly used to getting his own way, she thought, and why not . . . with all that charm?

She nodded and studied him coolly. His face was squarish, over a Roman nose; his brown eyes, set wide apart, seemed to twinkle more than other eyes. She wondered why that was. When he smiled his face broadened and the lines on his cheeks set into dimples. He was suntanned and strong and he had a clean-cut look about him. His hair was black and inclined to be curly, and it was cropped in a crew cut for that reason, she guessed.

Too good-looking by far, she thought, noting his strong white teeth. She tried to guess his age, but could not. Late twenties perhaps.

"Twenty-seven," he said.

She blushed. "Oh . . . was I that obvious?"

"I'll forgive you. What are you drinking?"

She smiled. "Scotch on ice, please."

When he had ordered, he said, "My name's Tony . . . what's yours?"

"Marika." She glanced around again. "I have a problem. I'm supposed to meet someone here . . ."

One thick eyebrow shot up into a broad forehead. He sighed exaggeratedly. "All the best girls are meeting someone," he said. "It's the story of my life."

"I don't believe that." She smiled and sipped her drink. "I needed a drink. It completes the day. Wonderful to feel warm inside and out after the snow."

"Who're you meeting?"

She frowned. "A business associate discovered I was here and sent a note. He asked me for supper, but I couldn't bear to spend the evening talking business with some old boor. Bit of a cheek, I thought, trying to cash in on business when I'm on holiday."

He nodded sympathetically. "Middle-aged, overstuffed and pompous-looking, is he?"

"Oh . . ." She smiled. "To tell the truth, I haven't met him, but I imagine him rather like that. Why . . . do you know him?"

"Guy called Palma collapsed in the foyer half an hour ago."

"You can't be serious. That's his name."

He shrugged apologetically.

"Oh my goodness."

"Well, since you've been stood up . . . how about dinner with me?"

"I'd love that," she said without hesitating.

"Good. Come and meet the others."

Half an hour later she wondered why she had spent three evenings alone. She now knew everyone and it seemed that they had all heard of her fashions. She felt happy and accepted and pleased with her reputation. They were all overachievers and here to have a good time and they tackled their leisure every bit as seriously as they tackled their careers, she decided, watching them.

There was a great deal of laughter, the food was superb and after dinner they gathered in a candlelit room with a bar in the corner where a glossy-haired young man was playing the guitar. The log fire crackled, burning pine cones filled the room with the scent of sap and Marika sprawled in an easy chair, dreamily listening to the gypsy's voice, halfway through her third whiskey and feeling more relaxed than she had been for a long time.

"There's a touch of the gypsy in me," Tony told her. "Give me your palm and I'll tell you your fortune."

"No, what a lot of nonsense," she said, laughing, and held out her hand.

Tony smoothed his hand over hers. Then he turned it palm upward and ran his fingers gently over her fingertips.

"Don't do that," she objected.

"It's all part of the mystique." He looked up with half a smile in his cynical brown eyes: "You are in grave danger," he said. "You have slighted an admirer and he will stop at nothing to tame you."

"Oh, silly," she murmured, tugging at her hand.

He held on. "He is rich and ruthless and he is mustering his resources to seduce you."

"Well . . . really . . . if he's that rich why should he bother?"

"I see him clearly . . . it's Palma . . . I think he's going to become a nuisance."

"Is that all you can see?" she asked, feeling disappointed. She had been sure he was going to make a pass.

"Isn't that enough? What a demanding woman you are."

"I had forgotten about Palma," she whispered, glancing around.

"Well, he hasn't forgotten about you."

Tony seemed to lose interest in telling her fortune. He grabbed the gypsy's guitar and sang haunting Italian lyrics in a near-perfect baritone. Obviously this was a nightly ritual. The gypsy wandered off and sat at the bar with a drink, talking to the barman.

Could Tony be a gigolo? she wondered. He was altogether too damned good-looking and knew he was the most popular man there.

He did not notice when Marika went to bed, and the last thing she heard before she fell asleep was his voice singing from the bar below her window.

She overslept and was woken at eight by a maid with coffee and a bowl of red roses. The card read: *Sorry to have missed you . . . taken ill unexpectedly. Can we make it tonight? Palma.*

"Oh no . . ." she muttered.

She met Tony in the ski lift later and told him about the roses.

"Watch out for Palma," he told her. "Nasty scandal with a film star eighteen months ago. He's bad news for women."

"I won't go," she said firmly.

"Come along with me if you like," he said. "I feel like a hamburger and fries and I sure as hell won't find it at that inn."

He was fun to be with. Marika laughed all evening and she was only too happy to spend her days with him. At the same time she felt her holiday was being spoiled by the gifts of flowers which kept arriving from Palma. She had asked Tony to check up on "this nut," as she called him.

When Tony disappeared for two days she felt let down and unaccountably depressed. After an afternoon skiing alone she returned to her room determined to pack and leave the following morning.

There, on her dressing table, she found an orchid. The note read: *Wear it for dinner tonight. Seven-thirty in the dining room. Palma.*

"What cheek!" she gasped.

She hurried to reception and heard Tony's voice behind her. "Hi, Marika, how're you doing?"

Her face lit up. Then she flushed. How could she be so stupid? she thought angrily. He was seven years younger than she and he had only befriended her because she was alone. "Oh, Tony," she said. "Look!" She held out the orchid. "Palma again. I'm sending it back. I don't know him and I don't want to know him. I've decided to check out tomorrow anyway."

"Scared of him?"

"No . . . good heavens, no . . ."

"You should be."

"I don't see why he should expect me to have dinner with him . . . just because he's one of the richest men in the world. How terribly gauche he must be."

She looked up smiling, loving the sight of him. Strange how Günter had faded into the past. Tony was more vital, more charming; besides, he was American and, even more to the point, he was here.

Right now his mouth was pulled back in a strange half smile and his eyes gleamed wickedly. At last she had found someone who attracted her as much as Günter did and for the first time in her life she wished she were ten years younger.

"Come with me," he said flippantly. And then more seriously: "Yes, why don't you?"

"Where to?"

"Further up the mountain. There's better skiing there;

food's more to my liking. You'll love it," he said, looking serious for once.

She made up her mind on the spur of the moment. Madness really, but still, why not?

"I'll come," she said decisively.

"We're leaving in half an hour. Don't be late. The road's not good enough for night driving." He frowned and looked at his watch.

Marika paid her bill, called a porter and found Tony in the parking lot standing next to a superb silver Maserati 5000S. She was surprised. Suddenly she realized how little she knew about Tony. "This yours?" she asked curiously.

He grinned wryly. "Company car. I've borrowed it."

"I must give a message to the porter," she said breathlessly.

"The guy's right here."

The porter straightened up from behind the trunk. "Yes, ma'am."

"Please tell Mr. Palma I've checked out and am unable to have dinner with him tonight or any other night," she said firmly.

"Yes, ma'am." His expression was a mixture of astonishment and amusement.

Let him think what he likes, she thought angrily. It was her business where she went.

"Oh, please, wait a minute," she told Tony as the car moved forward. She handed the orchid to the porter. "Give this to Mr. Palma with my compliments," she said.

"Certainly, ma'am." The porter plodded around the car and handed the orchid to Tony. "With the madame's compliments, sir," he said.

The Maserati shot out into the dusk.

"Oh no . . ." she said. "Oh, Tony . . ." She began to laugh.

"I told you Palma would get you, didn't I? And here you are alone with the bastard on a lonely Alpine road, lured to his mountain hideaway. Tut, tut! I tried to warn you, but you wouldn't listen." He glanced around, one black eyebrow raised, teeth gleaming in a Machiavellian smile.

The car skidded around a sharp bend and Tony turned his attention to the road.

"I've been taken," she said flatly.

"Not yet, but give or take a couple of hours."

"You want to know something?" she asked after a while.

"Uh-huh!"

"I'm going to enjoy every minute of it."

Chapter Fifty-five

Perhaps is was the isolation of the Swiss chalet perched among the pines in a valley between two mountain peaks, or the bizarre and unnatural situation in which she found herself, or even a desire to break the bonds that bound her to Günter, once and for all. Whatever the reason, Marika gave herself as she had never given before.

Tony was demanding, as a lover, as a man and as a friend. He took all that she had, but he was never satisfied. He was always ready to make love at any time of the day; one look from Tony and she would feel her resistance melting away. He would talk all hours of the night—philosophy, art, politics. He hardly needed to sleep; one or two hours was enough for him. He skied all day, or drove for miles at high speed, and Marika was soon exhausted. She did not mind as long as Tony was happy.

Sometimes she thought she was like a delicious orange and he would suck the juice out of her, then chew the pulp and the pips and even the rind and finally there would be nothing left of her . . . nothing at all. She was filled with a strange sense of fatalism and a feeling of belonging. He could love her or they could ski or talk, it was all one, just as long as she was with him.

All the time she craved more of him . . . more information about him . . . more understanding of the way he thought and reacted . . . and more, much more of his body. She was like an addict, she could not manage without him; his special, overpowering, demanding way of making love or just his presence in the same room or his voice shouting into the telephone.

She learned to cram a lifetime into a week, for she knew that was all they had. He must return to the United States; she was overdue at the plant. She had telephoned Tanya, tried to explain, but she was three days late and this had never happened before.

She counted the days left . . . and the hours . . . and skied . . . then she counted the hours left again . . . and rushed off to do silly, inconsequential things like taking the Alpine train to a village and buying souvenirs or skating on the lake and all the while time was dwindling away.

Did she love him? She had no way of telling. Sometimes she thought she was snared by his intense magnetism, like a moth to a flame. She was the essential mistress, devoid of modesty. She was in a state of conflagration, soon she would be utterly consumed. Sometimes she fought, or answered back in a flash of bravado, but it was all a sham. She wanted what he wanted; she had succumbed utterly.

She learned more about Tony from his long-distance calls than the things he told her. He was chairman of a vast multinational chemical and pharmaceutical concern that made at least half a dozen drugs which were household names; he owned four knitting mills and two clothing factories in the United States and Rome, one of which made Marika Magos Fashions under license; fairly recently he had acquired six oil wells in Texas and now he was trying to take controlling interest in an electronics company based in the United States but manufacturing in Korea.

He was amoral, she discovered, not immoral. He had his own code, which he stuck to, but normal conventional mores meant nothing to him. He created his own environment—one designed to suit Tony.

His power and his wealth took her breath away. Tony, which was his nickname, she discovered, shifted money from continent to continent the way others played with draughts on a board. Distance, too, had little meaning for him. A private jet and hired helicopter could transport him to his various enterprises in the minimum time and maximum comfort. He always traveled with a team of secretaries.

To Tony, business was a game. "Sometimes I think it's a game designed expressly for my pleasure," he told her one evening. "If I always won, the suspense would be gone—the game spoiled. Then I would give up business. But there's nothing else I really enjoy quite as much. Well, maybe fucking you. Yes, I think that's better."

She smiled the smile of the wiser, older woman. She was an interlude for him and he for her. It was a fifty-fifty relationship, no recriminations. She was enjoying it as much as he was. But she could not help counting again—three days, seven hours and forty minutes of paradise left.

"Lucky you inherited so much, since you love it so," she said one morning at breakfast.

"Yes, I was lucky," Tony admitted, giving her a quizzical look. "But I only inherited the clothing factories. My old man died when I was seventeen. I acquired the rest in the past ten years."

Tony was an enigma; quick-witted with a tremendous sense of humor and mischief which would sometimes prove quite cruel. But it was always for fun, she discovered—for kicks, for thrills.

His restless brain could not bear to be inactive for more than a few moments, and whatever he tackled he had to become an expert—art, philosophy, politics, finance, sports. Eventually she gave up trying to understand him.

It was Sunday, their last day; they were leaving early in the morning. They had been skiing the long, superb run from their chalet to the village below. It was this run which had persuaded Tony to buy the chalet, he told Marika.

She was not really expert enough for the steep curves, but she wanted to go with him. Recklessness lent her extra skill. Fear was abolished. She did not really care whether or not she survived. Life had been really lived, each moment had been savored; she had been living in a state of superconsciousness. Consequently she enjoyed the run as she had never enjoyed anything in her life and at the village Tony's chauffeur was waiting to drive them back to the chalet.

They were dining at home with the table pulled closer to the roaring log fire. Marika glanced around, thinking of how she had learned to love the chalet, the polished wooden floors and timbered ceilings, the small, cozy windows and huge stone hearth covering most of one wall.

Tony seemed unusually preoccupied this evening; no jokes, no teasing, just frowning and staring at his plate. All the same, she loved the sight of him, in all his moods. He was like the sea, she thought. Never the same, always changing, sometimes beautiful, sometimes harsh . . . even frightening.

At times she would look up and see him watching her, too, and she wondered if he felt as she did.

Impatiently he pushed his plate away. "I'd rather fuck than eat," he said.

"Funny you should say that . . ." She smiled, a secret, woman's smile.

"Here," he said. "On the hearth in front of the fire."

He undressed her slowly, caressing her skin, standing back to gaze at her with a mixture of awe and pride.

She watched him curiously. "Sometimes you give me the impression that I'm a statue you wish to put on your mantelpiece," she blurted out without thinking what she was saying.

"You read my thoughts," he said.

"Oh . . . I wonder . . . is that a compliment?"

"No. It's just the way I am."

"I'm real."

"No, you're not." He pounced and tickled her and she rolled on the rug, kicking and giggling.

"Maybe you're real. I've never owned a ticklish statue." He grinned at her, happy again. Her Tony! He was two different people, she thought. Or maybe dozens of people.

"Come here." He squatted on his heels and pulled her onto his lap. She loved his thick, broad, muscular chest and the tufts of black hair under his arms and his wide, sinewed neck.

She wrapped her legs around his waist and her arms around his neck and felt him nudging into her as she nuzzled his ear.

"Why are you so brown in midwinter?" she asked, seeing the contrast between her white breasts and his suntanned skin.

"Just came back from South America," he said. "Don't talk, just move your ass."

He lay back on the floor, caught her buttocks in his hands and moved her gently backwards and forwards.

"You're terrific," he said. "I wish you could see yourself from this angle. Your breasts are standing up twice as large as life and you've got that funny, dreamy look you get on your face. It turns me on . . . hopelessly. Hurry, or you'll miss out."

"Oh, oh," she gasped, the agonizing sadness of it. This was the last . . . the very last time. She began to moan gently and her moans changed to harsh wracking sobs.

"I don't regret anything," she said at last, and wiped her eyes with the backs of her hands.

"Finished with the banshee bit?" he asked.

"Finished," she said firmly.

He rolled her over until she lay beneath him, watching his face looking down at her with a mixture of need and irritation. It was a strangely ferocious look. He bent over and kissed her fiercely and a second later cradled her in his arms and gently came.

She turned her head and kissed his cheek, stroking the back of his stiff, curly hair. She knew the drill. She would wait and he would come for a second time in a few minutes. Once was for lesser mortals. Tony came twice.

Then he moved away from her abruptly, which was unusual, and sat cross-legged gazing into the fire. She watched the flames sending golden lights and shadows across his face. To Marika he looked like a Roman gladiator in ancient times with his jet-black hair, arrogant nose and cruel, brooding expression.

"Marika, will you marry me?" he asked abruptly.

She gasped, not only from his words but from the tension emanating from him.

"We've never talked about age, Tony," she began quietly after a long silence. "I'm thirty-four, you're twenty-seven . . . seven years' difference."

"Shit!" His voice cracked like a whip. "I don't want a lesson in arithmetic. I want your goddamn answer."

"Yes," she said firmly.

"Good. That's settled, then," he said as if he had completed a satisfactory business deal. "We'll be married by special license in London on Tuesday. There'll be a million details to fix—we'll tackle them later."

He stood up and walked into his office, slamming the door behind him.

She wondered why he always did that. Soon he would be yelling into the receiver loud enough for everyone to hear.

She stood up and knelt in front of the fire, watching the flames making curious patterns as the logs blazed, died down and blazed again.

From now on her life would be irrevocably changed, she knew. Perhaps fuller, more meaningful, but for now she was enjoying this small moment of silence and peace.

This was the division; the end of the old, the start of the new. She wished she would stay forever suspended in time; halfway between the past and the future, youth and age, freedom and submission; but there was no turning back. She had no choice, she knew. She could not . . . would not . . . banish love for a second time.

But still . . . she wished this small moment of nothingness could last forever.

PART
THREE

Chapter Fifty-six

Like a bloody orgy, Marika thought, gazing moodily around the garden, where traces of the party lingered under shrubs and hedges like the last remnants of snow. There had been too much gaiety, too much laughter, and their guests, drenched and dizzy with champagne, had screamed above the clamor of a Latin American band until 3 A.M., when the last stragglers had left, noisy and regretful. Then the servants had moved in.

Dawn was breaking. The swans had left the safety of the island and were gliding effortlessly over the lake, ethereal in the pale dawn light. Beyond them oak trees glimmered insubstantial against a glimmer of gray.

Only memories lingered with the debris, as obtrusive and disagreeable: Tony flirting with their guests, one hand held proprietorially on her shoulder—grabbing both options; John Sidwell obsessed with his hopeless quest of luring a model into his bed, leaving last, angry and deprived; a ballet dancer, stoned, but lovely, who had stripped, dived into the lake and swum to the island, where she had danced, naked and ghostly in the moonlight, disturbing the sleeping birds.

Their home was a converted monastery, set among the chalk hills of Kent, but to Marika it was the apex of their world—a transient, shrinking world. As she thought about it a thrill of insecurity touched her and she shuddered.

Distance was becoming meaningless. "Anywhere" was readily and quickly available. A helicopter transported them from their home to the airfield, where a private jet, piloted by a team of three, flew them to wherever they wanted to go at a moment's notice.

The world should be larger, she thought grimly, and her

feet should be solidly and enduringly placed upon the earth. Life was an unfulfilled promise, a fleeting grab at existence, and the tighter you grasped it, the quicker it melted and dripped between your fingers. This dwindling planet, the meagerness of the life-sustaining atmosphere and the impermanence of it all seemed to hit her harder when they were jet-setting around the globe and nowadays they were nearly always going somewhere.

All the pleasures of the world, infinitely desirable and infinitely accessible, were gobbled ravenously. Politicians, film stars, musicians, business tycoons—those who had reached the peak in their fields—were their friends. Dinner with the President of the United States one week, slumming in Haifa with a sculptor from Yugoslavia the next, then off to their Swiss lodge for a long weekend of skiing. When they were sick of snow, why then, the sun was always shining in Buenos Aires, where their friend Toledo, the bullfighter, gave magnificent parties. Only time was rationed. There was not enough of it. They wanted more and more—and still more.

Money ruled the world, she thought. Of course it did. Everything could be purchased: people, good times, health, even beauty. The whole world was for sale—a gigantic funfair—there for the pickings. Even revenge, she thought somberly. Gone were the days of vendettas. She fought with her money—more costly, but infinitely more effective, for lately a chain of informers and agents was scouring the world for Geissler. They would catch him eventually. The knowledge that this would happen was the nearest Marika came to joy.

"I am happy," she said aloud. When she frowned her enchantment vanished and she looked older. She was thirty-five and according to her moods she could look twenty or middle-aged. She glowered at her fingertips. "I could have been happy," she corrected herself.

Tony, who was approaching softly across the lawn, saw her frown and felt irritated. He loved beauty obsessively and covetously. When he saw a beautiful view or a work of art, he wanted to be a part of it, immerse himself totally into it, but he could not. Instead he fought and on those rare occasions when it was not for sale he was plagued with a sense of rejection.

To Tony, Marika was like a work of art and she should always look placid and beautiful; that was the way he wanted to see her.

"What's wrong?"

She jumped. "You startled me."

"You're frowning."

To Marika it sounded like an accusation. She made an effort to smile. She had come to terms with Tony's infatuation. Tony loved winners. Failure was unacceptable and sadness was failure. She valued his adoration and was afraid to be sad. "When I frown it doesn't mean there's something wrong," she said lightly, "I was only thinking . . ."

"I am the genie of the lamp." Tony's voice boomed over the lake; the swans turned and glided into the shadows. "Tell me your wish and it will be granted."

He clowned around on the lawn and Marika sighed as she watched him. To Tony life was simple. You decided what you wanted and you went out and took it—or bought it. In the end it was the same thing. Unlike Tony, she was unable to define the cause of her unhappiness or her fears and longings. Life was full; Tony was handsome and fun to be with; her business was successful beyond anything she could have envisaged; she was rich and famous. What else was there? Yet surely there must be something that could bring meaning to life, if not joy.

"Haven't you seen enough vacuous smiles for one night?" she retorted, buying time. Did sadness have a cause? she wondered. Well, if she had to put a finger on the one unhealable wound it was her family. Time and again she had begged Sylvia to live with her, if only for a few months a year, but she always refused.

"But, darling, I *miss* . . . positively *miss* my family." She smiled disarmingly as if to show that it was only a small thing, after all.

"Bring them over." He stopped clowning the genie and put his arm around her. "Marika, I'd love it. I mean it."

"They prefer Günter and South Africa."

"They'll come if you insist." He squeezed her shoulder and smiled.

Like a good-hearted schoolboy, she thought, watching him cynically, but she had seen him in action. Well . . . really . . . so devious. "Do you think I haven't tried?" she exploded in one of her swift and unexpected fits of temper. "You make it sound . . . well . . . so simple."

"It is," he said. "It's you that's complicated."

Tony's moral code no longer surprised Marika. To Tony it was enough to know what he wanted. He had no anxieties about the rights and wrongs of the situation, or what would be best for others. What was good for Tony had to happen. So far his desires had corresponded with hers. Slowly, but inevitably she had allowed herself to flow with him . . . bend the rules . . . or rather tailor them to fit like a glove, she admitted with a rare twinge of guilt. She closed her mind to vague misgivings.

"Do you love me?" she asked abruptly, looking over the lake. "I mean the real me . . . the person inside . . . not just what I look like."

"I'm nuts about you," he said.

Not the answer she had hoped for. Watching him, Marika could not help smiling. Tony was larger than life: powerful, headstrong, arrogant, but with a tremendous sense of humor.

"Maybe you're scared to bring her over—scared to make a father of me," he said with an infuriating smile. "Scared I might like it." He knew her fear of pregnancy and childbirth.

He was teasing, she knew that, but an icy stillness settled over her and, sensing her inner shrinking, he probed deeper. "Papa," he said musingly. "I like the sound of it."

He broke off, frowning, the game already forgotten as he stared moodily at the lake. Restless! She watched him

cautiously. Now he was back in his private business world.
He turned abruptly and sprinted back to the house.

She sat on the stone bench overlooking the lake and
watched. Clouds were gathering on the horizon. It would
then soon. They had been lucky with the weather for the

the distance she could hear Tony's voice as he yelled
the telephone. He had started his working day and he
could not sleep now, but she was exhausted. She would
go to bed soon. Never mind. John ran the plant nowadays,
or thought he did, together with Tanya in an uneasy alli-
ance. They had a team of economists to advise them, each
one handpicked, and under their covert direction Marika
had made a million and secured a major share of the British
and American clothing markets. Her name was internationally known for furs and fashions.

Well, at least in designing Tony could not help her, nor
John. She was on her own. Ultimately the group's success
depended upon the collections she produced twice a year.
The best business analysts in the world could not offset a
bad showing, she thought, smiling with satisfaction. In the
fashion world she was right at the forefront. She intended
to stay there.

"Where're you going, sweetie?" Tony yelled as she
passed the study.

"To sleep."

"I'll be up in five minutes," he called after her. "But
not to sleep. To hell with sleep."

"I'm tired," she called over her shoulder.

Watching her heavy eyes and drooping shoulders, Tony
felt irritated. Such physical perfection should be matched
by superior mental and intellectual abilities. Then she
would be perfect. But she was far from perfect. She was
too emotional, possessing a strange wayward temper which
could explode at the most inconvenient times; she would
cry without shame and when she did her face became
bloated and ugly. When she was happy she became quite
drunk with it; she could not handle happiness. She was a

prude, but her sensuality shone through her pai
guises and she was always posturing, yet she cou
conceal her thoughts or intentions. Sh could not bear
criticism. Her untidiness drove him crazy, could not bear
and untidy mind, he thought, watching her satidy nature
ing his dependence, yet longing for her. He felt his hat-
racing to his loins as he watched the full hips sw
from a narrow waist and long, golden thighs show
through the split in her dress.

Jesus! She was sensational. Not just her looks either,
but all that talent. Spread it around his various fashion
designers and every brand would become internationally
famous overnight. She had it! Boy, did she have it! Talent
and looks! But for the rest—she was a disaster. Sometimes
she looked her age, too, which was a shame. Right now
she was stumbling up the stairs as if she hadn't slept for a
week instead of a night. Soon her clothes would be strewn
over the carpets and she would be sprawled naked among
the sheets with that silly smile on her perfect classical
features.

The thought of her sleeping turned him on. He could
picture her hair spread over the pillow, rosy lips parted
with a glimpse of pearl gleaming between them. Her neck
was long and graceful, her skin pure and translucent,
unblemished—or almost. Lately traces of lines were showing around her eyes and mouth, but she was still the most
beautiful woman he had seen in his life. He should know—
he'd seen them all. She—only she—had penetrated his
defenses. She was like a drug and his dependence was
growing as the months passed.

He heard the switchboard operator's voice dimly through
the static of the Hong Kong connection. "Karl Bremen is
on the line, sir. I'm putting you through."

"Forget it." He replaced the receiver slowly and stood
up. Absurd, he thought, noting his quickening breath, his
dry lips and moist palms, I should get my ass back on that
chair and concentrate on the Hong Kong takeover. But he
could not. Sensuality was flooding through him and he
was running out of control. He was half undressed by the
time he reached the bedroom door.

Chapter Fifty-seven

Sunday lunch at Xhabbo was a ritual the family looked
forward to. Around ten they would drift toward the stoep
overlooking the swimming pool where Claire had put bowls
of fruit salad and fresh orange juice on the table. Then
they would laze away the morning and most of the afternoon discussing their news, swimming and lying in the sun
while Günter barbecued lamb chops and sausages and the
maids tripped in with ice-cold beer, platters of salads and
potatoes baked in their skins.

Sylvia was first this morning. She gazed around feeling
thrilled to be alive and young and living in Xhabbo,
which, she knew was the most beautiful place in the world.

It was a lovely highveld morning, the air sparkling and
warm, but not overwarm. The visibility was particularly
clear, so she could see the sky stretching hazy blue to the
distant horizon. Weaverbirds and mossies were chirping in
the trees and hopping on the lawn, to the annoyance of
two bullying myna birds who were doing their best to chase
them away. There was the scent of new-mown grass and wild
jasmine from the hedge.

Just perfect, she decided. She dived into the pool, followed by Pluto, her Labrador, whose ambition was to
catch her and drag her out of the water. "Oooh, ouch! No,
bad dog." Her laughter and screams echoed around the
house until Günter arrived.

"Your damn dog's hairs are clogging the filter," he
grumbled. "There's nothing worse than Labrador hairs."
He leaned over the fence frowning as he watched Sylvia
swimming.

She had suddenly changed; only yesterday, it seemed,
she was running around in pigtails, skinny and long-legged,

and now womanhood had settled firmly upon her; her breasts had become full and erect, her hips were firm and well formed. Günter had to admit that she was incredibly lovely with a look of sophistication which she certainly did not deserve, for she was anything but sophisticated. Behind the perfect classic profile, the huge, passionate violet eyes and the shining ash-blond hair lurked a shy child, unwilling to come to terms with growing up. He turned away, noticing her embarrassment as she scrambled clumsily out of the pool and hastily pulled on her beach robe. She insisted on wearing her plain black swimsuit from school, and her hair had been cut short and ragged recently. It didn't help. If anything, it suited her. Sometimes he wished he could be of more help to her.

When she was concealed in her thick terry cloth she put her arms around him and kissed him on the cheek. "Morning, Dad," she said. "You woke up on the wrong side, did you? Had you noticed what a lovely morning it is?"

He put his arms around her and hugged her. She smelled of chlorine and talcum powder and her fine hair tickled his nose. It was hard to be cross with his daughter. She was a living reminder of Marika. "You clean the filter," he said.

Claire came bustling out, green eyes glinting. She was fond of Sylvia, he knew that, but she could not help being jealous.

Nothing shy about Claire, he thought, noting her briefest possible bikini. She had never had much to hide and over the years she had not managed to gain weight. Her red hair shone in a dozen different shades in the brilliant sunshine as she dived into the water.

She swam a few lengths, then came out briskly and put on a hip-length green jacket. He thought: Everything Claire does is brisk and calculated. Like turning up at the right time when Marika refused the diamond. It occurred to him then that marrying Claire on the rebound was the silliest mistake he had ever made. He had married her out of guilt. She had been so faithful and so loving for so long and he had never reciprocated. He was quite sure that he was the only man in her life and always would be. That was the burden. Then he wondered why he was being so critical this morning. He had to admit she was a smart dresser; knew how to spend money, too.

Claire's shrewd blue eyes were watching Günter quizzically, trying to gauge his thoughts. Claire was permanently on edge—on guard—ready for the enemy assault. She loved him, but she knew she was never close to him, and consequently she was always looking for slights and she always attacked first.

"That old blue swimsuit of yours is a disgrace," she said. "It shows where Bertha sewed it when the dog ripped it. It's not as if we're short of money."

He grinned and pinched her ear. Top marks again, he thought, but he said, "I like it." Then he went to fetch the barbecue.

Claire watched him leaving with a pang of misgiving. She was so proud of him. Obsessed almost! There was nothing else in her life. When Günter was away, she would spend her time improving the decor or the garden, for Xhabbo was Günter, an extension of his personality, or so it seemed to Claire. It had been the home of one of the first mining tycoons in the days of the gold rush, a warren of oak-paneled rooms with embossed ceilings and old brass fittings. It was Günter who had renamed the house Xhabbo, which was Bushman for "Peace," he had told her, and the library housed his collection of African artifacts, said to be one of the finest in the world.

She looked around proudly. She had improved so many things, tamed the environment, just as she had tamed Günter. But now she was uneasy again. Günter had received a letter from Marika; so had Bertha and since then they had both been irritable. Marika was bad news.

She walked back to the stoep when she saw Bertha coming. "Hi, Bertha, you're early," she called out. Bertha looked tired. Her brown parchment-like skin, ruined by years in the sun, was more wrinkled than usual and there were bags under her eyes.

"I didn't sleep," Bertha complained. "Hardly a wink all night and then I fell asleep at four and, d'you know, those terrible sparrows woke me at five. I've never heard such a din. You can't call it birdsong, that's a fact."

"Oh, Boba," Sylvia grumbled, emerging from her book. "They're weaverbirds, not sparrows."

"Weaver, shmeaver, they're noisy, that's all."

"They're nesting," Sylvia said.

Bertha watched as a yellow bird swooped low over them and made a swift side turn into the pampas grass. It hacked away with its sharp beak and soared back into the sky trailing a long piece of pampas like a kite. Soon it was weaving it into its nest.

"I'll buy earplugs," she said. Silly to blame the birds. It was Marika's letter which had upset her and spoiled her night's sleep. She sat and pretended to read the paper, but all the time she was thinking: How terrible to leave all this.

She looked sidelong at Sylvia and sighed. How would the girl take to London? She looked like a million dollars, that was true, but she was a country lass at heart, never happier than when she was camping in the bush or looking after her pets. She was inclined to be intolerant, but really that was her only fault, Bertha thought.

Sylvia watched her grandmother narrowly. She thought she knew why everyone was in a bad temper; they had found out about last night's demo. Goodness knows how. She had held a placard on the pavement outside Wits University for three hours, until her arms were aching so much she thought she would pass out. She had been grateful when the police had asked them to go.

"Okay, let's cut out the guff," she began when her father had lit the fire and was sitting with them. "You're mad at me." There was a long silence. "Don't hedge, I know you're mad at me." She thrust her fist under her father's nose. "You taught me to stand up for what I think's right, Dad. Well, that's what I'm doing. Do what you like. I don't care." She glared aggressively, obviously caring very much indeed.

Günter stared at the chewed finger waving in front of his eyes and sighed. Perhaps London would do her good, he thought. Lately she had developed a rough way of talking to offset her increasingly feminine appearance.

"You're going to England," he said. "When you finish school. Your mother insists."

She gasped and spun round to Bertha. Behind her she heard Claire dropping a plate.

"Insists!" she heard Claire snarl. "Who cares if she insists? She has no right."

"No right," Sylvia echoed. For once they agreed on something. "I won't go."

She turned appealingly to Bertha. "You hate England, don't you, Bertha? Well, I won't go without you."

"It's not that simple," Bertha began uneasily. "Your mother has custody. She's let you stay here all this time, but she has every right to insist on having you with her. When she brought you to stay with me it was with the understanding that you would return when you were older and she was in a position to look after you—it just took a little longer than she expected. I can't stop you from going—even if I wanted to. And I don't. You see," Bertha explained unhappily, "if only I had stayed in England . . . well, you would have been there instead of here. I always felt guilty for not staying to help Marika."

"She sent me away," Sylvia said defiantly. "She never came holidays, like she promised."

"Your mother wants you to give London a chance for a year," Günter said. "After that you can come home. She's built up a very big business. You're to inherit it one day, if you want, but now she wants to know whether she should keep it going—for you. Otherwise she intends to sell out."

"Do you believe that?" Sylvia said, suddenly peering at Bertha with the candor of the very young. "Do you believe a word of that?"

"Your mother must be very lonely to make such a strong case," Bertha said.

"She needs you," Günter added.

"So my needs are to be overruled by Mother's needs and your needs," she said nastily. "Oh, don't try to pull the wool over my eyes." Her face was quite swollen with anger now. "You're both besotted with her. You always have been."

"You're being absurd," Bertha began. "It's a question of conscience. She's your mother . . ."

"She's nothing. Less than nothing. I hate her. You didn't know that, did you?" She flopped back in her chair and looked to Claire for support.

"I don't think she should go . . ." Claire began, and was silenced at a gesture from Günter.

"Your mother wants a chance to get to know you," Günter went on. "Just a year . . . then you can come home."

"If you send me away I'll never come back," Sylvia cried as she rushed through the house followed by her dog.

She heard them calling her as she ran to her suite and bolted the door of her study. She knew she would argue and fight and plead and cause no end of trouble, but finally she would be forced to go . . . and why? Because Dad would never take her side against her mother. She could never forget the look on Dad's face when he had pleaded with her bloody mother to marry him in that grotty Lüderitz hotel. He still cared . . . after all this time he still cared . . . the dumb fool! Now she was to be sent to her mother on a plate. Like a sacrificial gift to an implacable goddess.

"Oh, damn! Damn! Damn!" she cried as she threw herself on the floor.

Chapter Fifty-eight

A grizzling morning sky and the airport twice as gloomy. A ghastly place for a reunion! Her daughter was used to space and the newness of everything. Marika gripped the barrier railing apprehensively. For the last three weeks she had been vacillating from excitement to gloomy foreboding and now the weather seemed to echo all her fears. Goddamnit! Couldn't it have been fine, just this once? After all, it was April, but April in name only; the trees not yet in bud.

She felt Tony's hand gripping her shoulder and glanced sidelong at him. If only Tony had met Sylvia in South Africa; her daughter was bound to be tired and first impressions were so important. She had suggested to Tony that he remain behind and meet her family at the house, but he had been hell-bent on coming. "I'm Papa!" he had insisted laughingly. "Tell her to call me Papa." He was enjoying his role. He had bought a tandem bicycle and there was a new mare in the stables . . . She was not supposed to know about it. If only he would love Sylvia just a little; if only Sylvia would love him; if only they could be a family. Oh, please, please, she found herself whispering.

Over three years had passed since Marika had seen her daughter; too long and it was her own fault. She had been unwilling to meet Günter now that he was married to Claire; jealous of Sylvia being a part of their family and furious that Bertha stayed on so happily. Now she was longing to bridge the gap and build a bond with her daughter. Heal the scars! A second chance. That's all she wanted, just a second chance. Sylvia was seventeen, she kept reminding herself, no longer a child, yet Marika could only visualize her as a gangling teenager, taller perhaps, but otherwise unchanged.

The first South Africans were emerging: suntanned smiles, wider frames, and safari bags slung over their shoulders. She raised one hand and rested it momentarily over Tony's, felt his fingers pressing her shoulder. Now she was glad he had come. Irrational fears were penetrating her fragile aplomb. They had missed the plane, or they were not coming. Perhaps Bertha had changed her mind, or Günter had stopped them.

She shivered with fright. Then she looked up and saw Bertha. Mottled red face and swollen eyes. Marika was about to rush forward when she gasped, shocked and bewildered. The young woman clutching Bertha was breathtakingly lovely, from her wide cheekbones to her astonishingly direct eyes. She was unsmiling now, but her lips were full and perfectly shaped, her nose exotically curved, and there was more . . . so much more than beautiful features, there was passion in her huge violet eyes, while her ash-blond hair accentuated a certain purity of expression. Her short, ragged haircut, shift and flat sandals implied a certain reluctance to accept her exquisite appearance.

It had to be Sylvia. No one else possessed those eyes, but for the rest . . .

"Tony, she's . . . she's so . . ."

"Tired," he said curtly.

Marika called out, waved and rushed forward, numbed by a sense of unreality. Glancing back at Tony, she noticed he looked dazed and upset. For God's sake, what was the matter with him? She hugged her daughter tightly and felt the girl stiffen and step backward. Then she babbled a lengthy greeting. Enough words for two. She paused, breathless.

"Bertha's been so sick." They were the first words her daughter spoke. She made it sound like an accusation.

"Marikala, darling," Bertha began soothingly. "Don't

listen to Sylvia, I'm all right. Now we're on God's earth you'll see how quickly I'll recover.''

At least Bertha had not changed. She was always airsick.

Together they found the luggage and a trolley, exchanging silly trivialities to pass the time, and to Marika it seemed as if Bertha and she had been parted for only a few days. Soon they were driving home through the drizzle.

Glancing over her shoulder, Marika flinched when she saw Sylvia shooting disgusted glances at the gray houses dimly seen through misted car windows and the rain. Tony was withdrawn and strangely quiet.

"Tony wants you to call him Papa," Marika said laughingly, her face turned toward Sylvia, but her hand squeezing Tony's knee.

"No, I don't," Tony said flatly. "That would be absurd."

Marika gasped. Deflated and betrayed. "Perhaps it would be inappropriate after all," she said gaily, but her laugh sounded false even to herself.

Filled with confusion and close to tears, Marika endured Sylvia's hostility and Tony's remoteness and gabbled to Bertha of old times until the car approached Outwood Manor.

Then Sylvia suddenly flashed into life, oohing and aahing over their rambling country home with its old slate roof, tiny gabled windows, the barn and the lake.

"So English," Sylvia sighed, "so perfect. I would have thought this the last place you would choose, Mother," Sylvia said. "It's heavenly."

Why the implied insult? Marika did not answer.

"Wait until you see inside, honey." Tony's voice boomed in the car. He was grinning now, looking pleased and proud as he parked the car. Everything's going to be all right after all, Marika told herself. We just need time.

Lunch was waiting in the old wood-paneled dining room. It was a painful procedure with Sylvia smirking at the tablecloth and Bertha talking too much and too hurriedly as if to carry the occasion singlehanded. Tony was curt and withdrawn; it was quite unlike him. For Christ's sake—

Marika wanted to plead with them all—can't you even bloody try? She caught Bertha's eye and made a special effort to look calm and happy.

Sylvia was gulping her coffee unbecomingly.

"Can I go and look . . . by myself, I mean . . . just sort of poke around?"

They spoke at once: "Sure, honey," and "Why not unpack first, darling?"

Sylvia shot Tony a grateful glance, ignored her mother and went out into the garden.

"She's grown a lot," Marika said smilingly to Tony. "Why, she's turning into a good-looking girl."

Tony looked at her strangely, but did not answer.

"Wouldn't you say so?" she persisted.

"An understatement."

"What's got into him?" Marika said later when they were going up to Bertha's room. She linked her arm with Bertha's. "He was fine at the airport. Well, never mind Tony; it can't be anything serious; let's talk about you."

To Tony it was serious. It was her face which had over-whelmed him, so hauntingly familiar, yet unfamiliar. So much of Marika was there, but a newer, younger and even more exquisite version of the woman he had loved obses-sively and lusted over for the past two years. He felt like a man who has purchased a forged painting and afterward is confronted with the real work of art. Coveted, but not his. Thwarted! Surely it was she he had fallen in love with. Marika was the replica.

He was filled with anger, allied to a sense of guilt. Sylvia was flesh and blood, not a painting, and further-more his stepdaughter. He was afraid Marika had noticed the rush of blood to his face and the sensuality that had flooded his loins. He had been scared to talk or even to look. But later, at home, the sight of those long, quivering limbs, the slender waist, the candid, glowing eyes had set him swaggering like a callow youth. Then he had been glad she liked the house, glad of the tandem bicycle and dappled mare, unable to resist taking her part.

"Oh God," he groaned. "This can't be happening." He felt that he was drowning in something new and terrifying. It was a strange, unwelcome feeling that he could not define. He stood staring out of the window moodily, for once oblivious to the view.

That was how Sylvia found him. She tapped lightly on his open office door and when there was no reply she walked in.

"Hey, Tony, you really dig that view." The slang was incongruous when spoken in her top-drawer school accent. Her voice was soft and low-pitched and her magnificent eyes were gazing at him with a mixture of shyness and pique.

She stood too closely, peering up into his face, and he wondered momentarily if she was shortsighted. Then she put one hand on his arm.

"Tony . . . or is it Papa?" She laughed harshly and the sound upset him. "Poor Mama and her world of illusions. I came to tell you not to worry about Bertha and me . . . being here, I mean . . . we're not staying. I promised her I'd give London a try, but I hate it already and I can't say I blame you . . . being fed up, I mean. Imagine being landed with a grown-up stepdaughter."

Tony's eyebrow shot up. "Don't be silly, that was the last thing I was thinking." He stared down at her thoughtfully. She was a self-willed young woman who for two pins would pack her bags and leave today. The thought was chilling. He mustered a bantering tone: "You're not grown-up at all." Then he smiled. It was a slow, crinkling sort of grin that affected every part of his face.

A total smile, Sylvia decided as she stared up uncertainly. His voice sounded odd, or was it her imagination? She was suddenly overcome by embarrassment as her worldly-wise veneer melted. What an attractive man he was when he smiled. Brown eyes glinting, cheeks dimpling in the rough skin where stubble traced a darker shade to his suntanned skin. He was not unusually tall, yet he gave the impression of being huge, something to do with the vitality he beamed out, she supposed. In spite of his

charm there was a harshness there. His features were
strong, but when he was not smiling he looked hard, even
cruel.

Then she wondered why she should care. But still . . . it
bothered her. In Sylvia's world there were the goodies and
the baddies and she was uncertain of how to classify Tony.
With Mother it was easy. She had been classified "bad-
die" since Sylvia was eleven.

"Perhaps it's just that you were expecting someone
younger."

"What makes you think that?" She was dead right, of
course. Woman's intuition.

"You looked so shocked. I was watching you."

He spoke without thinking and regretted it. "You're
lovely."

She giggled. Then she moved away and stared out of the
window.

Watching her, Tony felt vaguely foolish. He understood
her all too well, a product of her exclusive environment.
Morals, like everything else, were a luxury; she would
have the very best and she would wear them on her arm
the way medieval knights had flaunted their colors—for
the world to take note of and admire. She was looking for
her dragon and he could well fit the role. The possibility
was unappealing.

"I know I'm beautiful," she said with unexpected candor. "I've been told so many times and I can see for
myself in the mirror, but d'you know something? I hate it.
Hate it!" She lowered her voice consciously. "I only want
the things I work for. Besides, it's too much."

"You don't know how to handle it?"

"Exactly."

"Oh, I think you do." He smiled, sure of himself
again. "You use it all the time. Perhaps unconsciously.
It's a very effective weapon and you are very young and
quite defenseless."

"I certainly hope that's not true," she said, meaning it.
She had the strangest feeling that she was out of her depth
and that Tony was quite unfathomable; a man in disguise.

Surely there was something missing behind that smiling exterior. But then he smiled again and put one hand on her shoulder. "You mustn't mind me teasing you," he said. "I'm a terrible tease. I think we're going to be friends."

"Oh, please," she murmured, feeling safer now. She glanced up at him and her eyes implored him to continue the deception.

"Tell me, should a woman as beautiful as you ride a tandem bicycle?" he asked, laughing.

She flushed. "Stop flattering me."

"Stepfathers don't flatter. They admonish."

She giggled and relaxed visibly. "I don't know about a beautiful woman, but your stepdaughter certainly can."

It had stopped drizzling. Necklaces of raindrops hung from every branch and glistened on spiderwebs in the tangled undergrowth. There was a delicious smell of fallen leaves and damp earth. They laughed a great deal and pedaled wildly uphill, racing down dangerously. Once they fell into stinging nettles and Tony showed her how to rub dock leaves over the blemishes.

They picked violets in the hedgerows and found primroses, and Sylvia fell in love with the English countryside. Wisps of cloud circled in the sky; swallows swooped low overhead; a skylark was twittering over celandine, clover and wild primulas—rising and falling purposelessly, as if in ecstasy with its own motion. When they saw a fox darting across the road Sylvia squealed with delight.

"Oh, it's too much, it's too much." She flung herself onto a damp grassy verge and clutched the grass with her hands. Then she rolled on her back, plucking a buttercup, and gazed at the sky.

Perfection—whichever way she turns, Tony thought, watching her carefully. She outshone every rare and beautiful thing he owned. He had never seen beauty like hers. It was more than good looks, but something to do with her warmth and the pure, childlike passion for life shining from her eyes.

"I'll show you Switzerland, and Italy," Tony said,

looking flushed and overexcited. He propped the tandem against a tree and sat on the ground beside her. "There's so much to see. Don't rush off too soon."

"You're frightfully rich, aren't you?" she said childishly.

"I'm frightful," he answered, pulling ferocious faces.

She giggled. "You don't look much like a business tycoon."

"That's the terrible thing about business tycoons, they fool everyone by looking human."

"So what's so special about you?" she asked.

"Nothing at all." He looked away, thinking that he could answer more truthfully, could have told her that he used people and sometimes he destroyed them; that he was afraid he would destroy her, too, and that for some inexplicable reason he would rather destroy himself than her. "I usually get my own way," he said.

When he looked at her she thought that he looked strange. She felt startled and a little confused. She flushed, but could not look away from him. "I'm terribly thirsty," she said.

"There's a pub down the road . . ."

"Oh, good. I've never had English beer."

"How old are you, Tony?" she asked when they were sitting at the long wooden bench in front of the old inn.

"Thirty," he said, and watched a small flicker of a frown hover between her brows.

"Mother didn't tell me that you were only twelve years older than I," she murmured.

"Why should she?" he said curtly.

"Why didn't you marry someone your own age?" she asked gravely.

"Because I never met anyone quite like Marika before, because at the time I thought she was the most beautiful woman in the world."

She looked away pouting. "And do you love my mother?"

"Yes," he said shortly, "and since you're her daughter it stands to reason that I'll love you, too."

The frown vanished. Suddenly she giggled. After that

she was full of laughter and babbling chatter as they pedaled home.

Tony was feeling vulnerable. It was the first time in his life he had experienced this unpleasant sensation. He could not believe it was happening to him.

Chapter Fifty-nine

She had drunk two martinis and then champagne while they waited for dinner in the exclusive nightclub which also housed London's most extravagant gambling table. The champagne dinner had been her own idea, to introduce Sylvia to London's nightlife. Marika wanted to show her daughter a world where money counted, where she was well known and where her furs would be worn almost exclusively. Then she would broach the question of Sylvia's future.

She had dressed with care. For some reason which she did not fully understand, Marika wanted to look young and seductive; she chose a Barrera creation, a sleek, short, clinging excuse for a dress which revealed her voluptuous figure while the shimmering dark green satin offset her amber eyes and highlighted the pale sheen of her skin. If nothing else Sylvia would see that her mother was still an attractive woman, she reasoned, for Sylvia had been openly antagonistic since her arrival and Marika was desperately anxious to win her daughter's approval.

She had been upstaged all the same, she thought without rancor. There was no antidote for the appeal of youth; that dewy glow more potent than the most costly makeup. With her incredibly sensuous features, the glowing warmth of her eyes and her striking ash-blond hair, Sylvia had so much more than mere youth. She was a sensation. She did not need the black Balenciaga Günter had bought her. This evening, in a place where most of the world's beauties had been seen at one time or another, all eyes had been surreptitiously glancing their way. Perhaps it was her prim expression, the short, ragged haircut or lack of makeup which said louder than any words: to hell with you and your world.

Now Marika was feeling overgroomed as she nervously sipped her champagne while Sylvia sat with a fixed small smile on her face, distastefully watching the diners, each glance a rebuke.

Everyone at the table was on edge, not the least Tony, Marika could see that. He was ultrasensitive, too quick with the repartee, the wisecracks coming faster than usual— his smile a grimace of tension. She wondered what was worrying him.

She noticed Bertha was watching her anxiously. Why, good heavens . . . she was not drunk . . . merely a little relaxed . . . the champagne seemed to have clarified her intentions. Whereas before she had felt uneasy about persuading Sylvia to join her business, she now realized that her daughter had a tailor-made future. She would have London at her feet and become a top model, achieving all that Marika had wanted but never accomplished. Together, mother and daughter would make a sensational team and their fashions would be unrivaled.

Bemused with happy daydreams, she said, "Sylvia darling, we must choose a fur coat for you tomorrow. White sealskin would look divine. Did you notice at least six women here are wearing Magos furs? You'll soon be able to recognize them."

Sylvia shuddered and looked down at her hands. "Oh, no, thank you, Mother," she mumbled.

"Why, darling, you must," Marika babbled on. "You should have a wonderful wardrobe. People will recognize you. Why, even here, everyone's noticed you; they're wondering who you are and where you come from." She chuckled, feeling happy and self-confident, and wondered why Bertha was kicking her on the ankle.

"Sylvia's very young," Bertha said softly.

"The younger, the better," Marika persisted gaily. "Some furs can only be worn well . . . I mean really well . . . by the very young." Let no one say she was ungracious about Sylvia's marvelous youth.

"But I could never . . . ugh!" Sylvia shuddered. "Just the thought of all those poor wild animals: trapped . . . dying in agony . . . just so that you can get rich . . . so that these women . . . these awful . . ." She faltered and broke off. "I'd rather die than wear a fur . . . and as for making money out of cruelty and pain . . . oh, I could never."

Marika sat bolt upright, puzzled and overpale. "I don't make money out of cruelty and pain," she said, stupidly echoing her daughter's words.

"I think you do."

Marika reeled with shock. A deliberate cut of the blade, cruelly administered, and war had not even been declared. How did her daughter learn to be so sure of herself, so scornfully self-righteous? Marika wondered. That was the advantage of youth . . . the reason for their arrogance . . . untried and therefore pure . . . innocent until proved guilty. If you want to be a saint, she thought foolishly, die very young.

"I hadn't noticed you were a vegetarian." Marika stumbled over the words, numb with pain. "You ate lamb chops for lunch, enjoyed them, I thought. I doubt the lamb suffered more or less than a fox or a seal."

"I'm becoming a vegetarian," Sylvia snapped back. "Besides, you could never understand . . . we live in different worlds . . . have different standards," Sylvia went on, each word a prod in the wound. "And quite honestly, I think it's best if we talk about something else." She turned to Tony for support.

Why him? Marika wondered. What was so goddamn pure about him? Blinded with tears, she drained her glass and the waiter instantly refilled it. By now she probably thinks I'm an alcoholic, too, she thought.

"I'd say the only thing safe to eat nowadays," Tony said seriously as he peered at the menu, "is a cabbage that died of natural causes. I believe it's their specialty." He raised an eyebrow as he shot Sylvia a derisive glance. "Would you allow me to order for you? Beware of the mashed potatoes. I've heard they gouge out eyes here."

"Oh, Tony." Sylvia let out a low gurgle and then, much against her wishes, burst into giggles. "You fool." Then she managed to look prim again. "Of course, you don't understand . . . how could you? You're older!"

Older! That dreadful word again. Was there some conspiracy among the young to retain morality for everyone?

Marika cowered behind the menu. Her ears were humming, her eyes stinging, and her cheeks were flushed with shame. They'll see I'm on the point of tears, she thought, grabbing her glass and draining it as she struggled to push the hurt away. For God's sake, this was supposed to be a celebration.

Marika pulled herself together and looked at her daughter with what she thought was a motherly expression. "Darling, I have good news for you," she said. "You've been accepted by the Lorraine Ashley school of modeling."

She sat back smiling gently, feeling that at last she had scored. Ashley's was the top modeling school in London. They took only a few novices each year.

Sylvia was looking at her with astonishment, her mouth slightly open, lips parted. Well, at least I've surprised her, she thought.

"But, Mother," Sylvia began. "I'm not going to be a model. I'm going to be a missionary . . . or at the very least a social worker. I could never waste my life with anything so frivolous as fashions and furs or coming to places like this." She looked around contemptuously.

Marika heard a low chuckle and glanced sidelong at Tony. He was enjoying the row. Incredible! Now she felt doubly rejected. She glanced wildly at Bertha for support.

"But you must," she heard herself stammering. "It's all for you . . . this world . . . these companies . . . a lifetime's work . . . my collections . . . Why, Sylvia, you can't understand how tough it is to get to the top and stay there. I'm proud of what I've accomplished. It's taken me fifteen years . . . '' Suddenly she wished she had not harped upon the years.

She slammed down her glass and the champagne frothed and spilled on the tablecloth. She could feel her cheeks burning with embarrassment and her eyes stinging.

"Marika, I think you've drunk too much," Tony said coldly. He turned to her daughter. "Would you care to dance, Sylvia?"

She watched astounded as Sylvia nodded. The next minute Tony and she were gliding on the small candlelit dance floor to the muted sound of the three-piece ensemble.

Turning to Bertha for support, Marika saw her mother wiping her eyes surreptitiously with her napkin.

"Oh, Bertha, it's really not important," she said in an attempt to look gay and uncaring. She reached out and squeezed her hand.

"She's just a child," Bertha said, sniffing. "But it takes a child to really hurt, particularly one's own children. You haven't seen her at her best . . . Marika," Bertha went on, trying to draw her daughter's attention away from her problems. "I'm moving back to Finchley next week. I've decided to stay on in London while Sylvia's here."

"You're so sure she'll need you," Marika said, feeling that once again she had failed as a mother.

"No, I'm afraid you might need me. Sylvia's not as vulnerable as you. Fortunately."

Marika looked startled.

"I don't want to be an interfering mother-in-law," Bertha went on in a manner that was typically her, "so I've made up my mind to live on my own! I'm going to look for a job to keep myself occupied."

"But, Bertha, really, I feel terrible. I thought you had plenty of cash."

"I have enough, but I wouldn't mind earning more. The point is, I need a job where I get to meet and talk to people. It's the job I want more than the money."

"Why, Bertha." Marika beamed. "I know just the job

for you. Would you be interested in personnel? I don't have anyone handling that at the factory and you're so sympathetic. Tanya complains that half her time is wasted sorting out the staff's problems. You know Tanya. She'd prefer to employ robots. She isn't interested in people's problems.''

"That would suit me admirably." Bertha replied. "If Tanya agrees, that is. Thank you, Marikala."

She broke off when she saw that Tony and Sylvia were coming back.

Marika flinched. Tony's hand was held proprietorially on Sylvia's shoulder. A familiar gesture. Sylvia was looking downcast and demure.

Marika fixed a smile in place, hoping that she looked wise and unaffected by her daughter's youthful hysteria.

"Hi, Tony." It was Bruce Rose, their stockbroker, and he was leaning back a little off balance, his cheeks flushed and gnarled with purple veins. He always affected a hearty manner, but tonight he was overdoing it. Without noticing Marika, he drooled over Sylvia. "God, but you know how to pick 'em," he roared. He winked lewdly, gripped Sylvia's hand and made a performance out of kissing it.

"My daughter . . ." Tony began coldly, but Bruce burst with laughter.

"Daughter! That's a good one. It might work with me, at my age, but you—you don't stand a chance, my boy."

"You're drunk," Tony said coldly.

Bruce looked bewildered, feeling rebuked and not knowing how to cope.

"Sure, sure," he said, and shrugged. "Aren't we all?" Then he caught sight of Marika at the table and flushed heavily. "I suppose you're going to say she's your daughter, too," he said, trying to recoup his position. "Ha, ha."

"She's my daughter," Marika said in a small, tired voice.

He frowned and gazed from one to the other. "Incredible," he murmured. He leaned over the table, blowing cognac and garlic fumes over Marika.

"She'll take some looking after," he said, his wits drowned in liquor. "Especially with your Tony. He's a sucker for beautiful women. Well, you should know that." He left abruptly.

"Tomorrow morning," Marika said firmly, "I'll get a new stockbroker and you, Sylvia, will learn a bit more about the world you are rejecting so energetically."

"There's no need to ride roughshod over the girl," Tony said soothingly. "We've had a talk, haven't we, Sylvia?" He placed one hand over hers. "Sylvia wants to go to university, but the new year is six months away. Meantime she's agreed to take the modeling course." He gazed at them smugly.

"Looks like you have influence," Marika said quietly.

Sylvia stood up, confused and watchful. Her mother looked haggard and Bertha was clearly angry. What had she done? Not that she cared, but still, it would be nice to know. She felt like a child who had grabbed a toy pistol and discovered it was lethal. Why this big deal about everything she said? If only she had not agreed with Tony, but it made sense. She knew he had flattered her to get his own way. "You're one of the loveliest women I've ever seen," he had told her while they were dancing, "but gauche! If only you would learn to walk properly and lose that childish slouch of yours. Why not spend the next few months learning to grow up gracefully? What have you got to lose?" Come to think of it, whose side was he on anyway? Sylvia thought resentfully. She no longer felt quite so sure of herself. This was not like home. She was in enemy territory.

"I'm tired. I should like to go to bed. No, please," she said as Tony stood up. "I'd rather take a taxi."

"I'll go with Sylvia," Bertha said heavily. "I'm feeling very tired."

"I couldn't possibly allow . . ." Tony signaled the waiter.

Sylvia placed a hand on his arm. "For me, Tony. Stay with Mother."

Why should her daughter have to beg Tony to stay with her? Marika thought grimly, watching Sylvia glide away.

Tony sat down, looking stunned.

"Quite a night," Marika said to break a long silence.

Tony turned his head and stared at her. There was something guarded about his expression; a secrecy she had not seen before. I'm imagining things, she thought.

"Quite a night," Tony agreed.

"I'm not very hungry." She looked at her melon without enthusiasm. Tony seemed quite unperturbed as he wolfed down his soup.

"You don't seem very worried about Sylvia's departure," she said heavily.

"Should I be?"

"Well, I am. Sylvia can be very hurtful," she went on, hoping to elicit some sympathy.

"It's quite simple—you don't understand her," he explained carefully as if talking to a child. "Can't be helped," he went on in a matter-of-fact voice. "It's called the generation gap. Don't let it worry you."

She stared at him hopelessly and then looked away. Folding her hands desolately on her lap, she tried to concentrate on the fashionably dressed women around them.

For the first time in her life she felt her age. It was no use telling herself she was only thirty-seven; pushing forty seemed to describe it better. Einstein missed one vital point, she decided. Time was relative, but the difference depended upon whether you were male or female.

Chapter Sixty

Sharp at eight the next morning Bertha arrived at Marika's factory. She wished she had not told Marika about her need to find work; she should have known her daughter would think of something. "Jobs for pals," she muttered scathingly. She had never been in favor of it.

Marika had wanted to fetch her in the afternoon and drive her to the plant, but Bertha had told her she'd get herself there. Let's keep family relationships out of the business, she had said. Who was she fooling? At fifty-nine she'd be lucky to find a job anywhere.

She would stay there a week, she decided, and see if there was anything useful for her to do. If she couldn't earn her keep she would leave. Once she had made up her mind about this, she did not feel so bad.

When she reached the corner she paused in amazement. The building was painted in shades of beige and chocolate. Sidersky Furs, Marika Magos Fashions and Furs, Magos Haute Couture—the outside was brimming with signs and it all looked very exclusive.

Bertha knew that her daughter had done well, but she was quite unprepared for the size and scope of the organization. She walked inside curiously. It was the same entrance Mendel had used, but that was all that was the same; inside was all glitter and glass.

"Good morning," she began. "I'm Bertha Factor, the new personnel officer. Do you know where I should go?"

"Personnel?" The blonde beamed at her. "That's a new one. We haven't had one of those before. I could do with a fire. I can tell you that now."

"I believe you," Bertha said. "It's freezing here. I'll . . . er . . . write that down." She took out her notebook.

"You get that past Mr. Sidwell and I'll think you're some kind of magician," the girl said, and sniffed.

She flicked a manicured finger on the intercom. "Mr. Sidwell, your new personnel manager is here."

"Please wait," she said.

Bertha waited, feeling increasingly nervous. She had a terrible feeling that Marika had forgotten about her.

She disliked John Sidwell on sight. He looked mild enough, but she could sense the steel behind his slight frame and nervous twitch. His pale gray eyes glittered furiously and cuff links twinkled in the fluorescent lights as he frantically waved his hands.

"Is this some kind of a joke?" he said. "Personnel! And you claim Ms. Magos hired you—at your age?"

"Tolerance comes with age," Bertha told him tartly. "One can learn to be considerate given time—maybe even you could, Mr. Sidwell."

"I wouldn't count on that. This is all very irregular," he complained. "I'm the managing director. Ms. Magos is the chairman. I do all the hiring and firing and I can't imagine why she should think we need a personnel officer."

Well, I can, looking at you, Bertha thought, and kept quiet with difficulty.

"I presume she went into your background, since she hired you."

"She knows it well enough," Bertha retorted.

"Well, let's see if you're any good," he said ungraciously. "There's a strike been declared by the drivers. It's most inconvenient right now—and don't they know it. Sort it out and you've got a job."

The drivers were in the yard. Angry shouts and waving fists. It was very intimidating, but not very helpful, she thought.

Bertha wondered what to do. She could not make herself heard. Finally she stood on a box.

"Shouting isn't going to help," she called. No one heard, so she tried again. Eventually a tired-looking man with a kind face and humorous brown eyes called up to her.

"Do yourself an injury, you will, standing on that box screaming your lungs out. I'd get down if I were you."

"But they won't listen," she said, red in the face.

He whistled, shrill and authoritative. There was a sudden silence.

"I'm the personnel officer and I'm here to listen to your grievances," she called out.

"Grievances, hark at 'er." The brown-eyed man cocked his thumb derisively in her direction. "I'm the shop steward here," he went on. "We ain't got no bloody grievances, ma'am. We've got two tickets for speeding that've got to be paid. Old shit-arse there, begging your pardon, ma'am, won't pay 'em. So we're going on strike till the blighter puts his hand in the cashbox and comes up with fifty bloody quid. That's how much he's docked off our wages."

"I see," Bertha said worriedly. "But why should the company be responsible? A traffic offense constitutes breaking the law, I believe."

"You've been listening to 'im, haven't you? The fact of the matter is, we've got schedules that are too tight to follow without a bit of speeding. If we don't make our schedules we don't get home in time, and what's worse— the customers don't get their goods. There's not enough vans and not enough drivers—that's a fact."

Was she being set up? Looking at the shop steward she didn't think so.

Finally the drivers agreed to go back to work on condition Bertha drove around London delivering furs with the shop steward.

They were right, she agreed five hours later. The schedule was hopelessly impracticable.

She saw John Sidwell at two. "I hope you enjoyed your lunch," she said. "I've had none, and neither have your drivers, as usual. The strike's sorted out, but you'll have to get another van and driver. I'll rework the routes for deliveries and I suggest you pay these fines personally. You're responsible for them, not the drivers. It is you who worked out these silly schedules, isn't it?"

For a moment John was too surprised to answer. Then he said nastily, "Giving in doesn't constitute success. I certainly have no intention of paying their fines."

"Then I'll take these delivery schedules of yours to the police," she said. "They'll be interested in the way you operate your fleet."

"Nonsense," he said, shrill and angry. "They're pulling the wool over your eyes." He peered at her over the top of his glasses. "I've just the job for you," he said. "The storekeeper wants insulated clothes and boots to work in the cold storage where we keep the furs. Spend the afternoon there, Mrs. Whatever-your-name-is; find out if he really needs them."

Marika had spent the morning in the New Bond Street wholesale shop and she arrived at the plant a little after four. She looked into John's office. "We'll have to refurbish the shop," she told him. "It's looking tatty lately. By the way, John, my mother has arrived in London and she's a bit lonely. She'll be popping into the factory one of these days. Put the red carpet out, there's a dear—find her a nice office, make her feel important. I'd be grateful."

"Marika darling, I can't wait to meet your mum. If she's like you she'll be divine. Oh and by the way, that bossy old tart you engaged for personnel is locked up in the cold storage cooling off her temper. I reckon she'll quit by nightfall."

Then he saw Marika's expression. "Oh no! So help me God!"

They raced to the stockroom.

"I'm glad this happened, Marikala," Bertha said firmly when she stumbled out of the cold room. "Now I know for sure you need me."

Thinking back now, Bertha decided that it had been the best introduction she could possibly have. The staff loved her, because they hated John, and consequently she was accepted by everyone from her very first day.

Now it was April again. She had been working at the

plant for a year. It didn't seem possible; the time had flown because she loved it and for the first time Bertha was enjoying England. The weather was milder this year; the leaves had opened earlier and the trees were covered in spring greenery. The parks were full of daffodils and so were the window boxes outside their factory windows. Bertha had ordered them, reasoning that they would be good for morale.

Inside, the factory walls had been repainted in warm, sunny tones, scientifically proved to enhance morale, and nowadays soothing, but lively music filled the plant from morning until evening.

Since she had joined the company almost a year ago, Bertha had been studying productivity and personnel part-time and she hoped to become a member of the Institute soon. She took her job very seriously. She knew she was successful because productivity was up by twenty percent, staff turnover was down and absenteeism cut by half.

She was happy and she knew why—once again she was needed. She had hired a secretary and with a little help from the many social welfare departments she now coped with broken marriages, lack of adequate crèches, housing loans, sickness—real and imaginary—and even the odd case of alcoholism.

Bertha liked to arrive at the factory each morning at seven. At that hour only Tanya was there and the two women usually had a cup of coffee before they began their busy days.

This morning there was no sign of Tanya and Bertha was surprised when she arrived late.

Nowadays she looked very different from the nondescript machine hand Bertha remembered from when Mendel ran the plant. She was always well dressed; this morning she was wearing a black tailored suit with a severe pin-striped blouse. Her hair was blond and swept up into a chignon on top of her head and her glasses were huge and diamond-studded. She looked the part of a successful, middle-aged career woman, which is exactly what she was, Bertha thought, for she ran the production of three different ranges single-handed.

Tanya sat down with a sigh. She said, "Oh dear."

"Don't worry," Bertha said. "Just talk."

"Believe it or not, I've been a real fool," Tanya began, looking embarrassed. "I was walking in the West End last Saturday morning when this really handsome man, sort of Italian-looking, in his thirties, came along and said I had just the face they were looking for and would I be prepared to let this beauty salon take some photographs of me, sort of suitably made up?

"I don't know what came over me, but I let him smooth-talk me all the way into the salon. There were all these pretty young attendants, oohing and aahing, and they gave me a free sauna and massage, plus makeup session. Then they took the photographs and I signed permission for them to use them."

She grinned a funny, lopsided grin. "Well, that's what I thought I was signing. Yesterday the bill came. It's over a thousand pounds. Can you believe that? Payable monthly, for three sessions a week. It seems the photographs were for a before-and-after series of pictures. The ones they took were for the before bit," Tanya said, overcome with embarrassment.

Well, what did she expect? Bertha thought. But the crooks should be taught a lesson. "Let me have your copy of the contract," she said. "I'm quite sure our company lawyer will sort them out . . ."

"That's just it," Tanya interrupted her. "I don't want anyone to know and I really don't want to have to see . . ."

"I know just how you feel—leave it to me," Bertha said.

Tanya settled down, looking more relaxed. Thank heavens for that. "Now, Bertha, about that new model, that dark girl from Jamaica who's supposed to launch the ethnic look. Well, I walked into the pressing room yesterday lunchtime and caught her with the cutter. Very compromising, very embarrassing. Have a word with her, will you? I don't want her fired. She's actually very good at her job."

Bertha made a note in her diary and Tanya left.

Maybe she could find five minutes after lunch, but it was going to be a hectic day: lunch with the company's insurance broker—he claimed he had found a better deal for the company's pension fund—after that there was an appointment with the sales manager of a flexitime company. She had best speak to the model first.

Tonight she had promised to watch Sylvia modeling Deidre Fashions' new collection at a do at the Dorchester.

She sat back thinking about Sylvia and Marika and sighed. They were so much alike; perhaps that was why they could not get on with each other. They were both single-minded, overachievers.

Since Sylvia had agreed to learn modeling for a year she had thrown herself wholeheartedly into the job. She did not go out with boys, or waste time. She had a tough routine of work, work, work. It was just the same with Marika. She had to be the best and she drove herself frenziedly from one collection to the next.

Right now she was preparing her lines for spring 1967, and Bertha could not imagine how Marika managed to keep up with Tony's hectic social life while working all hours at the plant. She wished she knew what it was that drove her daughter to push herself to such lengths. Surely now she was successful she could relax a little, but when she asked her one day her daughter had just shrugged. "There's more to life than happiness, Bertha," she had said, looking profoundly Slavic with her burning amber eyes so intense and bitter. It occurred to Bertha then that Marika had never recovered from the war. She carried her hatred inside her and she would not let go of it. "You have so much, Marikala," Bertha had told her anxiously. "You should be happy. I don't think you even try."

"Now, Bertha, don't start practicing your psychology on me," Marika had said, suddenly smiling again. "Of course I'm happy."

Well, she couldn't fool her mother. Come to think of it, of all the problems in the company none were quite as unsolvable as those of her own family, Bertha thought sadly.

Chapter Sixty-one

It was a Sunday morning and Marika was lying in bed half awake and half asleep, listening to the drip-drip of rain-drops falling from the roof to the gravel path and a thrush singing in the oak tree near their window.

Why was it so peaceful? she wondered. Then she re-membered; Sylvia was away "on location," as she called it, in Singapore, and consequently her tape deck was not blaring the latest hits by the Beatles and Elvis and there were no friends shrieking in their heated swimming pool. Peace!

It had been an eventful eighteen months since Sylvia arrived in London. Once she had agreed to become a model, albeit temporarily, she had thrown all her energy into the joy of succeeding. She was like Günter in that respect, always wanting to be the best in whatever she did. And she had been better than even Marika had hoped. But it was Tony who had persuaded her to put off university for another year and aim for the top. Marika had been both puzzled and pleased. Eventually, she hoped, Sylvia's world would be fashion and clothing and she would be able to lure her into her business.

Günter had been disappointed and Sylvia had flown home to see him several times, usually with Bertha, who valued her trips to South Africa.

This morning Marika had a slight headache, nothing serious, and she was feeling shamefaced, too. Yesterday would have been Irwin's sixty-fifth birthday and she had spent the evening at Bertha's Finchley house. She had stayed on long after the guests had left and poured out her troubles while drinking too much of Bertha's sweet home-made wine.

What was the point of burdening Bertha with half-truths and unproved suspicions? Admittedly she felt worried, although she was not quite sure why. It was something to do with Tony, but she could not decide what the problem was. They hadn't had a fight, so why was he so . . . so remote. Yes, that was the right word, she thought, she could not accuse him of being unfriendly. Most of the time she tried not to worry about it.

At first Tony and she had taken Sylvia on holiday with them, and it had seemed that they were turning into a family, but soon Sylvia's own commitments took up her time and she made friends with the girls at the modeling school. Although she had just turned nineteen, Sylvia did not have a steady boyfriend. Marika had asked her about this one day. "They don't measure up to Dad, so I'm not interested," Sylvia had told her. When she needed an escort, Tony usually had to help out. He never refused and that was a point in his favor, Marika decided. Or was it?

She snuggled under the blankets and was trying to fall asleep when she remembered that today the Sunday *Times* was publishing a feature article about her daughter in the color magazine supplement. There had been several articles about Sylvia in recent months, but a whole feature— Well, really it was quite breathtaking.

Not wishing to wake Tony, she tiptoed down to the front door and retrieved the papers from the doorstep. Half asleep, she laid them on the hall table and leafed through the pages.

There it was: three pages and nine photographs of Sylvia in various poses and costumes. She gasped with pleasure. It was far better than she had anticipated.

Sylvia Crashes the London Fashion Scene was the headline. Marika sank onto the nearest chair and read: *A South African model who came to England less than eighteen*

*months ago has become one of London's most sought-after
models.*

Lovely Sylvia Shaw . . . Marika stopped reading for a
moment and stared at the photographs. One of them was
well known; it was the best shot of Sylvia taken for the
Lavender campaign and it had been featured on the cover
of *Nova* magazine. "Shaw," she murmured. A disaster,
but Sylvia had refused to use her own name, claiming that
it would give her undue preference over others if she were
known to be Marika's daughter. Eventually Bertha had
chosen Shaw.

With a sigh she returned to the text: *Lovely Sylvia Shaw,
19, came to London with no intention of breaking into the
local modeling scene.*

*Yet today she commands a fee of between £200 and
£400 an hour.*

*Sylvia, the daughter of one of London's most successful
couturiers, Marika Magos, has been featured on the cov-
ers of some of Europe's top women's magazines and in
several international TV advertising campaigns.*

*Recently she was picked as one of the James Bond girls
for the new 007 film, but pulled out when she discovered
she would have to appear in the nude.*

*Sylvia began her career at the Lorraine Ashley school of
modeling and within a few months was much in demand by
free-lance photographers. Her work has taken her to Spain,
Germany, Greece and America. Currently she is in Singapore on the new BOAC Jet-East campaign. To British
women she is best known for the Lavender cosmetic account when she appeared nightly on ITV for several months.*

*Surprisingly Sylvia does not intend to model for much
longer. "I want to find something worthwhile to do," she
said when interviewed in Cannes last week. Strange words
from the girl who has become a household name on two
continents.*

There was much more, but Marika was shivering in the
drafty hall. She rang for coffee and took the newspaper
back to bed.

Tony was half asleep, but when he saw the paper he sat

up. "Unbelievable," he muttered, but of course it wasn't. Physical perfection as rare as hers was bound to be in demand.

If it were only beauty the photographs revealed, but there was so much more than that, he mused. Sylvia had a pure virginal loveliness, but underlying it was a sense of latent sensuality. One could feel the passion that would one day surge to the surface; it shone in her eyes and miraculously was transmitted to film and paper. Add to that her astonishing directness and openness—small wonder the world's advertising agencies were outbidding each other for her services.

He gazed long and hard at the photographs, wondering how she was making out in Singapore and wishing he could be there with her. Well . . . why not?

He turned to Marika. "Hate to think of her there alone," he said. "It's one of the most notorious ports in the world. Filthy! No place for a young girl. Well, I guess you've got someone keeping an eye on her."

"No, I haven't," Marika said, looking worried. "I never gave it a thought. After all, girls of nineteen do what they like nowadays."

"Ah yes, in the West, but Singapore?" He let his unspoken threat sink in as he leaned back and studied the photographs.

"Maybe I should join her, but the collection's at an awkward stage. Only ten days to deadline."

"If you like, I'll fly over," he said. "I've a couple of interests I can look into at the same time. Just so she doesn't think we're knuckling in on her world."

"Oh, Tony, really, that's not necessary." She leaned over and kissed him. "I'm sure she'll stick with the advertising team." She felt ashamed of her doubts as she went to bathe. "Well, if you really think that's best," she called out guiltily. Then she sat on the edge of the bath feeling hopeless and miserable.

It was noon, a sultry, clouded, tropical noon, and thirty-five top airline and agency executives were sweating in

Singapore's bird park, where it was even hotter under the
gigantic netting which stretched for several acres down the
hillside.

They were filming a thirty-second TV commercial about
family package tours to the Far East and it was intended
that wives, having viewed the commercial, would feel
enthusiastic and confident enough to insist on accompany-
ing their husbands on future trips.

But why should they suffocate under this damnable
netting among a lot of squawking parrots? the airline
marketing manager asked himself for the fiftieth time that
day. Because the art director said so, and because the
campaign was costing more than a thousand pounds an
hour, so why beef about a little discomfort?

The art director was standing in a huddle with the
photographer, and the pound notes were trickling away
like water in that damned noisy waterfall, the airline manager thought irritably. "What the hell is delaying us?" he
yelled. The photographer explained politely: "The problem seems to be that there is no palm tree here, sir." The
manager snorted. He knew the score as well as they did.
Sylvia was to emerge framed against a backdrop of mountains and waterfalls. She would pause to admire the magnificent plumage of the birds perched in a palm tree while
dainty Oriental extras in kimonos trooped past chattering,
bowing and admiring Sylvia. The idea was that among this
bevy of local beauties, scenic splendor and exotic birds, an
attractive Western woman would outshine it all and look
even lovelier.

Now the camera was turning, the executives looked
tense and unhappy, the manager's mouth dried, for the
airline's madly expensive illusion was about to be created.

There was no sign of Sylvia. She had been taking a nap
in the trailer parked nearby. He was becoming more and
more worried. His job could be at stake.

The entire fantasy depended upon the beauty of Sylvia,
whom he had never met. But she'd have to be bloody good
to compete with the little Malayan misses here, one of

whom he had a date with that evening. He began to sweat more heavily now.

Then Sylvia appeared and suddenly the theme was no longer silly; the heat no longer unbearable. He took a deep breath. Wives would be planning their trips eastward with confidence. The airline was getting its money's worth.

Sylvia's shoulder-length ash-blond hair, her flawless milky skin and her huge violet eyes shone with a blatant invitation. Yet she looked virginal and lovely against the exotic backdrop and beside her the Malayan girls looked sallow and earthy, their hair lank and unattractive.

The airline chief wondered whether he should break his date. Perhaps Sylvia . . . ? He watched her thoughtfully and gave up hope. "Just too damn pure," he murmured, but he had forgotten the discomfort of the flies and the smell of the birds as he watched her whirl down the hillside, pause at the palm tree, which had miraculously appeared from nowhere, and stroke the plumage of a lovebird, while a flock of dainty, but now unappealing kimono-clad extras watched her with unconcealed envy.

Chapter Sixty-two

She leaned back, sighed and ordered another iced Coke from a waiter in white uniform, fez and gloves, and stared dismally at the revolving fan hanging from the ceiling. For Sylvia, Singapore was one big disappointment. The English stamp their seal wherever they go, she thought gloomily, leaving little English replicas scattered across the globe. "If I see another Hollyhock Crescent I'll throw up," she muttered. As for the hotel . . .

She sighed. She had expected something Eastern and exotic, but instead the famous Raffles Hotel contrived to convince the guests they were back in colonial days and that the British sahib still ruled the world. "Archaic!" she murmured rebelliously, like the two airline executives who were moving purposely toward her.

She glanced around for an escape exit and instead she saw Tony walking into the lounge.

"Tony," she yelled. "Oh, Tony." She raced across the room and flung her arms around his neck. "Oh my, what a lovely surprise, and just in time, too." She gestured over her shoulder. "Those creeps were on their way." She sighed theatrically. "Where's Mother?"

"In London." He stepped away, disentangling her arms from behind his neck. "She can't leave the business right now."

"That's the story of my life."

"Grow up," Tony said curtly. "You're too old for the Orphan Annie act. Forget it."

"Don't snarl at me. You've just arrived." She pouted and stepped away from him.

When she behaved like a child he felt annoyed. She could be so damned naïve sometimes. These childish, boisterous hugs irritated him. He said, "I thought you'd be out having fun somewhere."

"Fun . . . here? You must be kidding. With this crowd of freaks?"

"You're spoiled."

"I know. Some of it's your fault." She grinned and he felt his irritation melting away.

"Where've you been so far?"

"All the clubs." She looked desperate and he watched her thoughtfully.

"Well, I'll show you the Chinese quarter and Geary Street and that's about it."

He took her to old Hindu and Buddhist temples, and to narrow streets between rows of Oriental houses where poles, slung out of every window like flagposts, hung wet washing as their colors. They watched coolies hauling barrows to a deserted car park which was transformed in a trice to the world's largest open-air restaurant with sizzling live crabs and prawns leaping on hot coals, sea urchin omeletes, seaweed salad, curries and pies—every conceivable dish to please every palate; and they wandered down miles of rickety barrows and bought records and gewgaws; and then to Geary Street, where the world's most famous transvestites emerge by the score from gloomy doorways, magnificent in their finery and brand-new, blown-up breasts, like so many termite queens with their virgin wings and their brief moment of glory.

Then they wandered back, arm in arm, followed by a skinny half-caste boy with pale face and desperate, greedy eyes. "You want young girl? You want boy? Beautiful young boy? You want to watch girl with men? Beautiful girl—young girl? Girl with cucumber?" He recited his repertoire without remorse. "You say what you want. They do it."

"Make him go away, I feel sick," Sylvia moaned.

"I'll take you back," Tony said, loitering and unwilling to let her go. "Or if you like we'll charter a sampan and cruise around the bay."

"It's so warm," she said, leaning back in the boat and closing her eyes. "I could dream I was in Africa."

"You're homesick," he accused her.

"Oh yes, terribly homesick. Don't you ever miss Italy?"

"I was very young when we left."

"Sometimes you seem very Italian," she said, "and sometimes the typical American male."

"Which do you prefer?" He looked intent and serious.

She flushed and stared over the bay. "Either. Both of you are nice." She laughed shakily. "It's the mixture that's so confusing. I never know where I am . . ." She could feel the tension emanating from him and suddenly she felt afraid of him. Or not of him, exactly, she told herself, but of the way he made her feel and act. Why had he come here? What did he want from her?

"I'm going home," she said abruptly. "To Africa—and soon. I hate being a model—I think you know that. I said I'd give it a try and I gave up university for another year because of you . . . you worked so hard to persuade me."

"It's paid off, hasn't it?" he said softly. "You've reached the top."

"But it's not what I want," she argued.

"It's always a good thing to quit when you're right at the peak," he said. If he were to push her too hard she would run home to Günter and he would lose her. He could not bear the thought of that. Softly, softly, he cautioned himself. Then, caught up with his own duplicity, he felt depressed and scowled.

It was not love, he reasoned. He had never loved anyone. It was his wild and uncontrollable passion for beauty. Sylvia was the loveliest woman he had ever seen and she had become an obsession—a need which never left him. Yet she was unaware of her own potential, still unfulfilled. At nineteen that was almost unbelievable, he thought. She was the fairy-tale sleeping princess awaiting the kiss that would awaken her. He knew she was half in love with him, but she was also a prude and his stepdaughter and all the money and influence in the world would never make him her Mr. Right.

But he could not let her go. He watched her guardedly. "I flew out to see you because I had a plan I wanted to discuss with you away from London and the family," he began, sensing her unease and wanting to calm her.

She smiled faintly, but said nothing, and for a while there was no sound but the soft swish of paddles in calm waters and far-off voices from the island fishing village half a mile away.

"I've wanted to bring this up for some time," he plodded on again, "but I knew it would ruin your career—as a model, that is—and I wanted you to be sure you were finished with all that."

"You're killing me with suspense, Tony," she said.

"All right." He laughed. "You know I own a large chemical group with a cosmetics division. It's one of my few failures—the cosmetics, I mean. It's never got off the ground. Yet it's a very lucrative field if you can get in." He leaned forward and grabbed her wrist. "I need a name—like yours—to launch the line.

"You're ideal because it's a top-market product, allergy-free, very expensive." His voice was hoarse now and he was talking too quickly. He broke off and took a deep breath. "Sylvia Cosmetics! Sounds good, I thought, but you'd have to give up other modeling."

The sweat was glistening on his forehead; watching him, Sylvia thought: He takes his moneymaking very seriously. Look at him—sweating with tension—no wonder he's so rich.

"I'd pay you two hundred thousand dollars," he was saying, "for a three-year contract, plus ten percent of the action . . . oh, and ten percent of the company for your mother just so she doesn't feel left out." He was afraid to stop talking in case she said no.

"With that much cash you'd be free—independent—pay your own way through college." He lurched forward and the boat keeled over. The boatman swore as he struggled to right it. "It would cost you a few hours a week—that's all—say, on Saturdays, or when it suits you—modeling at the agency. Well, what do you say?"

"Yes." Sylvia watched him and frowned. Why was he so uptight? Surely he could launch his cosmetics with or without her help. Still, it was a fair deal—more than fair. She thought regretfully of Xhabbo and Dad. Well, it was only three years away and by then she'd have her degree.

"As a matter of fact," he went on, "I brought the contract with me. Thought we might put it to bed here in Singapore. Perhaps over lunch tomorrow."

"What's the hurry?" she asked, sensitive to his fears.

"No hurry. It's just that your mother and Bertha will want to interfere and I think it's time you ran your own life."

"I agree," she said. Then she reached forward impulsively and squeezed his hand. "You know something, Tony? Sometimes you scare me. I don't know why that is. I think maybe you're just a scary sort of person."

"Maybe you're scared of your own feelings," he said. Then he leaned back and watched her carefully.

"That's not impossible," she whispered, and shuddered

at her own boldness. "Sometimes I wish you weren't married to Mother. It's sort of—well—limiting. No, don't say anything," she said quickly as Tony started to speak. "It's no damn use, Tony. No use at all. We'll have to settle for friends."

"Friends it is," he said, but he knew that it wasn't going to be like that at all.

Chapter Sixty-three

Bertha picked up the telephone and dialed "O" for a line. She heard talking. She was about to replace the receiver when she recognized Marika's voice.

"For God's sake—what's the matter with you? I told you I'd pay. You must go ahead—it's our only chance. We've tried everything else."

"Are you sure you can raise it all?" Bertha heard a quiet whisper reply. "It's a lot of money."

"Yes, I agree. Twenty thousand pounds is a lot of money. I don't keep that much lying around in cash. Give me time. No, really, I insist, but give me time to raise the cash." There was a small, impersonal click.

Bertha sat back shaking. What was going on? Was her daughter being blackmailed? Bertha worried about it all that day and the next and finally made up her mind to speak to Marika. Maybe she could help her. On Monday morning she buzzed Marika on the intercom.

Her daughter sounded busy.

"Marikala," Bertha began. "How about lunch?"

"When?" Marika snapped.

"Today?"

Marika was about to say that it was absolutely impossible when she realized that Bertha had never asked her to lunch before. Did she have a problem? she wondered.

Damn, she'd just have to fit it in. "That will be lovely, Bertha. Where?"

"Somewhere private," Bertha said. "Where do you suggest?"

"How about the Good Earth? I'll have to meet you there because I'm seeing a customer at the shop at twelve."

"Good," Bertha said. "Don't hurry. I'll wait."

Bertha arrived early and sat thinking about Marika. She had changed, although it was hard to say exactly how. There was a sadness about her more intense than before. At least she had her business, although sometimes Bertha wondered if that was such a good thing. Frenzied would describe her well enough, Bertha reckoned.

Sylvia had changed, too. There was a strange watchfulness about her. She was becoming secretive and at times she could be downright unkind.

London wasn't doing her granddaughter any good at all; she had been happier in Johannesburg. There was no love lost between mother and daughter, but Marika would not accept the truth. Hardly a day passed without her telling Bertha how much better things were going at home.

Bertha had planned to speak to Günter when she and Sylvia had flown back to Xhabbo for Christmas, but when she had seen how unhappy Claire and Günter were, she had decided to keep quiet.

Poor Claire, she couldn't help feeling sorry for her, although she had never grown to like her particularly. Claire had been pathetically pleased to see them both and Bertha could guess why. When Sylvia was there Günter felt happy at home; Sylvia filled the gap Marika had left. Nowadays Günter spent longer hours at the office and he worked most weekends.

Lately her adopted family seemed to be threatened on all sides. She sighed and then brightened up when she saw Marika rushing toward her.

"Darling, I'm so sorry I'm late," she said.

She leaned forward and kissed Bertha on the cheek; then she sat down, smiling curiously.

"Do you want to sit through lunch and worry about

whatever it is that's bothering you—or shall we have it out before we order?'' she asked. Then she smiled.

Bertha smiled back nervously. Marika would always be her special favorite no matter what happened. She didn't want to interfere, but at the same time she wanted Marika to know that she would always be there—right behind her.

''Marikala,'' she began. ''I picked up the telephone last week, and overheard your call. You have to find a great deal of money quickly. That's it—in a nutshell. I want to know what's wrong. If you can tell me, that is. Are you in trouble?''

Marika smiled sadly. ''It's nothing new, Bertha. To tell the truth, I didn't really want you to know.''

''Then we'll say no more,'' Bertha said too hurriedly.

''Oh, silly. You'd just worry.''

Bertha watched her expression changing. It was like watching the sun go in. When Marika scowled she looked quite cruel, she noticed for the first time.

''I'm paying an organization that specializes in tracking Nazi criminals. They've caught several so far. That makes me feel good. As if I'm involved in some way.'' She made an effort to smile, but it was unsuccessful. Then she scowled at her glass. She seemed to come to a decision suddenly. ''You see, Bertha, you'd never understand. Never! You've got this turn-the-other-cheek attitude, but not me. I intend to do everything in my power to find the criminals who massacred my father—and the rest of Oradour.

''Don't look so shocked, Bertha.'' She reached out and grasped her mother's hand. ''It's been going on for years. Since before you left London. I pay fifteen percent of my salary to them, but nowadays I find a good deal of extra cash for special projects.'' She looked up and frowned. ''You really disapprove. I can see by your face. But you want to know something? In 1954 they discovered that Major Otto Geissler is still alive.

''Makes you think, doesn't it?'' she went on. ''He's somewhere out there, living a normal life, disguised as a human being. Yet he slaughtered hundreds of people, women and children, burned them to death.'' She shuddered.

"The entire operation is run on charity, and when they have a lead which is too costly for them to follow up, I usually back them—well, most times." She smiled apologetically. "It's the least I can do."

"Is that all?" Bertha said flatly. "Hundreds of thousands of pounds later they've discovered he's alive."

Marika leaned forward and glared at Bertha. "It's something I have to do," she whispered.

She broke off and gazed absentmindedly at her glass. "Bertha, I sometimes wonder what I would do without this hatred, this need for revenge which I live with. It's like my crutch, it's sustained me so many times. In the past . . . when you were in Johannesburg . . . there were so many times when I felt like giving up the business. The struggle was just too much—but I couldn't and d'you know why? Because I'd be lost if I didn't have money. It's the only weapon I have in the war against Geissler and his kind. Take away my hatred and there'd be nothing left . . . just an empty shell. This hate—it's me—I think it's all of me."

Bertha was looking upset, and Marika noticed and felt guilty. "Don't take it to heart. I can easily afford the money," she said.

The money? Well, that was the least Marika was paying, Bertha thought, gazing at her daughter in dismay.

"In a way I'm letting myself off lightly and this worries me," Marika was saying. "I should be out there searching, instead of only paying. One day they'll find Geissler and I shall see him dying." Her eyes narrowed and for a moment she looked quite strange. "That's something I've promised myself," she said.

Bertha shuddered. Downturned mouth and glittering eyes. She looked a picture of malice. "I wish you would put all that behind you, Marikala," she said sadly, but she was thinking: Strange how you could love someone so much but never really understand them. Marika's Slavic intensity frightened her. Sometimes, like now, she had a glimpse of how very desperately Marika had loved her parents. She knew that most of the time she lived out a comforting illusion that she was the only real mother Marika had ever had.

"Don't be sad, Bertha," Marika said. Leaning forward, she kissed her cheek.

"This afternoon I'm going to have an advance show of the next look! Just John and Tanya with a couple of models and sketches. You must come. Please, Bertha."

That was Marika for you, Bertha reflected on the drive back to the factory. A strange, complex woman, loving or hating, creating or destroying, but always passionately.

Chapter Sixty-four

It was enrollment day at the London School of Economics. Courses would start tomorrow. After the shuffling and queueing and the shouts of club organizers touting for new members it was strangely quiet in the Robinson Room restaurant, the scraping of cutlery on crockery seemed overloud and grated on everyone's ears. There was little conversation; most of the students were new and felt strange, but already they were forming groups of twos and threes and getting to know each other—all except Sylvia.

She was being tacitly ignored and she tried not to notice their surreptitious glances and envious stares.

By now the tables were overflowing except for the space surrounding her, so she ate her hamburger and chips in silence, gazing at her plate. When she looked up from time to time she saw the students' faces hastily turn the other way.

Then she saw a young man ambling toward her, a book in one hand and a plate in the other. He was tall and big-boned, but thin. In spite of his sloppy clothes, he looked oversensitive and intelligent. His trousers were faded and torn, his checked shirt was open at the neck, revealing a bright yellow vest, but his curly dark brown hair was cut in a neat crew cut.

She found herself wondering what he studied—or was he a lecturer? No, he could not be more than twenty-two. You couldn't call him good-looking, she decided. His chin was too pronounced, his nose a trifle too long, but his eyes were arresting—they were large and dark blue, set wide apart under a high brow. Scottish? she wondered.

Aware of her scrutiny, he glanced at her coldly. "You saving this seat for someone?" His voice was deep, his accent American.

"No, no, please."

He turned his attention to his fish pie. "Jesus, English cooking!"

"What's wrong with English cooking?" He had been talking to himself, she realized, and now he looked startled.

"It's one of the penances you endure to get an English education."

"And the others?"

He frowned irritably. "What others?"

"That's what I was asking you." She flashed her warmest, £400-an-hour smile at him. "What are the other penances you are enduring?"

"Well, crazy women like you, for a start. This place is full of 'em."

The smile faded. "I'm sorry if I disturbed you," she said huffily. "It's just that no one wants to sit next to me." She wondered why he was so unfriendly. He seemed to prefer his book. "No one's said one word to me yet," she explained. "But everyone keeps staring. If only they'd say 'hi,' but just staring like this . . . it's sort of unnerving."

He sighed and laid down his book. "I think you've got a problem, pal. I'd have it seen to if I were you." He stared at her moodily and began munching his pie.

He thinks I'm crazy, she thought. Maybe I am. Maybe I just got too used to being the center of attraction. She stood up. "I'm sure you're right," she said, "I must be going anyway."

"Bye," he said without looking up.

She loitered regretfully at the end of the table, wishing she could at least have spoken to someone on her first day. "I'm Sylvia Shaw," she said. "Who're you?"

"Andy Stark," then, as an afterthought, "from Boston."

"I knew it . . . I told you so," an excited voice called from the next table.

Sylvia turned toward the eager young face gazing up at her. "We've laid bets on you being Sylvia Shaw and I won." The girl called to the next table, loud and shrill. "It's her. It's Sylvia Shaw. You owe me two pounds. Pay up."

Sylvia turned to her neighbor. "Well, at least that's broken the ice."

He looked slightly amused. "Well, it seems you do have a problem. Only it's a different kind of problem." He smiled. "Okay. I'm sorry."

Then he looked at her—really looked at her—and he could not believe his eyes. "Incredibly lovely. Yes—you really are," he said. "That must be a real problem to live with." He looked around the room. "You're right, of course. People stare. Can't say I blame them. The attraction of beauty . . . one of nature's motivating forces . . . you see it all the time . . . in flowers . . . in birds with their mating feathers. I don't know if you've ever seen . . ."

He broke off abruptly. "What the hell am I rambling on for?" He waved across the room to someone he knew. "I'm glad to see you're learning something useful," he said, "and not just content with being decorative. No credit to you, really, is it?

"Well." He stood up, looking bored. "I don't suppose we'll bump into each other again, so . . . good luck." He ambled away and Sylvia could not believe her ears.

She hurried after him. "That's just what I feel, too," she said, "but you're the first person to put it quite so bluntly." She had to struggle to keep up with him through the crowd at the door.

"Who's Sylvia Shaw when she's not playing at being a freshman?" he called over his shoulder.

"I gave up modeling to study sociology," she shouted, wondering if he could hear, for he was three paces ahead.

"Modeling," he said incredulously. "That's just about the silliest thing I can think of anyone doing."

"You and I have something in common," she said. "But I have a feeling Mother isn't going to like you."

He stopped abruptly, turned and stared at her—his face a mixture of annoyance and amusement.

"Sweetheart, I will never meet your mother."

"That's three mistakes in three minutes," she said. "I think you almost broke a record."

Sylvia could not wait to rush to tell Bertha about the LSE, but some of her exuberance vanished during the hour-long wait in a traffic jam and by the time she reached Finchley she felt tired and anxious.

Bertha revived her with hot soup and questions and Sylvia described her first day. She tried to make it sound exciting, but Bertha could sense her disappointment.

"Then there was this strange man. Sort of remote," she went on breathlessly. "Really, he was the only person to talk to me all day. He wasn't particularly friendly, either. A bit strange, I thought."

"If he's not interested in you then he must be peculiar? Is that it?" Bertha asked, looking innocent.

"Oh, Bertha," Sylvia grumbled. Then she smiled reluctantly. "I must admit it's a bit unusual. I mean . . . well, really . . . no point in lying . . . most men are falling over themselves to take me out."

"You've been mixing with the wrong types," Bertha said. "Do you good to meet some real people with real values for a change. You've been living too long in a fairy-tale world. Getting a bit above yourself lately. Don't think I haven't noticed."

"Oh, Bertha, that's not true and you know it." She put her arms around Bertha and hugged her. "Why're you so grumpy?"

"What makes you think I'm grumpy? Just because I

don't smile like a toothpaste advertisement or drool over you—I'm grumpy?''

"All right, all right, you're not grumpy. Anyway," she went on, "there's this society there which aims to teach people to care about wild animals and the environment and I joined . . ." Her voice prattled on while Bertha made supper.

I suppose this is what old is, Bertha was thinking. God knows, I don't feel any different and surely sixty isn't really old, but it's just that the young seem so much younger. Children, really.

Sylvia spent the evening looking through her textbooks while Bertha cooked her granddaughter's favorite South African supper: a sweet curry called babootie, pumpkin and yellow rice followed by milk tart.

Then Bertha settled down with the crossword puzzle, but she could not help noticing that Sylvia was not really concentrating on her books. She kept gazing up with a frown on her face. Obviously this young man had hurt her pride. Do her some good. Bertha had to admit that Sylvia was becoming very conceited lately.

Andy sat moodily staring at a pile of anthropological textbooks on his desk. *Sexual Practices of the Melanesians*. Heck! If he had to read that he'd be as horny as a billy goat. Sex was a word he tried to avoid thinking about. To Andy there were two types of girls: the ones who wanted his cash and the ones who wanted his time. He was short on both.

At least, that was the excuse he made for himself. The truth was, Andy was not very successful with the opposite sex. His eyes were too remote, his mind too questioning, and although he did not know this yet, he was also a perfectionist. His lack of success had made him shy.

Gloomily he decided he would probably never keep a woman for any length of time, although he knew the type he would choose if he could; a pleasant woman, trained as a nurse or a doctor, preferably from Boston, who would help him establish his research and development projects in underdeveloped countries.

Andy was twenty-two and in his second year at the LSE, studying for a B.Sc. in social anthropology. Before enrolling he had worked for two years as a game park warden in Rhodesia. Wildlife and filmmaking were his two passions in life and he made the occasional wildlife film when funds permitted. Once he had intended to become a scriptwriter, but after his African spell, as he called it, he decided to join the United Nations to help develop underprivileged societies.

He lived in a spartan attic flat and ate beans on toast, unless he was eating at one of the university canteens where meals were cheap. Most of the small private income he received monthly from a trust left by his mother went on his various campaigns.

What a day, he thought. He pushed the books aside and opened the fridge. He normally waited until seven for his one beer of the day, but drank it tonight while he was warming his baked beans on the gas stove, because he felt he deserved a break.

Moodily he gulped large mouthfuls as he gazed out of his window at a sea of London rooftops. He shivered and wondered whether or not to waste money on the electric fire. Finally he chose the duffel coat and shrugged into it.

His day had started to go wrong early in the morning when he and his friend Bob Israel put up the table and placards to attract the new students to join their Save Our World Society. He had founded the club at the beginning of last year, and Bob Israel, a second-year psychology student, had joined shortly afterward. Now they ran it together. But this year canvassing had gone particularly badly.

Then that incredibly silly model, whose name he had forgotten, chatted with him at lunch and he had made an ass of himself. When he escaped from her he had left his notebook on the table. It contained the names of all their new members. He went back later, but of course it was gone.

He and Bob had been in the main hall canvassing for members when she had turned up again and joined, to his annoyance. He liked genuine members. Bob had been taken in by her nonsense as she oohed and aahed over the placards. Anyone could see Bob had fallen for her. Well, good luck to him. He'd be sorry. Bob had even wanted to send her around canvassing for new members, but that was going too far. What did she know about it? Finally they had argued heatedly. "What are you, some kind of a misanthrope?" Bob had flung at him when she had gone. "D'you know who she is? D'you know how many members we could get through her?"

Goddamnit, he didn't want to think about his day. He opened a second bottle of beer and settled down to *The Bored Stones of Africa*. He was still at it at midnight.

Chapter Sixty-five

It was eight-thirty; prime viewing time on ITV. *The music was sultry; the scene exotic; tropical plants waved in a somnolent breeze. Tahiti possibly? Or Hawaii? In fact, it was Devon and the plants had been purchased from a nearby indoor tropical garden; they would die soon, but for the moment they created the ideal setting for a millionaire's island playground.*

Sylvia, looking breathtakingly lovely in a brightly colored sarong, appeared from among the foliage and, plucking a hibiscus flower, placed it behind her ear. She sauntered toward the sea. A bronzed, handsome male leapt off his million-dollar yacht and ran toward Sylvia as she unfastened her sarong. She paused for a moment in her bikini, waved and ran into the surf. The man picked up the fallen

hibiscus flower, crushed it in his hands, smelled the per-
fume and dived after Sylvia to the sound of gentle Hawai-
ian music fading to the roar of the sea. A bottle of perfume
with flowers on the label flashed on the screen. "Hibiscus,"
a voice whispered against splashing surf. "A new Sylvia
perfume, designed for the irresistible."

Andy stood up and switched off the television. Suddenly
his room seemed very empty. "Of all the corny, moronic
ads she's been in, that's the corniest," he said aloud.

So why did he watch them night after night? He knew
the answer to that question. Because he could not resist the
urge to gaze long and hungrily at her beautiful face and
body, without her even knowing. She appeared nightly in
one or another of these pathetic advertisements and each
one was engraved in his mind.

He began to pace his room, around the table to the bed
and back toward the cupboard. The students in the room
underneath were complaining about his habitual agitation.
Lately unhappiness had become a tangible symptom that
lived in a hard lump at the pit of Andy's stomach.

Insane! What the heck did he think he was doing,
dreaming about a girl like her?

Until now, Andy's work had been enough. He could not
afford to waste time. One-night stands were his specialty.
Madness with a girl like Sylvia, but thank God he was
saved from his own madness—she loathed him. Every
meeting they had erupted in an argument.

He turned to his textbooks with a sigh. *The Bored
Stones of Africa* was heavy going. He read for a few
minutes and then pushed his work aside and went out for a
beer.

The membership of the Save Our World Society was
growing and tonight there were over thirty students gathered in Andy's attic flat, which doubled as the club meeting room. It was late April, but still cold; the north wind
was racing around London's roof tops, penetrating the
cracks around the skylight. Sylvia was woefully aware that
the mohair poncho she was wearing was nowhere near

warm enough. She could not stop shivering, but if they could stand it so could she.

There were a number of items on the agenda and the students were full of exciting ideas: an expedition to film the slaughter of the harp seals; a protest delegation to Japan over the depletion of whales; distributing leaflets about companies who used animals for testing cosmetics. There was not enough cash to do any of these things and it seemed to Sylvia that they had their priorities wrong.

She said as much, when she eventually managed to make herself heard.

"Perhaps it's because I'm older than most of you," she began, "that I can see where we're going wrong." She glanced at Andy and saw him glaring at her. Tough! she thought. She was as keen on this society as he was. "We need cash. All these marvelous ideas—they're doomed to peter out without money. So why don't we make fund raising our number one target? Then, perhaps, we can do some of these things you've been talking about."

"Raising funds, Sylvia," Andy cut in on her, "is hardly something we're unaware of. Bob and I put almost all of our own money into the club."

"Well, that's absurd," she went on determinedly. "What you can raise individually is peanuts compared with what we can collect from businesses. If we really try, that is." She looked around questioningly. "If you don't believe me, just give me a chance."

Andy was scowling ferociously, but in spite of his doubts, it was voted that Sylvia would head fund raising. Four others volunteered to assist her. That was how she came to be sitting in Andy's attic after everyone else had left.

"I'd like to remind you that you've got this society into a whole new ball game. Now we'll have to register as a non-profit-making charity and have our books audited. Did you think of that?" He looked sour and she wondered why.

"Is that so important?" she asked, "Compared with raising the funds you need."

"Let's see the cash first," he said, knowing it was no sort of an answer and feeling stupid.

"You've got something against me, haven't you?" she asked resentfully.

"Yes," he said, quietly angry. "You're just too damned good-looking. I don't believe you care about this society or anything else. Least of all wildlife. You'd pass out if you so much as set eyes on a lion."

"So why d'you think I'm here?"

"That's what I'd like to find out," he snarled. "I bet you've got a cupboard full of furs."

"Funny you should say that," she said, smiling haughtily. "I have."

She left abruptly, not wanting Andy to see how hurt she was. He had wounded her in her only defenseless area. She loved animals passionately. She always had, ever since she was small and all the pent-up love for her mother had been lavished on her puppy. She could not bear pain in animals, and when she saw a lost cat or dog wandering in the streets, she just had to help them. In a way it was herself who was homeless and afraid. Those beautiful, horrible fur coats hung like corpses in her cupboard, a witness to her failure to stand up for what she believed in.

"Jesus! That freak! I mean, really freaky," Sylvia complained to Bertha the next evening. She recounted the discussion. "The pompous, opinionated, ego-ridden freak.

"I'm going to teach him a lesson," she told Bertha. "I'll flood them with cash. I'll show him who cares. He may find he's not so smart as he thinks."

"Trying to teach people a lesson can sometimes backfire," Bertha sad, shaking her head.

It was a week later and Sylvia, looking stunning in a black velvet suit and white gorget blouse, was gulping supper while reading her notes. She was about to leave for the Save Our World weekly meeting and Tony was looking belligerent.

"You should spend more time studying," he said, eyeing

her suit thoughtfully. "That's what you're there for, isn't it?"

"It's important to take part in the social activities," Sylvia retorted, as she always did. This was an ancient fight.

"Why dress up for a club meeting?" he went on.

Watching them both, Marika could not understand why Tony became so upset about Sylvia's evening activities. It wasn't as if she were sixteen.

Tony followed Sylvia to her car. "Skip the damn meeting," he muttered. "We could meet for drinks somewhere."

"I can't skip the meeting," she mumbled.

"You did last month and it's a pity to waste that outfit on a crowd of scruffy students." He reached out and grabbed her arm.

"Let go." She smiled nervously. "I have to give a talk."

"Honey, it's far beneath you," he said. "Okay, so you want a degree, but forget the rest. Work hard now," he said, trying to look confident, "and I'll take you to South America for skiing in the June holidays."

"I'm booked for the holidays," she retorted. Grabbing her files, she jumped into the car and raced out of the gate.

Her heart was beating too fast and her palms were moist. Damn and blast Tony. What did he want from her? He was married to Mother, wasn't he? So why did her heart pound and her knees weaken when he touched her. It was a crazy, dangerous, kinky situation and she wanted out.

She arrived early and sat humming to herself, hoping no one would notice she was shaking.

Andy eyed her with displeasure, as she had known he would. She could not help comparing Andy with Tony. Two opposites. Andy was not a bit devious, but absurdly straightforward; so bent on goodness. Unreal, she thought. He and Tony were like night and day. But night could be far more exciting.

But Andy was male, too. With her canny feminine

intuition she knew that her looks and her presence unnerved him and that he disliked her for this reason.

Strangely enough, Andy bothered her, too. When she was close to him a strange prickling in her skin brought out goose pimples. Sometimes she tried to work out why. Analyzing him, she realized that he should have been good-looking, but he wasn't. He was tall and broad; his features were regular and strong. The trouble was his damned, remote eyes that looked right through you and saw every flaw. At the same time a girl would know where she was with Andy, if any girl ever caught him, she thought.

The meeting dragged on, without anything new coming to the fore until Sylvia stood up to give her fund-raising report. Two thousand pounds from Sylvia Cosmetics. "Of course, I simply insisted," she said. One thousand pounds from a Canadian mining group who were willing to support their anti-trapping campaign, and there were various other sums still in the pipeline.

"These guys take a long time to make up their minds," she said. "Lastly, there's an offer from a South African mining company, who are the principal backers of the Namib Wildlife Fund, to pay five thousand pounds to the club. In return they want assistance in gathering public support toward the formation of a fund for the protection of wildlife in the Namib." She broke off. "They want public signatures, articles and pictures in the press. That sort of thing? They feel student support would help the cause—maybe just a small turnout with a few placards. Anyone interested?"

When the clamor died down it was decided that they could now go ahead with most of their projects and that Namibian wildlife would take top priority.

Andy felt that he hated her more than he had ever hated anyone.

"They seem pretty well taken by the Namibian campaign," Sylvia said smugly when the others had left. She was filing her reports in Andy's box files.

"Of course," he said spitefully. "Nowadays you tell the club what to think and what to feel," he said. "You've got it all worked out, haven't you? Just like you manipulate everyone else who crosses your path. Looks and money. You've got everything. Well, you can count me out."

"Suit yourself," she said sarcastically. "I suppose I'll have to look around for new premises. You're jealous and you're spiteful," she said. "I'd like to know why you resent me so much."

"How the hell do you think I feel?" He looked at her quickly and looked away again. "Why, I feel like a fool." He knitted his brow and shook his head. "Listen to me, Sylvia. You're too far removed from reality, real people's reality. The fact that you are here at all proves that the whole thing is a hoax. It's not real. The Namib Wildlife Fund is probably something dreamed up by Sylvia Cosmetics to prove they really *care*." He said the last word sarcastically. "Just to keep the public from snooping around their laboratories. I bet they torture rabbits. Wildlife. Ha! Ha!"

"It's real, Andy. Why don't you check up? It's a registered trust fund and nothing at all to do with Sylvia Cosmetics. Anyway," she concluded, "I'm only the house model."

"Well, I don't intend to be manipulated and I don't like being taken over by the jet-set socialites. Now, either you get lost or I get lost."

She flushed hotly and went home in a temper. It was quite unthinkable that Andy should leave his club. After all, he founded it, didn't he? She could not imagine it lasting for long without Andy and for some reason she felt a grudging admiration for the monster.

Sylvia missed the next few meetings; she met Tony in the city instead. Nothing wrong with that, she told herself guiltily. What was the harm in just talking? It was a relief to talk about things that mattered without Mother being there. And once, when Mother was in America on business, they flew to Paris—just for dinner and a show—and then flew home again in Tony's private jet.

But it worried her. She felt she was racing along the edge of a precipice . . . out of control and heading for trouble. She was scared. Tony made everything seem so right, so normal, so worthwhile, but deep inside she felt sick. Andy's arrogantly moral view of the world began to appear increasingly valuable. Andy, she knew, saw the world in terms of black or white and there was a clear-cut division between the two. To Tony it was just one glorious Technicolor happening.

One lunchtime, early in October, when she was sitting in the LSE cafeteria, Andy walked in and saw her. He ambled over and sat beside her.

He seemed a little odd, she thought. "I was expecting you at the meetings," he said by way of introduction.

"You didn't make me very welcome there." She glared at him, wishing he could say something witty or flattering, like Tony—just for once.

"Didn't worry you before. I think everyone misses you," he said. "I'd hate to think you dropped out because of me."

"Why should you care?" she said haughtily.

"Because I've been thinking a lot about the funds and I've decided I was wrong," he said. "I'm sorry. I mean, it's not the money I'm missing. It's you." She did not say anything, so he hurried on. "Say, I think I owe you some sort of a peace offering. Would you settle for dinner?"

"You don't owe me anything, Andy," she said softly.

"Damn it, Sylvia, don't always try to call the tune," he snarled. "If I say I owe you something then I owe you."

"And damn you, too, Andy Stark," she said, and her voice was high-pitched and quavering. "Either you want to take me to dinner or you don't. Now make up your mind what you're trying to do, date me or pay your imaginary debts."

There was a long silence while Andy looked at his hands. When he looked up there was a strange glint in his blue eyes.

"You're right," he said. "But just for once I wish you'd learn to let folks hang on to their dignity. I was trying to date you."

The met in town the following evening and dined in style. She felt guilty wondering about the hole the bill would make in Andy's pocket until she learned that he had a small private income.

He was absurdly correct all evening and only held her arm when they were crossing the road. "Funny, but you just don't strike me as a girl who would care about animals," he said over coffee. "Or anything, really, except having a good time."

"What do you know about me, Andy?" she asked. "You have an image based on all those silly perfume advertisements."

So she told him about home and the Namib and their farm in the Kalahari and how she was brought up by Dad and the camping and prospecting trips they had taken together and why she was so homesick. She did not tell him about Mother, or Dad's mines, or Tony.

"Now tell me why you're telling me all this," he said eventually.

"I just wanted to show you that being a model didn't stop me from being your sort of woman, too."

"My sort of woman?" he asked softly, and turned to look at her. His eyes registered amazement.

"Why can't we be friends?" she stammered. "Like you and Bob."

"Bob's a man," he said flatly.

"Don't you believe in platonic friendships?"

"No."

"Why not?"

"Things like desire and jealousy get in the way."

"Do you desire me?" she asked in a shy whisper.

"I'm not unnatural," he said. "Anyone would desire you."

"So why do you fight me off all the time?"

"Listen, Sylvia," he began, leaning with one elbow on

the side of her car. "One night, well, every night, to be honest, I switch on the TV and watch you in those dreadful commercials. The thing is, I just can't resist watching. And then I say to myself, what would a girl like that do with a guy like me?" He straightened up and stared down at the curb, kicked some paper into the gutter. "It's getting chilly," he said. "You want to come up for coffee?"

"Yes," she said. "Yes, I do."

"You know what I've planned for the future," he went on when he had the percolator plugged in. "I can't expect a girl like you—with your looks—to live in the African bush and you're hardly the one-night-stand type. Or are you?"

She watched him speculatively. "So how do you see my life, Andy? My future, I mean. A rich husband, a yacht perhaps, maybe like those ads you don't like?"

"Something like that, I guess."

"You think I should settle for the right life instead of the right man?"

"You'll find someone suitable and you'll love him."

"What would you say if I told you I love you?"

"I'd say you are mistaken, or possibly lying."

"Maybe you'd be right, but, Andy, I'd really like a chance to find out."

He poured out the coffee and passed her a cup. Then he sat down and his analytical eyes scanned her face. "There's something you're holding back. So many secrets, Sylvia. I've always sensed that with you."

She looked at him guiltily; she was longing to tell him about her fears and about her budding sensuality and her need to be loved which was driving her straight into Tony's arms.

Instead she said, "There's another man and he's married." To my mother, she might have added, but didn't.

He flinched. He had been so sure she was a virgin.

Something about his expression made her blush.

"You want to go to bed?" he asked.

"Yes. Love me just a little bit. Tonight. Please, Andy." Her knees seemed to have turned to jelly and a curious shooting sensation, half pain, half pleasure, was making it difficult to move.

Why isn't he pleased? she wondered, watching him peevishly. I'm throwing myself at him and I know he wants me. Can't he look a little bit glad?

She stood up and took off her clothes. It was nearly freezing, but she did not feel cold. She was burning all over. She knew she had a lovely body and for the first time in her life she was glad of it. She wanted to please Andy, but when she glanced at him he looked far from pleased.

"Are you sure this is what you want?" he asked harshly, and when she nodded he said, "I suppose models strip all the time."

"Of course this is what I want."

"Sex doesn't mean much to you, then?" he asked sullenly.

"No. Should it? Are you a virgin?"

"No," he admitted.

She felt strangely hurt as she slipped under the bedclothes.

Andy stared at her moodily for a while. Then he shrugged and stood up. "Heck, it's cold," he said.

Sylvia watched entranced as he undressed. How unexpectedly beautiful he was. Although he was thin, he was huge; all sinew and muscle. His brown hair curled on his long legs and groin and over his chest.

"I guess I had you sized up all wrong," he said mournfully. "It's that virginal look you wear."

"It's good for business," she replied.

Yeah. I guess it must be. Just tell me something. Not that it matters." He grinned painfully. "Is it over between you and this married guy?"

"Yes," she said firmly. "I need you, Andy. Love me. Help me."

He lay on her, cupping his hands around her breasts. Then he lunged into her. "Oh no," he groaned. He pulled back and stared frenziedly at her. He should have listened to his instinct. He'd known she was a virgin all along.

"Why didn't you tell me?" He sighed. "Oh, Sylvie, look what I've done."

He buried his head between her breasts and then he kissed her gently and moved his lips slowly over her skin.

He was a gentle, passionate lover and there was no more pain, only a soft falling away into sensuousness, and when at last Andy came she cried out with happiness.

For a long time they lay in each other's arms. Andy was thinking: This isn't for real and I must never love her. But still he was filled with tenderness. How beautiful she was. He could not tear his eyes away. He had wanted her from the day he first saw her. Why had she chosen him to be the first? He was too vulnerable, too prone to fall in love, and she was not for him. He knew that.

Sylvia lay in his arms examining this strange, new feeling of belonging. He wasn't as powerful or as handsome as Dad, or as exciting as Tony, but at least this time she did not have to share him with Mother.

Chapter Sixty-six

It was 8 A.M., but Marika had been at her drawing board for over an hour when the receptionist brought in the morning papers and coffee.

She scanned the pages eagerly. Yesterday she had addressed a group of feminists on the psychological impact of fashion on society. She had expected some adverse criticism, but the press had been kind.

She froze as her eye caught an insignificant report at the bottom of the page. Former SS officer Ernst Stuckler, sought since 1945 for war crimes in Polish concentration camps, was apprehended and arrested in Athens while en route to South America after a short stay in Geneva for medical treatment. The man behind his arrest, Klaus Greenstein, told reporters . . .

Marika flung the newspaper aside and buried her face in her hands. For a few moments she sat shivering. Then she reached for the telephone and dialed Greenstein's number. He would only be back after lunch, she was told.

The morning passed slowly and her efforts at the drawing board were particularly unsuccessful. Marika became increasingly tense and after snarling at her secretary she swallowed half a Valium with a glass of milk. It seemed to make her even more depressed.

She forced herself to wait until two-thirty before ringing Greenstein again. By this time her mouth was so stiff with suppressed anger she could hardly talk. "My money . . . my backing . . . you used me . . . you said you had a lead on Otto Geissler."

"A regrettable mistake," Greenstein said. "I warned you of this. But in any event we have brought to justice yet another Nazi criminal. That, after all, is what this agency is all about—not personal vendettas. I have told you that so many times." His voice became more feeble. "Marika, you know the score—we follow up every possible lead. You're assisting the agency in all its operations —we do all we can. If I could discover the whereabouts of Otto Geissler, I would arrest him tomorrow. Believe me, my dear. Yet I admit, I too had hoped . . ."

How old he sounded and his voice was hardly more than a whisper. A thrill of fear rushed through her. If he died . . . or if he gave up . . . why, he was her lifeline . . . at that moment she felt like a fetus hanging precariously at the end of a long and fragile umbilical cord. Only through Greenstein could she wreak her revenge. Her lack of control and helplessness angered her.

"You pick your criminals with care, don't you?" she snarled. "It's always the most notorious . . . the ones that attract the publicity and the cash . . . oh, I understand . . . business is business," she said nastily.

"My dear, if you feel like that I suggest you cancel your

payments," he said in a small, tired voice. "I'm so sorry that you feel we've let you down."

"Yes, I do feel that," she retorted. She felt no compassion for his obvious exhaustion; only anger. "I'm increasing my payments. Do something! Anything! Find better agents. I'll send a check in the mail."

She flung down the receiver before he could reply and sat shaking with rage. Greenstein's suggestion that she should pull out had frightened her. Her drive for revenge was the drug that sustained her, the foundation upon which her life—and fortune—was built. Take it away and she would crumble. What was she, after all? Why, nothing! Only emptiness.

Chapter Sixty-seven

It was almost six years since Günter had pledged the Kwammang-a to the bank to secure a loan of ten million dollars. With the cash had come power . . . to make more money . . . to open up new mines . . . to extend his diamond-dredging operation . . . and more important, to ruin Tex McGregor and regain those coveted uranium mines in the Namib Desert.

Günter had planned his revenge with the single-minded dedication which nowadays characterized all his ambitions. Secretly, Günter's broker had been buying Western Minerals Exploration Holding Company shares whenever they became available through the stock market. As with many other complex mining corporations, the Western Minerals board did not control the majority of the group's shares. In fact, Tex, who in reality was the board, held only twenty-five percent; the remainder was in public hands. If Günter could purchase the majority of Western Minerals shares he could oust McGregor from control and take over the group himself.

But during the past six years Western Minerals had also grown and acquired bigger and better mines in South Africa and Australia. Günter's plan was costing him far more than he had originally calculated.

It had been a long-term strategy and so far Günter had felt he was winning. Until now—for Tex's latest move would make the acquisition of the controlling interest wellnigh impossible.

In six weeks' time Western Minerals would be making a public offering to raise the capital Tex McGregor needed to develop the huge Namibian uranium mines—my goddamn mines, Günter thought angrily. Six weeks to go! If he did not wrest control from Tex within that time he would lose forever.

Right now he owned twenty-nine percent of the stock, four percent more than Tex himself. It sounded good, but it meant nothing, Günter reminded himself. The incumbent always had an advantage. And why? Because invariably the host of small investors gave their proxies to the man running the company. Even so—if it were not for the new public offering looming ahead, Günter might gamble on a proxy battle. Now he wouldn't stand a chance. Only a fool would try.

The maid came in with his breakfast, but Günter waved her away angrily. He had been in a foul mood since the offer was announced a few days ago, for it spelled disaster for Günter and his plans to ruin Tex. The public offering would increase the public's holding of Western Minerals by over sixty percent and greatly dilute his own holding. Right now uranium and nuclear power were the answer to the world's energy shortage, as Günter had always predicted; consequently, the new offer would be heavily subscribed. He would be lucky to capture five percent of it.

No, to succeed Günter had to make a swift and decisive coup before the flotation, and if he lost now, Tex would ensure that he never had another chance.

But how?

Günter picked up the telephone and dialed his stockbroker. "Have any Western Minerals shares come on the market?"

"For Christ's sake, Günter, this is the third time you've phoned in three days. If anything comes on the market we'll buy it." There was a babble of conversation in the background. "Hang on a minute, Günter. Hang on." He heard him shouting above raised voices. Then he said, "Look, Günter, you know as well as I do, what with you and McGregor holding fifty percent between you and the institutions another thirty, very little is being traded. You yourself insisted that we proceed very cautiously so that we don't tip off the other side that someone is trying to corner the market." He paused, waiting for Günter to speak. Then he said, "You've got to admit we only lost one parcel of shares since this caper began."

"Okay, okay," Günter said, "you've explained it all before."

He replaced the receiver and thumped his fist into the palm of his hand.

The day passed slowly and Claire irritated him more than usual. She wanted to know why he was not eating, and why he would not come to her trainer's stables to admire the new racehorse she had bought. Claire was getting very horsey lately. All her friends and acquaintances were connected with training or racing in one way or another.

By sunset only a few more shares had been acquired and Günter was so tense he could hardly move one leg in front of the other. If only he was a financier, instead of a miner, he thought, he would have found another way by now. After six years of scheming and planning, the bloody institutions owned more of Western Minerals' shares than he did.

Suddenly he jumped to his feet. "Shit!" he yelled. That was the answer. Here he was, buying up Mickey Mouse parcels of shares on the exchange, when the key to control was held by fewer than a dozen large investors, mainly insurance and investment groups. Somehow they must be persuaded to sell him their thirty percent. Why hadn't his broker thought of it? He'd fire the dumb bastard when this was over.

Since the time when Tex had swindled him out of his claims, Günter had used only top advisers. He picked up the telephone now and called the senior partner in a firm of international auditors who handled his company's affairs. Perhaps he should have brought them into it at the outset, Günter wondered uneasily, but secrecy had been essential.

By ten the following morning, he was sitting in a massive boardroom together with his accountant, his legal adviser and a merchant banker and it was soon apparent to Günter that he was going to require a great deal more ready cash than he had available. If he succeeded in gaining control of Western Minerals, he would still have to go ahead with Tex's announced plan of offering more shares to the investing public. Otherwise he would lose investors' confidence. Yet he must also retain majority holding. To do that he needed a massive cash injection.

His accountant and the merchant banker had a complicated scheme to put to him; they suggested creating a series of pyramid holding companies through which cash could be raised. Günter's own Namib Mining and Minerals Corporation would eventually go public, too, although Günter would retain control of the group with his majority ownership of the top holding company. In the meantime the merchant bank would advance Günter the funds for his bid and through their many contacts quietly sound out the willingness of the large Western Minerals investors to sell their holdings. Günter agreed at once.

Four days later his accountant came back to him. The Lifetime Assurance Company and the Commonwealth Commodities Investment Trust, which each held seven percent of Western Minerals, would sell their holdings to him outright, but at a price well above market. It was expensive, but worth it.

In addition, the Union Investment Bank, which controlled just over eight percent, through various client portfolios it administered, would not sell, but they would support Günter's takeover provided they had an option to exchange their holdings in Western Minerals for shares in Günter's companies when these were listed.

Günter raced to his auditors in a frenzy of excitement. His accountant had worked out a formula for the exchange and had drawn up letters of agreement. It was enough for Günter. At last he had control of fifty-one percent of Western Minerals voting rights. For Tex McGregor the night of the long knives had come.

Although Tex's London office was the most imposing it was mainly for show and housed his English directors and clerical staff. The mining nerve center was set in Johannesburg. From here Tex administered his mining and prospecting on three continents.

Early the following Monday morning, Günter and his solicitor arrived at Western Minerals' Johannesburg offices. Apart from Tex McGregor, who was out of town and would not return until later that afternoon, Western Minerals had four other South African directors, all full-time employees of the company.

Günter strolled into the financial director's office, armed with the proxies, proving that he controlled fifty-one percent of the company, and convinced the bewildered man that it was in his best interests to call a meeting of directors.

The meeting was held at once and Günter's message was blunt. Under the terms of the Companies' Act he had already called for a shareholders' meeting to be held and within a month he would have formal control of the company. The directors could choose to work with him in the intervening period, or spend that time doing the round of various employment agencies. Without hesitation the directors unanimously invited Günter to join their board.

When Tex returned late that afternoon Günter had already established himself in Tex's office, and was concluding dictation of the directors' minutes removing Tex as a bank signatory.

For a few moments Tex was beyond sanity. There was

murder in his eyes as they flickered this way and that for a weapon.

"Get out, Tex," Günter said. "Unless you want a beating like last time. I see your nose didn't quite make it. Or was it bitten off in a brothel?"

Tex was speechless and suddenly short of breath as he realized what a fool he had been. In his quest for rapid growth he had relinquished voting control, and now found himself a minority shareholder in Günter Grieff's company.

"Have the damn lot," he grunted. "Make me an offer."

Günter smiled nastily from behind his desk. "I already have control," he pointed out. "I don't want your shares. Try selling them on the open market, and remember, Tex, screw up the company and you'll lower the share price. You're the seller, I'm not."

Tex threw his cigar butt on the Persian carpet and ground it out with his heel. "By the way," Günter went on. "At the board meeting this morning I was given exclusive use of the company's Rolls-Royce and the company's London house. Leave the keys with my secretary on your way out."

The takeover bid, with its elements of intrigue and power politics, and the subsequent listing of Günter's company made international headlines.

Günter was well satisfied. He had set out to take revenge on Tex and he had succeeded. What he had not planned was the listing of his own company, the Namib Mining and Minerals Corporation, in itself an achievement, and the sudden acquisition of a great deal of wealth in the process.

Suddenly he was known and respected and to his delight he had enough cash to redeem his beloved Kwammang-a.

The following week he startled his bank manager by calling personally to collect his diamond.

"But my dear Grieff," the manager said. "You can't just put it in your pocket and walk out of here. Good God, man. It's priceless! Keep it in the bank's vaults, or at the very least have it transported by armed security guards to your safe at home.''

Günter tossed the diamond in his hand and thrust it into his pocket. "D'you know why I treasure it so? It saved my life once. And now it's bought me Western Minerals. I like the feel of it here.'' He patted his pocket. "It's hard to believe that it's been drifting off the Skeleton Coast for over a million years—or maybe longer. That's where I found it. It'll sure as hell survive the trip home in my pocket.''

The bank manager accompanied Günter to the door, envying him his jaunty step as he disappeared through the crowds. He shrugged. He's crazy, he decided. Well, you have to be crazy to get that rich. Then he thought about the Kwammang-a. He wouldn't mind being a little bit crazy.

Chapter Sixty-eight

After months of preparation, Marika was launching her new collection. The showroom was full to overflowing and all the important buyers were there as well as the fashion press.

Peeping through the curtains, Marika tried to ignore the twinges in her belly. She felt sick with fear; the tension which had started in her legs had reached her neck and it ached intolerably. She would never be free of this dread, she knew that; however much money she made, or famous she became, she would always crave public approval and acceptance—as she had years ago. Right now she was just as tense, just as scared.

She felt Bertha squeeze her hand. "It will be all right,'' Bertha whispered. "Don't worry.''

All right, she thought irritably. If it were just "all right'' she would shoot herself. It had to be the best, better than last year, better than anything she had done before. She did not know why, but she was just built that way.

Marika had to admit that everything was very well organized this year. The models were not shrieking at each other, nothing had been lost, the refreshments were on time and the compere seemed calm and competent. Bertha's influence. She wondered how she had managed without her all those years.

The show opened with a fanfare of trumpets, and to the music of Prokofiev eight models waltzed onto the stage and down the platform in her favorite creations. Flashbulbs went off, reporters took up their notebooks and the babble of conversation ceased.

When Marika heard the applause she felt the tension draining down into the floor, pulling her with it. The collection was going to be a success—after all the months of planning, hoping, working—and she would like nothing better than to curl up in a corner and fall asleep. "Bloody well should be," she muttered. "Bloody well should be." But you could never tell. Hard work wasn't enough—she knew that.

Several international photographers were there: David Montgomery, Tony Snowdon, Oliviero Toscani, as well as representatives from the top fashion magazines and women's press of three continents. She had not disappointed them; the seventies were looming ahead and Marika had succeeded in portraying the woman of the future with stark clarity and amazing sensitivity. Femininity was fading to sensuality; modesty to enthusiasm for life; there was bold, vigorous styling for a new decade.

It was nearly intermission now and Marika was peeping through the curtains again, feeling satisfied and remembering Mendel with nostalgia. She still used the same showroom; the old Persian carpets were laid out every year; the chandeliers washed and polished. How proud he would be to see her latest range. Tony would be, too, if only he were there, she thought wistfully.

It was then that she heard shouting outside; the porter's voice joined in. Doors were flung open and a crowd of scruffy students flung themselves into the showroom and sprawled on the floor. Several chairs were flung over as the students unfurled their banners and marched along the dais yelling, "Care for animals, don't wear them."

Marika shuddered as she huddled in the wings. The placards were horrible: foxes in traps gnawing their legs, a dog caught in a snare and starved, beavers drowned underwater. "Oh my God," she whispered. "Those horrible, horrible pictures."

Then she saw Sylvia, violet eyes brimming with fury. She, too, was carrying a placard and she was shouting with the rest.

Marika stood numb with shock, unable to move, and saw Bertha storm down the aisle and slap Sylvia's face. Then she turned to argue with a tall, young bearded man who grabbed Sylvia's arm and tried to pull her out. Too late! The press had seen her! They had recognized Sylvia Shaw and knew she was her daughter. The oohs and ahs changed to a hubbub of excitement. There was a story here.

Marika pulled herself together and signaled to the disc jockey to increase the volume of the music. The models were trying their best, but they could not push their way through the demonstrators.

Chaos!

Then the police arrived and shortly afterward the last of the students were hauled through the doorway.

The demonstration had lasted only five minutes, but then so does an earthquake, Marika thought sadly, which it could as well have been, judging by the damage it had done. Her show was ruined.

She crept sadly onto the stage and took the microphone.

"It's a sign of the times," she began, fumbling for words. "Pointless to ignore it. It's here. A new awareness." She broke off and looked around. A sea of faces gazed up at her and everyone was looking uncomfortable.

"Some of you are here because you are buyers and your livelihoods depend on furs. To you I say: Statistics prove that furs are gaining in popularity. To those of you who are representing the press I'd like to point out that we are witnessing a social revolution. For the first time in decades young people are banding together to eradicate evil and to foster good. They are searching, feeling their way, and they are making mistakes. Personally I feel that this evening was a mistake.'' There were feeble laughs from the audience.

"But that doesn't matter,'' she went on determinedly. "What matters is that they care. They really do care—and if sometimes they seem to overdo their missionary zeal and take the wrong direction—well, it's all in the cause of goodness.''

She glanced ruefully at the torn carpets, shattered chairs and broken door. "Just material things,'' she said with a shrug.

"Now for something more contentious. Is it wrong to wear a fur coat? I don't think so, but it's up to the individual to decide—like eating meat, or going fishing. But I must stress that we no longer deal with wild furs. All the coats you have seen this evening are from farm-bred animals.''

She finished to a storm of applause, but she knew that the show was ruined, and she was right.

When the show was over, Bertha, Tanya and John joined Marika for the customary glass of champagne with the rest of the staff and the models.

Bertha pulled Marika aside. "Don't take it to heart,'' She said. "Sylvia just wants to be like the others. All students hold demonstrations—it's a way of life for them. I must tell you, her friend, Andy Stark, was furious. He did not know her family was involved, or so he told me, and I believe him. He's a nice young man. So don't take it personally, Marika. It will all blow over, you'll see.'' She hugged her tightly.

"I didn't even know she had a young man,'' Marika said dully, wondering how she could possibly be so out of touch with her daughter. "I'm sure you're right,'' she added to please Bertha, but she had seen the fury blazing from her daughter's eyes.

"Presumably Sylvia won't be joining the business," John said scathingly when no one was listening. "What better way could she find to tell you, dear? Take my advice. Give up! You're kidding yourself if you think things are going to get better between you," he added with his customary lack of tact.

Marika tried to persuade Bertha to come back with her for dinner, but Bertha was tired and wanted to have an early night. Eventually Marika drove home feeling close to tears.

Tony was locked in his study yelling into the telephone. He came out briefly to eat, but Marika decided not to tell him about the demonstration. She was sitting alone in front of the fire, feeling confused and unhappy, when Sylvia rushed in.

"I know you're angry," she burst out, and Marika was surprised to notice that her daughter looked upset, "but I think I have a right to stand up for what I believe in. The fact that you deal with furs does not alter my views one bit. I'm absolutely against it."

"You made that very clear," Marika said coldly. "You also cost me a small fortune tonight. I expect you knew that, too."

"Money, money, money. Heavens, Mother! If only we could talk of something besides money . . . just once in a while. Didn't the demo get through to you at all? It's not money that counts, it's pain and suffering. Have you thought of how many foxes died to make that coat you were showing off so proudly? Have you ever thought?"

Marika was about to say, "Let's call a truce, shall we?" But before she could speak, Sylvia said, "Of course, you could never understand, you're quite insensitive to everything except your own ambition." After that it was no good trying anymore.

Marika burst into tears, screamed bitter, wounding gibes

she did not mean, and her daughter retaliated more cruelly, until the doorbell rang and Sylvia fled to her bedroom.

They had fought bitterly on the pavement. Why hadn't Sylvia told them it was her mother's show they were gate-crashing? If he'd known he would never have let her join the demonstration. Damnit! That was no way to treat your mother, even if she was Britain's fur queen. Andy was furious with Sylvia and even angrier with himself. He had known her mother was in furs, but he had assumed her name was Shaw, not Magos. He should have paid more attention.

Now, single-handed, she had ruined the demonstration— all their publicity, all their work, and the message they were trying to get over—overshadowed by the attraction of a stupid family feud. The press would make the most of it, he knew that. He had seen one photographer line up his sights to get Sylvia and Marika in the same shot. The generation gap! That's what it narrowed down to—thanks to Sylvia and her mother.

He had told her so and Sylvia had burst into tears and driven away. Andy had felt sorry when he realized how upset she was and he had run back to his car and driven after her, wondering where she was going as they raced along country roads.

Outwood Manor! And Sylvia had driven up the long, imposing driveway. Shit! A manor and a wealthy mother. No wonder she had never invited him home. For a moment he hesitated. Then he shrugged. He knew he had to bail her out. What a fool he had been to become entangled with her. He had nothing to offer a girl like her and he should have known better. Their relationship was doomed.

"Wow! What a place," he said aloud. He parked and rang a massive bell hanging by an equally imposing door, expecting church bells to peal, but he heard a discreet chime in the hall, then footsteps approaching.

The man who opened the door was tall, stately and silver-haired. He had a vaguely condescending air.

"I'm Andy Stark," Andy began uncertainly. "I'm a

friend of Sylvia's. I'd like to see her mother, Mrs. Magos. You're Mr. Magos, I presume. How do you do, sir.''

"I'm the butler and her mother is Mrs. Palma,'' the man said without a trace of a smile. "Here is Mr. Palma."

Andy nearly exclaimed with shock when he saw Palma. How could he be Sylvia's stepfather? A young man, not much older than himself. Regular dandy, Andy thought, with his florid good looks and his fancy track suit. He took an instantaneous dislike to him. A brief glance around the hall nearly took his breath away. Antiques, paintings and Persian carpets—Aladdin's cave!

"I'd like to speak to Mrs. Palma," Andy began.

"She's busy. She doesn't want to be disturbed," Tony said.

"Where's Sylvia?"

"You can't see Sylvia," Tony said. "She's gone to bed. Don't call again."

"I know she's in there." Andy pointed to a door across the hall. Beyond he could hear sobbing.

"No," Tony retorted. "She's not in there."

"You're lying," Andy said, hating him. "It's not her fault. I want to explain."

"Go and see for yourself," Tony said carelessly.

Andy strode across the hall and flung open the door. "Sylvia," he called. The woman who looked up at him was not Sylvia, although there was a great resemblance. She was Marika Magos, whom he had last seen on the platform, but now she was crying bitterly.

"I'm so sorry," he said. "So sorry. Really. I had no idea it was your collection—that is, I didn't know you were her mother. I can see how hurt you are. Please don't blame Sylvia. I organized everything."

Marika looked up. "Who are you?" she asked. Then she gave him a tremulous smile. "I know—you're Andy. Bertha told me about you." She liked him immediately, in spite of his wretched demonstration. Far too trusting for her daughter, she thought treacherously. He would be badly hurt.

"It's hard to believe you're her mother," he went on. "You look alike, but you're so young," he said.

"You've said your piece. Now get the hell out of here," Palma told him. Suddenly it all clicked into place. Angelo Palma, the industrialist: oil wells, chemical groups, cosmetics, clothing, factories, just about everything. Andy felt very sick. What the hell was he doing tangling with the jet set?

"The next time I see you," Palma said as Andy walked out the front door, "you'll be damned sorry." Then the door slammed.

Andy started the engine of his beat-up jalopy and gazed momentarily at the house. Jesus! What a house! There was an upstairs light on. Sylvia's, presumably. Well, he thought ruefully, he should have listened to his sixth sense when he first met her.

He would miss her. As he drove down the driveway he realized, for the first time, just how much he loved her.

Chapter Sixty-nine

It was a particularly cold January and the garden took on a fairy-tale appearance. In spite of her unhappiness Sylvia could not help marveling at the change: snow-capped firs ringed the frozen lake, dewdrops sparkled like diamonds from every twig and the air was crisp and pure. When she could not stand the gloomy atmosphere in the house she would go out and sit on the bench by the lake.

It seemed that everyone was set against her and she knew it served her right. "Oh, it's all too much . . . too much," she whispered to herself. But the real cause of her misery was Andy. Since the fur demonstration, he avoided her whenever possible, and when they met accidentally he was cold, but polite, which was far worse than quarreling.

She was badly hurt. She had tried to use Andy to save herself from Tony and instead she had fallen in love.

She was still sitting there when her mother found her. Marika wondered what fascination this bleak scene could possibly hold for her daughter: the swans were huddled on the island, cold and dejected; mist drifted over the ice; the sky was leaden. The original ice maiden, she thought, watching her daughter's white skin and ash-blond hair merge into the startling white background.

It was impossible to walk quietly as she had intended, for her footsteps crunched on the frozen snow. Sylvia glanced over her shoulder and frowned; her violet eyes looked as cold and remote as the wintry scene.

Was all that warmth merely an illusion, Marika wondered, ready on call, together with tropical plants and island breezes, for when the art director snapped his fingers?

There was no welcoming smile. "Oh . . . Mother," her daughter said tensely.

"I brought you this stole." Marika laughed shakily. "You must be freezing. And a bag of bread. I thought you might like to feed the ducks."

Sylvia took the bag and flung pieces of bread sullenly over the ice and soon they were surrounded with greedy, quacking birds.

"Poor things—they're starving," Sylvia began.

"They just like the bread; the gardener feeds them twice a day."

"Oh!" She looked taken aback. "I never thought . . ."

"Sounds like your theme song."

"Oh, Mother."

"Sylvia," Marika began, turning to her daughter nervously. "Do you remember? . . . We often used to feed the ducks down at the pond."

She tried to remind her daughter of the days they had spent together in London's parks while they sketched and picnicked under the trees. Happier times! They could not all be forgotten, surely.

Sylvia listened in silence with a slight derisive smile on

her face. Mother was trying belatedly to play "Mother."
She'd use anything to force her own way. Old memories,
feelings long forgotten. She'd have to dig deeply to find
them. "I remember," she said tonelessly.

"I made a mistake in letting you go, but Bertha loved
you so and I could not look after you properly. It seemed
the best solution for the time being." Her daughter was
staring at the ducks and frowning slightly.

"Then, somehow the years slipped away, and you were
happy with Günter." She almost choked on the word.
"Suddenly it was too late. I couldn't get you back. I have
never stopped regretting it. And that fight . . ." She leaned
back and sighed.

"It's silly to bring back the past, but I thought . . ."
She broke off, wondering where she had gone wrong. If
she had stayed in Africa, would that have helped Sylvia?
Perhaps if she had kept Sylvia in London—things might
have been different; she would have managed somehow.

Looking back, she became confused with the extent of
her alternatives. Only one thing was clear: Sylvia had
rejected her.

"I thought perhaps we could work on being friends,"
Marika blurted out in a rush, the words tumbling over each
other. "If we could start off by trusting each other?"

Sylvia turned and stared at her mother relentlessly. "Correct me if I've got it wrong. I must trust you to be a good
mother from now on. And you will trust me to be a good
daughter and not cause you any more business losses.

"Oh, I know about the losses," she went on, feeling
secure in her triumph. "Dad spelled it out to me at
Christmas."

Suddenly she realized that she hated her mother. The
idea was devastating—like a cyclone inside her—starting
in her stomach and moving up to blow her mind away. She
felt her face burning red, her eyes smarting.

But her mother was talking, hands over her face, voice
muffled, trying to exorcise her own phantoms. Stop it!
Stop it! Sylvia shrieked inwardly.

"I couldn't stand the desert, you see," her mother was

saying. "That lonely camp in the Kalahari. It was home, but what a dreadful home. All that sand . . . all that loneliness . . . But you know something? Nothing has ever seemed like home since. Not this place. It's lovely and I'm proud of it, but it's not home."

"Who cares?" Sylvia jumped up; her face was bitter and spiteful. "Who cares if you feel at home? I don't. You can't be a lily-white mother, after all. You blew it—years ago."

Sylvia ran toward the house and Marika lost sight of her in the misty dusk.

The lights were suddenly switched on. They seemed very far away. She heard the gardener's whistle coming from beyond the lake. The ducks and swans stood up and waddled awkwardly on the ice toward the whistle. The mist swirled in eddies and the fir trees bowed toward the night. Marika sat on, oblivious to the damp cold.

Chapter Seventy

Sylvia could not bear to stay in the house after the scene they had just had. Besides, her resentment of her mother was tinged with guilt. She grabbed her coat and car keys and escaped before her mother returned.

Driving to London was traumatic; she could hardly see five yards ahead in the thickening fog, but the cars kept racing past her. A foul and terrible night. A night for introspection, for burying grudges and dreams. She would corner Andy and demand the truth. He must tell her what was wrong; better to know than to waste her days with longing and silly dreams. "Damn the man," she murmured as she narrowly missed a pedestrian. The fog was getting worse. She should have stayed home.

It was past nine when she arrived. Andy had not locked

his door. He never did. The bed was rumpled, the dishes unwashed, jobs he hated, she knew, but the rest of the attic studio was neat as an army barrack—and as spartan. It was a long, low room with skylights, the walls covered with rough wooden shelving packed with books and box files; at one end a partition hid the darkroom and the cabinets where Andy kept his photographic equipment.

The room said a lot about him, she thought. A man who lived for his work, avoiding time-consuming emotional attachments. A man with a mission.

She began to clean up; it was something to do, but at twelve, when he had not arrived, she wished that she had not come. He should be back by now—he and Bob Israel and four others who had flown to Newfoundland and chartered a boat to the seal grounds to film the annual seal hunt. Sylvia had expected to go with them, but they had put her off. Eventually she curled up on his bed and fell asleep.

She awoke much later when the lights were switched on. Andy was home, looking cold, fed up and heartbreakingly familiar. For a moment she was confused. "Oh, Andy, I was expecting you ages ago." Then she remembered why she was there. She flushed and bit her lip.

His face became bleak when he saw her. "What the hell are you doing here?" he said coldly. He flung his bags on the floor and lowered his camera case more gently to the desk. Then he lit the gas stove and hung his duffel coat on a hook on the back of the door.

"I came to talk to you," she said. She sat up and leaned against the iron bedstead, watching Andy fill a kettle and place it on the gas ring. Then he leaned over it, rubbing his hands over the heat. His nose was blue and his eyes smarting. "You're back late," she said, avoiding the confrontation.

"Lucky I'm here at all," he said. "A catastrophe! They took my film. Tried to beat us up. Brutal beggars." Then he grinned. "But I had another film hidden. We were expecting them, you see."

"Andy, I don't want to know about the seals," she

said. "I want to talk about us." She stood up and caught
hold of his hand. It was icy cold. She placed it against her
cheek and pressed hard. She looked up pleadingly, but
Andy turned away, unwilling to meet her candid, searching eyes.

"Heavens, Andy. What a rotten way to behave," she
persisted. "You might have said, 'Get lost, I found some-
body new,' or 'I'm off blondes—it's my year for bru-
nettes,' or any bloody thing . . ."

"Honey, you're way off beam," he said gently. "The
fact is, you're out of my reach, Sylvia. Let's not kid
ourselves. There's nothing ahead but heartbreak—for both
of us. Best to break up now before we're hurt bad."

Andy looked around for the dirty cups and noticed they
were clean. He looked at her long and silently. Then he
shrugged. "Slumming again, were you?"

She gasped, jumped forward and slapped his face. Then
she flung herself on the bed, pummeling her fists into the
pillow.

The water boiled and he took two mugs and made some
tea. Then he wondered where to put the mugs and whether
or not she'd burn herself when she flung the tea at him.

"Okay, I'm sorry," he said. He put one hand on her
shoulder. "Please don't be upset. I can't bear to see you
so hurt."

"Don't lie, don't lie to me," she mumbled.

"You're just a child, really, aren't you?" he said gently.
"It's your face—you look so sophisticated—too perfect,
really. Most of the time I don't notice how you look—
you're just you—but then on TV. Well, I can't really miss
seeing you in those damned perfume spots every night."

Andy took her in his arms and tried to calm her and
eventually she stopped shaking.

"I love you, Sylvia," he whispered. "But I can't live in
your world and you won't want to live in mine. That's all.
That's it. I can't see a solution."

"Oh, Andy," she wailed. "I'm so miserable. I suddenly realized . . . it was like a light switched on in the
chamber of horrors . . . I hate my mother."

"There's no law says you have to love your mother, honey," Andy said gently. "But she looked like a real fine woman to me. She was crying. When I looked at her I suddenly realized that I've never seen you crying."

"I cried when she left me, but never again. What's the point? It doesn't change anything."

She shuddered. "I talked to her about the furs—the way we feel about trapping and clubbing. It was a few weeks ago. Do you know what Mother said?" Sylvia went on. "She said, 'Do what you have to do. As I must. I, too, have dedicated my life to a mission.' " Sylvia imitated her mother's husky voice. " 'You didn't know that, did you? And nothing in this world is going to stop me. It's somewhat different from yours. I pray to God you'll never have anything more than seals and beavers to worry about.' Then she looked at me. I swear I've never seen anything as terrible as Mother's eyes at that moment. She looked vicious—blazing with hate. She gave me the creeps.

"I need you, Andy. I don't want to get like Mother. I have this terrible feeling that somewhere along the way Mother made the wrong choice. She forgot about goodness. I don't want to get like her. Please, Andy."

She had never spent the night with Andy; never taken that final, irrevocable step.

It was a night which seemed to last forever. Moonlight poured through the skylight and she could see the moon, a blurred yellow globe crossing their narrow strip of private sky. In the dim, mellow light she watched Andy and his sensitive, clever face and his eyes so loving and concerned.

He was kind and sensuous, and he kissed her neck, her mouth and her fingertips, letting his lips brush over her skin. She drifted into a state of joy, scarcely able to talk, but she experienced it all with gratitude. Andy loved her. Nothing else in the world could be as important as that. Surely it would all come right eventually. He was being oversensitive.

She wanted to watch him, to examine his beautiful body, to see the way his muscles flexed and unflexed when he moved. She loved the sheen of his skin, the long hairs tangled on his legs and chest, the sheer beauty of every part of him, but when she sat up in bed, icy blasts made her dive back under the bedclothes, forcing them to snuggle up tightly together again.

When he made love he raised himself on his elbows and clutched her hands, while his eyes gazed into hers, leaving her helpless with desire. She could only murmur, "I love you . . . love . . . love . . . love." She had never known her body before this night; she had been unaware that she was a warm and passionate woman. Now she knew for sure she had been created for this one particular man—and he for her. When they climaxed together it merely reinforced her vision. They were one. Capricious fate alone had made them two—two halves of a whole. She and Andy. Home!

Then she remembered her mother and her pitiful words— her plea for charity—saw her eyes haggard and lonely. Softly, in the night, snuggled tightly against Andy, compassion brushed her and her eyes filled with tears.

Chapter Seventy-one

London, which Günter had always disliked, seemed suddenly delightful; the houses cheerier, the people gayer. He smiled as he walked down Piccadilly and everyone smiled back.

It was a crisp, misty morning and in the distance Günter could hear the drum of horse hooves approaching. Horse and guardsman appeared through the mist like a specter from the past. Flash of red and polished brass buttons. Then he was gone. Günter stood at the curb gawking like any schoolboy. "Unreal," he muttered. A toy soldier come to life. He walked on in a party mood.

Western Minerals! It looked delightfully English with its

granite gargoyles over the massive doorway and discreetly carved door. Western Minerals—at last it was his.

All things considered, it was a beautiful morning and Günter whistled merrily as he bounded up the imposing stone steps.

Once in the foyer, he paused and looked around uncertainly. The situation was entirely new to him. The doorman was advancing, or was he the doorman? He had enough gold braid for a general.

"Mr. Grieff, sir? Come with me, please. You're expected."

You bet the hell I am, Günter thought, as he strode along the corridors.

There were about thirty men in the boardroom. They were wearing the obligatory welcoming smile and looking uneasy. Behind them, on the long mahogany polished table, were three silver trays with sherry decanters and glasses. Tex always did things in style, he remembered.

He picked up the decanter and poured out the sherry. To hell with protocol. "Help yourselves, gentlemen," he said, holding his glass up. "To Tex McGregor, a gallant loser, but a loser just the same, and that, gentlemen, is the very last fight that Western Minerals will ever lose. From now on forget protocol. Just concentrate on winning. Now let's get down to business."

By the time Sylvia arrived with a reluctant Andy in tow, Günter had sized up his management team and sorted out their various responsibilities and priorities. He also knew which ones he would fire.

He was talking when the door burst open.

"Daddy darling," Sylvia said, and raced across the room to fling her arms around him. "They wouldn't let me in," she said incredulously. "So I just pushed."

"Good for you." His eyes glowed with pride. "Gentlemen, this is my daughter, Sylvia Shaw. I expect you've seen her on TV. It's the only way I get to see her nowadays, so if you'll excuse me I'll call a lunch break. See you at . . ." He glanced at his watch. "Two."

"You didn't phone," she complained when they were out of the boardroom.

"I did and you weren't home. Where the hell were you?"

"With Andy. Andy Stark. This is he and he's special," she added in case her father had not noticed.

Andy muttered something ineffectual. He was feeling foolish and inadequate to meet the situation. It was only when Sylvia had burst into the boardroom that he had realized that her father must be a pretty important person. Now he remembered reading about the fight to gain control of this vast mining group with assets as far afield as Canada, Australia, Africa and South America. It seemed her old man owned both this and his own South African mining group. He wouldn't waste much time considering Andy as a prospective escort for his daughter. Why the hell hadn't she told him before? Andy wondered angrily.

He endured an embarrassing few minutes while Günter plied him with questions, which Sylvia answered for him. Eventually he lost his cool and snarled, "Sylvia, will you stop talking for me? I'm quite capable of replying. To cut short a long inquisition, sir, and without disrespect, I can tell you categorically that I am quite unsuitable for your daughter. I cannot keep her in the style to which she is accustomed. In fact, I cannot keep her at all. It's my intention to join the United Nations and work for underdeveloped countries in Africa. Sylvia's very young and right now she thinks it would be romantic to return to the African bush. She has two choices, your money or my life. There's no way the two will ever be entangled."

"Well, that was quite a mouthful," Günter retorted with a wry smile. "I'll tell you something, Andy. My daughter's quite good at making her own money. Or d'you have old-fashioned ideas about women working, too? And there's nothing you could teach my daughter about the African bush," he went on, preventing Andy from answering with a wave of his hand. "She knew it all before you knew Africa existed."

"Stop bragging, Dad," Sylvia interrupted him.

"I sure as hell don't want to interfere in her life,"
Günter said, eyeing the boy shrewdly. He decided he liked
Andy.

"We're going steady," Sylvia told him solemnly. "But
we don't go out much. Andy can't afford it and he won't
let me pay." She pulled a wry face at Günter.

"Won't hurt you," Günter said. The boy was so young,
still testing the mettle of his masculinity. He wanted to be
the boss in his home and he saw Sylvia's money as a
threat. Well, why not? But he wouldn't be able to fight it
forever.

Over lunch Günter cross-examined Sylvia about Marika.
How was she looking? What was she doing? He never
mentioned Tony.

When Sylvia heard that Dad owned a company house in
London and hoped to live there within a year her spirits
soared.

"How's Claire?" she asked.

"She's in Ireland buying a racehorse," he said. "She's
developed a passion for training. She'll be here in a day or
two. You'll see her then."

When they left he stood watching them walk arm in arm
along the pavement. Suddenly he felt happy for Sylvia,
glad of her youth and her delight at being in love.

Then he turned and walked briskly back to Western
Minerals House feeling just about as pleased as he had
ever felt.

He was twenty minutes early, so he found his way to
McGregor's old office.

His secretary was hovering there, looking excited and
scared and pleased all at the same time. "This is the key
of the safe, Mr. Grieff," she said. "Mr. McGregor was
most insistent that no one should open that safe except
you."

She handed him the key as if it were the crown jewels,
hesitated and then backed out.

Curiously, Günter opened the door. The safe was empty
except for a note which read: *Screw you, Grieff, you*

bastard. You've won this round, but I still fucked Claire—
and boy, it was lovely. Ask her about it.

A poor revenge—just a spit in the eye from a bad loser.

He sat quietly at his desk for a while. Then he telephoned Claire in Ireland. She was out and he wondered whether or not to leave a message. Eventually he replaced the receiver. Who cares! Günter thought as he tore the note into small pieces.

He went to the boardroom trying to look jaunty and to recover the feeling of joy he had been carrying with him all morning. But it was no use—the day was spoiled and his triumph seemed negligible.

Chapter Seventy-two

Tony sat glowering out of the window. The sun's pale rays pierced the clouds, sending shafts of brightness on trees and grass; melting frost sparkled with rainbow prisms; a blackbird sang with gratitude from the bare branch of an oak tree and snowy swans glistened startling white against gray wintry waters. Who cared? Not Tony, for Sylvia had announced that morning that she was leaving home shortly and moving in with Andy. His jealousy was like a tapeworm devouring his entrails. So Tony was planning his revenge with the same cold efficiency that had built his empire.

"Problems are opportunities for correction," he murmured. It was a phrase out of his group's staff training manual, which he had mainly written himself, but it did not help him to think straight. His brain was addled with anger. One thought—just one thought kept beating in his head. Destroy! Destroy Sylvia and her pathetic world—her infantile, mucky, sordid world—and her queer boyfriend with his meetings and bonfires and all the rigmarole of an undisciplined society.

The house was in an uproar. Marika was moping somewhere, too stubborn and proud to argue; Sylvia was sorting out what she would take. Andy had flown home to Boston to see his father, who was ill. She would move in with him when he returned.

Tony sat down and put his head in his hands. He had never felt so bad about anything in his life. No . . . not even the death of his mother had hurt him so much.

She must be brought to heel—like an untrained puppy. That's all she is, he thought, in spite of her incredible beauty and her naïve ways. And now she had discovered her sexuality with another man. She had slept out three nights running. There lay the pain . . . the reason for his fury.

Sylvia arrived at dinner feeling defiant and on the defensive. She was running away, she knew that. Of course, she loved Andy, for his goodness and his fine, straight mind. He was a friend as well as a lover and she would marry him one day. Yet Tony still had the power to turn her spine to jelly if he so much as put a hand on her shoulder. Just to gaze into his eyes made her knees wobbly. So she was running away from Tony and she wished that Andy were here to help her when she needed him.

Why was everything looking so terribly normal? Sylvia wondered uneasily as she sat at the table. Unreal!

"Sylvia, I like Andy," her mother began. She had obviously rehearsed her speech. "Of course, I only saw him once. I'd like to see him more often. Let's make Friday our family night. You and Andy could come to dinner—and then there's the indoor swimming pool. I'm sure Andy would like that in winter." Mother was looking terribly sad.

"Yes," Sylvia said, feeling relieved. "Thank you, Mother." This was going to be easier than she had imagined.

Tony was grinning cheerfully, which surprised her. "Just as long as you don't neglect the modeling, Sylvia," he said. "But I know you won't. There's a million bucks spent on the campaign already. Since you're going to have your time taken up, I've suggested to the agency that they run the Swiss campaign earlier. They'll contact you. Of course, it depends on their plans, too, but since Andy's away . . . " He broke off and poured out the wine.

"Drink up," he said. "This is a celebration, isn't it? Even if the hero is absent."

Sylvia settled back and sighed with contentment. It was going to be all right. She had learned a valuable lesson, stood up for what she wanted and Tony had given in. What else could he do? After all, he was married to Mother. Otherwise . . .

She felt a flood of warmth toward him. "Of course I'd love to do the Swiss campaign," she said, smiling. "It would help pass the time until Andy returns."

Dusk settled quietly on the snowy slopes and through the mist the lights began twinkling from the village far below. The air was crisp, the sky a pale and watery blue, mists were gathering higher up the mountain and nearer fir trees trembled under their burden of snow. For a strange, unsettling moment it seemed that she was the only person alive in this quaint, Christmas-card world. She called out, "Tony, hello there," and her voice echoed in the distance. Then she turned and skimmed down the smooth, untrammeled snow.

It was their last run for the day and Tony was in sight now as he approached the chalet. He paused and, turning, beckoned her. She waved back, overbalanced and sprawled forward, enjoying the crunch as her body sank into packed snow. Clods of snow from overladen branches spattered silently around her.

It was almost dark as she skied to the shed, hung up her skis and unlaced her boots.

By now Tony would be mixing their drinks, the fire would be roaring in the old stone hearth and the housekeeper would have left a steaming casserole on the stove. Maybe there would be apple tart in the warmer.

Sylvia sighed with contentment. It had been a marvelous four days. The advertising agency had turned out in force and stayed in the inn at the village. She had had the chalet all to herself until two days ago when Tony suddenly appeared—just to check how the campaign was going, he had told her.

Naughty, she acknowledged, but harmless, and after all, no one knew. Tony had told her that "Mother," as he often called her when she was not around to hear, was in America visiting her distributors.

Of course, Sylvia was longing to see Andy, but since he was still in Boston she might as well stay for the weekend. Now she was glad. She had never imagined Tony could be such fun. They had skied, skated on the village lake, visited local inns and explored the shops.

Her fingers were frozen and it took her some time to unlace her boots, but eventually she managed and walked gratefully into the warm chalet.

Tony, who had been listening for her footsteps, held out her glass. "Cheers! Hope it wasn't too painful."

"You might have waited." She smiled softly as she sipped the steaming mulled wine fragrant with cloves.

"I thought you'd need this drink more than a piggy-back. That's my perfume you're wearing," he went on. "Bet you didn't know it was created just for you. That's why it's the top one in the range."

"Thank you, Tony," she said. She was habitually deft at handling compliments, but suddenly she flushed.

Tony smiled. "Come over here. I've got something special for you." He clattered around behind the bar. Very special!

For a moment he hesitated. Then he cleared his head of wasteful and unnecessary emotions. Action was necessary. He was taking the required steps; that was all. He saw himself in the role of an archaeologist who comes across a priceless relic being used by savages for their daily needs. It had to be placed in safer, wiser hands. The rare beauties of this world are not for the raggle-taggle. Sylvia must be cosseted and guarded—for her own sake.

"This is called the Tycoon Tickler," he said, grinning happily. "To get the right effect you have to swallow it in one mouthful. Like so." He flung the contents of a small liqueur glass into his mouth and swallowed it with a gulp.

She copied him and placed the glass laughingly on the bar. Then she frowned. "Oops," she said. "Quite a kick. I don't want to ski with a hangover tomorrow."

He gave her an odd look which made her feel uncomfortable.

"I'm hungry," she said.

They sat by the old stone hearth and ate veal cooked with port and herbs and drank red wine. Sylvia became unusually garrulous, talking about her father and home and the future she and Andy had planned together in a mission station somewhere in Africa. "Mother would never understand," she told him seriously.

But it was hard to be serious when the room was turning around her, although she tried, unburdening her hopes and plans.

"I think I drank too much," she told Tony, mouthing her words carefully. "It was that Tycoon Tickler. You're crazy." She burst into laughter and eventually subsided into a state of silence. She leaned back with a silly, vacuous look on her face, eyes glazed, mouth slightly open.

Tony turned away and pulled the table nearer to the fire.

"I don't know how to explain how happy I feel," she told him. At that moment it seemed to Sylvia important that Tony should understand. She tried again: "I feel strange. Sort of happy. No, sort of happy-go-lucky." Then she gave up and leaned back sighing.

But Tony had a rough idea of how she felt. He had experimented with mescaline and a few other drugs and he could describe in detail the state of dreamlike fragmentation she was experiencing. He even knew about those certain vital areas in which she was now undefended, such as love, modesty, sensuality—and the ability to distinguish between right and wrong.

"Have another Tycoon Tickler."

She giggled. "Such a mad name. I feel so close to you, Tony. Even as close as Dad . . . yes . . . even Andy." Her eyes took on a glazed, sultry expression. "Yes, I will have another," she said dreamily. "Can I sip it this time?

"If you like. Don't waste it. It's very *rare*." Unique, in fact; an ingenious blending of hallucinatory and other drugs devised by his best chemist.

Sylvia was gazing around apprehensively. The room had changed its structure, losing its three-dimensional aspect, so that the furniture towered over her. Colors throbbed and glowed like seaweed undulating in the tide. She had never seen so much beauty. The curtain's rich burgundy folds were moving and changing to violet, cerise, rose and purple in a never-ending kaleidoscope of breathtaking colors, more spectacular than a fireworks display and more startling by far. It was too much. Too painful. She shielded her eyes with her hands.

When Tony stood up Sylvia gasped with surprise. Then she giggled. "Someone painted you onto stained-glass windows," she gurgled. "It's a joke, isn't it?" Her voice drifted away and she was lost in some secret world of her own imagination, staring fixedly at the wall.

She leaned back and groaned with ecstasy. "Oh," she gasped. At that moment Tony brought his mouth down on hers.

Chapter Seventy-three

The first thing she became aware of was a splitting pain in her head. She tried to move, but the pain was unbearable, so she lay still, drifting in and out of unconsciousness, plagued by dreams—or memories?

Later—much later—she noticed the smell of vomit on

the pillow beside her and saw their Swiss housekeeper bending over her.

Sylvia lay back and closed her eyes. Eventually she fell asleep and when she woke next it was dark. She reached out and switched on her bedside lamp, but the light stabbed her eyes and she cried out.

She heard creaking floorboards and then the house-keeper was beside her. "Drugs," the old woman muttered angrily. "You're lucky you're alive, my fine young lady. I hope you've learned a good lesson."

When the doctor came she asked him what was wrong with her. He told her that she had been reported missing two nights ago and her stepfather had alerted the police before he went looking for her. He had found her in a room above the inn with a young student suffering from an overdose of drugs.

"Which inn?"

He didn't know.

"And what would you say," she asked the doctor, "if I told you that I never take drugs, have absolutely no knowledge of taking drugs and no memories of inns, merely of having dinner with my stepfather?"

"It's not unusual to suffer from amnesia, from hallucinatory memories," he said. "My advice to you, young lady, is choose your company more carefully."

She flew home the following day. Mother had just arrived back and she seemed surprised to see her.

"Tony said you'd flown on to America to stay with Andy. What happened? Did you fall out?"

Sylvia kept her teeth gritted and her mouth shut.

It was Friday. Andy was due back in a few days. Perhaps she should fly over. Put the whole sordid business out of her mind. Of course everything was all right. Yet these curious and horrible memories persisted.

Her anguish continued all day, with Tony playing the perfect husband to Marika and Marika being especially maternal to her.

"Stay home tomorrow, pet," Marika said after dinner.

"You look really sick. I have to be at the plant, we're racing ahead with the new range. Difficult times for everyone, but Tony's at home tomorrow."

She lay awake for most of the night, afraid to confront her stepfather without her mother's presence as a buffer, wondering what she would say to him.

The next morning before breakfast, Tony said, "I want to talk to you." They had both arrived in the dining room at the same time.

"And I want to talk to you. Is Mother gone?"

"Yes."

"Tony, you drugged me," she burst out the moment the library door closed. "It was the Tycoon Tickler. How could you do a thing like that? You know how dangerous drugs are. You could go to prison." She scowled at him. "I want you to know I've had three days of hell."

"Darling," he said. "So have I." He hugged her in his arms and pushed his open mouth onto hers.

For a few seconds she struggled and fought and when at last he released her she struck him a stinging blow on his cheek; saw the skin smarting red, saw his eye watering.

"Don't tell me you've lost interest so quickly after our dirty weekend in the Alps."

"What the hell are you talking about?" she shrieked.

"I think you remember. Or at least a part of it."

"I'm going to the police," she said quickly. "Andy will kill you—and Dad. I'll phone Dad."

She raced to the telephone, but Tony was quicker.

"This is where you learn to toe the line, Sylvia," he said. "Unless you have ambitions of being a movie star. I can hardly resist selling it. Boy, is it explicit! Better watch it first so you know what you're up against. It'll be released all over London by the end of the week if you go to dear Dad or anyone else. I hate to think how he'd react. Or Andy."

He walked into the study and pulled down the blinds. Then he switched on the projector.

She gazed as if in a trance at the horrible, terrible pictures. There she was grinning straight at the camera, while Tony did unspeakably dreadful things to her and she to him.

Her thoughts hurtled frantically at imagined avenues of escape like a wild bird in a cage. She could sue; she could explain; but what if she did? All the world would have seen her on her knees in front of Tony . . . And she . . . oh God . . . she looked so happy about it. She thought of killing herself, then she thought of killing Tony. She could destroy the film.

Suddenly she raced to the projector, grabbed the film and hurled it on the floor, panting with the effort as she trampled on it.

"There," she said. She looked up, feeling puzzled because Tony had not tried to stop her.

"What a shame, you missed the best bits. Never mind. It was only a copy. You'll see it at your local cinema—if you want to. Next week."

"Tony, you can't," she begged.

"I don't know much about love," he said, and his voice was emotionless, "but I'll tell you this now. I would kill you before I'd see you marry Andy. You're not leaving here—or living with him. Forget it."

"But I will marry Andy." She felt bewildered now and more frightened than she had ever been in her life.

"Honey, I have the means to keep you with me for just as long as I want and the way I feel now that'll be one hell of a long time."

He's mad, she thought, watching him. Only a madman could plan such a revenge. Random thoughts ran through her mind. The police, Dad, Andy, killing Tony. But nothing . . . no one would stop him from releasing the film, even if it was underground. The truth would still be her sitting naked and giggling astride Tony. There was no escape from it.

"What do you want from me?" she said hoarsely. "Just to stay here?"

"For the time being . . . yes. We'll play it by ear."

Now she could sense the power play, the lack of humanity, the ruthless drive to get what he wanted at any cost, but it was all so well concealed beneath his grinning, boyish good looks. That was his strength, she thought sadly. Everyone underestimated him.

"Very well," she said. She would play for time. Something must turn up to help her. She walked quietly from the room.

"Oh, Sylvia," he called as she opened the door. "Don't lock your door nights. Remember that, won't you?"

Chapter Seventy-four

Marika had just finished bathing and the bathroom was steamy and scented. Everywhere she looked was pleasing—unless, of course, she looked in the mirror and then she was plunged into despair. Muttering angrily, she wiped a hole in the misted glass and peered anxiously at her face. "I must be a masochist," she told herself mournfully. The fluorescent light emphasized every line and imperfection. Hastily she grabbed her moisturizer, which, she had read somewhere, weight for weight cost more than gold. She tried to rub away the lines, but it had little effect other than making her face red. "Damnit," she muttered.

She splashed her face with ice-cold water from the kitchen. It was no use—none of it—the costly creams, the weekly massages, the vitamin E pills—nothing worked! She sighed, wrapped herself in the bath towel and was soon absorbed in ghastly introspection, a nightly ritual which she tried to avoid, but never could.

"Why does it hurt so?" she muttered. "No one else seems to care quite as much as I do." She knew the answer: failures dare not grow old. So every day Marika dieted, endured extremes of hunger—no, not hunger, starvation—but she was never thin enough and she hated every particle of flesh on her body. She knew she was looking gaunt and bony; everyone told her so and her clothes hung loose and shapeless, but still she starved. Food had become an anathema; a constant reminder of the impermanence of her flesh.

A week ago, Klaus Greenstein had telephoned. He was seriously ill, he had told her, and was forced to close his agency. Her direct payments from the bank should be canceled. He was sorry.

Nightly, Marika took stock of her life's achievements. It was a destructive operation: her marriage foundering, her daughter alienated, her business success meaningless to her, and worse, Geissler still free. Beside that overwhelming failure all the rest was insignificant.

This evening they had dined with a well-known film producer and his house had been filled with nubile young women. She had hated them all.

"Watching them makes one feel ancient, doesn't it?" the producer had said, as if divining her thoughts. She had smiled gracefully, trying not to hurl her glass at him. Then, glancing across the room, she had noticed Tony's hand on Sylvia's shoulder—there was something wrong about that; and what the hell had happened to Andy and all of Sylvia's zany friends?

Suspicion clouded her mind and for a moment she thought she would be sick there and then, but the idea was too terrible even to contemplate and in self-defense her mind rejected it.

Yesterday she had cornered Sylvia in the library. "You're not losing weight, Sylvia," she had said in a poor attempt at humor. "You're shedding bone. I'm so worried about you. Please tell me what's wrong. Perhaps I can help." But Sylvia had turned away with something close to hatred in her eyes.

Then Tony was so remote . . . so cruelly ignorant of her existence. How long was it since they had made love? Six months at least. They shared a bedroom, but Tony spent most nights on a divan in his office. He did not need much sleep and he was always busy with calls and telexes to his managers all over the world.

She heard Tony walk into the bedroom and found herself trembling. What was she afraid of? That was an easy one. Tony! Or rather his indifference, which hurt.

She put on her pink housecoat and brushed her hair. It was still long and beautiful and she arranged it to fall softly over her shoulders. Then she switched off the fluorescent light. She could be in her twenties, just as long as the pink shades covered the bulb. She decided to have the fluorescent bulb removed. It was bad for her ego.

Tony was standing in his pajamas reading an article in the newspaper she had left lying on the bed.

"Cernik's urged the intellectuals to leave Czechoslovakia. You read this?" He looked up. "Thank God there's somewhere for them to go."

It was hard to believe she was born Czech. She could not even remember her mother tongue.

Encouraged by his sympathetic smile, she said, "Tony, I wish you would give up business for a few hours."

He tucked the newspaper under his arm and flung her a quick smile. "It's this Canadian deal," he explained. "It'll keep me on the phone all night."

"You never sleep."

"Never seem to need much. Not like you."

She walked up to him, wound her arms around his neck and hugged him.

"Tony darling, please come to bed," she said. "D'you know how long it is? Six months. What's happened to our marriage?" She wanted to dam the flow of emotion, but the words kept pouring out; she was frustrated and lonely, she could hardly concentrate on her work. If there was something wrong, surely they could talk about it. Start again!

At last Tony put his finger over her lips and hugged her tightly against him. She was so relieved she burst into tears and sobbed on his shoulder, leaving a damp patch on his brown silk pajamas.

"Feeling better?" he said. "I've got to make a call."

"Like hell you will," she burst out indignantly. "Typical! Damn you, Tony. Say something, can't you?"

"What is there to say? I know what you want, but I don't feel like it."

"Force yourself," she screamed. "I've got my rights. I can divorce you for this. Cruel! Cruel!"

This was not the way to woo Tony, she told herself sternly.

"If you want a divorce I won't stand in your way," he said. "I quite understand."

She gasped. Then she caught sight of herself in the mirror. She looked agonized and she covered her face with her hands.

"Look here, Marika," Tony said unhappily. "It's the sort of thing men can't discuss. Try to be understanding."

She peered anxiously at him. "Who needs sex?"

"You do."

"No," she said. "Just the occasional snuggle."

She tried to smile winsomely, but Tony left and Marika fumbled in her drawer for her sleeping pills. Tonight she would take two, she decided. She deserved them. She could hear Tony's voice yelling into the telephone as she drifted into a deep, drugged sleep.

Sylvia was lying tense and sleepless. She knew Tony was coming, because he had told her so, and she dreaded the sound of creaking stairs. She heard her mother and Tony shouting at each other and Tony's office door slamming.

It was six months since that terrible weekend in Switzerland and Tony had come to her room almost nightly. What was she to do? How she longed for Andy. His straitlaced ethics had irked her, but now she longed for goodness. She knew that she loved him, but she felt so vile. Andy would never forgive her if he knew, so she could not run to him. At times she had even considered appealing to Mother for help, but Mother would never help her, and besides, she would tell Dad.

Sylvia had seen a lawyer and plucked up courage to tell him about the drugs, the rape, the nightly forced sex. He had watched her with his penetrating blue eyes and she had felt exposed and soiled. He did not believe she was as innocent as she protested. She could see that and everyone would think she was to blame—just as he had.

"Miss Magos," he had told her gravely. "You would have to sue your stepfather for seduction and gain a court order preventing him from releasing the film. You would win the latter, but I have my doubts about the former. The publicity would be excessive and if your stepfather is as ruthless as you tell me then doubtless the film would be released illegally. There are a thousand places where it would be shown in London alone.

"My advice to you is leave the house immediately and I will apply for an urgent court order to prevent the film's distribution. Let's call his bluff."

She had followed his advice and the following Sunday the back pages of the newspapers had shown Sylvia stark naked, but from the back view. Impossible to tell if it really was her, unless you knew about the birthmark on her back.

Is this the famous model Sylvia Shaw? Film distributors of a new porno film about to go on circuit say it is and that Sylvia takes the star role. Sylvia says it certainly is not and so do her family.

There was much more, but Sylvia threw the paper away in disgust. She felt she would kill herself if Dad or Andy found out. She returned home the same evening and her life resumed its former terrible routine.

She heard footsteps and seconds later Tony came in and locked the door behind him. "Why aren't you in bed?" he asked. He leaned forward and put his arms around her, tried to cover her mouth with his so that she could not speak, but she pushed him back. She had made up her mind.

"No more," she said. "You must give me the film or I'll kill myself."

"Stupid bitch," he said lovingly.

"I mean it," she said.

"Nothing's changed, not even you. You know something? You should have been a missionary after all." He stepped back and scowled at her, feeling hurt and angry.

"Miss Prim and Proper to the end. You could have kept it up while the locals raped you. But I happen to know how many times you've come."

"That only makes it worse," she said miserably. "Keep away or I swear I'll scream. I don't care anymore."

"Why didn't you scream six months ago?" He grinned. "Marika knows how long I haven't been fucking her. D'you think your father will understand—or Bertha?"

Her eyes filled with tears. She always lost. Tony was stroking her hair, her breasts, and running his lips over her cheek.

"Sylvie, Sylvie, I love you. Don't be so cruel. I can't live without you."

He grasped her knees and wrenched them apart, and in spite of her resolve, she felt herself falling . . . falling . . . as her body took control of her mind.

Chapter Seventy-five

Shameful and despised body! Loathsome flesh! She wanted to damage herself. Destroy the beauty that had destroyed her. She lay in bed shuddering while Tony stood up, yawned and put on his pajamas, moving lethargically— sure of himself—while Sylvia lay drowning in self-disgust.

When he left she pulled on a track suit and went quietly out of the house.

The moon shone brightly in the clear sky; the lake was a sheet of burnished metal; there was a glimmer of white among the trees on the island. It was still warm, but a trace of autumn showed. She heard the hoot of a barnyard owl close by and saw it clearly in the branches of a dead tree. She did not see a man walking quietly through the trees, watching her.

Andy nearly let her go. He hung around undecided,

hating her and not really caring why she was wandering around disheveled and unsteady in the middle of the night.

It was six months since she had broken their romance. At first he had tried to play the gentleman, asking to meet her new boyfriend, suggesting friendship in a civilized manner, not wanting their friends to see him as a jealous fool. When he recovered from his hurt sufficiently to think, he noticed how thin Sylvia had become, how she was dropping out of classes and was no longer interested in their club functions. After that she had disappeared, but he had still seen her nightly on the TV screen, for the compulsion to switch it on was more than he could resist.

Then he had checked on her from time to time, desperate to know who had destroyed their relationship, but he had been surprised to find that she seldom went out, except with her parents. After that he thought of illness— God knows, she looked sick enough. Lately, after days of misery, he had taken to hanging around the house, waiting for a chance to confront her. Then tonight, when he was feeling desperate enough to break in, he had seen her light switched on, and heard a murmur of voices—sounds that kept him shuddering with rage, but unable to go—and saw Tony's unmistakable outline as he put on his pajamas.

She was having it off with her stepfather! What a fool he had been. Still, some sick compulsion kept him lurking in the woods beside the lake.

The frailty of women, he thought, watching her slim shape disappear toward the road. Where the hell was she going now?

He hesitated, undecided, and then followed her toward the village where she stood on a hill, irresolute, before veering toward the motorway.

Half an hour later she was waiting by the side of the road, intent and white-faced, peering toward the north.

Funny time for hitchhiking, he thought, or was Tony picking her up? He saw distant headlights as she moved forward like a sleepwalker. She did not hear his footsteps and he felt like an interloper.

When the car was only yards away he understood and hurled himself on her.

For a long, agonizing moment that seemed to last a lifetime, they struggled on the edge of the motorway. There were sounds of squealing brakes and Sylvia's screams as she fought him with the strength of madness.

The car stopped, the driver ran back, scared and angry. Together they bundled her into the back seat and raced her to the nearest hospital, where she was sedated. With Andy prompting her, she told him about hatred and degradation and her terrible fear of exposure.

He might have lost her. What if he had not been there tonight? The question plagued him and he knew he loved her more than his ambitions. He would find a job, earn a living, look after her.

But what was he to do now? That was the problem that tormented him through the long night hours. His alternatives seemed as limited as Sylvia's had been. For the first time in his life he was faced with a problem he could not solve.

Her stepfather was powerful, crazy and vindictive. If he released the film Sylvia might never recover from the shame of it.

At dawn, when he was still unable to think of a solution, he telephoned Günter, who, Bertha told him, was in New York on business.

Chapter Seventy-six

It was a balmy late-summer evening; a hint of a breeze—warm, but not hot; the oak trees gently rustling their new autumn colors; the ducks and geese waddling up from the still waters of the lake while from the lounge came the gentle chords of "A Penny for a Song," played by a string ensemble Marika had hired.

Marika and Tony were sitting at either end of their dining-room table; between them sat their guests: a visiting American congressman and his wife; some dancers from the touring Royal Danish Ballet Company; two managers of Tony's British chemical company and their wives; an infamous, but amusing British poet; the president of a vast South American group with whom Tony was trying to do business and his wife and teenage daughter.

It was the type of dinner party in which Marika usually excelled, and as always the food was superb, the service impeccable and her dress stately, but stunning. Yet tonight Marika was feeling depressed and longing for dinner to be over and their guests dispatched.

She had too much on her mind. She was worried about Sylvia. Bertha had telephoned that morning to say that Sylvia had arrived there and was not feeling well, so she had persuaded her to stay at Finchley for a few days. Fair enough! Yet something about Bertha's voice had disturbed her. A hint of hostility.

She mentioned it to Tony and he had been unusually curt. Why? Watching him playing the host at the end of the table, she could tell he was keyed up; his aggression was badly concealed and his grin was taut and unnatural.

Marika tried to look vivacious and dismiss her fears, but something about the stillness of the evening reminded her of the Namib before a storm. She was discussing the cancellation of the Bolshoi ballet tour when she noticed the guests were staring toward the French window. Looking up, Marika saw Günter framed in the open doorway.

She was flabbergasted and for a moment could not say anything. How wonderful he looked—she had not seen him for years—she had forgotten how huge he was and how handsome. But he looked angry. Ferociously angry. Then confusion fell away and she wondered indignantly why he was gate-crashing her dinner party.

"Friend of yours?" Tony called, smiling from the end

of the table. But she could see from the slant of his eyes he was prepared for trouble. Then she remembered that he had never met Günter.

"It's Günter," she blurted out. Suddenly the room was very quiet.

The joyous strains of "Napoli" came drifting in from the lounge. Wrong music, she thought, altogether wrong.

Günter was striding across the room toward Tony, fists clenched, fury blazing in his eyes.

To Marika it was all happening in slow motion. He's going to kill him, she thought, but she could not move or speak. For a moment she felt a strange sense of pity for Tony. He looked so confident. She knew he prided himself on his fitness, fancied himself a boxer. How could a boxer cope with the unleashed fury of a goaded bull?

Tony saw him coming and he knew why—knew he was fighting for survival. As Günter's fist rocketed toward him, Tony leapt sideways, swinging his chair into the path of the blow. The Chippendale chair shattered like matchwood and Günter's momentum sent them both sprawling across the floor to crash heavily into the fireplace.

Struggling to his knees, Tony ripped the iron fire poker from its wall mounting and swung it at Günter's head.

Günter deflected the blow with his forearm, ignoring the pain. Tony's wild swing had left him off balance and as he sprawled forward he was unprotected.

Like a bolt from a crossbow, Günter's fist shot forward, catching Tony full in the mouth.

Tony choked and spat blood and teeth on the carpet.

It had all been so quick. No time for thought or action. Marika watched Tony's face swelling as he writhed on the floor.

Now her guests were beginning to react. Some of them stood up. The wife of the South American industrialist was clasping her emerald necklace with both hands.

"He's not a gangster," Marika wanted to say, but when she opened her mouth no sound came out. The butler raced across the room holding a silver tray and beat Günter across the head with it. Günter looked surprised—as if he thought that only he and Tony existed.

Then Andy walked in from the other door. Impossible! Insane! Marika thought. Andy did not know Günter. "Ladies and gentlemen, would you please go home?" he said in his broad American accent.

"They'll kill each other," the congressman gasped.

"I told you they were Mafia," the industrialist's wife said.

Tony had got to his feet by this time. He made a sudden dash across the room and grabbed the telephone. It was dead. "You bastard—you cut the lines," he lisped.

"I did," Andy said smugly.

Marika found her voice. "Stop it . . . stop it at once," she screamed, shrill and terrified; she was on the verge of hysteria. "How dare you come here? . . . How dare you cut the telephone? . . . Will someone tell me what's going on?" She appealed to her guests. "I'm sorry, but please go."

"I came here," Günter said loudly and clearly, "to see a porno movie. I hear you have a very good one—so good Palma's thinking of having it released on the public circuit. Anyone here with a taste for blue movies?"

"You want to see a blue movie, Grieff?" Tony yelled from the corner, but he had difficulty saying the words. "Watch it on circuit next week, you and the rest of the world, and see your goody-goody daughter fucking her ass off. Now get out." He was holding the carving knife in front of him and grinning ferociously.

He knows what all this is about, Marika thought. She flung herself at Andy and hammered on his chest. "Will you tell me what's going on!" But Andy pushed her aside and leaped at Tony.

Günter kicked the boy's feet from under him and he fell on the floor, swearing at Günter and rubbing his shins.

"I told you to leave the rough stuff to me. Keep out of it," Günter snarled, "and make yourself useful. Get this lot out of here." He gestured toward the diners.

Marika stared around helplessly, but their guests, sensing a scandal, were unwilling to leave.

"He's been fucking Sylvia," Günter's voice roared at Marika across the room. "Every night while you were sleeping—or were you sleeping, you lousy bitch?" His voice sobbed suddenly. "He drugged her . . ."

Günter took a deep breath. "Made a film and he's been blackmailing her with it. Why d'you think she dropped out of classes . . . gave up Andy . . . or don't you ever think?"

Tony sprang at him, swearing violently.

Günter swung his body backward, avoiding the knife thrust, and using the force of Tony's onslaught, thrust him headlong into the wall.

A picture trembled and toppled to the floor as Marika stood mesmerized with horror. She was only vaguely aware of Andy ushering their guests out and the butler imploring them to fetch the police. She heard cars start up and leave, but the congressman was arguing in the hall and she heard a scuffle break out there as well, and Andy shouting.

As Günter bent to pick up the knife, Tony kicked him in the side of the head, sending him crashing into the sideboard, smashing dishes and plates and the Venetian glassware Marika had just bought.

Tony made as if to follow up, but thought better of it and turned and ran out of the French window onto the balcony. He was at the top of the steps when Günter caught him with a rugby tackle. They rolled down the steps, punching, kicking and grunting.

Tony was fitter and more agile than Günter had imagined, but nothing could withstand the merciless assault of Günter, with all the ferocity of a vengeful father. He was no longer human, but a fighting machine as he pummeled and pushed Tony over the lawns, through the shrubbery and down to the lake.

Tony could take no more. He collapsed, too exhausted to care what happened to him. Günter grabbed him up by the remnants of his shirt, dragged him to the lake and

dumped him in. When Tony used his last reserves of
strength to push his head above the water, Günter pushed
him under again.

"I'm going to kill you—you fucking faggot," he muttered, "but first I'll have the evidence."

Marika could not banish a sense of unreality as she
stood watching Günter hoist Tony out of the water and try
to make him stand up, but Tony was unconscious and
almost unrecognizable. His eyes were lost in the swelling
flesh that had been his face and his clothes were in shreds.

Günter was almost too exhausted to hoist Tony over his
shoulder. He staggered back to the house in a shuffling,
zigzag course.

He used to be fitter, Marika thought treacherously.

Andy rushed forward to help him, but Günter waved
him off. He dumped Tony in an armchair. "Bring the
bastard round with brandy," he told Andy.

Marika was crying now. "I don't believe this," she
sobbed. "You have no right . . . no right to come here
and make these terrible accusations. Who have you talked
to . . .? Did Sylvia tell you this?"

"You'll see for yourself," Günter told her harshly.

Tony gagged on the brandy and opened his eyes fractionally, but he could hardly see.

He would not tell them where the film was until Günter
smashed his fist again and again into the pulpy mess.
Eventually he screamed and told them.

Andy had difficulty operating the projector, his hands
were shaking so badly. He hated violence, he had never
seen the cause for it—until tonight. Now he was forced to
admit he admired Günter.

Marika did not want to watch the film and neither did
Andy, but Günter insisted. He made her sit near the front
and keep her eyes open. She cried at first, but after a while
she was too shocked to cry.

When the image of Sylvia came on the screen, Andy
forgot about the rights and wrongs of beating Tony and
only wished he had done it himself. The poor child was so

obviously drugged—her eyes wide and staring, her mouth hanging slack and loose.

Five minutes later, Günter decided enough was enough. Marika was sitting trancelike, staring at the screen, but no longer recording what she was seeing. Andy was crying. He took some papers from Tony's desk, lit a fire and burned the film, taking a long time about it.

"And did the naïve child really believe that Tony would put this film on circuit when it so obviously shows himself?" Günter growled to Andy. "Well, this is from Sylvia."

Then he struck Tony. It was a last, savage blow—all the sadness, all the anger, the longing for revenge and the rage of a shamed father was in that blow. Tony catapulted from his chair and fell unconscious to the floor.

Andy wondered if he was dead, without really caring. "Marika needs a doctor," he told Günter. "Let's go."

Chapter Seventy-seven

It was over a month since Günter had brought Marika and Sylvia to his Hampstead house and now he was restless and impatient to be gone. Early days yet, he told himself daily, but his inactivity irked him.

Pushing the heavy net curtains aside, he stared moodily out of the window at lawns, shrubs and two magnificent beech trees, but Günter was seeing the desert stretched out to a far horizon under a hazy blue sky.

That was where he would go when this was over. He had decided to ask Claire for a divorce. The marriage had been a mistake from the start. Then he would go prospecting. As to the future—that would depend upon Marika.

He had been in New York on business when Andy called him. Somehow he had managed to avoid Claire during the past few months. He had telephoned her in

Johannesburg and told her a business crisis had arisen in
London and he would be away for some time. She did not
complain. Tex's note in the safe had put the lid on their
marriage. Günter did not understand why that was, but he
knew he was being a bastard. It was one of those occasions in life when he had to make a decision. Goddamnit,
he reasoned, there was no choice. He would not abandon
Marika when she needed him.

She was ill, hovering between sanity and a nervous
breakdown. At times she seemed to be recovering and then
she would become deeply depressed again.

He prowled the length of the study and back again. He
felt like an intruder and this irked him. After all, it was his
house. It had been part of the fringe benefits of the Western Minerals takeover, together with six company cars,
one a Rolls, and a private box at Covent Garden. It was a
vast, gloomy place and it depressed Günter. He wondered
how Tex was making out in Australia. He had tried to put
a mining group together again. No chance! He had lost his
credibility; Günter had taken care of that. Now he was
working as a manager on a platinum mine in the sticks and
good luck to him. He did not expect to see Tex again.

He rang the bell and eventually a maid arrived.

"See if you can brighten the place, stronger bulbs,
better lamps, and take these net curtains away. Any damn
thing! Oh, and breakfast in here, coffee and toast—unless
of course Mrs. . . ." He could not bring himself to say
Palma.

"Madam will not be coming down for breakfast, sir."

"Has Mrs. Factor arrived yet?"

"She's at the factory. She'll be here by lunchtime."

"That's it, then."

Günter tried to immerse himself in the group's accounts,
but eventually he pushed the books aside and began to
riffle through the drawers and shelves, trying to achieve a
feeling of ownership.

This had been Tex McGregor's British home. More fool
him to keep all his assets in the Western Minerals stable.

After years of preparation the takeover had been so

quick. Tex had been out before he had time to pack properly and since then the house had been empty, except for the servants.

Breakfast arrived. Günter buried himself behind the newspaper and munched his dry toast. Then he heard the doorbell. That would be Grainger, his London solicitor, a strange, introverted man, but clever. Günter did not like him, but this morning he welcomed the intrusion.

Grainger was shown in. He looked paler than usual, his graying hair looked thinner, his gray eyes even more remote behind his large, horn-rimmed glasses. He was well built and Günter wondered why the man looked slight. Perhaps because he was tall and walked with a permanent stoop.

This morning he was looking particularly pained to be there. "A number of problems . . . most distasteful . . . hardly my area of the law . . . however, under the circumstances . . ." His voice was too high-pitched. Günter often wondered if it was that which irritated him so.

"Coffee?" Günter interrupted him impatiently.

"Thank you . . . no." He cleared his throat. "I mentioned at our last meeting that Angelo Palma is suing his wife, Marika Palma, for divorce, citing desertion. Well, he has now put in an alternative plea of adultery, citing you as . . ." He looked up awkwardly.

"Fine. Let him sue. I like that."

"If I may be so bold . . . the question is—what would Mrs. Palma like me to do about it?" Grainger peered shrewdly over the top of his glasses. "The lady is blameless."

Not really, Günter was thinking. In fact, she was entirely to blame. She belonged to him—perhaps not legally, but morally. She had always belonged to him—and she had married Palma, thereby ruining all their lives.

"She says," Günter said forcibly, "let him get on with it."

"I would prefer to speak to her myself."

Günter sighed and rang the bell. The maid seemed to be hovering on the other side of the door. "Tell Mrs. Palma that she has to see the solicitor and we'll be up in twenty minutes," he told her.

"What's next?" Günter asked.

"Palma is suing you for one million pounds: disfigurement, loss of earnings, pain and discomfort, doctors' and nursing-home fees . . . Evidently he'll be there for some time—two months at least, according to his lawyer."

"We'll fight that one," Günter said tersely. "I'd like to face him in court."

The solicitor frowned and adjusted his glasses. "This one may come as a shock to you," he began. "Palma is suing Sylvia, your daughter, for ten million pounds: the loss he claims he will sustain as a result of the Sylvia Cosmetics campaign coming to an untimely halt. There's a list here; advertising, research . . ."

"Spare me." Günter held up his hand. "We'll fight that one as well. Let him sue."

"I don't quite follow your reasoning," Grainger began.

"Quite simple," Günter said. "I don't intend to pay that bugger one cent."

The lawyer pursed his lips and scribbled in his notebook. Then he gazed anxiously at Günter. "He'd probably settle for far less. If the matter goes to court the publicity might be quite embarrassing."

"Not a penny," Günter repeated. "He's a bully and my daughter is going to learn to stand up to bullies. Tell his lawyer," Günter said, and for a moment his chin sunk onto his chest and he peered belligerently from under his broad brow, "the moment the summonses arrive we'll lay charges of drug dealing, blackmail, and on behalf of Marika we'll sue him for adultery."

Watching him, Grainger felt quite sure that he would never give in. A dangerous man, he decided. Clever, you could give him that, but emotionally speaking, the fellow was positively Neanderthal.

"Okay, let's go up to Marika," Günter said reluctantly.

The door was locked. Günter tried the spare key, but Marika's key was in the lock. Then he called a warning and kicked the door open with a single well-placed blow.

Marika looked horrified and untidy. She jumped up for her gown and smoothed her hair nervously, but the brush fell on the floor.

Günter sighed and picked it up for her. Marika's face was swollen, her eyes red, and her hands were shaking.

"I was just having a rest," she said, trying to sound carefree and girlish. "Such a sad day and I couldn't be bothered to get dressed, but of course I'll be down soon." Then she laughed brightly and falsely.

Günter seemed to crumple. He crouched in front of Marika and took her face between his hands. "Don't laugh, Marika, not when you feel like crying." He gazed compassionately into her eyes. "Cry!" He sighed and then lovingly brushed her cheek with his hand. "And stay in bed if you want to. Do what you like. You don't have to please anyone—not ever again. Only yourself. I love you and it doesn't matter to me what you look like." He turned to Grainger. "If only she knew how lovely she is," he said quietly.

Grainger, who was not married, had never experienced such an intensely personal scene. He flushed a deep red and backed toward the door. Then he remembered why they had come.

"Mrs. Palma, your husband is suing you for divorce and citing Mr. Grieff as corespondent, with desertion as the alternative plea. Do you want to defend the action?"

"No," she said tonelessly. "Let him do what he wants. Just as long as we're free of each other.

"How's Sylvia?" she said, turning to Günter.

"A damn sight better than you," Günter told her. "She's much tougher . . . more resilient."

"Younger," Marika sighed.

Shit! He'd said the wrong thing again.

Then she looked up and smiled in a poor imitation of the reckless, enticing smile he had loved so. "Well, that's just wonderful," she said overbrightly.

At that moment the doctor arrived and they all felt relieved.

It's Marika who's damaged, not Sylvia, Günter thought,

and somehow it seemed strange to him. Surely it should have been the other way round. Sylvia's recovery had been astonishingly fast. She had insisted on having her womb scraped at a private nursing home. After that she dismissed the whole affair as if it were an ancient nightmare best forgotten. Andy was calling daily and she was back at university, although she would have to take the year again, she told him.

Strange creatures, women, Günter thought as he went through the routine business problems with Grainger. They could take rape, seduction and even whoring in their stride. It was part of life, part of survival. But rejection! That was a killer. Marika was still beautiful, for all the good it did her, and only a little thinner. Years ago, in the Namib, he had known she would improve with age. Her bone structure was still fine and delicate-looking; her eyes were still wide and candid, and her broad brow unlined. For the life of him, he could not imagine why she was so depressed. A waste of a lovely, vibrant woman, he thought.

Günter was in his study when Sylvia burst in, towing Andy behind her. The boy looked embarrassed and anxious.

"Dad!" She flung herself at Günter, winding her arms around his neck and pressing her lips against his cheek. "We're going to be married. Next week. Isn't it wonderful! Aren't you happy for me? I'm deliriously happy."

"I believe you," he said, disentangling her arms from his neck. He glared at Andy, hating him at that moment. He had always known that this would happen one day, and God knows, he liked the boy—well, hardly a boy, he admitted. Nevertheless . . . He scowled and turned away.

"Dad?" Sylvia said, always quick to spot his moods. "You're angry. But you like Andy, you said so."

"Like," he said gruffly. "What's like got to do with it?" Strange, but he felt almost as hurt as when Marika had married Palma. Absurd, he told himself, but somehow marriage was an irretrievable break and inevitably she would grow away from him. Well, that was what it was all about, this strange, heartbreaking business of rearing a daughter.

"So what have you got to say for yourself, Andy?" Belatedly Günter clapped his shoulder with a heartiness he was not feeling. "I guess this calls for a bottle of the best. Wait till I fetch Marika."

"If you're going to fetch Mother, then I'm leaving," Sylvia said stonily.

"That's not very charitable of you," Andy said.

Günter glanced sharply at him. Reprimanding Sylvia was exclusively his territory. Can't he wait until he's married? he thought jealously.

Marika refused to join them and they celebrated solemnly, and hastily because Sylvia was in a hurry to go shopping.

When they left, Günter felt twice as unhappy as before they came.

Then the telephone rang. It was for Marika, and when Günter went upstairs to tell her, she refused to take the call.

"I'll take a message," he said gloomily. He picked up the receiver next to her bed. "Mrs. Palma is sleeping. . . . Yes, I'll take your number. . . . Klaus Greenstein . . ."

Marika grabbed the receiver and Günter hung around, feeling surprised and curious. Something—or someone— could still get through to her.

"It's private," she snapped. Günter left, looking sulky.

Greenstein sounded ill and Marika wondered why his voice had faded to a whisper. She could hardly hear him.

"I knew you'd like to hear that the money you've paid out all these years is paying off at last," he began. "The French police have information which will most probably lead to the early arrest of Otto Geissler."

Marika could hardly hear him, but between the coughing and whispers she learned that in the course of their investigations about a French forger, who was about to be brought to trial, the police had discovered hidden files containing all the work he had undertaken for the SS toward the end of the war. The forger had provided new identities for several wanted Nazis—including Geissler— and the files gave their false identities and nationalities together with passport numbers. It was only a matter of time before he was arrested—if he was still alive, Greenstein promised her.

Marika thanked him and replaced the receiver. She felt dizzy and quite overcome with emotion. She found she was crying and she wondered when last she had cried. She desperately wanted to tell someone—share the good news— but there was no one who would understand what it meant to her. She walked over to the window and looked at the leaves glistening with rain and the garden looking so fresh and English. Then she flung open the window and leaned out. What a delightful smell of damp earth and wet grass. She wondered why she had stayed cooped up in this room for days when she could have been walking over the heath. She must get out more and now would be a good time to start, she decided.

It was midafternoon when Claire arrived in a taxi.

"Günter darling," she said, offering her cheek for a husbandly kiss while she pulled off her gloves. She was trying so hard to pretend that nothing had changed, but her hands were shaking and her eyes were glittering with fear. "I missed you so much," she babbled, trying to smile. "Not much of a holiday without you, so I thought to myself, why not pop over and spend a few days with you, catch up on shopping, while you finish all these mysterious affairs."

Top marks, Claire, he thought, admiring her performance and feeling sad for her all at the same time. She looked tremendous with her emerald-green suit tailored to fit snug against her trim frame, and her emerald jewelry. The miniskirt suited her admirably. "You look superb," he said, "and there's nothing mysterious about what I'm doing, because I told you before I left."

She brightened and some of the glitter left her eyes.

"Darling," she began, and the pretense was suddenly gone. "How much longer . . .?"

"How did you know Marika was here?"

She shrugged. "I checked up on you—I even hired a detective." She smiled grimly.

"Claire," Günter began clumsily, in the manner of a callous schoolboy. "I'll see you're all right. You won't ever have to worry about money . . . or anything like that. But I'm not coming back to you."

For a moment she looked like a wild animal at bay and he thought she would spring at him. Instinctively he stepped backward and put one hand in front of his face.

She laughed. "Oh, I'll get you, all right," she said, and her voice was harsh, her expression ugly, "but I'm not quite as brutal as you are."

She spread her hands over her face—a quick, decisive gesture, wanting to hide her anger and regretting her hasty words.

"Günter, I love you," she began tremulously. "Let me move in here with you. I'll help you look after Marika and Sylvia. You can count on me.

"That's impossible," he said heavily.

"Marika doesn't love you," she pleaded. "Not like I do. Surely you want to be loved?"

"I want Marika," he said quietly.

"She'll throw you over." Her words came faster, bubbling, confused, muddled and desperate. "She always has; she always will . . . I mean . . . you know how it always was . . . when she doesn't need you . . . love . . . why . . . she can't love . . ."

"She needs me," he said, feeling like a heel and wishing he could do otherwise.

"Good God, so she needs you!" Her voice was taut, on the edge of hysteria. "She needs you—temporarily—and I get flung in the shit. My marriage . . . my life . . . ruined! Ruined, I tell you." She was furious now, caution flung aside. "I'll sue you—you bastard—I'll take you to the cleaners. I'll name her as the other woman."

Anger broke through his resolve. "You're the other

woman, Claire,'' he said. ''You always have been and you always knew it.''

Then she struck him. Using every ounce of strength, she pummeled her fists against his face and dragged her fingernails through his skin. ''I hate . . . hate . . . I'll kill you . . .''

Günter pushed her away too savagely and she fell against the table and sprawled on the floor. ''Cut it out,'' he said, wiping his face with a handkerchief. ''It's over. Damnit, Claire, if I wanted to be with you, I would. Can't you understand that?''

She crumpled into a chair, looking tattered and forlorn, and all Günter could see were her skinny knees and her red hair bobbing up and down as she shuddered and sobbed.

Her cries went on and on. ''I'll make you some tea,'' he said miserably, and crept shamefully out of the room, but when he returned five minutes later Claire had gone. He ran into the street, but there was no sign of her and eventually he returned to the house.

''No doubt I'll be hearing from her lawyer,'' he said aloud to assuage his guilt.

In the late afternoon the doctor arrived. ''She's up in the clouds today,'' he told Günter sadly. ''Typical symptoms of a manic-depressive. She refused to take a sedative. Not much more I can do, but if she doesn't soon pull herself together we'll have to consider shock treatment.''

''No, we damn well won't,'' Günter snarled. The doctor shrugged and left.

The clock on the mantelpiece ticked loudly; the rain dripped from the ivy to the windowsill; there was a dreary sound of wheels whooshing on wet roads and the drone of an aircraft far away. The room was filled with the smell of leather upholstery, stale tobacco and dusty books. What a bloody awful day!

''Shit!'' Günter yelled. He slammed his fist on the leather-top desk, but even the thump was muffled and ineffectual. ''Shit! Shit! Shit!'' he roared. But the wheels went on whooshing and the clock ticking and every second seemed to last an hour.

He stood up, walked to the door and locked it. Then he returned to his desk, buried his head in his arms and wished he were dead.

Chapter Seventy-eight

Blinded with tears and mascara, Claire missed her footing and stumbled down the pavement to sprawl in the muddy gutter.

"Oh!" she gasped. "Oh, Günter! Oh, you bastard!" She groped for her bag and felt herself being lifted by her elbows.

"You all right, love?"

Claire dried her eyes and examined the damage: two bleeding knees, torn panty hose, a broken marriage and her life irrevocably ruined. Then a taxi drew up beside her.

Afterward she could not remember the drive to the hotel, only the image of Günter's cold eyes as he said, "You're the other woman, Claire. You always have been and you always knew it."

"Oh dear!" Her misery was too great to bear alone, but there was no one—no one at all to tell. She flung herself on the bed and sobbed a great torrent of tears.

Eventually, at dusk, she called a well-known newspaper.

"Claire Grieff," she told the news editor. "I'm the wife of Günter Grieff. You ran a story on the Western Minerals takeover a few months ago. Yes . . . that Grieff. I can tell you why he wanted the company so badly . . . and why I'm divorcing him." She tried to smother a sob. "And why his daughter, Sylvia Shaw, has broken her contract with Sylvia Cosmetics. I'm at the Hilton if you're interested." She flung down the receiver.

"Hit him back. Hurt him like he hurt me," she muttered. She knew she could only wound him through Marika
and Sylvia. There was nothing else he cared about quite as
much; not money, and certainly not herself.

By the following evening, a team of reporters had checked
out Claire's story, and the news editor decided to go ahead
and publish. The scoop of the year, he modestly called it.

Günter shuddered when the morning papers arrived. The
best pictures ever taken of Sylvia as well as the nude shot
Tony had sent them from the film he had taken. *World-
famous model forced into midnight orgies by famous industrialist stepfather*, the page was headed, and underneath:
Mining magnate dad sends Palma to hospital. And next to
it: *Fur queen Magos cited for adultery in coming divorce
suit*.

Well, at least that was both untrue and actionable, Günter
thought furiously as he skimmed through the columns.

The lurid, staccato prose read more like a paperback
then a newspaper: *Stealthily, in the dead of night, wealthy
industrialist Angelo Palma left his nuptial bed for that of
his stepdaughter, the fabulously beautiful Sylvia Shaw,
and forced her to endure his unwanted sexual demands,
until dawn sent him creeping back to his wife* . . . Günter
was shaking so badly he could hardly read the paper.
"God damn that bitch," he muttered. "Now she can fight
for every penny she gets."

The telephone rang and Günter rushed to answer it. It
was Andy; he sounded incoherent with rage.

"Sylvia's here," he began.

"So I gathered," Günter said angrily, "You're not
married yet, you know."

"I've had to lock her in the bathroom," Andy went on,
ignoring the interruption. "Can you hear her yelling? She's
trying to break out. She wants to kill Claire. Hang on."

Günter heard Andy shouting in the background. "I'm
bringing her home. I'll stick around your place for a
while—if you don't mind, that is. All we need is another
scandal."

We! Günter noted. He liked the "we." "You do that, Andy," he said. "Come right over."

He heard a gasp behind him as he replaced the receiver. Damn and blast! Why did Marika get up so early these days? She looked distraught as she skimmed the pages of the newspaper. Günter wished she had not seen them. She was so tense lately, always hovering near the telephone and rushing to answer it. He'd like to know what she was waiting for. Surely not Tony! If that bastard showed his face here, Günter knew he would kill him.

"What are we going to do?" Her hands were trembling. "This will kill Sylvia."

"What about you? Let's worry about you."

"Me?" She looked puzzled. "I'm all right. Who cares about me?"

"I care about you," he said gruffly.

She was not listening to him. "I forced her to come here," she said softly, "and I let her down."

She gasped. "Look there!"

Günter wheeled around and through the window saw reporters dodging behind the trees; two photographers were dashing up the driveway pointing their cameras at the house.

They were still there half an hour later when Andy arrived. He saw the boy fighting his way through the crowd, dragging Sylvia behind him. Andy turned and swung a punch at one of them.

Günter hurtled into the midst of the fight, smashing to the left and right. A few cameras toppled and the press retreated to the gate.

"You're trespassing," Günter snarled, dazzled by the blaze of flashbulbs. "Get the hell off my property."

The three of them walked to the house in silence, trying not to show their feelings.

Shortly afterward they heard voices raised. Günter looked out of the window and saw Bertha forcing her way through the crowd with her umbrella. By the time he reached the front porch she was already there.

"They asked me for a statement. Statement! I said:

You'll get nothing from me. You want to wait? Wait! Catch a cold, I told them. That's all you'll catch here.''

It seemed as if the reporters would never go and articles would never stop appearing. If it weren't for Bertha, Günter often thought, they would all go crazy, for Sylvia was not speaking to Marika, Marika was sulking in her room most days and Andy was in a fever of impatience for the wedding. But Bertha's biting sense of humor kept them laughing and her staunchness made them ashamed to complain.

On Wednesday morning the family left in separate cars and met up at the magistrate's court, feeling pleased with themselves, for they had evaded the reporters. After the wedding the couple left for a short holiday in Spain and Bertha went back to her Finchley house.

What a strange evening it was, with just the two of them together for the first time in years. They were at dinner when they heard the doorbell ring.

"They're back again." Marika laughed harshly.

Günter looked at his watch. "Bit late, isn't it?"

The maid opened the door and shortly afterward she walked in looking curious. "Two detectives to see you, sir. They're waiting in the hall."

"Well, show them in," Günter told her. "I suppose Tony's got around to laying charges. Don't worry about it." He smiled ruefully, trying to reassure Marika.

The moment she saw them, Marika knew it was not about Tony. They were too senior and too serious. She felt a flutter of fear in her stomach.

They were very polite and self-effacing as they introduced themselves and showed their warrant cards.

"We'd be obliged if you would accompany us to Scotland Yard to answer a few questions," the inspector said in the manner of a helpful undertaker. "We suggest you contact your solicitor before we leave. I must warn you, sir, that you're not obliged to say anything, but that anything you say will be taken down and may be used in evidence against you. It's a question of war crimes, sir."

Günter reeled back in shock and knocked over Marika's glass.

Marika bent to pick it up, not wanting the police to see the fear on her face. How polite they were. They might have been asking the time, but a voice inside her was screaming: War crimes!

"We have a request for your extradition from the French authorities."

"You must have the wrong man," Günter was saying. He was stammering badly and he looked confused.

"That's what we hope to establish at the Yard, sir."

"Well, then . . . I'll fetch my coat."

"I'm afraid Sergeant Williams will have to accompany you, sir."

Marika looked up into Günter's shocked face. "Get hold of Grainger; ask him to come down to the Yard right away," he said. He looked so vulnerable she wanted to cry.

She nodded, unable to speak, and watched Günter being led away between the two men. She heard their car engine start up and then it faded in the distance.

In all her life she had never before felt so alone.

It was almost dawn when Grainger arrived to tell her that Günter was in good spirits and he had spoken to the Chief Superintendent.

"It's the most unlikely story I've ever heard," he recounted to her. "You mustn't worry. I'm sure it's a straightforward case of an identity mix-up. Happens all the time." He took off his glasses and peered myopically at her while he polished them. "After all, Günter's not even German."

"Who do they claim he is?" she managed to ask eventually. He looked up sharply and saw the fear on her face.

"Well, they don't say he's anyone right now. They're feeling their way," Grainger hedged. "The normal procedure in these cases is to hold their suspect for about a week, pending inquiries. When they've proved to their satisfaction that the French claim is justified they hold extradition proceedings, really like a short court case, but of course we both know that it won't get that far."

"Who?" Marika persisted.

He flushed, wishing that he had never set eyes on Günter. "Well, actually, Otto Geissler of Oradour fame."

Grainger was more athletic than he looked. He caught Marika before she struck the floor and lifted her onto the couch. Then he called for help.

"Poor lady," he muttered as he telephoned the doctor.

Most disquieting, Grainger thought as he drove home. He decided to engage the best French criminal lawyer available first thing in the morning.

PART FOUR

Chapter Seventy-nine

Paris
February 1969

So this was her moment of triumph, Marika thought bitterly as she loitered in the courtyard of the Palais de Justice, feeling afraid to go inside. At last her father's murderer was to be brought to trial. There had been six months of waiting while Günter was in prison, first in London and lately in Paris, and all the time she had hoped that he was not Otto Geissler. But as the date of the trial had drawn near, she had lost hope.

It seemed to Marika that Günter would endure more of an inquisition than a trial in the French court. Pierre Guedi, Günter's defense lawyer, had patiently explained that the procedure was quite different from that of British courts. The case had already begun with a preliminary inquiry by a magistrate into the available evidence. This information had been summarized and submitted to the court in the form of a prepared brief, on whose merits the case was to be heard. Now there would be a sifting of facts by the defense and the prosecution and then a decision—not a verdict—delivered by the Presiding Judge, based on the votes of his assisting judges and the jury.

"But surely he's innocent until he's proved guilty," she had muttered.

"But no, it's a different approach entirely," he had told her. "Really no better nor worse than the British system, because the end result is justice and to dispense justice one must find the truth. That is what both methods are after. Personally speaking, I prefer the Continental approach; admittedly the British sporting instinct is missing, but that can be an advantage. Your exaggerated desire for fair play has freed many a criminal."

*   *   *

She was remembering this conversation clearly now as she
plucked up courage to emerge from behind the pillar and
walk toward the antechamber. Flashbulbs dazzled her as
she pushed her way through the crowd. The press were
there in force from all over the world and they were as
intrigued by Günter's private life as by his trial. The
divorce had been resurrected, as had Sylvia's part in the
scandal. For weeks their family had been dissected and
exhibited piece by piece.

Thank God for her friends. Tanya and John had been
right behind her since Günter was arrested and so had
Bertha. She would have gone crazy without them. As she
remembered now, tears blinded her eyes; she tripped and
nearly fell and flashbulbs exploded around her again.

Claire was there, discreetly dressed in navy and white,
and smothered with jewelry as usual. For a brief moment
her bright blue eyes turned toward Marika. Pools of hatred! Marika shivered and looked the other way.

She felt a hand on her shoulder and, turning, saw Andy
with one arm around Sylvia. He nodded, but her daughter
ignored her. Andy was glaring at Marika, willing her to
speak. What was she supposed to say? She almost began: I
deeply regret . . . but it sounded like a dirge for the dead
and Günter was about to fight for his life.

There was nothing left to say. She turned and pushed
her way toward a seat near the front and was surprised to
see that Andy had followed her, pulling Sylvia behind
him. Andy looked so tense. Too young to cope with
joining their family, she thought. Son-in-law to a Nazi war
criminal would take some living down. She wondered if he
regretted his hasty marriage. She could see Sylvia's fingers
pressing into his arm. Beyond them, at the end of the row,
Claire was holding a handkerchief to her eyes.

There was a hush in the hubbub of voices as the doors
were thrown open. This is a French courtroom, Marika
thought uneasily; a place where truth is captured, stripped
and raped without mercy or compassion—as a nun is raped
in a lonely mission station. The naked truth! Suddenly she
understood the expression.

Marika turned and took her daughter's arm. "I'm sorry
. . ." she began, but Sylvia pulled her arm loose. They
must write those words on my tombstone, Marika thought
bitterly.

After ten minutes, when the crowd had been quieted,
the Advocate General for the prosecution came in. He was
a short, homely-looking man with a shock of white hair
cut short and pink freckled skin. He sat at a table to the
right of the judges' rostrum and glared at his legal team
when they sat down around him. Then came the Partis
Serville, a team of three top advocates, representing the
rights of the victims' next of kin, and shortly afterward
nine jurists. Last of all came Pierre Guedi, Günter's defense advocate, and his team. Marika did not like Guedi.
He looked too emaciated to inspire her confidence. Only
his voice was rich and deep and seemed to come from a
man far larger than himself. He was followed by his two
colleagues, looking insignificant and ridiculously young.

The court was hushed as Günter was brought in and
taken to the prisoner's dock. How pale he was. There were
shadows under his eyes. He looked older than his forty-
five years and so sad. She could not tear her eyes away
from him as she rose and waited for the Presiding Judge
and his two assessors to enter and sit on the rostrum. The
Advocate General stood up to speak. The trial was to be
held in French. Beside him the translator waited patiently.

May it please the President and members of the court; the
Republic against Günter Grieff, the charge premeditated
murder against the people of France."

The Advocate opened his case. Marika spoke French,
but she knew that Günter did not. Then the translator
stepped forward and spoke softly to Günter:

"You were born Otto Geissler in Hamburg, in 1915,
and were, in 1944, a major and commander of the 1st
Battalion of the Führer Regiment, since when you have
been known as Günter Grieff, Swiss, and currently are a
South African national."

"I am Günter Grieff, I acknowledge," Günter said

quietly. "I am not Otto Geissler." There was a pause for the translator.

"Günter Grieff, the court has fully investigated your plea of mistaken identity. According to the indictment before me, there is no possibility of doubt and you are in fact Otto Geissler. However, your submission will be taken note of at the proper time.

"You are charged with the willful murder of six hundred and fifty French men, women and children on the afternoon of June 10, 1944, at Oradour-sur-Glane."

The words were hardly out of his mouth when the court broke into a frenzy of booing and shouting that even the frantic police were unable to stem.

The anger, the frustration, the longing for revenge—it was there around her and within her. At that moment Marika felt at one with the crowd and she watched sympathetically as the police removed the offenders. They were respectable, middle-aged country people, unused to scenes or rowdiness, and they were muttering and confused now.

Marika's fingers gripped the sides of the chair. As she listened to Sylvia weeping, she felt she would be torn apart by the force of the conflicting emotions raging inside her.

Chapter Eighty

When, at last, the courtroom was silent the President said, "Are you represented by counsel or do you require the assistance of a public advocate?"

Pierre Guedi stood up. "The accused is represented, Mr. President . . . Pierre Guedi, advocate for the defense."

The President made a brief note on his paper and turned to the prosecution. "The Advocate General may present his case."

The Prosecutor took his place in front of the judges and

began speaking softly. "Mr. President, gentlemen of the court, the events in this crime are well known; Oradour-sur-Glane has become a public monument to one of the most hideous crimes of World War II.

"Every French man and woman is familiar with this dreadful story. I will not waste words condemning the prisoner's crime. The fact that Geissler went far beyond his commander's orders and took a personal initiative in ordering the massacre is a matter of history and cannot be regarded merely as an excess. He did not take hostages as he had been told to do and the destruction of Oradour cannot, therefore, be blamed on the leadership of the Führer Regiment or the Reich Division, or in any way on the German authority, but rests fairly and squarely upon the shoulders of Otto Geissler."

He turned toward the dock with a sweeping, dramatic gesture. "You, Otto Geissler, are guilty of ordering your troops to destroy the men, women and children of an entire French village." He put down the papers and stared at Günter as if on the point of tears. Then he sighed, looked around the courtroom and finally at the judges.

"We have here documents giving Otto Geissler's own version of the massacre. I shall read an excerpt from the history of the Führer Regiment, compiled by Major Weidinger, Geissler's superior officer." He cleared his throat.

" 'Late in the afternoon of June 10,' " he began reading quietly and without inflection, " 'Sturmbannführer Geissler returned to the regiment and reported the following: The company met resistance in Oradour and came across several bodies of murdered German soldiers. The company then occupied the town and promptly started to search the houses. They discovered hidden ammunition and weapons, so Geissler had all the men of the town, whom he identified as Maquisards, shot.

" 'Meanwhile, the women and children had been locked into the church and the town had been set on fire. Hidden ammunition exploded in nearly all the houses. The fire suddenly spread to the church, which also had ammunition hidden in its steeple. The church burned very quickly and the women and children died.' "

The court was so silent you could hear the footsteps of the police sentries in the courtyard outside. Then a rustle that was more of a sigh ran around the benches.

The Prosecutor spoke solemnly, his voice vibrant with underlying tension. "A terrible story. But how much worse will be the true evidence offered by our witnesses?" Then he laid down the papers and looked directly at the judges.

"Geissler's CO, Colonel Stadler, was deeply shocked at this report and told Geissler . . ." He paused and shuffled the papers again. " 'Geissler, you could pay heavily for this. I shall request that you be court-martialed immediately by the division. I cannot let something like this rest on the shoulders of the regiment.' At the time Geissler did not defend himself, but he obviously expected to do so at the military hearing. A court-martial was arranged to be held as soon as possible."

The Prosecutor placed the papers on the desk before him. He looked depressed. Then he sighed. "So long ago, but the documentation is precise and accurate . . ."

There was a long silence as he stared earnestly at the assembled courtroom.

The President leaned forward and spoke to Günter: "Otto Geissler, do you now, twenty-five years later, wish to challenge or withdraw this statement?"

Pierre Guedi stood up quickly. "We do not wish to withdraw or challenge the statement made by Otto Geissler, Mr. President. We are satisfied that it has no bearing on the charges against my client."

The President gave him a reproachful stare. "You fully understand its incriminating character?"

"Fully, Mr. President, but it is our submission that for justice's sake this statement must remain unchallenged. We hope to convince the court of my client's innocence."

"You may continue," the President told the Prosecutor, who turned with a flourish of impatience toward the judges. "With the permission of the President, I intend to present my witnesses to prove, in the first instance, that the prisoner, Günter Grieff, and the former Major Otto Geissler are in fact one and the same person.''

"Permission granted."

First he called Klaus Greenstein.

Marika was saddened to see how old and frail he had become. Greenstein walked with a permanent stoop and his voice was hardly more than a whisper. Nevertheless, his answers were swift and to the point. He identified himself and explained the nature of his work, pointing out with more than a little pride a number of notable Nazi criminals he had been responsible for unmasking. He outlined the events leading up to the discovery of Günter Grieff, which began with Marika's visit to his office.

"I told her at the time that there was every chance that Geissler was dead," his relentless whispering continued.

"The records showed that Major Otto Geissler was killed in action on June 30, 1944. His supposed death, witnessed by his comrades, seemed to us to hold sufficient doubt to warrant an investigation."

He broke into a coughing fit and had to be revived with a glass of water before he could continue. "There was, of course, the very real possibility that this was a cover-up by his comrades, who knew that he would very soon face the wrath of the Allied victors for his crime at Oradour."

He paused and looked around. Then he saw Marika and for a moment his gaze rested compassionately upon her. "Previous investigations had told us that his family were killed in the Berlin blitz. It was impossible to find his grave; therefore we could not check dental records or other details. However, she . . . Mrs. Palma, that is . . . insisted that we keep every possible avenue open.

"Then in September 1954 we were instrumental in capturing another Nazi war criminal in Argentina, who told us—under some duress, I might add—that Geissler had not died; although he claimed not to know what became of him."

He sighed and glanced apologetically at the President. "I contacted Mrs. Palma—Miss Magos, as she was then—

and she decided to increase her financial support. But in spite of lengthy inquiries we were not able to obtain any further leads. However, we passed this information to the French authorities, including details of Geissler's past life prior to World War II."

The Prosecutor interrupted him: "Would you care to give the court some idea of the information you uncovered?"

"Well"—the old man stood blinking, stooped more heavily now—"it was a lengthy document."

"Perhaps I could help you to remember some relevant details. I think you went fairly heavily into Geissler's early youth; on his mother's side, I believe, his grandparents had lived in South-West Africa, and Geissler frequently told friends that he would eventually go to Africa; his parents were divorced when Geissler was sixteen and he lived for a while with his mother, prior to joining the University of Heidelberg, where he studied geology, gaining a B.Sc. prior to the outbreak of the war. That is correct?"

Marika stirred restlessly. She felt sick. Africa! Geology! She hardly dared glance at Günter and when she did she saw how his eyes were staring in shock and his mouth hung open stupidly. She had never seen him look like that before.

By the time the prosecution had finished with Greenstein the old man could hardly stand and had to be assisted to his seat. The defense declined to cross-examine him and he went off coughing and leaning heavily on his stick.

A new witness was taking the oath. It was Sergeant Breyton of the French police, a once handsome man who had gone to seed; his stomach bulged, his hair was balding and his cheeks drooped. His voice sounded as tired as he looked when he recounted events leading to the application for extradition of Grieff.

He explained how—after a ten-year search—they had uncovered the operation of a forger, a certain Maurice Mousson, who had been producing passports for leading criminals. One of these criminals had talked and Mousson had been arrested.

"Subsequently," Breyton told a hushed courtroom, "on a routine raid of Mousson's home and premises, we discovered a tin box hidden in the attic containing details of work undertaken for the SS toward the end of World War II."

He paused dramatically, well aware of the importance of his words. "Under interrogation, Mousson admitted that for years he had feared that his former SS clients might be tempted to do away with him, for he alone knew the new identities and nationalities of several wanted war criminals. And why?" He looked around triumphantly. "Because it was he who had furnished them with their identity papers and passports. So he had kept the evidence hidden in the roof of his house as a type of insurance. His brother had instructions to deliver the box to the police should Mousson disappear or die in suspicious circumstances.

"Included in the files were details of the false papers sold to Otto Geissler in December 1944. From this we learned that Geissler had taken the name Günter Grieff and assumed Swiss nationality."

There was a roar of satisfaction in the courtroom. Breyton wiped his forehead with a large handkerchief and stared at the Prosecutor apologetically. Order was soon restored and there was only a mumble of conversation as Breyton stood down.

The President frowned, but said nothing. Once again the defense declined to cross-examine the witness.

It was nearly one when the President announced: "The court is adjourned until three o'clock this afternoon."

The President left the court with amazing agility for such an old man, followed by his colleagues. Günter Grieff was led away by a guard and then the courtroom became an uproar, with everyone shouting and pushing at once.

Chapter Eighty-one

It was inevitable that they would call Mousson to the stand after lunch. He was sworn in as soon as the afternoon session opened. He was a flamboyant man: vain and unrepentant.

"Your name is Maurice Mousson and you are serving a ten-year sentence for forgery?"

"Yes, Mr. President."

"During your activities as a forger you have undertaken work for a number of political groups and particularly for the SS toward the end of the last war?"

Mousson looked around uneasily.

"You may answer the question without fear," the President reminded him, "since it is not you who are on trial. You are merely a witness and whatever you say will have no bearing on your sentence."

Eventually, with a good deal of prompting, Mousson admitted that he had met Otto Geissler in November 1944. He described how he had been brought to see Geissler, who was in hiding after being listed as killed in action. He took a great deal of time describing the house, the attic room and the condition Geissler was in. "A cynical bastard," he said, and was reproved by the President. "A tough customer, that one," he added later, "not someone you'd care to double-cross."

Mousson went on to explain how he had been paid by the SS to forge Geissler a Swiss passport based on a genuine Swiss birth certificate for a certain Günter Grieff. He had given Geissler these papers in December 1944, and he had not seen Geissler again.

"Monsieur Mousson, can you identify the prisoner in

the dock as the man for whom you made those forged papers in 1944?'' the Prosecutor asked.

"Well, you're asking a lot." He glanced at Günter and quickly looked away again. "It's over twenty years, you know." He smiled quietly and shrugged. "I can only say that he was about the same height, with blond hair, blue eyes and a pleasant-enough smile." He shrugged again and gestured with his hands palms upward. "In the name of God! People change, don't they? Don't we all? That's life."

"Monsieur Mousson," the Prosecutor said, rubbing his hands gleefully. "If you cannot identify the prisoner conclusively, would you be able to recognize whether or not this passport is your own work?"

A gasp ran around the court and all eyes turned surreptitiously toward Günter, whose hands were gripping the rail. He looked horrified.

The Prosecutor could not resist a sly glance at Günter and for the first time a wintry smile showed on the old man's face.

Watching Grieff, Guedi felt old and angry. He sat silently for a moment, toying with a pen. There was no time to prepare a new case, suicidal to change tactics at this stage. Grieff had told him that after he married Claire Grieff, in Johannesburg in 1962, he had decided to apply for South African nationality. He had handed in the papers to the authorities and when they were sent back they were lost in the post. Guedi could have sworn Günter was telling the truth.

Without those papers, the prosecution's case had been flimsy. It rested on identifications by witnesses who had not seen Geissler for over twenty years. Now they had the evidence to guillotine Grieff. He swore silently under his breath. There is nothing an advocate fears more than a client who lies. A case can be constructed for the most heinous crime, but the unexpected cannot be anticipated. Günter was a fool. He shrugged, already dismissing the case as one of his rare failures. One in twenty! Not a bad percentage, he thought ruefully.

The Prosecutor picked up an old and battered passport and handed it to the witness. "This is Günter Grieff's Swiss passport," he said. "Can you identify it as one of your creations?"

Suddenly the court was silent. Everyone peered forward, intent and anxious. The footsteps of the guards outside the courtroom sounded frighteningly loud.

Mousson stared at the passport, and his face burst into a rare smile. "Look at this," he cried, holding it up. "Twenty-five years and it's still unsmudged and unfaded. I tell you, even the government can't make them as well as I."

"It's one of yours, then, is it? Can you swear to that?"

"Oh yes, undoubtedly." He was smiling confidently for the first time.

A man who loves his work, Marika thought, watching him with horror.

"I have my little tricks, my trademark. I—Mousson—could never make a mistake about such a matter."

The Prosecutor was smiling happily. He waved his hand nonchalantly and beamed at Mousson. "Tell me, Monsieur Mousson," he said as if he were addressing a mischievous child. "Why Günter Grieff? What made you choose that name?"

"But I explained to you already," Mousson said, looking pained. "That's nothing to do with me. Oh no! My job was to forge papers." He looked around anxiously. "The SS used to find the names and produce the birth certificates. They were always valid. Don't ask me how they dug them up. People who had died, usually without surviving relatives." He shrugged. "Of course, they always took identities from camp inmates, but Grieff being Swiss?" He gestured eloquently. "They paid well."

Marika was too upset to concentrate on what he was saying. There was a loud babble of voices in the courtroom. The President banged his gavel. Then Sylvia burst into tears and ran from the courtroom with Andy hard behind her. She would have liked to go after her daughter and comfort her, but she was afraid.

She saw Claire sobbing into her handkerchief. All at

once Claire jumped up and called loudly: "Pigs! Pigs! You tricked me. I gave you his papers to prove his innocence. He's innocent, I tell you." Sobbing bitterly, she was escorted from the courtroom by an official.

The lengthy cross-examination by Guedi merely confirmed Mousson's implacable faith in his own work. He was positive that he had forged this passport, he could prove it, and no amount of persuasion could instill even a trifling doubt into the minds of those assembled in the courtroom.

When the Prosecutor brought in the next witness, an official from the Swiss Embassy who swore that the passport was forged, there was no reaction from the courtroom. It was an anticlimax, no one needed convincing. He pointed out that the birth certificate was valid, but Swiss records also had a death certificate for the same person. Günter Grieff had died of consumption at the outbreak of the war, aged twenty-four, and had no surviving relatives. He had been an orphan from a state institution.

"Just be thankful for small mercies," Guedi told his colleagues. "At least Grieff hasn't testified yet, so he doesn't have to change his story." There was still time to get together and tunnel a way through this morass of evidence heaped around him.

"Call Mrs. Marika Palma."

Marika stood poised and tense, as if to flee from the courtroom. She was not surprised when her arm was taken firmly by a court official and she was propelled to the witness stand. The moment of truth was approaching. What was she to say? A thousand memories flashed before her eyes: the Germans marching into Czechoslovakia—jackboots, swastikas and frightful inhumanity; her father being dragged to the train; her mother crying; and finally no one left alive at all.

She had spent thousands of pounds and for what? To bring about this moment of revenge. There stood Günter, the man she loved. What strange twist of fate had made her love her father's murderer?

"Your name is Mrs. Marika Palma, previously Marika Magos, and you are the owner of Marika Magos Furs and Marika Magos Fashions, wife of Angelo Palma, industrialist?"

"Yes."

"Mrs. Palma, how long have you been married?"

"Over six years."

"And this is your first marriage?"

"That is correct."

"In 1947 you gave birth to a daughter, named Sylvia Magos?"

She nodded silently.

"And the father was known to you as Günter Grieff?"

"Yes." Her mouth was so dry she could hardly speak.

"Is the prisoner in the dock the father of your child?"

"Yes."

"Would you tell the court how you met the prisoner."

She began shakily. "I visited the hospital with fruit for the patients. I saw him. We fell in love." How feeble words could be at times like this. How could she explain the magic which had raced between them, so that they were inextricably entwined before even they had spoken a word to each other. She remembered Günter in the hospital, holding her hands, begging her to come back again. And later, she remembered making love among the sand dunes—conceiving Sylvia. It was only fitting that Sylvia should be so very beautiful, she thought, as she stumbled to find the words to explain. "We became engaged, but afterward we broke it off."

"I would like you to tell the court your reasons for breaking your relationship with the prisoner. After all, at the time you were pregnant and engaged."

Marika glanced at Günter. He was watching her with such tenderness. He had never stopped loving her, not even now when it was she who had brought all this misfortune upon him. "Yes." She replied tonelessly. She wondered who had been giving them this information.

"Please answer the question."

Her thoughts were jumbled and confused. This was where she plunged the lever that would bring the guillotine crashing onto Günter's neck. Well, that was what she wanted, wasn't it? After all the years of paying and hoping, her father's murderer stood before her. It was her duty . . . No, she corrected herself, her pleasure to tell them that Günter was in fact a German and that she had always known that. Not just German, but a German who fought in the war and earned the Iron Cross. A war criminal.

"Would you please answer the question?" The President glared at her impatiently.

"I don't understand," she murmured, licking her lips.

What if she lied? How would that help Günter? What could she say? The papers had been proved false. Whatever else Günter was, he was not Günter Grieff. Sadness ran through her and she nearly cried out. The truth, dissected and exposed. The naked truth. If Günter was her father's murderer he must pay for his crimes.

"I loved him," she began quietly. "I loved him so much, but then we fought. He refused to work in my mother's store. He wanted to go prospecting in the desert. I hate the sand, sand, always sand." She broke off and stared at the President.

"Is that all?" he asked gently. "Are you sure?"

"That's all."

"Marika." She heard Günter's voice speaking quietly from the prisoner's dock. "Tell the truth, Marika."

The President slammed his gavel on the bench. "If you speak again I shall have you removed from the court."

Slowly Marika looked up and her eyes met Günter's. For a long moment they stared at each other. Then she shook her head. "That's the truth," she lied, and gazed timidly at the President.

The defense declined to cross-examine her and she fled through the courtroom and out into the cold and misty afternoon. Why had she lied? She sat on a stone bench outside the courtroom and tried to sort out her confused thoughts and warring emotions.

Sylvia found her there. She looked wild and angry. Her violet eyes were blazing with indignation.

"I was standing at the back. I heard what you said."

"So?"

"So what did Dad mean? Tell the truth! What was he trying to make you say?"

"I don't know," Marika stammered, lying badly.

"You do know. I saw your face and I saw his face," she went on. "He loves you, but you have destroyed him. I despise you," she began slowly, her voice rising in crescendo. "All of this—it's your fault. Right from the beginning. And all because you don't like sand." She stepped forward and gave her mother a stinging blow on her cheek.

Marika crumpled onto the stone bench and raised her hand protectively to shield her face.

"Yes," she said. She looked up and her eyes filled with tears as she watched her daughter, distraught and disheveled, rushing back to the courtroom.

Soon afterward the court adjourned until the next morning and Marika left hurriedly to dodge the press who were pouring out of the doorway in search of their next victim.

"Why did you lie to me, Günter?" Guedi said wearily. He was waiting in the cell when Günter was brought back from the dock.

Günter sighed and stared long and hard at his lawyer; watching him, Guedi could sense the defeat in the man.

Eventually Günter said, "I thought he was Swiss."

"Who?"

"Grieff, or whoever he was . . . he seemed so genuine . . . so . . ." His voice tailed off disconsolately. "It was I who was German. I felt guilty . . . I have always felt guilty . . . Besides, how could I admit that I am German . . . living under a false name . . . when I am facing a charge of war crimes?"

Guedi sighed. "So you admit you are German?"

"Yes."

"You are, in fact, Otto Geissler."

"No!" Günter looked up, shocked and scared. "Surely you don't believe that. I was in submarines in the war. But that was so long ago. Since then I grew into the name Grieff. It really seems like me. All that Günter has achieved, the mines, the money, the reputation, well, I did all that. It's me. I felt it would be safer just to deny everything. I couldn't believe that Grieff . . ." He broke off.

"But why did you tell me your passport and birth certificate were lost?"

"I thought they were." Günter said, frowning. "Claire told me they were never returned by the Department of the Interior. We made inquiries for a while and eventually forgot about it. I no longer needed them."

When Guedi did not answer he went on. "Years ago, in another age, another lifetime, there was a war and I was a young engineer in a U-boat and then I was called Hans Kolb." He sighed. It was all so long ago. He sat down and recounted his story. It was late when he finished, but neither of them noticed.

"That's the truth," he whispered eventually, when he had told Guedi all that he could remember. "But I swear to God, it seems more like fiction to me. Günter Grieff . . . Well, that's real enough. Besides, I felt secure with Grieff's papers." He sat down and buried his face in his hands. "Claire kept the papers all that time," he said brokenly. "Why? Why did she do that?" He broke off and lapsed into silence.

"So only Claire knows the truth."

Günter scowled. "Only Claire."

"All right," Guedi said. "Let's get to work. There must be someone who can identify you."

Two hours later Guedi was feeling desperate. "I'm sure I don't have to remind you that the guillotine awaits you . . . unless you can prove your identity."

Günter nodded.

"Think, man. Think! And from now on stick strictly to the truth. I'll try for an adjournment, but it's unlikely I'll succeed. You've been interrogated enough times. They're bound to think this is a last-minute fabrication to save your neck.''

Watching him, seeing his bleak eyes, Günter felt an acute burning sensation around his neck and began to rub his hand against it.

Guedi noticed and smiled mirthlessly. ''Think harder,'' he said, and left.

Guedi sat late into the night wrestling with his problem. The real Hans Kolb had disappeared as surely as if he had never existed. Günter's parents were killed in the blitz, their farm sold; there were no surviving relatives and Hans's school and all its records had been destroyed during the blitz. Prewar records at the Stralsund naval training school had also been destroyed.

It could take months to find anyone who remembered the youthful Hans Kolb, if indeed anyone did.

For a brief, depressing moment the defense lawyer wondered if Hans had ever existed—or was he merely the fabrication of a desperate man? Claire was the key. She had exchanged and destroyed the papers, according to Günter. Well, it would all be revealed tomorrow, he thought. But Claire's story alone would not be enough to save Günter from the guillotine. Only his real papers could do that.

Chapter Eighty-two

Marika passed the newsstand on the way back to her hotel from the court and morbid curiosity won through her determination not to look. She approached nervously, glancing around, but no one noticed her. When she ventured into the streets nowadays she wore dark glasses and a large scarf over her head—an obvious disguise, but this evening it was raining and pedestrians were wrapped in their own gloom as they hurried home.

There was a front-page photograph of Sylvia looking frail as she fled from the court clutching Andy. *Famous model flees trial. Internationally known model Sylvia Shaw fled from the court this afternoon when her father's Swiss passport was proved to be forged. Mousson, a forger serving a ten-year sentence, alleges* . . .

Marika sighed and skimmed down the columns. She flinched as she turned the page and saw a dreadful picture of herself arriving at court that morning. She stared at it sullenly before turning the page.

Grieff's alibi crumbles, she read. *Not Swiss, says state expert.* There was more, much more, and glancing at the headlines on every newspaper, Marika began to feel sick.

A picture in the London *Daily Mail* caught her eye and she flinched. *Claire tells her story* . . . *"I will stand by my husband to the end,"* says . . .

"End! My God!" Marika fumed. In Claire's mind Günter was as good as executed. She flung down the newspaper and turned away.

"Cruel, cruel," she muttered. The ponderous conveyor belt of the law was thrusting Günter slowly, but inexorably toward the guillotine.

Well, that was what she wanted, she thought. An eye for an eye . . . Feeling confused and guilty, she called a taxi and when she was safely in her room she flung herself on the bed and wept.

She was still crying when she heard knocking on her hotel bedroom door. It was Bertha.

"Oh God, Bertha, you shouldn't have come," she said. "You promised to stay in London."

"How could I stay? The waiting nearly killed me. Besides, you need me. I've seen Sylvia," she went on. "She's very upset, naturally, but she's surviving. Thank God for Andy. It's you I'm worried about."

"I don't know what I feel the most,' Marika blurted out. "Hate or pity. It's killing me."

Bertha sent down for some tea and mixed a tranquilizer

with Marika's sugar. Sleep! That's what she needs, Bertha thought. Just as long as she can survive each day, who knows what tomorrow will bring?

Günter was alone in his cell, huddled in a blanket for warmth, but he could not stop shivering and he knew that it was not just from the cold. It was something to do with Claire's eyes and the way she looked at him. As if she personally was responsible for his plight. She was enjoying her revenge, yet she had played her trump card—produced Grieff's passport, condemning him in the eyes of the entire court. So why did she still smirk so arrogantly and confidently from the courtroom bench? Why did she feel that she alone could dole out life . . . or death . . .? Günter was haunted by the malicious contemplation in Claire's shrewd blue eyes.

All evening a terrible suspicion had been tormenting him. Years before, Claire had told him that Günter Grieff's passport had been lost. Why? What neurotic insecurity had driven her to conceal this evidence all those years?

Now, in the solitude of his cell, he recalled that nightmare swim from the submarine to Walvis Bay; he remembered seeing the moon in a haze just above the horizon and he remembered the pain of the shooting cramps which had tormented him. He had discarded his life jacket because it impeded his arm movements and then . . . God . . . the pain had been killing him. But he had taken such trouble to transfer his papers from his belt to his shirt pocket before he discarded his trousers as well. They had been wrapped in oilskin and it was only because of his papers that he had not discarded his shirt. Later, when he recovered in the hospital, Claire had said there had been no papers. But Claire had said his passport was lost and Claire was a liar. He thought about his naval papers for a while. Photographs, fingerprints, it was all there . . . all he needed to prove his identity. Had Claire hidden them all this time? The thought was driving him crazy.

He was not surprised when Claire was admitted to his cell late that evening.

"Oh, Günter," she cried. "Don't be angry. I wasn't to know; how could I possibly guess the passport was forged?"

He stirred uncomfortably and gazed at his hands, unwilling to look at Claire. If he looked at her—really looked at her—he might kill her.

After a while he said, "Why did you lie to me? You told me the passport was lost in the post. I remember quite clearly. What else are you holding back, Claire?"

She moistened her lips nervously. "I only hid the passport in case you needed it one day."

Or in case you needed it, he thought. His eyes narrowed speculatively as he looked up. Suddenly he knew what she was going to say.

Claire saw the expression on his face and stepped backward. "Günter, I'm your wife. You know how much I love you."

He looked away again and stared out of the cell window.

"I've stopped the divorce," she whispered. "I made a mistake. I was so jealous." She grabbed his hand and held it tightly, laying her cheek against his palm. "Surely you understand?"

"Oh, I understand," he said sadly. "I have always understood. Your tragedy is me."

"It doesn't have to be a tragedy," she said. "Let's start again." She looked up hopefully, sure that she could win him over with the force of her passion. "Eight years, Günter. Eight terrific years. Don't let's throw them away."

"Claire," he said softly. "It's over. That's it. You must understand."

She stepped back and stared at him shrewdly. "All right," she said at last, plucking up courage. "How much is your life worth? Is it worth putting up with me?

"Two choices, Günter. Me or the guillotine. Give up Marika, come back to me. I can save you." Her face was white as chalk, eyes glinting.

Snake's eyes, Günter thought, and shivered. Now he knew without doubt that she had his papers.

"What you're doing is wrong, Claire. Evil! Don't you understand? Evil attracts evil."

She was not listening. "To me you're not a man, Günter, you're a god, and I can't live without you." Her voice rose, trembling on the edge of hysteria. "I'd rather see you dead than with another woman. Give up Marika. Within forty-eight hours you'll be free."

"And if I say no?"

"Oh, Günter, don't make me make that terrible choice."

She was unprepared for the blow which sent her flying across the cell.

"Get out," he said quietly, "while you're still alive. And, Claire . . . don't ever come back, whatever you do. I never want to see you again."

"Goddamn you, Günter," she said. "I'll see you at your bloody funeral."

Chapter Eighty-three

The next morning Marika arrived at the Palais de Justice an hour before the session was due to open, but the antechamber and pavement were crowded with press and spectators clamoring to get in. It took all her charm and persuasion to gain entrance to the court, where she found Sylvia and Claire were already seated on the crowded benches.

At last the doors on either side of the courtroom opened and the prosecution and defense teams settled themselves at their tables.

When Günter was led in between prison officers, there was a frenzied burst of conversation. Like sharks, Marika thought, they can smell blood and it excites them. Günter looked haggard and near the end of his endurance.

Then the President and his judges filed in, looking alert and pleased, as if they knew the case would be over shortly. The Advocate General stood up with a smile.

"Mr. President, gentlemen of the court." He paused and gazed earnestly at each of the judges and the jury. "We feel that the evidence we have produced is sufficiently valid to prove that Günter Grieff is indeed Otto Geissler and that on June 10, 1944, he was responsible for the murder of six hundred and fifty French men and women. We have produced evidence from both the forger, Maurice Mousson, who made Otto Geissler's passport in the name of Günter Grieff, and a Swiss authority, both of whom testified that the passport was a fake, and we were told that the real Günter Grieff died many years ago.

"In each case the defense has left our testimony unchallenged. I do not intend to waste more of the court's time by dwelling further on these accusations, but to bring in evidence to prove that the crime was both premeditated and willful."

What followed was a nightmare for Marika. For the first time she heard eyewitness accounts of how her father and countless others died in Oradour. A succession of witnesses were called from neighboring towns to identify Geissler—as they all did. Some were more positive than others; all of them mentioned the passing of the years, their failing memories, the way people change. "He looks familiar," one of them said. "He has the same build, the same skin coloring, the same eyes and hair. Of course, he's changed. What can one expect in over twenty years?"

There was only one female survivor from Oradour. Her name was Madame Grandjean. She was a small, gray-haired woman of about sixty with a complexion like unbaked clay. She was having treatment for depression and had been in and out of mental homes since the disaster. She sobbed when she was asked to recall the massacre.

"We share your grief with you—a terrible experience—and we regret that you should be exposed to the pain of questioning. Nevertheless, you must try to compose yourself and answer the questions concisely," the President told her.

Haltingly, between sobs and sips of water, she described how four hundred women, children and babies were herded into the church and locked in while the SS remained inside covering them with machine guns. They waited in silence for a long time until the doors opened and soldiers carried in a heavy box, which they dumped at the nave. The soldiers lit a fuse sticking out of it and ran out.

Madame Grandjean became hysterical at this point and had to be calmed by a policewoman. At last she continued: "We watched in horror as thick black smoke poured from the box. Then we screamed and tried to escape, but the Germans cocked their weapons. When we heard the first bursts of fire in the town the SS began hurling grenades and emptying gunfire into the throng of women, children and babies.

"Oh Lord," she whimpered. "I can still see it . . . still smell it . . . and the blood, Babies!" she called shrilly. "I ask you—babies!" Her voice fell to a low-pitched grumble. "I saw my daughter fall dead. I, too, slipped and fell to the ground. I lay in the blood. Horrible! It will haunt me forever."

Surreptitiously Marika tried to wipe the tears from her cheeks with the back of her hand. When she looked at Günter she saw he was crying, too. Remorse? Guilt? Fear? What was making him cry?

The Prosecutor stood up. "Mr. President," he said quickly. "We have Madame Grandjean's story here, one which she has had to recount any number of times. Would it be appropriate to read it aloud and she could acknowledge its authenticity?" The President inclined his head and Madame Grandjean sank gratefully into a chair.

Reading rapidly, the Prosecutor described how the woman had hauled herself to the stand where the Abbé lit his candles and from there flung herself out of a window; although hit five times by bullets she had managed to hide in a pea garden until nightfall.

He turned to his witness. "Thank you," he said simply. "You are a very courageous woman."

A low mutter of sympathy ran around the courtroom. The President frowned. "Does the defense have any further questions for this witness?"

The President glanced at Guedi.

He appeared to be lost in thought. Then he said slowly, "Mr. President, I should like to cross-examine this witness later, when I present my defense."

"The witness may step down, but will be recalled later."

"Thank you, Mr. President," Guedi said quietly.

Next the Prosecutor called one of the only five men to survive the massacre. He recounted to a shocked courtroom that fateful afternoon when all the men of the village were marched to garages and barns and shot; then their bodies were burned.

One of them was her father and Marika burst into tears and unashamedly sobbed into her handkerchief. But why was she crying? She knew the horror movie well enough. She had played it to herself nightly for years. An entire population had been killed as a punishment for an act of sabotage which had been committed somewhere else. There were no arms or ammunition found in Oradour, nor in the church. Her father, who was in the Maquis, had been there by accident. Was she crying for her father, or for the six hundred and fifty innocent victims, or for Günter, looking so pale and agitated as he leaned against the rail in the dock?

The Prosecutor had taken the floor and in mournful tones was addressing the judges. "Mr. President, gentlemen of the court, the indictment is straightforward: willful and premeditated murder against the people of France. A crime so heinous that it will be remembered with repulsion for centuries to come. We have submitted proof of the crime in the form of evidence written by the prisoner himself when he was preparing a statement for his regiment; we have brought forward a series of witnesses to recount the authenticity of our allegations.

"Furthermore we have produced evidence to prove that Günter Grieff is a fictitious character; the real owner of the name and birth certificate has been dead for thirty-two years.

"The fact that Geissler went far beyond his commander's orders and took a personal initiative in ordering the massacre is a matter of history.

"The testimony of all the witnesses is so concise and damning that I do not wish to waste the court's time in bringing forward any further evidence available to us."

"In that case," the President said, "the defense may present its own testimony, but as it's approaching four, I think this may be a good time to call a halt for the day." He picked up his gavel. "The court is adjourned until ten tomorrow morning."

Chapter Eighty-four

It took five hours to gain permission to visit Günter, but eventually Marika found herself being led down cold, echoing corridors to the maximum-security block, where his cell door was flung open. Günter was huddled in a blanket at the end of his bed.

"Don't worry, no one will disturb you for half an hour," the guard told her without a change in his expression.

Günter seemed dazed, as if he could not believe what he was seeing. Then he tried out a pallid grin. He stood up shakily like an old man, looking stiff and old and without hope.

"I've come to tell you I love you and I forgive you," Marika said, trying to find a strength she did not have. "No matter what you have done or why you did it, I forgive you. If I could get you out of here, I would. Can you believe that? I think I must be mad."

He smiled and his eyes looked so compassionate. What right had he to look compassionate? she wondered.

"Marika, I never had the chance to explain—how it all happened," he began, but his teeth were chattering so badly he broke off and sat on the bunk, pulling the blanket around his shoulders.

"I don't want to know," she said quickly. "We have half an hour and I want you to make love to me." Because, she thought, because maybe this is all we shall ever have, but she could not say that, so she smiled and said, "I need you, Günter."

"I don't think I can," he said sadly.

"Oh, but it's cold." She took off her clothes and, seared by the cold, her skin became pink and blotchy. She was oblivious to the guard's footsteps pacing the corridor, or the cold stone beneath her naked feet.

She walked softly to Günter, knelt in front of him and ruffled his hair with her hands. Then she took his face between her hands and kissed his forehead, closed his eyes and moved her lips down to his mouth. He was cold; rigid with tension; unable to give, or participate; but wanting her desperately. "Love me, Marika," he murmured.

She undid the buttons of his shirt and gently removed it. He was never cold, she remembered, but now he was cold. She undid his trousers and made him stand so that she could pull them down and then his underpants. There was no desire in him, no passion; he was a shivering shadow of the man she had known. She stifled an impulse to cry, and pushing him down on the bed, she moved her lips over his belly and down to his groin, taking the maleness of him into her mouth and gently kneading and caressing. Her tongue felt the gentle stirring and stiffening and he groaned softly, and began to cry like a child, and then he twisted around and buried his face in the mattress.

She understood and lay beside him, pulling his head down between her breasts. Günter groaned and clutched her and she tried not to flinch with pain as his fingers dug into her shoulders and his lips bruised her neck and her mouth.

"Oh, Marika! Oh, my love, my love."

He was like a man lost in the desert—she the oasis. He clutched at her—groaning, thrusting his face into her breasts, her stomach, her navel; tasting the sweetness, the God-given sweetness of her. Woman and survival—they were synonymous. And she was all woman—and every woman; a haven of peace; a brief respite from his perilous road to extinction.

And when he pushed into her it was his roots he was pushing down and down into the fertile earth; searching for nourishment and strength; quivering, pulsating, sucking the goodness from her; feeling her life force flooding into him. The eternal woman—lifeline to survival. Through her was the beginning; through her was the joy; through her was fulfillment and the key to salvation.

And she gave all that she had; all her love; all her body; all her compassion and womanly healing.

He came at last, shuddered and pulled her close against him.

She smiled. He was male again and ready to fight another day.

"Time's nearly up. You'd better get dressed." He stood up, grinning, and dumped her clothes on her lap.

They heard footsteps approaching slowly and loud whistling in the corridor.

"So French," she murmured, putting on her coat. "So humane."

"Marika," he called as the door was closing. "Go and pray . . . pray for a miracle."

"Oh yes," she sighed. "I will."

"Pray for him, Günter had said. How naïve, how gauche. Yet she had promised and she must pray for him. There must be a church somewhere near. She walked out into the night, not sure of which direction she was taking. Unwilling to arrive at her destination. It was so long ago since she had prayed in a church.

The wind was stronger now, a biting, damp wind that seemed to soak into the marrow of her bones. She turned up the collar of her coat and hunched her shoulders, looking straight ahead at the ground in front of her feet; the cobblestones seemed to be leading her into the past.

Perhaps if she found a mosque or a synagogue she could

beseech some foreign God firmly entrenched in the minds
of the believers . . . but how could she go back—back to
spurned faiths, broken creeds, forgotten vows and . . . far
worse . . . anger and heartbreak?

She had been sixteen when her father was killed. The
anger and the disillusionment which had driven her from
her faith had long since dwindled. Often she had tried to
go back, but the beliefs of her youth clashed with the
maturity of her adulthood and she was too honest to pretend, too proud to hang on to the last shreds of a tattered
faith.

So finally she had clung to her own ideas, which were
not ideas at all, but merely an accumulation of facts—
things she could see and touch, things she could trust in:
the evolution of life, the inevitability of birth and death.

Deeper down and hardly acknowledged burned the slow
fires of resentment and the fuel was terror. Life—the
tormenter; a fleeting glimpse of paradise, the paradise of
existence, passing like the wind. Matter would endure, but
she—Marika Magos—would not. As far as she was concerned, all the rest was insignificant against that one final
judgment. Extinction! But sometimes she wondered: Was
that all? Was that the end of the story?

And now, as her footsteps led her aimlessly through the
night streets of Paris, she felt sadness welling up from
deep inside and drifting around her like the damp mist
contaminating all within reach. But not bitterness, she
thought. Oh no, not bitterness. If anything, the trial had
filled her with a sense of wonder at the communal struggle
to uplift humanity—through truth and justice and a striving
for goodness. Why? she wondered. Why does man long
for goodness even while failing?

At that moment it seemed to Marika that all sin was one
sin—denying goodness—the rest extraneous detail.

She found a church at last. It was set back behind
narrow streets and mean shops—a workingman's church.

Inside the smell of incense hit her in the stomach and
she was overcome with a sense of poignancy as memories
flushed through her. Mama praying for Papa after he was

taken away; a young and idealistic girl on her knees in Walvis Bay, whispering while wind and sand pummeled the walls; the roughness of the wooden step against her knees as she pleaded with the statue of the Virgin Mary, who, in some strange way, was also Mama—two in one— who must make a miracle and bring Papa home safely at the end of the war. All those prayers! Wasted time and scraped knees! And here she was again, about to pray for her father's murderer. Absurd. But Günter believed and she could not let him down.

She wandered down the pews, feeling the polished wood under her fingers, noting the altar, achingly familiar, with the candles burning. A figure at the nave was moving slowly with a lighted taper.

Marika knelt and said, "Please save Günter." Then she recited a prayer. " . . . forgive us our trespasses . . . as we forgive . . ." She broke off.

It was no use. What a lot of rigmarole. Here she was, talking to herself like the old peasant sitting alone at the back of the church. She stood up and, drawn as if by a magnet, walked slowly toward the woman, noting with compassion her gnarled hands pressed tightly together, her wrinkled face, yellow teeth showing as she muttered fervently.

She felt a hand on her arm and, turning, saw the priest watching her, lighted taper still in his hand.

"Would you like to confess, my child?" he asked.

"There's no point, since I don't believe in God," she replied sadly.

"Even so . . . you are here." He smiled gently.

"The Church cannot help me," she said. "I need twentieth-century answers." She walked away.

Outside the wind was harsher; it was whining uneasily around the rooftops. She would find a taxi and go back to her safe, luxurious hotel. But the thought that it was only transient—that life, with its modern comforts, could only offer a temporary harbor—and that she was quite alone, obsessed her and frightened her. She loitered on the pavement.

"Help," she whispered to the heedless night. "I need help."

She heard footsteps approaching and turning, saw the woman hurrying behind, her lips still moving and her feet surprisingly heavy.

She held out her hands, mumbling still, but Marika could not understand what she was saying. She fumbled in her bag for all the money that she had and gave it to her.

Why not? Tonight she loved her with a fierce, burning love, and her children, and her children's children, and all those who had come before and those who were not yet born. They all struggled and hoped and were extinguished in their turn and if she could she would have granted them all immortality.

Then, for a brief, glorious moment, she was not herself at all. She had slipped away from her own precarious ego and merged with the sea of living energy which was all around and within her. She was the peasant and the stark bare branches of the trees set into the pavement; even the pavement itself; and the wind which howled around the old walls; and the sleeping people within. She was them—part of a vibrant, living force of energy and love. Home! This was real and all the rest ephemeral.

The moment passed—or was it an hour? She had no way of telling. Suddenly she was alone again, imprisoned in her evanescent shell. But not forever. She walked on slowly, trying to understand. She thought about the human condition, and about her own disillusionment and her fear of annihilation. Yet all the time God was there, around and within her.

What was it that had led to this sudden revelation? She did not know; knew only that she had received something precious. A gift!

Unable to reason or even to understand, but suffused with joy, she hurried back to the hotel.

Chapter Eighty-five

Long before the day's session began Marika was in the front row with Bertha, waiting impatiently for Günter to be brought in. When he came she saw him searching the seats anxiously until he saw her. Then he smiled. It was a smile she remembered from the past—from the Namib—a smile of infinite tenderness. But his face was gray and he looked old and gaunt.

Günter seemed surprised when Guedi called him. He took the oath in an absolutely silent courtroom: the coughing and shuffling ceased and the footsteps of guards in the corridor echoed eerily along bare walls.

This was the moment they had all waited for—to see the monster threshing like a shark in a net.

"You are known as Günter Grieff, naturalized citizen of South Africa, and you are chairman of the Namib Mining and Minerals Corporation? Recently you took over Western Minerals, a multinational mining group with headquarters in London?"

"That is correct."

"Will you please tell the court why and when you assumed the identity of Günter Grieff."

A sigh that was almost a gasp ran around the courtroom. Marika turned to Sylvia, but her daughter remained rigidly staring at the dock, her fingers gripping Andy's arm frenziedly.

Günter frowned. "Where shall I begin?" he whispered. He looked at Marika and she gained the impression that he was staring through her into a long-lost world.

"It's so unreal," Günter was murmuring, "so very long ago. As if it happened to someone else—someone I read about."

"The prisoner will confine himself to the facts," the President said sharply.

Günter nodded and squared his shoulders. "I was born Hans Kolb, the only son of Karl and Frieda Kolb, on March 13, 1923, in Weyer, Austria," he began. "I attended the local high school and at the outbreak of war entered the naval academy at Kiel and later at Stralsund. I became an engineer on U-boats and served in the Atlantic from 1940 until 1942, when I was recalled to Germany for special training on a new type of submarine fitted with revolutionary Walther diesel engines. I trained at the Walther plant for six months and returned to active service in September 1942 aboard the U-boat XLII as chief engineer. We operated along the Atlantic seaboard from Walvis Bay to Gibraltar.

"On April 14, 1945, our commander, Captain Max Erath, engaged an enemy convoy and we succeeded in torpedoing a Swedish cargo boat, which caught alight and sank.

"The British destroyer sent down depth charges and one of them exploded close to the stern of the XLII, damaging the plating.

"Water flooded in . . . " He broke off, remembering the lights fading, the smell of the fumes, the sound of water gushing into the battery room, Schmidt with his neck broken and his own terrible demoralizing fear. Günter's hands were clutching the rail, his face shone with sweat. Then he looked up and stared at the courtroom. "I thought I was a dead man," he said softly. "Since then every day has been a gift."

"The prisoner will kindly refrain from introducing extraneous details and stick to the point," the President repeated sternly.

Günter nodded. "I was ordered to the conning tower, together with the first officer, and told to abandon ship through the escape hatch. As we did so the submarine flooded and that was the last I remembered until I recovered consciousness some hours later in the sea. I swam toward the shore and was picked up by the crew of a British lifeboat and transferred to the Walvis Bay hospital.''

Günter broke off and saw the hostile faces of the judges and the President watching him skeptically. They did not believe him, he could see that clearly enough. Hopelessness engulfed him and for a moment he could not find the courage to continue.

Watching Günter, Guedi was struggling to control his mounting anger. Time . . . all he needed was time . . . if Günter's story was true he must be able to find some verification. But Günter had produced his unlikely and therefore probable story on the last day of the trial. No one believed him now. Guedi's only hope lay in Claire. If she corroborated Günter's story he might be able to gain an adjournment.

Grieff seemed to have dried up. He was looking around sadly and licking his dry lips.

"And then?" Guedi prompted him.

"Five survivors from the stricken ships were transferred to Walvis Bay for emergency treatment,'' Günter went on more quietly. "One of them was Günter Grieff, who was traveling on a Swedish cargo boat to South Africa. He was dying and the nurse who administered first aid on the wharf, Claire McGuire, who is now my wife, was sympathetic to my plight and suggested that we exchange papers. She said we looked alike, Grieff and I—that is. I took his papers after he died.''

He sounded unconvincing, as if he, too, could not really believe his story. "It's all so long ago—like a dream,'' he apologized.

Judging by the muttering in the courtroom, no one believed him.

"Tell me, Mr. Grieff,'' Guedi went on. "The war was almost over; you must have realized that the worst you could expect was interrogation followed by a brief spell as a prisoner of war and then repatriation to Germany. Why did you commit a crime and take papers and a nationality which did not belong to you? You had nothing to hide.''

Guedi stepped back and waited tensely. He was taking a

chance, he knew that. If Günter refused to tell his story, just as he had the previous evening, then he would just create more doubts for the judges and the President.

"I wanted to stay in South-West Africa," he said, stuttering badly.

Guedi swore under his breath. "Please tell the court why you wanted to stay."

"It's not relevant," Günter muttered.

"I think it is," Guedi replied quickly.

"I had seen her and I loved her," Günter muttered, gesturing briefly toward Marika. "I was afraid to leave, afraid she might not wait; I knew it might be years before I could get back to Walvis Bay. I might lose her."

"Carry on."

"So I took the papers, that's all. It worried me, but as the years passed I began to think I really was Günter Grieff. I was employed as service manager of fishing boats at the local canning factory."

"A job for which you were ideally trained."

"Of course."

"And subsequently you became engaged to Marika Palma?"

"Magos!"

"As you wish."

"We became engaged, but she broke off the engagement when she discovered I was German. It's hard to understand now, but she suffered terribly as a result of the war. All her family were shot and her father was killed at Oradour."

"You told her you were German?" Guedi interjected.

"No. I could never pluck up courage. Claire told her."

Suddenly there was lively interest in the court, and a hubbub of voices filled the room. Sylvia's white face was turned toward Marika—a question in her eyes. Marika was too stunned to pay attention. She was tormented by an image of an Iron Cross—his Iron Cross—lying at her feet. Where was that and why had she forgotten everything except the awful realization that Günter was German?

"Thank you. Mr. President, I have no further questions for the prisoner."

Günter looked depressed and upset.

The President struck the desk with his gavel and the court quieted.

"Claire Grieff, wife of the accused," the court official announced.

Günter was staring searchingly at Claire, but she looked away and buried her face in a handkerchief. Günter's shoulders sagged and he bowed his head. It was the first time he had shown positive signs of defeat.

"Your name is Claire Grieff and you are the wife of the accused?"

Claire murmured, hiccupped a sob and clasped the hand-kerchief over her mouth.

The President spoke clearly, like a schoolmaster to a wayward pupil. "This is a most painful occasion for you and the sympathy of the court is with you, but you must try to compose yourself and answer questions clearly so that we can hear your replies."

"Yes," she whispered.

"How long have you been married to the accused?" Guedi began.

"For eight years."

"Would you call it a happy marriage?"

"Yes." She sobbed again and made an effort to control herself.

"And before you were married, how long had you known the accused?"

"Since 1945—twenty-four years," she replied.

"Please describe to the court how your first meeting took place."

"I was a nurse at the Walvis Bay hospital," she stammered. "Günter was traveling on the Swedish cargo boat which had joined the convoy. The ship was torpedoed by a U-boat some miles off the coast and Günter was the only survivor."

Guedi stepped back and regarded her carefully, but

when he spoke his voice did not betray his anger. "You are aware that your husband claims that he was a survivor from the U-boat, that his real name is Hans Kolb and that you and he exchanged papers with those of the dead man, Günter Grieff, so that he would not have to go to a prisoner-of-war camp. Did you exchange these papers or have any knowledge of them?"

Claire looked around wildly, as if torn in two by the question.

"I . . . I can't . . . I really can't . . ."

"I must remind you that you are under oath," the President said sternly.

"The survivor from the U-boat was buried at Walvis Bay," she said, her voice low and husky. "I thought my husband was Swiss, I have always thought that . . . until . . . until he was arrested." She burst into a flood of sobbing again.

Marika sat up sharply. That was a lie. She was flooded with sudden recall. She was running . . . running toward the cemetery because of the note she had received from Claire. What was it? Goddamnit—what was it? *Günter Grieff is dead. Come to the cemetery.* "She's lying," she called out loudly, leaping to her feet. "Günter Grieff is dead. She wrote that . . . she wrote that to me and that's how I found out . . ." Her words were drowned by the call for order. "He's innocent, I tell you. He's innocent," she yelled.

Bertha took her arm and dragged her down onto the seat. "Hush, Marikala, hush," she whispered.

"Liar! Liar!" Marika sobbed.

There was an uproar around her. The President quieted the court and said, "One more outburst, Mrs. Palma, and I will have you removed from the court." He looked displeased as he sat frowning.

"Did anyone else, other than you, Mrs. Grieff, speak to Hans Kolb when he was conscious at any time?"

Claire hesitated, unwilling to answer. "No one else," she admitted eventually. "I was the only nurse at the wharf."

"So it is true to say that apart from the prisoner in the dock you alone hold the key to the accused's real identity?"

"He has been identified by many people in this court," Claire said sulkily.

"Is it true that at the time of the arrest you had filed divorce proceedings against your husband, naming Marika Magos, mother of the prisoner's natural child, as correspondent?"

"It is true," she murmured.

"No further questions," Guedi said.

"Thank you, madam. That is all."

Claire turned and gazed at Günter.

Something about her expression caught the President's eye. He peered sharply at her and scribbled in his notebook.

Claire returned to her seat, pausing momentarily beside Marika. Briefly the two women stared at each other. Jealousy blazed out of Claire's eyes as she smiled triumphantly.

Chapter Eighty-six

The court was recessed for lunch. In a daze Marika followed Bertha through the crowd to the pavement. It was cold and she wrapped her coat around her. She felt a hand clutching her arm.

It was Sylvia and behind her Andy. Sylvia's face was red and swollen, her eyes brimming with tears. Andy hung back and took Bertha's arm and suddenly the two of them were alone together.

"Oh, Mother." She put her hands over her mouth and choked back the sobs. "You must tell me everything. He's not guilty, is he? You know he's not guilty." She looked imploringly at Marika and then away again.

"He's innocent," Marika said firmly. "They buried

Günter Grieff in the Walvis Bay cemetery." Suddenly she remembered watching him groaning in the ward and the thought came: So I saw my father's murderer dying, after all, just as I had always planned. It did not seem very important.

"What are we going to do?" Sylvia cried out.

"We're going to save him," Marika said. "Guedi will try for an adjournment and even if he doesn't succeed there's a good deal of time before . . . before . . ." She could not say the word "guillotine." Instead she tried out a taut smile.

"We can appeal, that will give us time. We'll find evidence to prove his identity," she went on firmly. She tried to look confident. "All we need is time."

"If only I had understood why you and Dad . . ." Sylvia broke off, looking sad and confused. "You see, I always blamed you for not marrying Dad. I thought you had put your career first." She broke off and took out a tissue to dab her eyes.

"I never wanted to burden you with war stories," Marika told her as they walked along, hunched against the wind. "And I could not tell you your father was German. I was very bitter for a very long time. Looking back now, I see my mistakes."

"There's something I want to tell you," Sylvia said nervously.

"And that is?" Marika asked, trying to sound light-hearted and prepare herself for the next blow.

"I'm sorry. Really sorry." She reached out and lightly touched her mother's arm. "Let's start again," she added shyly.

The afternoon session opened with a sense of urgency and the courtroom was crowded with press from all over the world. They were hoping for an early judgment, and from the whispered comments it seemed that everyone expected the maximum penalty to be imposed.

They were all surprised when, instead of calling the next witness, Guedi stood up and said, "I beg the indulgence of the court and request that this hearing be adjourned for two weeks in order to present the final evidence for the defense in an orderly manner.''

The President scowled at Guedi. ''The defense counsel has had adequate time available to research and present his case. I must remind him that the prisoner spent three months in prison awaiting trial. How would justice be served by delaying the hearing for another two weeks?''

''By uncovering the truth, Mr. President,'' Guedi argued hotly. ''That, after all, is what this trial is all about . . . truth and justice. My client is on trial on the most terrible of all charges and I submit that his evidence, which has only just come to light, should be put to the test. If Günter Grieff is indeed Hans Kolb, then I must request your leave to fully investigate his claim.''

''But the prisoner has sworn on oath that he is Günter Grieff,'' the President argued.

''I'd like to respectfully submit that this proves him a liar, not a murderer,'' Guedi said, and was rewarded with a scalding glance from the President.

''My point is that my client thought it had been lost. His wife had kept its existence hidden from him for several years. In spite of her sobs and protestations in this courtroom, she handed this damning evidence to the prosecution, not to her husband's defense lawyer, and I knew nothing about it,'' Guedi said, staking his reputation on this last plea.

''Surely that proves a malicious intent to damage her husband's case.'' Guedi's bony finger shot out to point at Claire. ''Yet it is her evidence, and her evidence alone, which has entirely discredited my client's defense. And I submit respectfully that French justice must surely be above the reach of a spiteful, jealous and forsaken wife.''

The President's face registered shock and then disapproval. ''You exceed yourself,'' he said angrily. He scribbled again in his notebook. Then he conferred with the judges, ignoring for a moment the babble of conversation which had broken out in the court.

At last he looked up and the court was silenced. ''This

court is adjourned until ten o'clock on Monday morning at the request of the defense,'' he announced.

"Thank you, Mr. President," Guedi said, frowning impatiently. It was Wednesday afternoon now. That left only two more working days. Two working days! What the hell could he do with two working days when the Walther plant's records were now behind the Iron Curtain?

Chapter Eighty-seven

Early the next morning Marika was pacing Günter's study in his Hampstead house when the telephone rang. It was from a pay phone and the caller could not get through. Eventually the line went dead. Disappointment flooded through her and she resumed her restless walk.

When the trial was adjourned the previous day, Marika returned to London with Bertha and Sylvia, who were staying together at Bertha's house. Guedi and his colleagues were in East Germany, searching for some proof of Günter's real identity, and Andy was there, too, looking for relatives. So Marika returned to Günter's house, where she had been living since he was arrested. How she wished she could do something to help. Waiting was worse—much worse, Marika considered, and she wondered how she would endure the next four days.

Then the telephone rang a second time, and when she answered she heard a strange voice on the line.

"I'd like to speak to Mrs. Grieff." It was a harsh, deep voice with a trace of a foreign accent.

"Who's speaking?" At first she thought it was a call from Western Minerals.

"Is that Mrs. Grieff?"

Marika gained the impression that the caller was about to hang up. "Yes," she lied, curious.

"Mrs. Grieff, I hold certain papers which concern your husband."

Marika could sense the hostility behind the words.

"What papers?" She needed time to think. Who was he and what was he talking about?

"They must be very valuable to you, since you went to such pains to conceal them. Just how much are you prepared to pay?"

"How much do you . . .?" she managed to say.

"The Kwammang-a, for a start," he said. "A trifle . . . compared with the stakes in the game you're playing."

There was a pause and Marika could not think what to say. What papers? For God's sake!

"Wouldn't you say so, Mrs. Grieff?"

"Yes . . . that is . . . of course," she stammered. "Where did you find them?"

"In your safe, Mrs. Grieff."

"I'll pay . . . I'll pay well, but first tell me what the papers are," she stammered.

There was a brief, frightening click. He had hung up.

Marika replaced the receiver, feeling terrified and furious with herself. She had said the wrong thing. Why? Why had she been such a fool? Claire would have known what papers they were, since they had been in her safe. Were they Hans Kolb's naval papers?

She crumpled with shock and sat with her head in her hands. What was she to do? This burglar, or whoever he was, would find Claire and she would pay him.

Oh God! She was too panic-stricken to think clearly.

She raced to the telephone and dialed Bertha's number. She was out of breath with fright as she tried to repeat everything the man had said.

"Oh, Bertha. What am I going to do? How can I stop Claire from getting the papers?"

"Claire's in Paris," Bertha pointed out. "She stayed overnight to try to see Günter again. I know for a fact, because she told Sylvia. She's returning to the Hilton this morning. It will take this man some time to find out where she is."

"Will he be able to find her?" Marika broke off. "Damn, yes, of course he will. He only has to check with Günter's lawyer or his company. Perhaps if I . . . I'll ring you back," she told Bertha.

Marika knew of only one detective agency, but it was the best, naturally, since Tony used them constantly for bodyguards and business information.

They were very busy, the secretary told her. She could make an appointment in a week's time. Marika had to bludgeon her with Tony's name before she was put through to Jim Renwick, one of the managing partners. She remembered him. He had called on business at Outwood Manor. She could not forget his loud, conceited voice.

"Money's no object," she concluded, when she had told him everything she could.

Marika telephoned Bertha to tell her and then she settled down for a long wait.

It was half past nine.

Three detectives were installed at the Hilton in a room next to the one booked by Mrs. Grieff. One of them was Renwick. Normally Renwick did not go out on a job, but it paid not to take chances with Palma's work, he reasoned. Palma's group accounted for over fifty percent of Renwick's business.

At exactly 10:30 A.M. Claire Grieff entered her room, flung a suitcase on the floor and poured herself a drink. She was in the bath and still drinking when the call came at 11:05.

Renwick was wearing headphones; he scribbled in his notebook in shorthand.

Caller: "*Mrs. Grieff? I've got those papers you were trying so hard to suppress. They must be worth an awful lot of money to you, so you won't mind paying to get them back. When your husband is guillotined you will be a wealthy woman, Mrs. Grieff, but of course you know that.*"

Mrs. Grieff: "*How dare you? Who are you? What do you want?*"

Caller: "Let's say my name is Jones. I'm an agent. These papers were passed to me by a client of mine who removed them from your safe in your Johannesburg home. If you want to buy them, be at Charing Cross cafeteria at noon exactly."

The line went dead.

Leaving his colleagues to monitor further calls, Renwick went down to reception and called his office.

"Call Mrs. Palma at this number and tell her we have located her target. He's contacted Mrs. Grieff and arranged to meet her at twelve at Charing Cross cafeteria. We'll be tailing him."

Renwick's secretary made three attempts to get through to the number, but it was busy and eventually she telephoned Outwood Manor, where Tony convinced her that Marika had asked him to take a message.

Just after noon, the telephone rang and Marika grabbed the receiver. It was Renwick.

"Sorry I couldn't get through to you before," Renwick told her, "but I asked my secretary to call you."

"Well, she didn't," Marika said angrily.

"I'm sorry. We couldn't contact this man, this Jones, as he's calling himself, until he met Mrs. Grieff, because we didn't know what he looked like. Jones met Mrs. Grieff and they talked, but no papers changed hands. They appeared to be arguing. She ran after him when he walked out. Seems like he's playing hard to get to push up the price. Two of my men are tailing him now."

"They talked," Marika gasped, feeling disappointed.

"Yes, but as I said, nothing changed hands. Presumably he's still got the papers. But there's a third party involved. Two men followed him when he left Charing Cross. We know them both. Unsavory types. Hit men who'll take on anything. Someone besides you wants the papers. We'll have to move fast. What do you want us to offer him?"

Marika was repelled by Renwick's slick manner and his voice, which was overbearing. "I would prefer you to bring him here," she said. "Tell him you have a buyer who can outbid Mrs. Grieff."

There was a long silence. "We'll check him out first," Renwick said eventually.

An hour later, Sylvia burst in and grabbed her mother. "For goodness' sake, what's happening?" she gasped. "We've been waiting . . . waiting . . . Oh, Mum. Can't we do something? Just waiting around like this I'll go crazy," she moaned.

Marika tried to comfort her daughter, but they were both on edge when Renwick's next call came shortly afterward.

"Things are moving nicely," Renwick began. "He told Mrs. Grieff his name is Jones, but in fact his name's Kramer. British subject, but foreign accent. Out of his depth in this caper, if you ask me. Operates as an armaments wholesaler—does a bit of gunrunning in Africa from time to time. He knows the territories because he's been a mercenary twice. Keeps his nose clean in England."

He paused, expecting Marika's approval, but eventually he carried on.

"We tailed him home. He lives in St. John's Wood in a mews house." He gave her the address. "Quite a nice place he's got. Name on the door on a brass plaque and that sort of thing. He's even in the telephone directory. Funny, that!"

"What's funny about it?" Marika asked.

"Well, he doesn't seem to be taking care—that's all. He seems to think he's got something that's worth a fortune—whatever it is—but he doesn't seem to be very cautious." He rang off.

Marika turned to tell Sylvia, but her daughter had left. The door was open and the telephone receiver in the hall was swinging at the end of the line.

Sylvia was at her bank, fuming and throwing her weight around. She wanted to withdraw her savings at once. The manager sent an armed messenger to another branch to collect the balance Sylvia required. Eventually he had given up trying to dissuade her, or to find out why she wanted the money, and he handed her a small suitcase packed with bundles of twenty-pound notes. The bank was closed by this time and a clerk let her out of a side door.

It was almost pitch dark and a blizzard was blowing up, by the look of things, Sylvia thought apprehensively. So much bloody time wasted. By now the car was probably towed away. But it was there, with a ticket on the windshield.

After she had skidded twice on newly fallen snow she slowed down and half an hour later she found the mews cottage in a tiny cobbled cul-de-sac.

"He better bloody be there," Sylvia muttered several times without noticing that she was talking aloud. She was more conscious of her heart beating loudly in her chest and her mouth, which was so dry she could not swallow.

She tried to lock the car, but her hand was shaking. So she swore, rammed the key in her bag and hurried to the door. She was determined to extract the papers from this Kramer—even if she had to promise another million.

No one answered the bell. Strange, she thought. She felt sure that she heard footsteps in the house. After a few seconds she rang again and crouched against the wall of the porch, trying to shelter from the wind, which was bitterly cold.

When she tried the handle the door swung open. It was dark inside. She walked in and found the light switch.

Chaos surrounded her. The room was knee deep in papers and books. She could see that it might have been a pleasant room before, with bookshelves of natural wood and modern Swedish-style furniture, but now the upholstery was ripped to shreds and so were the mohair rugs. Two speakers were lying on the floor and torn open, the hi-fi equipment was in pieces and even the pictures had been wrenched from the frames. They had been pictures of ships and they were scattered everywhere. Half of the room had been an office, with a large desk, a filing cabinet and rows of files. The cabinet was on its side and the files were strewn over the floor. She had never seen anything quite like it.

Then she heard a noise behind her and wheeled around. There were two men with stockings over their faces running toward her. She opened her mouth to scream, but a vicious punch on her cheek sent her reeling backward. Then came another explosive blow on her temple and that was the last thing she remembered.

Chapter Eighty-eight

Kramer awoke with a jolt. Where the hell was he? He saw Bertha Factor watching him intently. She was puzzled and there was a hint of compassion in her eyes.

He sat up and ran his hands through his hair. Then he remembered the previous day in disjointed fragments: Claire Grieff at the cafeteria with her arrogant eyes and bouncing red hair, Marika Palma and her desperation and lastly that incredibly beautiful child lying unconscious on his doorstep.

He looked up and saw Bertha Factor. Of course, he was in her house in Finchley with the mezuzahs and the candlesticks. Then her story came flooding back so vividly it seemed as if he had lived through it with them—well, he thought, he had for the last week. Was it only a week? Looking back, it seemed much longer. He felt annoyed with himself. Why the hell had he fallen asleep?

She nodded. Then she stood up. Although she was stout she was remarkably agile, he noticed. "You slept for over an hour," she said.

"I'm sorry." He felt uncomfortable with those intelligent brown eyes questioning him. "How's Sylvia?"

"She seems all right. She's going for X rays later." Then she hesitated. She wanted to ask him something, he could see that. Instead she said, "Would you like some coffee?" The questions would come later.

"Please," he murmured. There wasn't much you could conceal from Bertha Factor, he decided. The old girl was right; they were streets ahead of him. All of them! Tougher; shrewder. A clever family. No wonder they were all so damn rich. But he would still get the diamond.

Bertha went into the kitchen and lit the gas stove. She made a pot of hot coffee and put some biscuits on a plate. When she returned Kramer was gone.

Outside it was snowing again and the blizzard had worsened. A pity he had to leave without the coffee, he thought. God, but it was cold. He began to jog toward the station and as he ran he thought about the last few hectic days.

Kramer knew now that it was Angelo Palma's hoods who had ransacked his house and beaten Sylvia. He had a score to settle with Palma, but later. His first priority was the Kwammang-a.

Kramer slowed down as he neared the tube station. He went to the public telephone and dialed Claire Grieff's hotel. She sounded surprisingly alert when his call was put through and he guessed she had been lying awake for most of the night.

"I want the diamond," he told her. "The diamond for the papers."

"It's disappeared," she said. "But I can pay you any amount. I told you before. You can name your price."

"I just did," he said. "The Kwammang-a, or it's no deal. You're the only one who could have removed the diamond from the safe. Where is it?"

She paused momentarily. Then she said, "In Johannesburg, Mr. Jones, where you'll never find it."

He glanced at his watch and swore. The earliest they could get there was Saturday morning. "Midnight, Saturday night at Xhabbo," he said. "Have it ready or it's no deal. I've had a good offer from Mrs. Palma." He rang off without waiting for her reply.

*   *   *

It was hot, and the night air, heady with the scent of hibiscus and tobacco flowers, trembled with the sounds of the African night.

Claire stood on the patio overlooking the lawn and the pool, trying to keep her mind clear; it was important not to remember, but every plant, every piece of furniture, every picture screamed Günter. "Darling," she sobbed. "Darling Günter. Oh Christ, Günter." Betrayer and betrayed and she cried out the grief of both.

She could never live here again, she thought, struggling to regain her composure. She would sell the place—lock, stock and barrel. She'd be a millionaire many times over and she was still young. She would emigrate! To France perhaps, but no, that would remind her of the trial. America! That was far away. Fleetingly she thought she might never find anywhere far enough away.

She had a sudden image of Marika at the trial with her huge amber eyes so red and swollen. There was a certain balm in remembering her fear. Nothing could save Günter from the guillotine. No other woman would ever know his body pressing down on her, his lips so warm and sensuous, the touch of his muscular neck beneath her probing fingers.

She became aware of pain in the palms of her hands. She had pierced the skin with her nails and she was bleeding. Carefully she took a tissue from her bag and held it over the cuts.

Beyond the wild chestnut grove, lights were extinguished. Their housekeeper was going to sleep. Claire had given her the evening off and told the caretaker not to disturb her for the night.

Nevertheless, there was no fear in Claire at the coming encounter. It was a straightforward business deal. She would destroy the evidence. She should have done so years ago, but even Günter's papers had seemed precious. Would she ever forget? she wondered.

Later she heard footsteps behind her and spun round. It was he. "How did you get in?" she asked angrily.

"Through the door."

"It's customary to ring."

Kramer ignored her. He took an envelope out of his pocket; tossed it on the table. "Where's the diamond?"

Claire reached forward, but suddenly the man was pointing a gun at her. It lifted fractionally.

She stepped backward. "I don't understand," she said. "Don't point that damn thing at me."

"Put the diamond on the table. Then we grab together," he told her. "That's the way." He was smiling, but there was no humor in his face. Just anger, she thought, and she wondered why.

She fumbled in her bag for the key and walked into the study.

"You don't have to follow me," she said.

"I prefer to." He sat down and watched her reach into one of the masks. "Will this fetch much?" he asked, gesturing toward the collection of masks and statues leering from every side.

"I've had an offer of five million dollars," Claire said, looking satisfied.

"So you've already found a buyer?"

Suddenly she flushed. "Go to hell," she snarled. She fumbled inside a mask—*Headpiece from Udi,* the plaque said. It was hideous, but Kramer hardly noticed it beside three hundred carats of dazzling perfection.

"Put it on the desk," he said. He flung down the envelope for a second time and picked up the diamond.

Something in his voice caught her attention—something was wrong! An idea was growing in her—a terrible idea. She snatched the envelope, tore it open and tipped the newspaper clippings and plastic disk on the table. She wanted to scream, but instead she sobbed. "Why? Why? Why?" Her face contorted with distress. She felt stunned with a sense of outrage. Looking at Jones was like looking into a mirror—the loathing and the revenge—it was all there in his face.

For a long time after he left she was too shocked to move. She felt weak with the force of the loathing pouring from her and the knowledge of what she was bound to do.

Later, she had no way of telling how much later, she heard footsteps in the driveway. Suddenly she felt alarmed. How foolish of her to remain alone here without the guards or even dogs for protection. Xhabbo was a natural target for any thieves, with all the recent press reports of the family's wealth and the Kwammang-a and the knowledge that Günter was in prison.

The footsteps were approaching. Perhaps it was the caretaker checking the house . . . but she had told him not to.

She forced herself to move and every step was an effort. She leaned out of the window and called. "That you, Hackett?"

There was no reply, but instead of the sound of footsteps racing away, the limping, shuffling tread kept coming toward her.

"Who's there?" she called out into the darkness. "Who is it?" She had a strange presentiment that it was not a person at all but the personification of her own malevolence—that evilness itself was approaching from the shrubbery.

She ran to the lounge and pressed the burglar alarm, but it was dead. Then she locked the sliding doors. After that she went quickly and clumsily from room to room, shutting every door and window, squashing her finger and blundering into the furniture in her panic.

Then she grabbed the telephone receiver. It was dead, too. Someone had cut the line. What should she do? Hackett was always armed, but he was an old man and asleep. She thought of leaning out of the window and screaming for help, but the housekeeper was deaf and the neighbors beyond earshot.

Claire always kept a gun in her handbag for protection, particularly in the car at night, but because she had just returned from London, her gun was locked in her safe in the bedroom.

It was when she mounted the stairs that she smelled the sweet cloying stench of sweat and her stomach contracted with spasms of fear. They were waiting and she had nearly gone up there. Perhaps even now they were watching her.

They must have been there for a long time, even before
Kramer came. She turned and walked slowly back. The
few seconds that it took to cross the marble hall seemed to
last forever.

At last she reached the front door and swung it open.
She screamed and eventually the scream died with a sob of
fear. The face in the porch was hideous. Once he had been
black and he still had the features of his race, but his skin
was horribly eroded and of a brilliant pink color with here
and there a strip of ebony. One eye was blind and milky,
the other stared at her with a malice which she had never
before seen.

"Get out," Claire said roughly as the figure lurched
toward her. "Get out or I'll sound the alarm,"

"Dead," he said laconically. "And the telephone."
Then his arm shot forward like the shaft of an arrow,
striking her face. She spun back and fell on the floor.

"Günter, Günter," she cried out, trying to pretend there
was someone in the house.

"Grieff's in prison. I can still read the newspapers—
with this eye." He smiled and pointed to his face. There
was something horribly familiar about him. Recognition
dawned as he limped in and with it memories of the copper
mine and that awful camp in the Namib; the convict
clutching his eyes and screaming as he rolled down the
stony mountainside enveloped in flames.

It was Jason. Suddenly she realized that the reports of
the trial had led him to Xhabbo, scenting wealth and
vengeance like a shark scents blood. "Oh my God," she
murmured. In desperation she lunged past him, fighting
him off with the strength of madness, but he kicked her
feet from under her and she spun across the room, caught
her hip on the corner of the table and crumpled onto the
floor, doubled up with pain.

He locked the door—called out and three others came
down the stairway.

"We want the Kwammang-a," Jason said, and she was
amazed that he knew its name, and could pronounce it
with the correct Bushman accent.

"I gave it to the man . . . Jones . . . you saw him . . . you were here." Her voice shook with fear.

They would not believe her. They forced her into the bathroom and pushed her head into the full bath and when she was half drowned they pulled her out and beat her and then they pushed her back again.

She pleaded and cried and begged them to stop. She opened the safe in the study and showed them the one in her bedroom, but they wanted the Kwammang-a; nothing less. Swearing quietly, Jason thrust his fist into her face.

Claire heard her nose crunch sickeningly. Pain dimmed her fear as she gagged on the blood. She passed out momentarily and when she came to she was lying on the floor. Jason was dragging her by her feet across the study floor and into the museum.

Obscene masks leered at her; ebony lips mouthed obscenities; black eye sockets watched fascinated as the four men stripped off her clothes, and pushed her—screaming and kicking—onto the floor, where they tied her legs to the heavy mahogany table and her wrists to the door until she could only jerk spasmodically as they raped her again and again.

Faces from a nightmare! Inhuman, terrible faces and they were doing terrible things to her. She was only dimly aware that they had bitten off her nipples and ripped at her stomach with their knives. Or was it them? Or the masks— hideous in their ritual rage? Scarred cheeks grinned obscenely, wooden teeth clattered, but worst of all was the mask with the livid, raw face. He hurt her badly—and he was insatiable. She seemed to hear tribal chanting and the far-off beat of drums. Revenge! Revenge! Revenge!

She lay there for hours, bruised and bloody. Sometimes she was left alone and she would try to scream for help, but only a croak came. She heard them dragging pillowcases and blankets, filled with things that bumped and smashed, out of the front door.

Then Jason came and pushed his foot hard on her stomach until she found the strength to scream. He grinned at

her and something about the look in his eyes banished
hope.

I'm dead, she thought. I'm as good as dead now. All
that's left is the degree of pain I must still bear. She began
to cry and not because of the pain, but because now she
would never be able to have her revenge on Günter.

Chapter Eighty-nine

It was a bleak Monday morning in Paris. The last remnants
of snow loitered in gutters and the north wind was bitterly
cold. Nimbus clouds hung low overhead. It would rain
before noon.

The three women sat silently in the taxi bringing them
from the airport to the courtroom. They had learned about
Claire's murder on Sunday morning when the caretaker at
Xhabbo had telephoned Bertha. The police, who were
called by neighbors during the night, had caught the gang
before dawn, but they were too late to save Claire. It was
a horrible story and they were feeling shocked and disgusted.

When they reached the Palais de Justice they found the
roads to the court were blocked by policemen on motorcy-
cles and there were armed guards on every door. The
authorities were taking no chance of a disturbance on what
was predicted to be the last day of the trial, for feelings
were running high.

The weekend press had resurrected the Oradour massacre in detail: photographs, interviews with bereaved relatives, statements from those who had uncovered the charred
bodies and buried the dead, nothing was spared; while
Günter's claim to be Hans Kolb was being treated as a
last-minute fabrication invented by a desperate man. Claire's
death received scant attention.

Sylvia was looking very sick and the sunglasses could

not hide all her bruises. Bertha and Marika had tried to persuade her to stay in London, but she had refused. They did not know where Andy was. Nor did they know if the defense team had found proof of Günter's identity.

Shortly afterward Andy arrived from Germany and joined them in the courtroom. He had not slept and they could see by his face that he had failed to find a trace of Kolb's relatives. He looked older and sadder, as if he had learned for the first time that truth and justice will not necessarily triumph.

By nine-thirty the family were sitting in the front row of the courtroom, where Guedi sent a messenger to warn them that the East German authorities had been polite but unhelpful and he had not been given access to the wartime files of the Walther plant. Many documents had been destroyed in the blitz, he had been told. Every avenue he had explored had drawn a blank.

Tense and haggard, the three women sat waiting for the trial to be resumed.

The court was humming with excited whispering as the legal teams entered and Marika felt a stunning dread settle on her when Günter was led in. He looked sick and scared. Damn the man, she thought. One look at him was enough to convince the judges of his guilt.

The spectators became tense and quiet as the President entered and sat down. He gazed for a moment at the judges and the legal teams and finally stared long and hard at the defense team.

"Mr. Guedi . . ."

Guedi stood up. "Mr. President," he began apologetically. "The time given was not sufficient to verify my client's story. After all, it was only two working days and the evidence lies behind the Iron Curtain." He raised his hands in despair. "I must humbly submit that in the interests of truth and justice, we should be given more time. I admit that my client made a bad mistake in misleading the court as to his real identity. Valuable time was wasted. I must beg the indulgence of the court, Mr. President."

"You have been placed in a most unfortunate position, since your client obviously did not hold you in sufficiently high regard to place his trust in you," the President said. "I sympathize, but cannot see how another adjournment could in any way further truth and justice."

A sigh ran around the court as Guedi sat down abruptly and wiped his forehead with a handkerchief.

Suddenly there was a commotion in the back of the court and the sound of a man's voice raised in argument.

An official hurried to the President and handed him an envelope.

Something about the President's manner caught the attention of the spectators and for a moment the coughing and rustling ceased. Looking over her shoulder, Marika saw Kramer framed in the doorway, two court officials on either side of him. Then Günter leapt to his feet. "Steen," he roared. "Steen."

Guidi asked permission to call another witness for the defense and Kramer was sworn in. Glancing at Günter, Marika saw that his cheeks were wet with tears.

"You will tell the court your name, your occupation, your relationship with the accused and the nature of the documents you have handed to the court."

"I'm Steen Kramer," the witness began. "Born in Hanover, Germany, on May 13, 1923. Hans and I were friends at school and afterward we served together on board the battleship *Schlesien* in the Baltic. Later we were transferred to submarines and we spent two months on the U-977 during the so-called Battle of the Atlantic. We lost touch with each other for a while because Hans was chosen for training on the top-secret Walther diesel engines at their plant. He was an engineer while I, at that time, was a sublieutenant.

"We were both surprised when toward the end of September 1942 we found ourselves together again on the maiden voyage of the U-XLII. Hans was chief engineer. Quite a promotion for him because the U-XLII was the only one of its kind in operation at that time . . ."

"We do not need the technicalities of the U-boat explained to us," the President said gravely.

Steen nodded. "We patrolled off South-West Africa for six months until our captain engaged an enemy convoy off the coast of Walvis Bay at precisely 1800 hours on April 14, 1945. The XLII was badly damaged and sprang a leak in the battery room. Captain Erath ordered Hans and me to attempt an escape."

He broke off and glanced toward Günter. "I'll never forget that night," he said as if he was talking to him alone. "Visibility was only a few feet in the dense fog. I lost consciousness quite quickly and recovered hours later to find that I had been picked up by a searching fishing vessel and transferred to a British tanker en route to Cape Town. I was flown to Britain for interrogation and spent six months in a prisoner-of-war camp.

"Years later I bumped into Hans in South-West Africa and he agreed to lend me enough cash to set up my own business. I was successful and nowadays I operate a small armaments wholesale business in London."

Kramer paused, wiped his forehead with a handkerchief and looked around the courtroom. Then he saw Marika and smiled at her. It was a strangely mocking smile and she felt uncomfortable.

"When the trial began last week," he said, "Hans contacted me and asked me to retrieve his old naval and identity papers, which his wife had hidden somewhere. He only discovered that his papers were still in existence when Mrs. Grieff attempted to blackmail him with them at the beginning of the trial."

There was an excited hum in the court and the President struck his gavel on the desk several times.

"I have just given you those papers, Mr. President. They include Kolb's engineering certificates, his passport and his security pass. You will notice that the latter contains his fingerprints as well as his photograph. It was issued in January 1942 by the authorities for access to the top-secret Walther plant."

"Dismiss the witness," the President said. He stood up

looking grave and the court rose hastily as he put the papers into their folder and placed them under his arm. "The prisoner will be held in custody pending the verification or otherwise of these papers," he said. Against the rising clamor in the courtroom, the President left hurriedly, closely followed by the judges.

By the time the family had excitedly congratulated each other and calmed Bertha, who was crying, they had difficulty pushing their way through the crowded courtroom into the street.

Kramer had disappeared and they were disappointed.

"Long life to him, long life to him," Bertha was muttering. "But I guessed," she whispered in Marika's ear. "The night he came to my house he was talking in his sleep, muttering about the water pouring into the U-boat and the need to save Günter, so I guessed . . . but still, I was afraid to raise your hopes."

The press were leaving hurriedly, their story ruined. After this there could only be an anticlimax. Only a few reporters followed the family.

They returned to the hotel in silence, feeling dazed with relief. No one felt like talking. It was too soon to be happy. The shock and fear still hung around them.

Bertha and the children were returning to London at once, but Marika planned to stay in Paris until she saw Günter. Someone had to tell him about Claire.

They had a drink together in the hotel; just a small celebration. Then Marika walked out to the street with them. Bertha was looking better already. Her head was erect, her eyes were shining, and Marika knew she would be back at the factory before the week was out. Sylvia was clutching Andy's arm and smiling. Suddenly she had recovered her provocative walk and her famous smile.

The resilience of my family is truly amazing, Marika told herself.

Chapter Ninety

It was late afternoon before Marika gained permission to see Günter. He was sitting with his head in his hands, but when he saw her he stood up, smiled sadly and folded her in his arms. He hung on and she guessed he was afraid to let go.

"So you know," she said simply.

"Claire? Yes. The police told me yesterday morning." He took a deep breath and exhaled it through pursed lips. "Thank God it's over," he went on after a long silence. "I expected Steen days ago."

"You should have told us," she said. "We were all trying to buy the papers from him. Then he disappeared and I guessed Claire had offered him the Kwammang-a. That was what he wanted all along."

"That was the deal," Günter told her. "Grainger contacted him on Monday night. Offered him the Kwammang-a for the papers, gave him the combination, but the diamond had disappeared from the safe. You see," he went on, "it was only when Claire tried to blackmail me that I learned they were still in existence. She always denied it. All those years ago . . . I wonder why."

"You never mentioned Kramer," Marika said curiously.

Günter scowled at the floor. "We used to be close friends, but Steen turned out to be a bit of a bastard. He changed, I suppose. He was a mercenary; imprisoned for a while in Zaire, but he escaped and made his way south through Angola to South-West Africa. When he came across a farm called XLII he realized there must be a connection. He traced me to Johannesburg and asked for fifty thousand dollars to set him up in business. He said he would reveal my identity unless I paid up. I had lots of loans at the time and had to borrow the cash. All the same, when I met him and saw the state he was in I was glad to pay. He never asked twice and I never saw him for years, but I made it my business to know where he lived and worked, just in case he should get greedy."

Günter smiled sadly. "Morals are a luxury. Hardly anyone can afford them nowadays." He grinned ruefully. "I didn't know whether or not Steen would show up with the papers."

"I like him," Marika said defensively. "If you were down and out I'm sure he would have done it for nothing. D'you think he has the Kwammang-a?"

"I have no doubt," Günter said. "Poor Claire," he went on. "It was my cruelty that killed her. The funny thing is, I loved her in a way. Can you believe that? But you were the prize. Goddamnit! I always have to win."

"Now you've won," she said flatly. "Here I am."

"Marika," he said slowly, overcome with remorse. "I don't know if I'm ever going to be able to claim that prize."

She watched him sadly, sensing his guilt and wishing she could help. "You'll work it out," she said. "I'll always love you, no matter what you decide to do." She picked up her bag and left.

Outside she found Kramer waiting. She was not surprised to see him.

"We all wanted to thank you, Steen," she said, "but we couldn't find you."

He grinned and she could not help noticing what an attractive man he was in spite of his lines and his careworn expression.

"You don't have to thank me. I was given a job and this was the payment." He felt in his pocket and drew out the Kwammang-a.

Whenever she saw it Marika felt uneasy. "Once Günter gave it to me," she said. "It was all that he had and I turned him down. I thought he would never forgive me and I'm not so sure he has."

Kramer put the diamond in his pocket.

"I wanted to tell you that I've straightened out Palma," he said. "But don't let it worry you; he'll be fine after a couple more days in the hospital." He laughed harshly. "He'll be dropping charges against Günter and Sylvia as soon as he's well enough. He won't try anything with Günter, I promise you."

Marika put her hand lightly on his arm. "The first time I saw you I had the feeling you'd be a wonderful friend or a terrible enemy. I hope you're my friend."

Suddenly she was caught in his arms. He kissed her hungrily, like a man who seldom kisses a woman and wants it to last for a long time.

"No, I'm not. You're my friend's girl," he said. "That's all."

Then he left. His long, loping stride carried him through the crowded hall and out of sight.

Chapter Ninety-one

It was over two months since Günter's trial ended and when Marika had first returned to London she had thought that her life would be irrevocably changed. But strangely it was not. She worked as hard as before, planned her collections, became absurdly upset by the smallest setbacks, fought the supervisor and the machinists with all the passion she could muster, lost her temper, was unkind and endured agonies of remorse afterward.

But still, something had changed and anyone could see that. "It's love," they all said at the factory, but no one saw her lover. Yet, lately her eyes sparkled, her hair shone, her designs were more vibrant and her fights were more passionate.

They were right. Marika was in love—she had fallen in

love with life, with every last particle of it: the trees, the flowers, the tiniest insect and every man, woman and child . . . and particularly with the creator of all this magnificence.

It was May and Marika's Hampstead garden was caught up in the carnival of spring; a riot of green shoots had appeared, intent on spearing the sun, the grass was shuffling and swaying to the rhythm of the music, the delicate buds bursting out in hosannas of joy, and the birds were wild and gay, overflowing with song. Marika loitered in the garden, touching the shrubs and trees, feeling grateful to be part of it all.

She smiled as she thought about Sylvia, who was pregnant, and her happiness with Andy; and Bertha's joy over the coming baby. She would be a great-grandmother. Not bad for someone who couldn't have children, Marika thought.

She heard footsteps and looked around. Günter was walking along the path toward her. She was not surprised; she had been expecting him. He looked magnificent. She could see he had been in the Namib from his deep tan and lean frame and she felt a sudden, fierce stab of pride.

"I've been worrying about you and wondering where you were," Marika said, "but now I can see you've been prospecting."

"That's what I told everyone," he said, "but I didn't do much work." He paused. "I was thinking. Trying to find a reason for all that happened to us."

He felt shy and tongue-tied. Absurd! After all, he was middle-aged. But still! He sat on the bench beside her and clumsily reached for her hand.

"I had to come," he said.

"Of course."

"I'm going to stay here with you."

"I was expecting you."

"Why, you're trembling," he said.

"It's cool today." she whispered eventually.

"Cool it is," he repeated oafishly. Cool! He was on fire, his lips were dry and his hands were sweating and his blood was racing through his body.

He reached out and touched her face; felt her shuddering beneath his fingertips.

"Oh yes," she said, hardly aware of the words tumbling out of her mouth. "It was warmer yesterday."

Suddenly Marika was tossed back in time and she knew that they were right at the beginning of everything. For her there was only Günter; nothing else counted. She could feel his fingers rubbing at her hand, at her very existence, filling her with spasms of joy and breathlessness.

Günter was nearly passing out with desire. "Perhaps if we went inside," he murmured, nuzzling his mouth against her neck.

"Yes, let's," she gasped, feeling quite overcome with the force of sensations ravishing her body.

She knew this had happened before, long ago in the Namib, and she had thrown it all away, but lately she had learned to love.